Praise for the Horngate Witches series

"Strongly crafted world building, with exciting nonstop action and main and supporting characters that are vivid and varied."

—*Sci Fi Guy*

"One of the most intriguing and compelling urban fantasy series around."

—*RT Book Reviews*

"A series to remember."

—*Fresh Fiction*

"The tough, feel-good supernatural fights . . . will keep action fans coming back for book after book."

—*Publishers Weekly*

"Outstanding writing and characters. A must read."

—*HubPages*

"Reading a Horngate Witches book is a bit like watching a big summer movie. Action! Explosions! Impossibly tough characters doing awesome things! It's a heck of a ride."

—*Fantasy Literature*

BITTER NIGHT

"This lush urban fantasy populated with witches, angels, Sunspears, and Shadowblades contains all the decadent delights of dark chocolate. One taste, and you'd devour this book."

—Ann Aguirre, national bestselling author of *Grimspace* and *Enclave*

"Once again, Max proves to be one of the top urban fantasy heroines. She's tough, actually cares about people, and is big enough to admit when she's made a mistake. I loved watching her grow in *Crimson Wind*, both as a leader and a woman."

—*Bitten by Books*

SHADOW CITY

"Amazing, fascinating, spellbinding. . . . Francis has a gem of a series in her hands, and this book is top-notch action and fantasy rolled into one. . . . A must read series for all urban fantasy readers."

—*Paranormal and Urban Fantasy Reviews*

"Max is an awesome heroine. She packs a lot of punch and is kind of a bad-ass. . . . There was never a dull moment. Francis does a wonderful job at keeping the reader in suspense throughout the book."

—*Boekie's Book Reviews*

"The latest Horngate Witches thriller is a great entry due to the actions and reactions of the lead characters. . . . Readers will relish this strong urban fantasy."

—*Genre Go Round Reviews*

Also by Diana Pharaoh Francis

Bitter Night
Crimson Wind
Shadow City

Available from Pocket Books

BLOOD WINTER

**A HORNGATE
WITCHES
BOOK**

Diana
Pharaoh Francis

Pocket Books

New York   London   Toronto   Sydney   New Delhi

Pocket Books
A Division of Simon & Schuster, Inc.
1230 Avenue of the Americas
New York, NY 10020

This book is a work of fiction. Names, characters, places, and incidents either are products of the author's imagination or are used fictitiously. Any resemblance to actual events or locales or persons, living or dead, is entirely coincidental.

First Pocket Books paperback edition January 2013

POCKET and colophon are registered trademarks of Simon & Schuster, Inc.

For information about special discounts for bulk purchases, please contact Simon & Schuster Special Sales at 1-866-506-1949 or business@simonandschuster.com.

The Simon & Schuster Speakers Bureau can bring authors to your live event. For more information or to book an event contact the Simon & Schuster Speakers Bureau at 1-866-248-3049 or visit our website at www.simonspeakers.com.

Manufactured in the United States of America

10 9 8 7 6 5 4 3 2 1

ISBN: 978-1-4516-1386-5
ISBN: 978-1-4516-1388-9 (ebook)

To Tony, Q-ball, and Syd. I love you all dearly.

Acknowledgments

I HAVE SO MANY PEOPLE TO THANK FOR HELPING ME with this book on so many levels. To start, I'd like to thank my wonderful and supportive family. Your patience and support mean the world to me and have kept me sane. Tony has been a rock, and Quentin and Syd are the light in my life.

Thanks also go to Lucienne Diver for being an amazing agent; Adam Wilson, who is a fabulous and patient editor; Wendy Keebler, who is an amazing copy editor; Julia Fincher, who makes sure things get done; and to everyone else at Pocket Books who helped make this book happen.

For those of you who contributed to the book in other ways, like beta reading, critiquing, helping with the title—thank you: Barb Cass, Christy Keyes, Megan Glasscock, Paula Richey, and Missy Sawmiller.

I've had a lot of support from my fellow writers in the war room. Thanks to all of you for the companionship and the cheerleading and the commiseration when needed. Thanks also to the folks on Twitter, LJ, FB, and my blog. Your support and camaraderie have been so important to me.

And last but not least, thank you to my readers. Thank you for reading my books and spreading the word. I could not do this thing that I love so much without you.

I

"WHAT IS THIS STUFF?"

As Tyler complained, he brushed at his clothing. A streak of bright red dust clung to the shirt wrapping his lean, muscular frame. His long blond hair was tied at the base of his neck, and he sported a Three Musketeers-style mustache and beard.

Max sipped at the concoction in her glass, wincing at the thick, syrupy taste. Now that food was getting a lot harder to come by, Magpie, a Circle-level witch and the covenstead's cook, had come up with a high-calorie drink made from honey, berries, and who knew what else. It tasted like the worst kind of cough medicine, but Shadowblades and Sunspears didn't have much choice. They needed a minimum of twenty thousand calories a day each to fuel the spells that created them, and going to Costco or Walmart for tubs of peanut butter and pallets of power bars was no longer an option. The Ugly Juice, as everybody was quietly calling it when Magpie's back was turned, was the only answer they had come up with.

"Maybe you rubbed up against something," she suggested unhelpfully as the red smudge refused to budge. "Or someone." She lifted a brow suggestively.

"The same something—or someone—you rubbed up against?" He glared at her arm. His blue eyes burned in his narrow face, and he spun a knife around the fingers of his left hand. It never seemed to leave his grip anymore. Like a deadly security blanket. He was perpetually angry, always needing to move. As if he was hunted.

Max glanced down at herself and frowned. A streak of red dust ran down her forearm. She wiped at it. The stuff might as well have been spray paint. She shrugged and gave up. "Probably something one of the witches concocted. Likely Kyle," she said, wincing again.

Her brother had all the power of a Triangle witch and all the training and self-control of a toddler. He tended to experiment with spells before considering the consequences, with frequently messy and some-times dire results.

"He needs a keeper," Tyler said, taking half a biscuit drenched in gravy and offering it to the beast lying at his feet.

The Grim stared up at him with unworldly green eyes for a long moment, before closing Tyler's entire hand in her jaws and scraping off the biscuit, leaving welts across his skin. The creature was at least two hundred fifty pounds of pure muscle and stood about three feet tall at the shoulder. Her bearlike fur was blue-black, developing into a ruff behind her heavy, square head. Her tail curled around her legs.

"Nice doggy," Max said, eyeing the scrapes on Tyler's hand. His healing spells kicked in instantly, and a moment later they vanished. "What's she do when she's pissed off at you?"

He looked down at the Grim. The beast looked like a cross between a dog and a bear, but she was something far more magical and dangerous. Not to mention unpredictable, moody, and very possessive of Tyler.

He grimaced, and then the corner of his mouth turned up reluctantly. "It's not what she does when she's pissed that's the question, it's what she does if she isn't. *That* I'm still waiting to find out."

Max snorted. "You do seem to attract sketchy women."

"Like you?"

"I was thinking of the witch-bitch herself. Giselle."

He chuckled. "You've got a point there. Apparently, I like hard-assed women with vicious tendencies."

"Good thing, too, given that you're surrounded by them. And sleeping with one," she said, jerking her chin at the Grim. "Does she hog the bed?"

Tyler winced. "More like I *am* the bed. I usually wake up with her sprawled across me and with a mouthful of dog hair."

"Sounds romantic."

"Shut up. What about Beyul? Alexander's Grim doesn't exactly strike me as the sort to sleep at the foot of the bed."

"He likes the couch."

"What about Spike?"

Spike was a Calopus and looked a lot like a silver wolf, except for the two thin horns that curved from her skull and the multitude of poison spines along her

back, chest, sides, and tail. She had taken a liking to
Max and had become her regular companion. Just at
the moment, she slept under the table, her chin resting on Max's foot.

"The couch is big enough for her and Beyul both."

"You and Alexander are probably too loud and en-
ergetic for either beastie to sleep well if one of them
tried to share the bed. But maybe they like to watch,"
Tyler said, waggling his brows up and down. His knife
still spun between his fingers.

Max flushed despite herself. She wasn't used to having someone special in her life and in her bed. Ever
since becoming a Shadowblade, she'd kept everyone at
arm's length, resorting to one-night stands to scratch
her sexual itches. But then Alexander had come along
and changed all that. Sort of. She was still trying to
figure out how not to fall back into the habit of closing him out. During the days in bed, when she could
float on the amazing feelings he awoke in her, things
were just about perfect. But then nights came, and she
had to deal with all her fears and knee-jerk patterns of
shutting down rather than dealing with too many con-
flicting emotions. Alexander had a lot patience, but it
was running out. After that—after that was something
that was starting to give her nightmares.

"Maybe they do watch," she said with a shrug.
"'Course, I wouldn't know. I keep busy, you know."

"Which reminds me, where is the fair Alexander
tonight?" Tyler glanced around at the other tables in
the covenstead's dining commons, where several other
Shadowblades and Sunspears were eating. "You didn't
forget to unlock his handcuffs, did you?"

"No, just wore him out. Turned him into a puddle of satisfied man-goo."

"Way too much information," Tyler said, sitting back and making a face.

"You asked."

"My mistake. Let's change the subject. I don't need to hear any more about your sex life. What's the schedule for tonight?"

Max sipped her Ugly Juice before answering. Tyler was going to hate her answer. "I am leaving you in charge of the Blades for a while."

He straightened, and his knife stopped spinning as he held it tight in his fingers. Like he was about to cut someone's throat. "Why? Where are you going?"

"Well, that's the fun part. I'm going to town."

Tyler scowled. "Town? What for? Every idiot in Missoula has formed up into armies and gangs, and they've been fighting over food, gas, water, and territory. They don't take to strangers. They shoot first and ask questions later. You know as well as I do that the last time we sent anyone into town, they barely got out in one piece. You can't dodge a rifle bullet, and you won't see it coming." His words spilled out in a froth of worried anger.

Max kept her voice even. "The problem is, we have no idea what's going on down there. Giselle wants me to find out." She hesitated. "I'll be fine. I'm not going to get hurt."

"Right. That's what Niko thought, and now he's dead, along with how many others? I bet our indestructible angel friends thought the same thing, and where are they? Laid out in a stone vault like corpses, neither dead nor alive. It's bullshit. We should stay the hell out of Missoula until they sort themselves out. When the dust settles, we can go find out what's what. Most people think the only good witch is a dead witch—and the Change has only made them believe it more."

She sighed quietly. Niko had been her best friend. Tyler's, too. Losing him was beyond painful, and Tyler had reacted by being both wildly reckless with himself and more protective of everybody else. But Max wasn't made to stay locked up safe; she was a weapon. She still had a job to do, and hiding in Horngate wouldn't get it done. She told him as much.

"Then I'm going with you."

She shook her head. "I'm taking Alexander. You're staying here."

He stared at her, his chin jutting. The Grim beside him rose and growled, her green eyes lighting with emerald sparks. Max wasn't sure if the beast was threatening her, threatening him, or just generally commenting on the noise.

"You don't trust me to have your back," he said finally. "Is that it? You think I got Niko killed."

"No," she said emphatically, leaning forward and grabbing one of his hands. "Bad luck got Niko killed. Bad luck and bad magic." She sat back, her fingers tapping restlessly. "Besides, Alexander was there, too. I don't blame either one of you." *I blame me.* "The fact is, I'm saving you from living hell. You really don't want to come with me today."

He didn't give an inch. "Oh?"

She sighed. "Remember what you said about Kyle needing a keeper?" Max lifted her hand to her brow in a casual salute. "Head keeper reporting for duty."

His lips slowly widened into a grin. "That *does* sound like a good time. Let me know when you're ready to bury the body. I want to help." Then he frowned. "He's a liability in town. Why take him?"

"Oh, it gets better. Tory and Carrie Lydman are going, too."

He goggled and shook his head. "Explain to me why you are taking a stupid witch and a pair of teenagers—one of whom is a bitch on wheels—into a war zone. Use small words. I'm feeling slow."

"Because Giselle wants me to mingle and spy, and Kyle and the girls are about as close to ordinary people as you can get for Horngate. Add in that Tory and Carrie have been threatening to sneak off by themselves, and Giselle figures that they'll get it out of their systems and be useful at the same time."

"That's insane. I can't believe their parents agreed."

"The girls are of age. And as crazy as it sounds, Giselle is right. We need intel on what's going on in Missoula. Not knowing is like having a bomb in the backyard and just guessing when it will go off."

Tyler rubbed his lips with his knuckles. "Kyle's a loose cannon. He's just as likely to chase butterflies into a hornet's nest as help you."

"I'll handle him," Max said. "Even if I have to club him over the head. But he's good to have around, just in case. His magic could come in handy if we run into serious trouble."

"Trouble? Tory and Carrie are nothing but trouble. You won't be able to escape it," Tyler scoffed.

"The girls are excited to help. They think it's all a game. And since we're going to start at the River Market, I'm sure they're hoping to find a new pair of shoes or some makeup." Max rolled her eyes. Teenage girls. Pre- or postapocalypse, their priorities never changed.

"Aren't you ready yet? We're all waiting for you."

Max glanced up at the nineteen-year-old girl standing in the doorway, keeping her expression neutral. Tory was her niece—a walking tornado of hormones and emotion. As Tyler said, a bitch on wheels. She was stubborn, angry, resentful, and mouthy, and she had a knack for getting on Max's last nerve.

She scanned Tory slowly from head to foot, taking in her fashionably ripped skinny jeans, her low-cut rhinestone-studded shirt revealing the top of her lacy bra and a healthy amount of cleavage, and a pair of spiked boots. Her golden hair hung loose to her waist and was curled and teased. Her full lips sparkled with gloss. She looked, in a word, sexy. Sexy as hell. Max glanced at Tyler. He stared with widening eyes, his mouth dropping open.

Men. They were so easy.

She looked back at Tory. "You know you aren't going hooking on the Vegas Strip, right? You may want to tone it down. We're trying *not* to attract a lot of attention."

"You may be, but I'm not," Tory said, jabbing her thumbs into her back pockets so her full breasts thrust out. Tyler nearly choked. "You want information. Boys see a hot body, and they do nothing but talk. Their brains drop to their dicks, and they get diarrhea of the mouth."

Max couldn't argue with that. If she needed proof, there was Tyler. She shook her head. "Your mother is going to love this. She'll kick my ass."

Tory tossed her hair. Her face was rounded and sweet. Camouflage. Max was pretty sure that at nineteen, the girl could chew up most people and spit them out without breaking a sweat.

"You know, the world doesn't revolve around you," Tory said.

"Are you sure, Buttercup?" Max drawled, clamping down on her irritation. "You want to go into town, but you're not going anywhere without me. That pretty much means I'm the center of your universe tonight, doesn't it?"

Tory's cheeks flushed red, and her eyes snapped with fury. She dropped her hands to her sides, her fingers curling into fists. "Yeah? Well, you need my help, too—besides, once I talk Giselle into making me a Shadowblade, I'll be able to do anything I want, whenever I want, just like you."

Max met her niece's gaze for a long moment and then glanced at Tyler. His body was chiseled in stone. She could feel his emotions flaring hot and wild. It had been just over a month since Niko had died, adding to the too-long tally of Shadowblades and Sunspears Horngate had lost since the Change—when the Guardians had flooded the world with magic. Both Max and Tyler knew that those supernatural warriors needed to be replaced in order to protect the covenstead, but the reality was too much to handle right now. The grief was still too raw.

Abruptly, Max swigged down the last of the Ugly Juice and stood. "Let's go," she said, and led Tory out of the dining commons. Spike trotted behind them.

Tory kept abreast of Max despite her aunt's fury. It

was actually impressive. Most humans cowered around an aroused Blade, much less a full Prime like herself. But then again, Tory was a burning ball of anger and resentment. Fear was a foreign concept to her.

Max slowed, reaching down to scratch Spike's ears. "You ready to give up going out during the day?" she asked. "Because Shadowblades fry—literally—in the daylight. *Poof!* Burn to ash in a matter of seconds. Or Giselle could make you a Sunspear, but they have their own problems. The dark poisons them. Sometimes slowly, but within an hour or so if they don't get inside."

"You just don't want to give me the chance to be like you," Tory said, stepping in front of Max with her hands on her hips. "You still hate Giselle for turning you, and you think just because you don't want to be a Shadowblade, nobody else will, either."

Max considered the accusation. Six months ago, there might have been some truth to it. But things had changed. Max had changed. She no longer resented being turned. She liked what she was. It allowed her to protect the people she cared about.

Except for Niko.

A worm of grief wriggled through her heart. At least she could protect them better than if she were still human. And if Tory were turned, the girl could at least protect herself. Still, Max doubted she had the slightest clue what being a Shadowblade really entailed.

"You won't be able to have kids," she said. "So you'll want to think about having one before you're turned. You have to eat a minimum of twenty thousand calories a day, more if you get into a battle or have to run thirty or forty miles or toss around a few cars. That's not so easy with food getting scarcer. You'll have healing spells, but you'll need them. You'll end up hurt a lot, and I'm not talking hangnails. Broken bones are easy, but you'll get shot, knifed, burned, mauled, shredded—all in a day's work. That will happen with depressing regularity for your entire life.

"The healing spells won't help with the pain. That's all yours. Let's hope you have a high tolerance. You won't age, as you can tell." Max gestured at herself. At fifty years old, she still looked the way she did when she was twenty-one. She looked more like Tory's sister than her aunt. "That means you probably shouldn't fall in love with any ordinary humans. They'll age and die long before you do. Then there's the binding. Most witches bind their Blades and Spears. There are some good reasons for that—Giselle will know when you've been hurt, she'll be able to summon you when she needs you, and she can help you heal faster through the binding. On the other hand, you won't be able to ever get away from her, and you'll be stuck serving her unless she releases you. Or you die. That works, too."

"You're trying to talk me out of it," Tory said. "It's not going to work."

Max shook her head. "That's not it at all, Buttercup. Giselle got me drunk and asked if I wanted to be superstrong, never age, never get sick, all that sort of thing. I said sure—who wouldn't say yes? But I thought it was all a joke. Next thing I knew, it was months later, and I was a Shadowblade, chained to serve her. I was a slave. Things might have been different if I'd really been willing. I just figure you ought to make an informed decision."

Tory sniffed and pushed her hair behind her ears. "Don't call me Buttercup. I know what I'm doing. But Giselle says she's not going to do it. I know why, too. It's *you*. She doesn't want to piss you off, for some reason." Despite the defiant edge to Tory's voice, Max could tell the girl was thinking about what she'd said.

"I'm not going to stop you. Turns out I'm pretty happy being a Shadowblade."

"So you'll talk to Giselle?" Tory's expression suddenly glowed with passionate hope, the kind only the young and naive can really feel.

"Sure. But don't be in a hurry. You've got to wait until you're twenty-one."

Tory's joyous triumph collapsed. "What? Why?"

Max shrugged. "It's a magic number."

"But people don't *have* to be exactly twenty-one, right? Alexander was twenty-five when he was made."

Max's brows rose. How the hell did Tory know that? She swallowed her curiosity and the sharp jab of jealousy that accompanied it. It wasn't like Alexander didn't have a right to tell people about his life. "He was turned more than a hundred years ago by a flesh witch. Maybe she didn't care about the numbers. Giselle does."

"Couldn't Uncle Kyle do it if Giselle won't?"

"Only if he wanted to be banished from Horngate— or killed. Giselle won't tolerate anyone stepping on her toes."

"*Killed?*" Tory repeated, her eyes widening.

"Yep. Oh, that's another thing about being a Shadowblade, Buttercup. You'll be killing things. Maybe people, maybe creatures, but you'll be spilling a lot of blood. Sometimes you'll use weapons, sometimes you'll kill bare-handed. Get used to the idea. That's a major part of the job. If you want, I could take you out hunting to see how you do with that."

Tory swallowed and didn't answer. Instead, she spun around and started up the corridor in silence. Max fell in beside her.

The heart of the Horngate covenstead was a mountain fortress west of Missoula. Giselle and the coven witches had carved a warren of rooms and passages, enough to house hundreds of people, with room to expand if needed. Max and Tory headed for a newer chamber on the northeast side of the mountain.

It was an expansive space with low ceilings. Vehicles were parked in rows. Max headed for a dark green Suburban. Kyle, Carrie Lydman, and Alexander were already waiting. Carrie was dressed much like Tory. Together, the two were stunning. Max had little doubt that men would certainly get diarrhea of the mouth upon seeing them.

Kyle was bouncing on his toes like a five-year-old at Disneyland, and Alexander stood at the rear of the Suburban, the back doors open as he checked supplies. At six feet, he was just a few inches taller than she. His skin was the color of tea, like he spent all his time in the sun. His short hair was black. A close-cut goatee framed his mouth. He was lean and muscular, and it made Max drool just to look at him.

He looked up as she and Tory entered, his dark gaze smoldering. Max shivered, resisting the urge to drag him off to a closet and have her way with him.

She took hold of herself, suppressing her reaction, keeping her face from showing her hunger. She was

Horngate's Shadowblade Prime, which meant she was in charge of Alexander and the rest of the Blades. She needed to stay focused on her job. She didn't need anybody else dying on her watch.

She crossed to glance inside the back of the Suburban, sidling away from his hand as he reached for her. He pulled back, his mouth flattening, his eyes flashing hurt annoyance. Max clenched her teeth. What the hell did he expect from her? But she knew the answer. He wanted public acknowledgment of their relationship. The trouble was, she was still trying to figure out exactly what their relationship was. She cared about him—*loved* him, she corrected herself acidly. She might as well admit it to herself, even if she was too much of a coward to tell him.

She didn't have much experience with long-term relationships. She'd only had one serious boyfriend before Giselle had turned her, and she'd fumbled that. She was like a child figuring out how to do calculus.

With a silent sigh, she pushed aside her internal turmoil. She'd work on fixing her head later. Now she had to get everybody in and out of Missoula alive.

Inside the back of the Suburban was a row of six shotguns upright in a rack. Beside them were six bandoliers with shells and grenades. The latter were witch-made. There was also a chest containing a variety of other weapons, including handguns, clips of bullets, knives, witch chain, canisters of salt, iron filings, mixes of herbs, tubs of healing salve, bandages, charms, light and dark sealed sacks, and duct tape, plus jerky, homemade high-calorie energy bars, and two jugs of Ugly Juice.

She and Alexander were both already wearing tactical vests, the pockets bulging with a variety of supplies. Max's .45 was holstered on her hip, and she had her two favorite flat-bladed knives strapped to her arms. Around her neck was a gold torque that could stretch itself into a garrote, a wire-thin rope, and other useful shapes. She had a Glock 9mm tucked into an ankle holster and a combat knife in her waistband.

She glanced at her companions. "Ready? Remember, we're going for the single purpose of intelligence collection. We'll have to park away from the River Market and walk in. We don't need anyone noticing that our vehicle runs on magic. Once there, try to blend in. The word is that the market stays lively late into the night, with a lot of buying and selling, not to mention gambling, whoring, drinking, and who knows what else. It can turn into a free-for-all pretty quick. Stick close to me and Alexander—and Kyle? Don't do anything witchy unless you have to."

Her brother looked at her innocently. Kyle never planned to be stupid and reckless, he just followed his idiot impulses. Babies had more sense than he did sometimes.

Max's eyes narrowed. A smudge of the red dust streaked Kyle's pale blond hair above his left ear. "What is that stuff?" she asked. "Do you know?"

"What stuff?" he said, even as Alexander came around the front of the Suburban. Beyul, another massive Grim, padded at his side.

"It's on you, too," she said, pointing at Alexander's boot.

He glanced down, his brow creasing.

"What is it?" Max held up her forearm to show her splash of red.

Tory and Carrie examined each other. "We don't have any of that junk on us," Carrie said with clear relief, no doubt relieved that she didn't have to worry about it staining her clothes.

"It doesn't come off," Max said. "Tyler had some on him, too."

Kyle ran a finger over her arm. Pale blue magic flickered along his fingertip, and Max's skin tingled. He pulled away, looking intrigued. "Could be magic-related. I need to do some experiments . . ."

"Not now," Tory said, grabbing his arm and shoving him toward the door of the Suburban. "We'll never get to town if you go off experimenting, Uncle Kyle. After all, it's just a little color, right?"

Max had to agree. The stuff didn't seem to be dangerous, and if Kyle went off on a mad-witch-scientist tangent, they might not get to town for another week or two.

"Load up," she said as she slammed the two rear doors shut. The two girls pushed into the front seat beside Alexander, who was driving. Max let Spike and Beyul into the rear seats and then slid in beside Kyle.

She was just shutting her door when a jolt shuddered through the air and a hail of needles ran along her nerves. The walls of the mountain fortress trembled and groaned. A split second later, the alarm chime vibrated through the air. It reverberated through Max's skull, making the marrow in her bones ache. Something had crossed the covenstead's outer ward line, something magical that didn't belong.

"What now?" Tory demanded. "Let's just go."

Max hopped out. "Trip's canceled," she said, her Prime rising hard. Her humanity flattened beneath the predator, her senses sharpening. With that came blinding rage. No one—*no one*—was going to get away with attacking her home again. She didn't care what she had to do to protect it and the people within. This was her home, her family. She'd kill anyone who threatened them.

"Tory and Carrie, get to the Great Hall with everybody else," she ordered hoarsely, her lips curling back from her lips in an animal snarl. "Kyle and Alexander, you're with me."

"I want to come with you," Tory said, her voice tense but resolute as she stepped in front of Max.

"No chance, Buttercup," Max replied, her fingers curling in an effort not to pick the teenager up and toss her out of the way.

"I can handle myself. Give me a gun."

"When pigs fly. Get back to the Great Hall before you get yourself killed," Max said. "That's something else Shadowblades do—obey orders." Max shoved past her, Spike loping at her side. Alexander and Beyul followed close on her heels, with Kyle bringing up the rear.

She pushed out into the night air. She could feel the wrongness in the wards and smell Divine magic. It came from the south.

She led the way around to the front entrance. The rest of her Blades had spilled out into the night, waiting for her, all armed to the teeth. A few Grims nosed around curiously.

Max turned to Tyler. "Where's Giselle?"

"On her way with Gregory and Judith."

She looked over her Blades. She probably ought to wait for them. "Tyler, Alexander, Oak, Nami, and Simon, you're with me. We'll scout ahead. The rest of you follow with the witches." She looked around at them all. She scowled as she realized that each one was smudged with some of the red dust. She'd have to ask Giselle about it later.

"Whatever's going on out there, watch one another's back. Nobody dies tonight. Got it?"

Sober nods went all around the group, and a minute later, Max and her companions were loping across the steep ridges south of Horngate, each one a messenger of death for whatever lay in wait.

2

ALEXANDER WAS SPOILING FOR A FIGHT. ANYTHING to relieve the tension knotting tighter with every second he spent with Max. For weeks, she had been blowing hot and cold—one minute she was wrapped around him as if she would never let go, the next she was covered in steel spikes and driving him away on the end of a spear. It was getting old. Like being on a roller coaster that never stopped running. Something had to change and soon, or he was going to go insane.

He had lost control of himself once. Doing it again would be his death sentence. He had managed to come back one time, but he was certain the next time he would have to be put down.

The smell of Divine magic grew more dense as they ranged closer to whoever or whatever had penetrated the ward line circling the Horngate fortress at a circumference of about five miles. Uncanny creatures like Shadowblades and Sunspears were made of magic but had no ability to create spells or cast magic. Only Divine creatures could, such as witches and angels and a host of other beings.

The group came up over the final ridge above where the ward line crossed the road into Horngate.

"What the fuck?" Simon said, and was cuffed on the side of the head by Nami.

"Shh!"

The road below snaked through a narrow channel between tall, heavily treed ridges. A broad arch of elk, deer, and moose horns over the road gave Horngate its name. It was blackened, and an acrid smell of burned horn drifted upward.

A line of people carrying torches and chanting stretched out of sight along the road. They marched through the gate—something the wards should have refused to let them do—and poured into a flat, wide area just within. In the center was a small cleared space surrounding what appeared to be large crosses with people hanging from them, crucified in biblical fashion. The base of each cross was stacked with wood. Two of the victims were children.

Alexander's stomach clenched and rage made the edges of his vision cloud. He sucked in a deep breath, trying to keep his Prime under control.

"Is that what it looks like?" Oak whispered in horror.

"It looks to me like a good old-fashioned burning at the stake," Max said, her voice cold as frosted iron. "With a dose of crucifixion to add that shine of historical glamor. Is that what it looks like to you?"

"That's fucking sick. They're going to burn kids?"

"No," Alexander said.

"You got that right, Slick," Max said.

Though she seemed to be taking the situation in stride, her Prime told another story. It had risen to the killing edge and the air crackled with her white-hot fury.

"What are they doing *here*?" Nami asked.

"Sending us a message," Max said.

"Like 'Please come kick our asses'?" said Simon. His eyes had narrowed, and his hands flexed into claws, like a cat kneading the air.

"I would say they want us to know that they do not like witches, except that they clearly have at least one down there," Alexander mused, watching as more and more people crowded into the small clearing below. The string of lights coming up the road had not thinned. There had to be a couple hundred people gathered already. How many more could there be?

"Wish we had the angels for a flyover," Max muttered, and then she clamped her jaws together.

But both Tutresiel and Xaphan lay unconscious in a stone vault inside Horngate, neither dead nor quite alive. No one knew how to wake them or if that was even possible. They had fallen when a Fury arose and unleashed her rage. Their loss, along with Niko's, had wounded Max to her soul. She had nightmares from which she awoke in a killing mood and after which she and Alexander usually had mind-blowing sex. Alexander did not know if she slept afterward out of satiation or exhaustion. The question bothered him more than he liked to admit.

"All right. This is what we're going to do. Simon, Tyler, Oak, and Nami, get across to the other ridge and wait for orders. Get down close but not so close they can see you. When the witches get here, we'll go in. Wait for my signal."

The four peeled away into the darkness, Tyler's Grim loping along beside him on silent feet. Whether she would choose to help or just watch was the never-ending question.

"Let's go back to the road and wait for the others," Max told Alexander.

They climbed back over the ridge and dropped down to the road, out of sight of the torch army.

"Who the fuck are they?" Max wondered aloud as she paced restlessly. "What are they up to?"

"We will find out soon," he said, hearing the crunch of tires as two vehicles drove closer. They ran on magic now, making them mostly silent.

The Suburban that Max had intended to take to town pulled up first, followed by a pickup. The rest of her Blades piled out, followed by Kyle, and Gregory.

Gregory stepped out of the Suburban and shook himself as though to straighten out his lanky body. Like Kyle, he was a Triangle-level witch. His powers were considerable, and he had far more experience than Max's impetuous brother.

His eyes were sunk deep beneath his black brows, his nose protruding like an eagle's beak. He carried himself hunched, like a slave awaiting the bite of the master's whip. Max and Alexander had rescued him and several members of his coven a few months back, and although his body had recovered from the experience, his mind had not. His eyes were always roving, searching for trouble. He rarely spoke, and when he did, his statements were terse and to the point.

He glanced up toward the bend in the road that hid the gathering and started walking in that direction.

"Thor," Alexander said, and he jerked his head after the witch.

The blond Shadowblade was wearing his usual battered straw cowboy hat and scuffed boots. Like all the other Blades, he was bristling with weapons. He nodded and caught up to Gregory. Flint and Steel, twins from Gregory's original covenstead, joined them.

Giselle stepped out last. She looked almost fragile, like fine china. She stood about five foot five in her stockinged feet, with waist-long chestnut hair and a heart-shaped face. She reminded Alexander of a hummingbird.

But her appearance was deceiving.

She was a powerful witch who had no problem killing anybody who might stand in her way. She could be brutal and vicious, and she frequently was. She could also be generous and loving, which made her extraordinary among witches. Most of the ones Alexander had known tended to be selfish and unconcerned with who suffered and died, so long as they got what they wanted.

"What's the story?" she demanded.

"There's a mob of torch-carrying village idiots on our side of the ward line. Hundreds of them. They've got five people hanging up on crosses, and it looks like they are planning a human barbecue," Max said. "They have to have at least one witch with them, probably more, given that they blew out our wards."

"Who are they? Where did they come from?" Kyle asked.

"More to the point, what do they want?" Giselle said. She glanced at Max. "Let's go ask. Then kick them the hell off our land."

For a moment, Alexander thought Max was going

to protest. She had been protective of everyone, especially Giselle, since Niko had died and the angels had fallen into their comas.

Max just scraped her teeth across her lower lip and nodded. "All right. Ivy and Jody, collect up Flint and Steel and work around the left side of the gathering. Wait for my signal."

The two Blades hurried off.

Max looked at Kyle. "This could get bloody," she said. "Stay with Giselle, and do what she tells you."

His excitement dimmed, but only slightly. Alexander shook his head. Kyle had no idea what real trouble looked like. He was about to find out, up close and personal.

Max started up the road and Alexander fell in beside her, with the two witches slightly behind and between them. Beyul and Spike trotted ahead.

At the bend in the road, they found Thor with Gregory perched on a pile of boulders in order to get a better view. As the others approached, the two clambered down. Gregory was shaking, his mouth bracketed with white dents. Green magic flickered around his hands as if he was having trouble keeping himself under control.

"They're going to burn them," he said hoarsely.

"No they aren't," Giselle said.

He did not seem to hear her. "Why don't they do something to escape? How can a horde of ordinary people snare witches like that?"

"They may not be witches," Alexander pointed out.

Gregory's head whipped around. "Of course they are. Why else would those bastards burn them? They have two *children* up there," he said, his voice dropping to a ragged whisper.

That rocked Giselle back on her heels. Her eyes widened, then narrowed to slits, and her hair rose on invisible currents as magic swelled around her. Her lips tightened and white dents bracketed her nose and mouth. The air turned thick and hot.

"We will not let them burn," she assured Gregory. "But Alexander's right; they may not be witches. They might just be unlucky. Don't go expecting them to be able to help themselves or us."

That took Gregory aback. Apparently he had forgotten his history and how often innocent people were taken for witches in the Salem witch trials and the Spanish Inquisition. After a moment, his fury flared hotter. His throat worked, and his face turned red, but the words refused to come. Magic sparked from his hair and ran in threads over his exposed skin. Like Giselle, Gregory did not believe witches were better than normal humans. Like her, he believed they ought to be protected. Alexander was still not used to that mentality in even one witch, much less two of them.

"Hold that thought," Giselle said. "Let's go."

Thor fell in on the other side of Max, while Gregory walked behind with Kyle and Giselle. A moment later, Tyler and his Grim stepped out of the trees, his knives glinting in the moonlight.

"Going to the party?" he asked. Despite the casual ease of his words, he was stretched tighter than a bowstring and near to snapping. "You weren't planning on going without me, were you?" His tone was accusing.

"I figured you'd crash," Max said. "You have all the manners of a buffalo."

He was not in any mood for humor. His Blade was frothing. He was losing control of himself. The next step was to go feral, and Alexander was the only person he knew of to ever come back from that insanity. He was not going to let Tyler try it.

Alexander loosened his grip on his Prime. Instantly, his vision went ghostly as the world turned from solid matter to living lights. He could see his companions' spirit flames and those of the gathered people. The earth, trees, rocks, animals, and air shimmered with life and magic. It was his unique talent to see the world in this way. An aftereffect of going feral. He brushed a hand over Tyler's shoulder, letting the power of his Prime surge. He pressed down on Tyler's wild rage, tempering it, making it controllable.

It took all of a second, and then Alexander dropped his hand. The other Blade looked at him and shifted closer to Max, like a child clinging to his mother. Which was true in its own way.

She was Horngate's official Shadowblade Prime. Alexander had come from another covenstead and had been allowed to stay and serve, but as far as he knew, no other covenstead had ever had two Primes at one time. Generally, there would be a fight for dominance, and the lesser one would be killed. But Horngate was different. The world was different. Besides, he was happy serving. There was no better Prime than Max. He would not have challenged her for anything.

Max reached back and touched Tyler's cheek reassuringly, flashing a swift smile at Alexander that was gone as fast as it formed. She was not jealous or threatened by him. She trusted him with her Blades. The knowledge warmed him.

"What's the plan?" Kyle asked from behind.

"Don't get dead?" Tyler said.

"That's a good plan," Max said. "I always like that one."

"Then how come you always go with the plan that includes death?" Tyler complained.

"I've only died once, and I did wake up from it," Max pointed out. "It's the rest of you—"

She broke off, and the tension instantly ratcheted up. The air felt so brittle that Alexander wondered if it might shatter.

"Seriously," Kyle said, unaware that he was taking his life into his own hands. "What do we do?"

A moment passed. Then another. Finally, she spoke. "Since we don't know what's going on and since we probably don't have a lot of time to waste before they start cooking their prisoners, we're going to walk into the middle of the shindig and ask questions. Your job is to protect us and yourself when things get ugly."

"You think there's going to be fighting?"

Max sucked an angry breath between clenched teeth.

"Yes, expect fighting," Alexander answered for her. "These people did not come here to be friendly. So that means you had better be on your A game. This is serious. *Deadly* serious."

"I know," Kyle said defensively, his pale cheeks flushing.

Cherubic. That was how he looked, with his peach-fuzz bristle, rounded cheeks, strawberries-and-cream complexion, and wide blue eyes. He should have been a kindergarten teacher. Instead, he had the ability to wield powerful magic and a stomach made of tapioca. He was more likely to freeze than fight. Alexander gave a quiet sigh and resolved to guard Kyle closely in the next few minutes.

Without a word, the four Blades arranged themselves in a diamond formation around the three witches, with Max in the lead, Tyler and Alexander on the left and right points, and Thor bringing up the rear. Beyul, Spike, and Tyler's Grim trotted just ahead.

As they turned the bend, Giselle broke ranks, stepping up beside Max. The road descended before them in a long, shallow slope. The ridges on either side rose almost vertically. They were thick with trees and stone outcroppings. With his altered sight, Alexander could see all of the Shadowblades hiding in the trees on either side of the gathering.

It appeared that the last of the parade had pushed beneath the charred horn arch. The crowd circled around the five crosses and swayed back and forth. They chanted, arms hooked together, their faces glowing with an unsettling blend of animal hunger and beatific rapture.

Max approached from behind the circle and pushed people apart. The small group wedged through the crowd. For a few seconds, the chanting faltered, and then it flared with new life. But now a corridor opened for them, giving them passage to the center ring. It was almost choreographed. Alexander's spine itched. This felt like a trap.

Bolts and wire bound the five victims to the crosses.

The bolts passed through their hands and crossed ankles, and wire looped their shoulders, cutting through their clothes into the flesh beneath. Blood ran from their wounds. There were two women in their twenties or thirties, a man closer to forty, one teenage girl, and a boy who couldn't have been more than ten. The boy and the girl were incoherent with pain, unrelenting keening sounds slipping from their cracked and broken lips.

The adults stared glassily at the surrounding group in fear and desperation, begging to be released. Tears and snot crusted their faces and clothing. Flies and mosquitoes buzzed eagerly around the blood.

Alexander's mind thinned to a hard wire, his Prime surging up hot and hard. Gregory's magic turned to a green nimbus around him as his rage increased. Kyle bent and puked. Giselle's eyes had turned black as magic pooled in her eye sockets. It danced around her fingertips.

The chants of the crowd nearest them stumbled and turned to mutters, and then angry growls. The path widened and then they were surrounded, the torches turning to weapons as the invading people prodded the air and began to shout.

"Witches!"

"Devils!"

"Demons!"

The words swelled and garbled together, then suddenly shifted to another chant that swept like wildfire through the mob, growing louder with every repetition: "Kill them! Kill them! Kill them!"

Each word was punctuated by a shake of a torch.

The witches and Blades fell back to stand at the base of the crosses. The torch flames reflected in the fanatical eyes of the horde, turning them into the devils they shouted about. They pressed forward, expressions frenzied, flinging their torches toward the Horngaters and the dry fuel at the base of the crosses. Alexander batted aside the missiles, fire searing his skin where they hit. Behind him he heard crackling sounds and screams of the five desperate victims on the crosses.

Magic swelled in the air as Giselle swore. "Take them down," she ordered as magic billowed from her hands, snuffing out every flame within a hundred yards.

The Blades leaped forward to yank the crosses out of the ground. Before they could make contact, columns of red smoke rose around each of the five victims. Acrid and sweet, it smelled like jasmine and battery acid. When Alexander touched the smoke, his hands blistered and blackened. He pushed against the crimson wall, but it did not give. He stepped back and looked up.

Above him, the woman on the cross twitched violently and screamed as boils covered her from head to foot. They burst, and her skin ran with blood and pus. She was not the only one. All five victims thrashed under similar attacks. It was a relief when the two children passed out and their heartrending cries ceased.

The four Blades looked expectantly at Giselle and Gregory. But at that moment, a sudden hush fell across the crowd.

"The faithful shalt not suffer a witch to live! It is the obligation of every God-fearing, God-loving human soul to stamp out the devil's minions!"

Although the voice was buttery soft and almost mellow, it echoed from the ridges, repeating and growing in intensity. The gathered crowd picked it up and started stamping their feet in time to the rhythm of a new chant, shouting, "No witches! No witches!"

A slow-whirling cloud of red smoke erupted from the ground behind the crosses. It grew denser, rising twenty feet in the air. Then it collapsed back down, revealing a man.

He wore sandals and long beige cotton robes belted with rope. Except for the fact that he had short reddish hair and was clean-shaven, he could have been attending a Halloween party dressed as Jesus. His hair stuck up in wild tufts. He lifted his arms with slow grandiosity, his palms turned upward. The crowd noise increased. Then he turned his hands outward, and the noised ceased as if someone had hit an off switch.

He smiled, and a feeling of joy radiated outward. It was physical. It caressed and warmed. Alexander snarled and shook himself. Beyul nosed his hand, and the feeling dissolved. He pet the Grim and glanced at his companions. Kyle looked slightly starstruck. The other two witches were irritated. Max was scowling.

"The Lord of Heaven and Earth bids us not suffer a witch to live," the man declared in a singsong cadence. "We must not suffer evil in our midst, or we will become evil; we will defile our Lord's name by our very existence. We must do His work, no matter the cost. He sacrificed His only son for us; we must be willing to sacrifice no less for Him!"

Alexander could not help but gawk at the brazen hypocrisy. The bastard *was* a witch.

"Mother of fuck . . ." Max whispered.

"Now, that's what I call the pot calling the kettle black," Thor drawled.

Tyler said nothing. His gaze was fixed on the boy on the cross, his hands clenching and unclenching. A thin line of yellow ringed his eyes. He was crossing into feral territory.

"My brothers and sisters, we have come here to the heart of the devil to show that we will not be corrupted; we will root out evil in all its shapes and forms. We are God's army, the last stand for all of Earth and humanity. God has made me His right hand. His might flows through me. Let it be done!"

His words pulsed through the air, throbbing with magic. His worshippers sighed and moaned and shouted "Amen!" and "Hallelujah!"

An instant later, fire erupted around each of the crosses, filling the red columns with hellish flames. The people within screamed. At once, the four Blades leaped forward, smashing at the magic barriers, while Gregory and Giselle unleashed a torrent of magic on the obstructions. Alexander slammed one flaming column with all his might. He bounced off, his clothing smoldering. He leaped forward again, this time with Beyul beside him. The Grim broke right through, and Alexander passed into the heart of the fire.

Flames caught his clothing and hair. They scorched his skin and burned away his eyelashes and eyebrows. Pain seared his body, and he could not breathe.

He plowed through the pile of firewood around the base of the cross, driving his shoulder into the upright. The cross shuddered. Changing his approach, Alexander wrapped his arms around it and lifted. It slid easily out of the rocky dirt. He twisted and stumbled blindly out of the fire, the massive beam tight against his chest. A moment later, coolness enveloped him, and familiar hands eased the heavy cross out of his hands.

The rest of Horngate's Shadowblades had joined the fight.

Alexander dropped to his knees, coughing raggedly. His body was a mass of pain. All around, he heard screams and running feet. He smelled blood and cooked flesh, and through it all spun that odd sweet-acrid scent.

It was not a good time to rest. He stood again, tottering as his head whirled. Beyul wuffled his hand, and he gripped the Grim's fur. His spirit sight told him that the other four columns had been breached and the other crosses had come down.

The crowd frothed and boiled as Shadowblades drove them back. They fought efficiently. The invaders were ill-equipped for their skills or their fury. Some of the invaders fought with knives, bats, shovel handles, and axes. More had guns. A barrage of shots rang out and bodies fell—none were Blades. People screamed in fear and agony. It sent the mob over the edge. People exploded into a frenzy as they fought to get away. Cowards. They pushed and shoved at one another, desperate to escape. More people fell and were trampled beneath their stampeding companions. In just a few minutes, the entire crowd had vanished, scuttling away down the road, leaving behind a couple of dozen bodies, some still alive.

There was no sign of the redheaded witch.

Alexander blinked, feeling his healing spells kicking into high gear. He hurt, but it was nothing he could not handle. He limped to where Gregory, Nami, and Oak were trying to detach one woman from her cross. She was badly burned. She whimpered with every touch and movement.

"Fuckers drilled straight through her shin bones. They glued the nut on the bolt with Loctite and sawed off the excess," Oak said. "Can't get a grip to break it off."

Gregory made an animal sound, and his green magic sliced through the back of the bolt like it was made of butter. The nut fell off, and Oak pulled the long metal shaft out from the front.

As he did so, the woman screamed. "Stop, please please please! I'll do anything you want. Anything! Oh, God, don't do this to me, please!"

Gregory touched his fingers to her forehead, and she slumped. "Should have done that first," he muttered.

They proceeded to remove the bolts from her hands and the wires holding her shoulders and torso to the wood. The wires had cut her to the bone. Blood spurted and ran. The witch stopped it with his magic, then stood.

"Watch her," he told Oak. "Holler if she has trouble. I'm going to stabilize the others."

It was too late for the girl and the other woman. Both had died from burns and smoke inhalation. Giselle was looking after the man, and Kyle and Tyler were working on the boy. Gregory went to help them.

Kyle's fingers shook, and he looked as if he might faint. Still, he was pumping healing into the boy as Tyler wrestled to free him. Gregory cut away the bolts and wire, and a moment later, the boy was lying on the ground. Blood bubbled from his lips, and his skin was black and melted. He was barely breathing.

"Get the vehicles," Max ordered, and a few minutes later, the truck and the Suburban pulled up.

"Load them up," Giselle said. "Careful, now."

In two minutes, it was done. Steel and Flint took the wheels of the vehicles and drove away with the three witches and the surviving victims. Tyler went, too, a silent shadow clinging to the boy's side.

"Are you okay?" Max asked.

Alexander looked at her. Like him, she was bruised, blistered, burned, and bloody. All in a day's work. "I could use a shower," he said. He itched to reach for her, to pull her tight and taste her breath, but she would only pull away. He was not up to dealing with the rejection just now.

She nodded, her expression visibly relaxing. She reached out and brushed the tips of her fingers down his cheek. She closed her eyes and nodded again before turning around. "Let's get these bodies in the ground. Simon, go fetch the backhoe."

As the others obeyed, she and Alexander wandered around, accompanied by Beyul and Spike. They came to the spot where the red-haired preacher had suddenly appeared. Max stared at the broad circle of red dust on the dirt road. She squatted and touched it, rubbing it between her fingers. Where it touched, it didn't come off.

Beyul sniffed it and padded through it. None of it clung to him. Spike sneezed and edged carefully around the circle.

Max slowly stood and looked up at Alexander. Her expression was troubled. "This is the stuff that's all over Horngate. It's all over us. Somehow that crazy preacher got inside the mountain. *Before* the wards broke. He got in without tripping any alarms."

"How is that possible?" Alexander asked, unease prickling along his neck.

Max shook her head. "That's just it, Slick. It isn't possible." She looked back down at her fingers. "What the fuck are we dealing with?"

3

THAT NIGHT, MAX WOKE SUDDENLY FROM A DEEP sleep. Her body was clammy with sweat, and her breathing was ragged. She'd been dreaming. A nightmare.

Filled with a primal need, she slid on top of Alexander, kissing him with a desperation born less from lust than from a need to disappear, to vanish. Alexander's hands rose and pressed hard and hot against her back. They glided down over her hips, butt, and thighs and then back up. She squirmed, grinding herself against him. He groaned and clutched her, his hips bucking, his cock hard between her legs.

She purred with the power she had over him and raked her fingernails along his ribs, thrusting her hips back and forth. He sucked in a breath, his hands tightening painfully. Suddenly, he lifted her, then drove himself up inside her. She gasped and clamped his hips between her knees, lifting herself up and down, riding him in a hard, fast rhythm. He cupped her breasts and thumbed her nipples, making her moan and ride him harder.

Her body was awash in glorious sensation. Alexander sat up, holding her hips still as he sucked on first one breast and then the other. Max whimpered and tried to move, but he held her fast and thrust up in short, staccato motions.

She bent and kissed him, her tongue delving inside his mouth. His lips seared hers. His hands rose to fasten on the back of her head as he deepened the kiss. Their teeth ground together as they devoured each other.

With her hips freed, Max began to move on him again. Sensation spiraled tight in her belly and sent sparks racing down every nerve. She flung her head back as she gripped the headboard for leverage, driving herself onto Alexander. He went back to teasing her breasts, licking and biting.

She whimpered more as the tension in her body wound to a single aching point at her core.

Her world exploded. Pleasure washed through her. Her muscles spasmed with the bliss. She fell against Alexander, letting the waves of pleasure wash over her again and again. She sat there for a long minute as she caught her breath, her arms around his neck. He rubbed her back, soothing away the storm of her passion. She was caught up in the feeling of rightness, of happiness.

Then she remembered.

The feelings she'd chased away came flooding back. Loss, fear, hurt, worry. They gnawed at her, and she had to move.

Wordlessly, she pushed herself away and climbed off the bed. She went into the bathroom, skirting the tub carved into the stone of the floor and heading straight to the shower. She turned it on to its hottest and let the spray pound her. The bite of the water did nothing to alleviate the knots of tension in her shoulders and the throbbing headache that threatened to split her skull. She braced her arms against the wall and let her head dangle, the water sluicing over her.

She glanced at the door, half expecting Alexander to join her. He didn't. She grimaced. This wasn't the first time she'd woken him that way, and it wasn't the first time she'd abandoned him without a word. She sighed. *What is my problem?*

She couldn't help but keep a wall up between them. She was doing her best to tear it down, but it was hard. She kept thinking of the what-ifs. What if he died like Niko? What if he quit wanting her? What if she couldn't keep this up? What if she got someone killed because she was too attached to Alexander?

The what-ifs were endless. Then stir in the awkwardness of actually being in a relationship with someone day to day. Public displays of affection or no? How was she supposed to fit him into a life where she was his boss and her lover?

Max rubbed her forehead. It really wasn't that complicated. But she felt like everyone was watching her, and it made her crazy. But the worst was knowing that she could get him killed. And not just him—everyone. If she chose the wrong strategy, if she didn't train them well enough, if she sent them off on a mission when they weren't ready, if she led them into a trap . . .

It was just dumb luck that no one had been killed the night before. Steel and Jody had both taken bullets, but luckily, their healing spells had been able to fix them.

"You didn't used to worry like a fucking mother hen," she muttered to herself, grabbing her scrubby and soaping herself up. She washed away the stink of her sweat and fear and dried herself.

Back in the bedroom, Alexander was asleep. Or pretending to be. Whichever it was, she let him. She didn't know what to say.

She dressed quickly and slipped out into the other room. Beyul watched her from the couch, his head on his forepaws. Spike rested her head on his back, her ears pricked up. Neither moved. She grinned at them both and left.

All thirteen of the Shadowblade apartments opened onto this passage, deep in the mountain fortress and well away from the deadly sunlight.

Max started toward the stairs. She wanted to check on the torture victims and see if there was any information about who the mysterious preacher had been. She found herself hesitating outside a door, knowing there was no one on the other side of it. Niko was dead.

Pain seized her, and she gasped. She caught herself against the jamb. Jagged sobs lodged in her throat, and she clamped her lips shut to keep them from escaping. Her Prime rose swift and hard, spurred to ferocity by the depth of her grief. Power exploded from her. Instantly, several doors slammed open, and her Blades launched into the hallway.

Not Alexander. She didn't know if that was a good thing or not.

Each had tumbled from bed ready to fight. They homed in on Max with a pack instinct. Tyler wasn't among them. She was pretty sure he was in the infirmary with the injured boy.

She held up a hand. "It's okay," she said, straightening up. But she could not so easily rein in her grief. Hot tears slipped down her cheeks.

Thor pushed through the others. He wore a pair of low-slung fleece pants and nothing else. His blond hair was long and loose, and his pale body was cut like crystal, a blond arrow of hair darkening as it disappeared inside his waistband. He eyed her from head to toe. His gaze flicked to Niko's door and then up the corridor behind her as if he were looking for Alexander.

"You all right?" he asked in his slow Texas drawl.

Max stiffened and lifted her head, swallowing down her emotions until she felt herself turn calm. It was no more than a thin shell of calm, but it would do.

"I'm fan-fucking-tastic," she said. "I always have public emotional breakdowns before breakfast." She drew a deep breath and blew it out in a gust. "Clears the sinuses. Gets the day off to a hell of a start. You should all try it. But first, why don't you all go back to bed before I'm any more humiliated?"

She didn't wait for them to disperse but hurried up the steps.

She went to the infirmary first. Judith, another Triangle-level witch, was sitting in a chair beside the man, who lay pale and still. The woman was in a bed on the other side and looked none the worse for wear. At least, her body did. Tyler sat beside the boy, staring at him like tiger stalking his prey. His face was stony, and his Blade filled the air with stifling power. His nostrils flared, but he didn't look up as Max entered.

"What's the word?" she asked Judith.

"They'll all live," the witch said with a tired smile. She'd cut her brown hair short recently, and it curled unexpectedly, making her look about twenty-five. But her eyes were old. She'd seen a lot of betrayal, a lot of death, and it had tempered her. Just like Gregory. Both preferred to heal, but out of recent necessity, they had grown adept at killing.

"When will they wake up?" Max asked.

"Maybe by tomorrow. Depends. They suffered a great deal." She glanced at Tyler and the boy and frowned. "Their bodies are healed, but their spirits are in shock. It may take them a while to decide it's safe to come back to the world."

Or they might not. Max could almost hear the unspoken words.

Judith reached over and smoothed the sheet over the man, then stood and went to do the same for the woman. "Some people just need killing," she said softly, then looked up at Max. Silver magic swirled in the hollows of her eyes. "And soon," she added.

Max saluted. "Yes, ma'am."

With that, she went to find Giselle. It took her a while. She wasn't anywhere Max expected her to be, and no one seemed to know where she was. Finally, she thought of the angel vault. It was the only place she hadn't looked.

THE ANGEL VAULT WAS A SMALL ROOM DEEP DOWN AMONG the roots of the mountain. The space had started as a small cave, and by using magic, Giselle had enlarged it.

As Max approached the entrance, she heard voices

within. Giselle's was one, and the other—Kyle? What was he doing in there? With Giselle?

Anger coiled in Max's chest. She drew closer. She could be wrong. She'd damned well better be wrong about what they were up to.

She wasn't.

"There's every possibility," Kyle said enthusiastically. "We'll have to experiment and see, but just look at what one of Tutresiel's tiniest feathers has done for Max. What a witch could do with the same feather I can't even begin to imagine."

Except that judging by the tone of his voice, he was imagining, and by the sound of it, he thought it was the holy grail.

Max gritted her teeth, her jaw muscles knotting. She rubbed her thumb absently over the palm of her hand. The feather Tutresiel had given her allowed her to jump huge distances. If she caught a breeze, she could glide a long way. It had been a gift, but Kyle was talking about mining the angels' comatose bodies for magical gold.

Her hand clenched.

"It's risky," Giselle said. "I don't know that we should take the chance. There could be recoil issues and dangerous complications. We can't afford to lose any more witches. We're too depleted already."

"But isn't that the point?" Kyle argued. "You said it yourself. That preacher wielded impossible power. He pierced the wards without any of us knowing about it. You need to use every weapon you have. You can't be squeamish about taking advantage of them. They wouldn't want to see Horngate destroyed."

They wouldn't want to be used like groceries in the pantry, either, Max thought. She waited for Giselle's reply.

"Horngate isn't so far in trouble," she replied dryly. "I have the Fury Seed."

The Fury Seed had been created when a Fury was born recently in Horngate. Sacrificed by her father, an enemy witch, a teenage girl had been reborn with a Fury's insane rage and thirst for vengeance. In order to keep the explosive power of her birth from destroying Horngate altogether, the coven had created a matrix to collect the magic. The matrix was like a pit at the center of a magical fruit. The Fury Seed, as it had come to be called, was an extraordinarily powerful reservoir of magic.

After the Fury's birth, the seed had been sunk deep under the fortress. It now fueled the day-to-day needs of the covenstead, the greenhouse heat, the phones, and some of Horngate's other necessities, although Giselle liked to keep its power in reserve against future problems. Maybe the future was now.

"Of course," Kyle said. "But that's raw and unformed. Angel magic could enhance specific abilities and allow you to do spells you never could before. You need both to protect this covenstead."

Max had heard enough. The angels were in these bizarre comas because they'd been defending Horngate against the rage of the Fury. They deserved better than to become ingredients in Giselle's spells. Or Kyle's.

She strode to the door and leaned against the jamb. "You two can stop arguing now," she said quietly, her jaws aching with the effort to keep herself from screaming at them. Her Prime was wild. She didn't bother restraining it.

Choking power flooded the room. Kyle staggered back toward the wall, his mouth falling open. Giselle stood between the stone slab tables that held the two angels, her arms crossed. She had the grace to look guilty, no doubt for getting caught, not for her plans to harvest angel parts.

The thought spurred Max's fury. In a minute, she was going to rip Giselle's arms off. "Let me make something very clear. Neither one of you is going to touch so much as a single hair on their heads. Not now, not ever. Understand?" She didn't wait for the answer but sauntered inside. "I suggest that if you're interested in surviving to your next birthday, you both ought to get the hell out of here. Now."

Kyle practically ran out. Max could smell his fear.

Giselle lowered her arms. "Feel better?"

"I'll feel better when you go get yourself run over by a truck. Feel free to have at it right now."

Giselle's head tipped to the side, her lips curved, and then the smile faded. "Like it or not, your brother is right," she said. "We have to use whatever weapons we have, no matter how distasteful it might be. Using the angels might become necessary."

"*Might be distasteful?*" Max lunged close, hands closing on Giselle's biceps hard enough to leave bruises. "You coldhearted bitch. They are my friends. My family. You. Will. Not. Touch. Them. Ever."

Giselle stared at her a moment, then wordlessly shook Max off and stepped away. She stopped at the door and turned back. "You know better, Max. I'll do anything to protect Horngate. Anything. So don't be surprised when I do just that."

With that, she left. Just in time. She wasn't going to survive if she stayed much longer.

Max took several breaths and then went to look over Tutresiel and Xaphan.

The two angels lay parallel to each other on two basalt tables. In between, a tiny waterfall trickled through the roof and dropped down into a basin on the floor. On the left lay Tutresiel. He was pale as ice, with long jet-black hair pooling around his head. His eyes were closed, his chiseled face looking as if Michelangelo had carved it. His expression was savage in its beauty. Silver wings folded beneath his back, the edges of each feather sharp as a scythe. They were tarnished a dull gray now.

A sheet covered him from the chest down. Beneath it, his body was beautiful and perfect—the epitome of pure masculinity. Too bad he wasn't breathing.

On the other slab lay Xaphan. He was equally beautiful, with white-blond hair and iridescent black wings. The flames that usually flickered along the edges of his feathers were doused now. Like Tutresiel, he wore nothing but a sheet and looked like a corpse. And, also like Tutresiel, he was in some sort of angel coma, and nobody had any idea of how to wake him. The pair would remain in the vault until either they rotted away or someone found a cure for them.

They looked undamaged, except—

Max scowled. Red dust sprinkled the sheets covering them and outlined their torsos like tiny bulwarks of powdered crimson chalk, although strangely, it didn't seem to touch their skin. It almost *avoided* doing so, in fact.

More layered the floor and had turned the waterfall basin to blood. It was scuffed where Kyle and Giselle had walked, but even as she watched, the dust swirled up and then settled back down in a pristine blanket.

"What the hell?" she asked. Her voice sounded loud.

Annoyed, she brushed at the heap surrounding Tutresiel. The dust coated her hand, then slid up over her fingers and forearm like a bloody glove. Max turned her hand, splaying her fingers. It was thick as velvet. She scraped the fingernails of her other hand through the compacted dust, and it slid up over her fingertips and congealed around that hand, too.

As it skimmed over her palm and the scar left behind when Tutresiel's feather had pierced her skin, the tide of red dust halted, and then the edges recoiled. Her palm glowed, the feather a shining shape inside its nest of tendon and muscle.

Light flashed, and the dust dropped to the floor in a sprinkle of black ash. The heat and light from her hand flared and ran like a jolt of lightning up her arm into the rest of her body. For a moment, Max felt like the center of a star. Her vision went white. Her body was incandescent. Every cell vibrated with elemental force, the kind that had sparked the birth of the universe.

For an instant, she felt the entire world on her skin; she felt every death, every birth. Fire and water poured through her veins. Salt, earth, and ash swirled on whirling wind.

It stopped.

She blinked and drew a slow breath, surprised that it didn't hurt. Her body throbbed with the fading memory of the pulse of power. She looked down at her hands. The dust had fallen away, and all that littered the vault was gray. Which meant that even though he was comatose, Tutresiel had enough residual juice to incinerate the invader.

Max smiled a smug smile. It faded just as quickly. This just added fuel to Giselle's argument for using the angels to power spells. As a necessity.

Fuck that.

She reached out and slid her palm over Tutresiel's cheek and down to rest on his chest. "Never," she said, and bent down to brush his forehead with her lips. She did the same to Xaphan, momentarily resting her head on his chest. She hoped to hear a heartbeat. Something to say he was still alive. But, as ever, she heard nothing. She straightened. She had better hearing than a bat on super-steroids. If his heart was working at all, she'd hear it.

Then again, he wasn't exactly dead. That was something.

She turned to leave, and as she did, a flicker caught her attention. She froze. What was *that*?

She stared, stepping closer. She saw it again.

A gleam of silver along the edge of a feather.

It flashed and was gone. There was another. And another.

Max lost track of how long she watched. The shine moved over Tutresiel's wings without any pattern. She waited for it to vanish like a blown candle. But it didn't. Hope lurched in her chest. Could he be waking up?

But nothing more happened. Max waited, the minutes ticking by. Still nothing. She sighed. She had things to do.

Max turned and left, scuffing at the gray ash on the floor.

Her stomach rumbled, and she headed for the dining commons to calorie load. After that, the first order of business was to go down into Missoula and figure out who the preacher witch was and find him.

And if possible, kill him.

4

ALEXANDER LISTENED TO MAX SHOWER, DRESS, and leave. A moment later, he felt the spike of her emotions and the surge of her Prime. He leaped out of bed in response but stopped himself from exploding through the door. He could feel her grief and knew that if he went to her, she would only push him away.

Instead, he showered and dressed. Most of his clothing was still in his apartment, although he slept every day in Max's bed. He did not think she would welcome anything more permanent.

As he was putting on his shirt, he felt her Prime rise again. He went still for a moment, then finished dressing. Every particle of his being was homed in on her. But whatever had set her off, she was safe enough inside the fortress. She would not want him showing up to help her. His mouth twisted. Lately, she seemed to want him in her bed and nowhere else.

As he strode out of the bedroom, Beyul and Spike lifted their heads, cocking them. A strange flash of energy burst through the room and was gone. It tingled over Alexander's skin, leaving behind a faintly itchy sensation.

Beyul gave a low bark and stood up, shaking himself. He went to the door and walked through the wood as if it were not there. Spike, who had followed him, barked at Alexander to open the door so she could follow.

Alexander did as commanded and followed them out into the corridor. Beyul was already at the steps, bounding up. Spike flowed after him like a silver shadow. He followed the pair.

They glided through the fortress, clearly heading for the outside. More Grims joined them, until all thirteen trailed behind Beyul and Spike. They were silent as ghosts, their green eyes lambent. Unease prickled down Alexander's back.

The Grims spilled out of the fortress into a whirl of thick snow. The flakes were heavy and wet. A thin layer already covered the ground beneath his feet. The temperature had gone from the sixties to the twenties since the night before.

He brushed the snow from his eyes. The Grims had spread out, all facing the southeast. Their noses tipped up into the air as if smelling something.

"What's going on?" Thor stepped out into the snowy darkness beside Alexander. "What's up with the puppies?"

"I do not know."

Alexander felt Thor's long stare but ignored it. He was feeling unsettled and violent. He needed to move, to hunt. He needed to let his Prime off its leash.

"Go get Max," he told Thor quietly, ignoring the cell phone in his pocket. "Giselle, too."

The other Blade slipped away without protest. Alexander edged through the Grims, stopped beside Beyul. He crouched, his shoulder rubbing against that of the tall beast.

"What is it?" he asked.

Beyul had the power to answer. Alexander knew the Grim could communicate telepathically, but whether he chose to was always an entirely different question.

He waited for some response. A minute ticked past. Then another. Alexander waited, snow mounding on his shoulders and thighs, dampness trickling down his forehead and neck.

Thor returned. Max arrived a few minutes later, and then Giselle and several other Blades showed up. He ignored them all.

Finally, Beyul turned and nudged against Alexander's ear with his nose. An image flashed through his mind. A crack in the ground with fire pouring from it. The flames were blue, purple, green, red, and orange. Within them, lizardlike creatures wriggled. They had frills around their heads, mouths like alligators, and wings that folded compactly to their long, sinuous bodies.

The image vanished. As fast as it went, so did the Grims. They trotted off into the snow. Spike went with them. Alexander straightened, watching them disappear behind the heavy curtain of snow. His stomach tightened. Would they be coming back? Or was that good-bye?

"Did Beyul tell you anything?" Giselle asked.

He turned. Snow had turned her into a ghost. "I got a picture of a crack in the ground, colored fire, and lizards with big mouths and wings. That is all."

"Salamanders?" Giselle wondered aloud. "Nobody's seen anything like them for centuries."

"Nobody's seen a lot of things that have suddenly come back," Max pointed out. "But they are the sort of thing that would make the Grims curious. Convenient timing, if you ask me."

"You should follow them," Giselle said, looking at Alexander. "If they are here, we need to know. They can cause a lot of damage, and they aren't easy to stop. Take Thor." She paused, frowning, then shook her head. "I can't spare anyone else. You'd better hurry before you lose them." She glanced up. "This snow isn't going to stop soon. It's not natural. Take a truck."

The witch walked away before he could answer, not that he had anything to say. His entire body had leaped at the chance to go after the Grims and get away from Horngate and Max.

He glanced at Thor. "Better eat first," he said. No matter how big a hurry they were in, they needed at least twenty thousand calories a day just to function. It was asking for trouble to leave without eating.

Max fell in beside him. She smelled of Divine magic. And the angels. Alexander wrinkled his nose and then quickly forced the expression away before she could notice.

"Something happened," she said quietly, so that only he and Thor could hear.

Alexander stopped, waiting for Giselle to disappear around a corner. "What?"

She related what had happened inside the vault, ending with a description of the gleams that had appeared on Tutresiel's wings. "He might be coming closer to alive," she said.

For her sake, Alexander was happy. He despised

the angel, but Max liked him. And Tutresiel *had* been trapped in his coma as a result of trying to help Horngate.

"What do you think caused the dust?" Thor asked, examining himself for evidence of it.

"It has something to do with that preacher witch," Max said with complete certainty. "When he disappeared, he left a pile of it behind. Can't be coincidence. Somehow he got it inside before the wards, and even though Giselle reinstated them, the dust was still attacking me in the vault. I think it's gone inert now that Tutresiel's magic reacted to it. But we need to take the preacher down before he comes after us again. Who knows what else he has up his sleeve?"

"You have not told Giselle?" Alexander asked.

Max's expression went cold, her eyes flat with hate. "Not yet."

"Why not?" he asked, sensing that something had happened between them. Something else. The two women had a long history of hate and love between them. Mostly hate.

"I came across her and Kyle working out a way to use the angels in their spells," she said. "An angelic pantry of magical supplies."

"Shit," Thor said.

"They think the angel ingredients will help fend off our enemies?" Alexander asked.

Max glared at him, her mouth pulling down. "You think it's a good idea, *too*?"

"I confess I would not mind seeing Tutresiel rammed into a jar and his guts sprinkled into a cauldron," he said. "But I would miss Xaphan."

"She's not getting her hands on either one of them," she declared, and spun around. "I'll see you in the dining commons in fifteen. I'll warn Magpie you're coming so she'll have food ready. Get your gear together."

PRECISELY FIFTEEN MINUTES LATER, ALEXANDER AND Thor dropped their packs outside the door of the dining commons. They both wore tactical vests, the pockets stuffed with ammo, food, and emergency supplies.

Max sat at a table with Simon, Jody, and Nami. They were already eating stacks of pancakes with sides of eggs, potatoes, sausage, bacon, and steak. In the past weeks, Giselle had sent people to harvest the Wheat Montana farm fields over near Three Forks. There were thousands of acres going to waste. They had brought back truckloads of it, thanks to engines powered by magic. Everybody everywhere was hoarding fuel.

Alexander loaded his plate and wished for fresh fruit. But the greenhouses would not produce any berries for another month or so, and tree fruit was another year off, if not more. There was canned fruit, which he spooned into a bowl. It was better than nothing.

He sat across from Max and dug in.

"What we should have done is clean out the Costco," Nami said in a low, throaty voice. "Or locked it down." She took up the saltshaker and sprinkled a snowstorm on top. "I'm not looking forward to running out of peanut butter and chocolate. Magpie's a genius with food, but I'm not sure she can make those."

"Should have done it with all the stores in Missoula," Simon said, shoveling a pile of cheesy potatoes into his mouth.

He and Nami were both small. Nami stood about five six and probably weighed about a hundred forty pounds soaking wet. She was mixed Mexican and Japanese, with ripe curves and black hair that fell to her waist in a starched silk curtain. Simon was maybe an inch taller and looked as if he had some Native American somewhere in his background. His hair was straight and dark brown. His eyes were nearly black, and his face was sculpted like wind-cut stone. He moved like a whip, sharp and fast.

"Might have upset the locals a little bit," Thor drawled. "What with starving to death because we hoarded all the food."

"Survival of the fittest," Simon said with a shrug.

"Seriously?" Jody asked. She was close to Max's height, with rippling muscle beneath her toffee-colored skin. Her hair was close-cropped, and she looked like a model. "The people in Missoula are looking down the barrel of cold, starvation, sickness, not to mention that insane preacher witch, and here you want to come steal what little food they have. They'd drop like flies."

"That is exactly what the Guardians want. To cull the human herd," Alexander said, feeling Max's fury rising and her control starting to slip.

"So why not let them?" Simon asked, either totally clueless that Max was about to rip his throat out or not caring. He could not be that stupid.

Thor stared. "Think about it. Maybe you'll come up with something," he said.

Simon opened his mouth to say something else, and Nami punched him in the thigh. He yelped and leaped to his feet, his chair careening across the floor.

"What the fuck did you do that for?" he demanded.

"Because you weren't going to survive the next few minutes without help," she snapped. "Sit down and eat, if you can pry your foot out of your mouth."

The boy glanced at Alexander, who had leaned back in his chair, his eyes hooded. Then he caught Max's gaze. He turned white. Retrieving his chair, he sank down and ducked his head over his food.

Max shook her head, her jaw clenched so tightly Alexander wondered if she would need a crowbar to finish eating.

The rest of their meal passed in silence. They all seemed to find themselves full at the same time. Almost as one, they rose.

"Everything set?" Max asked Thor, her gaze sliding past Alexander.

"Got everything we need, Sugar," Thor said with a wink. "Unless you want to come along to sweeten things up a little."

She snorted. "Tempting, but word is you're all talk and no action."

His mouth fell open, and Alexander chuckled.

"Who said that? It's an absolute lie!"

"What was it that Shakespeare said about protesting too much?" Alexander asked.

Thor clamped his mouth shut, and he flushed red. Then, "Anytime you want to go for a ride, Sweetness, let me know, and we'll see who's 'all talk.'"

"I will cut your balls off first," Alexander said without an ounce of humor.

Thor and Max looked at him, and Thor nodded and backed away, lifting his hands. "I'll meet you at the truck." He grabbed both packs and disappeared down the hall.

Jody, Nami, and Simon glanced from Max to Alexander, and all three trotted off without another word.

"Gather everybody," Max called after them. "We're heading into town." She looked at Alexander. "I'm not your fire hydrant to pee on and claim."

"But you are mine," he said quietly.

"Am I?" she said, her chin jutting.

He tipped his head to the side, and impatience and annoyance kicked hard in his chest. When was she finally going to choose him? Maybe she was never going to embrace him fully as her lover, her mate, her other half. Maybe this was the best he would ever get from her.

Pain and fury slashed through him. His body went taut, and he stepped back, his mouth curving in a bitter smile. "I had thought so. But maybe I was wrong. I tell you what. You let me know when I get back from chasing down the Grims. I would like to know where I should be sleeping."

With that, he spun and strode away, feeling her gaze drilling into his back.

5

"WHEN ARE WE LEAVING?"

Max turned around, still reeling from her exchange with Alexander. What had happened? Why did she have to keep shoving him away?

Tory and Carrie stood waiting, both practically bouncing off the floor with their excitement.

"Leaving?" Max repeated stupidly. Of course, she was Alexander's. She didn't want anyone else. Didn't want him having anyone else. And yet—

She couldn't go that extra distance to make it real, make it permanent. She kept holding on to the wiggle room that it was just for now.

"Going into Missoula," Tory said, as if speaking to a mental patient. "To look for information with you and Uncle Kyle and Tyler. We're going tonight, since last night there was all that other stuff going on." Tory waved her hand vaguely.

She didn't have any idea what had really happened. Time to buy her a clue.

"*Last night,* a witch broke into Horngate with a mob and burned five people at the stake in front of us,"

Max said baldly. "So today I'm taking a team to try to hunt them down. You are staying here until he's been taken care of, maybe longer. It's too dangerous for you to go into Missoula now."

Carrie and Tory stared at her, uncomprehending. Then the news slowly took on meaning.

"Burned them at the stake?" Carrie whispered, turning pale and clutching her fingers together.

"Tortured them and then burned them. Two died," Max said. "The others we got to the infirmary, but they aren't out of the woods yet."

"That's too bad for them," Tory said, recovering herself. "But it won't happen to us. Kyle, you, and Tyler won't let it happen. And we'll help you find out what you need to know. You said yourself it was a good idea."

"*Was* being the operative word," Max said. "It is now a very stupid idea. So go find some other way to contribute."

She stalked away, pulling her mind away from Alexander and the girls to focus on the preacher witch.

A half hour later, she joined her Blades, who had assembled in the lounge outside the Great Hall. They were all armed to the teeth. Max had put on her tactical vest and buckled her .45 to her hip and her 9mm to her ankle. She strapped her flat-bladed knives to her forearms and had two more sheathed in her boots. Another was stuck into her waistband. She'd donned a long drover's coat made of oiled canvas, and beneath it, over her shoulder, she'd slung a sawed-off shotgun. It hung down at her hip. A bandolier of shells slanted across her chest. If she had to do insane-mob control, she was ready.

She had also buckled a sword to her other hip. There

was nothing like a yard of steel to make magical creatures stop and think. They did *not* like iron.

Tyler sauntered in a minute later, his knife spinning around his fingers.

"The boy?" Max asked.

"He woke up enough to eat." His beast was still raging inside him. His face was shuttered and bland, but he was seething. "He lost it when he started remembering what happened. Judith made him sleep."

"We'll make the fucker pay," Max promised.

Tyler's expression turned brutal. "Damned right we will."

"All right, everyone. This is what we're going to do. We need information on this preacher. We're going to break into three teams of three. Flint, Steel, and Tyler, you take Rattlesnake Canyon and Rose Park and the university district. Oak, Ivy, and Jody, you've got south of Highway Twelve across to the university. Simon, Nami, and I will take the central and west sides. Don't call attention to yourselves. Find out everything you can about how the local politics have evolved and who this fellow is. Be back here by sunrise. The snow's coming down hard now—that will work in our favor. One more thing—"

"Max."

Giselle stood in the doorway. She motioned Max over to join her. "I got a call from Frank Bryce. He's one of the farmers we're working with out on O'Brien Creek Road. He says something's moved in up in the hills south of his place. He's found dead bears, elk, and deer. Says they've been ripped to shreds. He's afraid for his stock. Our deal with him says we'll protect him in exchange for lambs in the spring. It takes priority."

Lambs over a psychopath burning people at the stake? Was she serious? "You can send the Sunspears in the morning to help him. We have to find out what's going on with this preacher witch. Who knows when he'll attack us again."

"I agree, but I promised Frank and I can't have any of our few farmer allies thinking we won't respond when they need help." She made a chopping motion with her hand when Max started to respond. "No arguments. No matter what happens with this preacher witch, we are going to need those lambs to survive the long term."

Max's mouth twisted, but she only nodded before turning back to her Blades. "You heard her. Let's go save some animals."

LEADING THE WAY TO THE NEAREST EXIT, MAX TOOK HER team out on the north side of the mountain fortress, facing the river. She didn't pause but leaped down the slope and broke into a loping run. She didn't bother with vehicles. It was faster to go as the crow flew, rather than back out around the highway and up to Missoula and west again.

The snow continued to fall in a thick, heavy blanket, making it difficult to see. She angled across the valley and northwest. Tyler flanked her on the left, and the others trailed in a long V. The ridges were steep, with sharp spines and towers of rock. Secreted within the folds were pocket valleys, cold mountain lakes, and swift-flowing rivers. Max was well used to traversing the terrain. The harsh edges and jagged contours of the Montana Rockies had been her home for thirty years.

As she ran, she let her Prime rise and flow outward. Her senses heightened, and her humanity flattened. Her predator instincts took over. She smelled the musky scents of animals and the pungency of plants. Beneath them, the stone and dirt were a cool metallic flavor. Birds chirped, and a bear sow growled a warning to something. A moose bellowed, and chipmunks chattered merrily. Woven through it all were the scents of the Uncanny and the Divine.

Until the Guardians had loosed a flood of wild magic into the world, the smells of magic around Horngate had been infrequent. But now they were everywhere. It put Max constantly on edge. It was impossible to tell whether or not something was a threat. It was safer to assume that everything was.

As they approached the area south of Frank Bryce's place, Max slowed down. She could smell carrion and something else, something rank and wet, a mix of black mold, stagnant water, and rotting flesh. The smell wafted from a canyon just ahead. Max eased up to the lip and crouched by a pile of granite boulders. Tyler hunkered down beside her, with the others gathering behind.

Below was a long canyon with a narrow bottom, like it had been hacked into the ground with a god-sized ax. Trees filled it, and between them and the snow, it was impossible to see the bottom. The rush of water from a waterfall smothered quieter sounds. Max stiffened. Mingling with the natural smells, the scent of magic, and the rank stench, was human scent. She frowned. Who would be down there?

Shouts erupted, and branches cracked like someone

or something rolling down a hill. A squeal echoed up the canyon. It sent spiders crawling down Max's spine. It was like the cry had come from the other side of the grave. Then everything went preternaturally quiet. The hairs on the back of Max's neck rose.

"What's going on?" Nami whispered.

"We're looking at the same things you are. How the hell should we know?" Simon snapped.

Max twisted to glare at him, and he flushed, his lips pinching shut. She turned back to Tyler.

"Take Oak, Nami, Ivy, and Flint. Go around the other side, and work your way down. We'll do the same over here."

Tyler scowled at her. "I don't like it."

Her brows rose. "Why?" But she knew why. Since Niko's death, he'd hardly been willing to let her out of his sight. He was afraid he'd turn his back and she'd die or disappear.

"We don't know what's waiting down there," he said. "You could be walking into a shitstorm." His knife spun like a shining pinwheel in his fingers. "Being a Shadowblade won't matter if someone puts a bullet in your head."

Max gave him a long look. She didn't like letting him out of her sight, either, but in the end, that was beside the point. "This is what we do." She was telling herself as much as she was telling him. It didn't make her any less terrified that something might happen to him or anybody else for that matter.

His lip curled. "We don't have to take stupid chances."

"Got another idea on how to handle this?"

He said nothing. Simon muttered something, and

Jody elbowed him. He yelped loudly. Max shot him a violent look, and he wilted.

"Got a problem?" Tyler asked, his expression flat and dangerous.

"No," Simon choked out, looking like he wanted to dig a hole to escape.

"Then why don't you share with the rest of the class?" Tyler's head tipped to the side, and his spinning knife came to rest in his hand. The threat was all too clear.

"I just said—" Simon flushed and looked away. "It wasn't anything."

"Must've been something. Enough for you to squawk like a chicken and tell the whole world we're here. So tell me. Now."

"It was just a joke."

Tyler waited. Max didn't interrupt. This had to be settled, for Tyler and for Simon, who clearly needed a spanking to settle him down to work. She watched to see if any of the intruders had noticed their noise.

"I—I just said it was hard to believe you were wearing granny pants under your jeans," Simon muttered at last.

Tyler leaned forward until his nose brushed Simon's. "Let's talk about my wardrobe when we get back to Horngate, shall we?" he said in a silky voice.

Simon blanched and shrank into himself.

Tyler swung back around. "Don't get dead," he told Max harshly, and then started off. Nami, Oak, Ivy, and Flint followed. Tyler grabbed Oak's arm. "You stay with Max. Simon, you're with me."

"But—"

Whatever Simon was going to say was cut off by Jody

smacking the back of his head and shoving him after Tyler. He staggered off and fell into line behind Ivy.

Oak settled down beside Max. "Tyler has a point," he said.

She rolled her eyes at him. He'd only been at Horngate for a couple of months, but he was already too full of himself by far. "You, too? Seriously, did you both drink the same Kool-Aid this morning?"

"Somebody has to be the voice of reason," he said, entirely unabashed.

"You're saying I'm not reasonable?"

"That pretty much sums it up."

She eyed him sideways. "Does Simon need to worry about your panties, too?"

He smiled slowly. His brown hair flopped down in his eyes but did not hide the hard glitter there. "It isn't funny."

She nodded. "I know."

"You should give in a little to Tyler."

She grimaced. "That isn't the way our world works. We take risks. We get hurt, and we die. The threats are only coming faster and harder. He knows that."

"He could break."

She stared. "If you're trying to tell me something, say it straight, and stop playing games."

He drew a breath to speak and then shook his head. "You know him better than I do."

"That's right," Max said, but worry chewed at her. She couldn't lose Tyler.

"You might remember he'll take stupid risks to keep you from doing it first," he added.

Max's hands clenched, and she forced them to relax. Then, without another word, she stood and skimmed along the top of the rimrock. She stopped at the top of a deep crack that cut down into the canyon. It was full of tumbled rocks, trees, and scrub, now layered with a couple of inches of snow. From unseasonably warm to full-on winter in a matter of minutes. This had something to do with the red dust and the preacher witch. She was sure of it.

But that was a problem for later.

She jumped down lightly, careful to make no noise. Her Blades followed. Max winced as one of them kicked over a rock and tipped off a small avalanche.

She kept moving, going for speed rather than stealth. She angled out along the steep side of the canyon. It was quieter going there. The ground was damp and thick with needles. Their footsteps made little sound, and the low-hanging branches masked their movements.

A breeze ruffled the trees overhead, and Max swiveled her head, sniffing the air. Uncanny magic pooled thick in the canyon. It was an odd combination of bitter and sweet—like a mouthful of salt and cigar butts all drenched in honey. The Divine magic wafted through in thin curls. It was both caustic and sweetly pungent, like lye and patchouli. Mixed in were human smells—salt, blood, and flesh—and that nose-burning rank stench that coated the back of Max's throat.

Suddenly, shots rang out, and a ghostly wail coiled through the canyon again, sending splinters of ice through Max's gut. Her eyes momentarily glazed with a gray film as the sound increased in pitch and intensity before ending on an ear-shredding shriek. Max blinked to clear the grayness and dodged behind a tree. Her Blades scattered, finding their own cover.

An odd white mist was creeping over the ground. It was about ankle-high and rolled up the sides of the canyon like a layer of wet cotton. It met the falling snow like a tide of poison. Max hopped up onto the top of an outcropping to avoid it. She crouched, scanning the thick trees. More shots rang out, then violent animal sounds, like a couple of wolves fighting. Max grimaced. She didn't want to get down into the mist if she didn't have to. It was just as likely to dissolve skin as anything else. But it sounded like she needed to see what was going on down there.

She decided on the high road, and swung herself up into a tree. She trotted out along a branch and leaped to the next tree. Her Blades followed suit. They swiftly worked their way down toward the shots and the fight.

The hail of bullets burned faster, and the sounds of fighting escalated. Suddenly, it seemed as if it wasn't just two wolves but an enormous pack. The wailing became unceasing. The sound hurt deep down in Max's being, hooking and tearing. Her vision blurred, and it was like trying to look through underwater murk. *Perfect.* Tyler sure as hell couldn't blame this on her. But he would.

There seemed to be only one throat making the wailing noise. So once they strangled it, they should be able to see. Max turned to Oak, who was on a branch just below hers.

"Oak?" Max whispered.

His face turned up at her. There was something odd about him. Max squinted and blinked, and for a moment, her sight cleared. Oak's eyes were disks of shining pearl. *Shit.* That couldn't be good.

"Stay here," she said.

"Where are you going? You can't see. Can you?" The last was hopeful.

"Better than you," Max said. She could still make out shapes. That with occasional real glimpses might be enough. They sure as hell couldn't sit in the tree till they became targets.

What was odd was the absolute lack of sound from anything human. The fact that the rapidly fired bullets seemed to be hitting things and weren't ricocheting randomly suggested discipline.

She slipped the drover's coat off to keep it from tangling in her legs and eased forward. She leaped to the next tree, scrabbling as she hit with her forearms instead of her hands. She grappled her way onto a branch and skirted around to the other side, feeling her way carefully.

The tree stood on the edge of a clearing. Max could just separate the sound of rushing water in a creek from the wailing. She blinked and shook her head, trying to clear her vision. It didn't work.

The smell of rotting death smashed her in the face like a bat. It was a cold, claustrophobic smell, stagnant and sticky. She fought the urge to throw up, swallowing hard. Movement sounded all around, thrashing and scraping followed by a low snarling.

She froze at the sound of someone moving along the tree line. Whoever it was stopped a few feet away. He was human and stank of sweat, grime, and gunpowder.

"Liam, this mist is chewing through my boots and gaiters. I'm gonna have to get up a tree in a minute." Pause. "Yes, sir. No, sir."

There was a military snap to his voice. He remained where he was and began shooting again. He was firing some sort of submachine gun. Maybe an HK. But how the hell could he still see?

Max blinked and shook her head, trying again to clear her vision. She picked his shape out from beneath the scrub. He seemed to be wearing camo and was lumpy all over like he was dressed as she was in a tactical vest and a lot of weaponry. He shot his weapon in careful spurts.

He swore. "Dammit! Why won't those things just fucking die?" A few seconds later, he gave a harsh bark of laughter. "Right, Dawson. You could scare them to death, maybe."

Max blinked and squinted and finally caught a better glimpse of him. He was wearing camo greasepaint and a military helmet with a set of heavy earphones over it. A microphone branched down along his cheek. That answered the question of how he and his buddies could still see. The headphones were smothering the blinding sound.

She dropped silently to the ground. In a quick move, she snatched him around the neck, yanking away his helmet and headphones and catching him in a sleeper hold. He stiffened and twisted, but she had supernatural strength. In a matter of half a minute, he slumped. She picked him up and hoisted him over a branch to get him out of the mist. Then she felt around on the ground for the helmet. She pulled the headpiece off and pulled it down over her own ears.

Instant relief. The wailing cut off abruptly, and her ears were filled instead with the crackle and hiss of the radio and the sounds of breathing and sputtering voices from whoever else was online.

It took a minute for her vision to clear completely, and when it did, she sucked in a soft breath. She was looking out over a rocky basin with a handful of scrawny birch trees. A fast-running creek snaked through the bottom. Fangs of rock thrust up from the frothing water. Just on the near side was a collection of creatures that looked as if they came out of some sort of apocalyptic disease movie.

Their stooping forms were more than seven feet tall, and their gray-green skin was ulcerated and weeping with something that looked like bloody pus. Long black hair hung in greasy, lank hanks. Their faces were long, with pointed snouts and curving teeth. Round yellow eyes bulged from beneath heavy brow bones. Long, sticklike arms ended in enormous spidery hands. They looked like they could grasp a man's head in one fist and pop it like a tick.

They circled around a bloated white sac that sat ten feet from the creek bank. It billowed and stretched like something was struggling to get out. The mist rolled off it like dry ice in water, and whatever it contained was making the ear-ripping noise.

Max counted fourteen of the creatures, and they were Divine. That meant they had the ability to cast magic, which didn't necessarily mean much. It could just be that their toenails could grow into instant trees if they were torn out and planted. On the other hand, maybe they could cast wards and other nasty spells.

Either way, they didn't belong in Horngate territory. She rolled her head on her neck to crack it and loosen her muscles. Max had a feeling they weren't going to move easily. First things first: she had to shut that damned noise up so her Blades could get their sight back.

"And they say crying babies will drive you insane," she murmured, forgetting her headphones. "Babies could learn a thing or two from these beasties."

Silence filled her ears, and a flat, cold voice spoke. "Who the hell are you?"

"We, my friend, are your friendly local nine-one-one responders," answered Tyler, much to Max's surprise. "We've come to pull your asses out of the fire. You can stop shooting anytime, by the way. You're wasting bullets. Lead doesn't bother them."

"It does when it blows off their heads," someone said.

Max scanned the clearing, looking for Tyler. "Where are you?"

"North and west in the trees."

In fact, he was halfway up a tree, crouching on a branch and wearing a set of headphones.

"What have you done with my men?" demanded the first voice.

"Nothing they can't recover from," Max said. "You didn't kill yours, did you, Tyler?"

"He'll live. But my Blades are up the hill. Blind as bats."

"Same here. We have to shut down the noise," she said. "Think you and I can get in there and kill that thing?"

"Do we have a choice?" came Tyler's reply.

"Just one fucking second. Who the hell are you?"

"We own this land. You're trespassers," Max said.

"Kiss my ass. This is Frank Bryce's land," someone said.

"Seal those lips, Foster," snapped the leader. Then, "He's right. This land doesn't belong to you."

"By the laws of magic, it does. Which means you

need to cease fire. If you shoot me, I'm going to be seriously annoyed," Max warned.

"Laws of magic?" Max could almost hear his lip curl, and she did hear him spit.

"That's right. It's a new world. Get used to it. Now, Tyler and I are going in. Don't get in our way, and quit shooting, and you just might survive the day."

She glanced over her shoulder. The soldier was starting to twitch and moan. Oak was edging down the slope behind her. Farther up, she could see the others trailing down, arms outstretched as they moved toward her voice.

"Did you hear?" she asked Oak. His eyes were now glassy white.

"Yep. You can see?" At least, that's what she thought he said. She wasn't exactly a lip reader.

"Earphones," she said by way of explanation. "Wait here. Once the noise stops, your eyes should heal up."

He lifted two fingers to his brow in a casual salute. "Yes, ma'am."

"Bite me," she said with a grin, and focused back on the clearing.

"How do you want to handle this?" Tyler asked. "Ask them politely to leave?"

"Think they'll listen?"

"It's possible."

"But not likely. Still, should let us get close enough to attack. I don't think the snow is thick enough to give us cover. And there's no sneaking in on our stomachs below the mist. It will probably eat our faces off. As it is, my boots are half gone," Max said. "But watch out—they are Divine."

"Bullshit. There ain't nothing holy about them but maybe what we shot through them," a man's voice growled into her ears.

It irritated her. "I didn't say *holy*, Ace. I said Divine. Better learn the difference, or you're going to end up dead. I might even kill you myself."

The demons—Max was sure they were demons, though of what variety she had no idea—turned to watch her as she strode across the clearing. They could see her perfectly, since as soon as she set foot on the floor of the canyon, the snow drew back to the tree line, clearing the entire bottom of the canyon. Definitely not natural.

She drew her sword with her right hand and kept her left on the shotgun. This was likely to go south quickly.

Tyler slunk through the mist on the other side of the creek. A few demons eyed him but didn't seem to think he was a threat. They didn't like running water—most demon kind didn't. Most couldn't cross it without a bridge or transportation, and even then, it was horrifically painful, if not fatal. Maybe they thought he couldn't cross, either, and therefore wasn't all that threatening.

Max stopped just out of reach of the three that came to meet her. They stank like a landfill on a hot and humid day. It was enough to make her eyes water and her throat burn.

"You're trespassing," she said. She held the sword casually, but she could chop through all three of them before they'd be able to grab her.

"Puny human. We eat you." The creature's voice was

like boulders grinding together. It didn't wait for Max to answer but darted its long arms out at her.

It moved faster than she expected. She jerked her sword up and around, chopping through its wrists. She whirled in a circle, ducking low to avoid the swiping hands of the other two. Hands? They were more like rakes with hooked talons.

She slammed into one, knocking it sideways, then hacked through the neck of the other. Purplish blood fountained, and her skin erupted in blisters and burns wherever it splashed. She felt poison leaching into her flesh and veins. Claws ripped down her thigh, shredding her pants and cutting deep. She kicked and wove in a desperate dance as the full company of demons descended on her. She blasted them with the shotgun, but even though the blasts tore holes in them and took off one demon's head, they kept coming.

"Destroy that thing fast," she gritted through the radio to Tyler. "I won't hold out long."

But instead of going after the giant Hefty bag of bloodcurdling screams, he was suddenly at her side. He had knives in both fists and moved with liquid grace as he sliced and cut, ducking and lunging.

"What are you doing?" Max demanded. She dropped her shotgun. It was empty, and she had no time to reload. Now it was just getting in the way.

"What does it look like?"

He grunted and doubled over as a demon leg smashed into his ribs. He jammed a knife deep into the leg and jerked away before the gout of blood could drench him. Jaws snapped next to Max's ear. One of them grabbed her ankle and yanked, dangling her in the air.

Twisting, she levered up from the waist and chopped through its arm with her sword. The limb separated, and she fell hard on her back. She rolled away, grunting as the creature's tail lashed across her back. Her headphones twisted, and the screaming wail instantly drilled into her skull. Max's eyes glazed gray. She wrenched away from an eviscerating slash at her gut and leaped to her feet, hooking her headphones back into place.

Voices crackled through the radio, offering a storm of advice. She ignored them. Suddenly, the leader's voice blasted through.

"Cut the jaw-jacking!"

Instant silence. Max could have kissed him.

She dove back into the fray, standing back-to-back with Tyler. Bit by bit, they chipped away at their enemies. Literally. A few fingers here, a hand there, a head, a leg, a foot, a tail. Blood and gore slicked the ground beneath them. The falling temperature was swiftly turning the wet to ice, making footing that much more difficult.

Suddenly, Tyler went down, falling beneath the level of the mist. Two demons dove on top of him, their jaws snapping. Without thinking, Max abandoned her own battle. She snatched one of the beasts by the shoulder and pulled it up, smashing her knee into its face. Its blood spurted, and it grabbed her thigh with both claws. Its bony fingers skewered her flesh. Talons scraped bone. Max clenched her teeth, biting back a yelp of pain. She clubbed the creature in the head with the hilt of the sword before it could strip the meat from her leg.

Its skull caved in, and the demon fell backward. Its fingers gouged through Max's thigh, turning it to hamburger. She kicked it away as best she could, but her leg was next to useless.

Something struck her from behind, knocking her flying. She flew over Tyler and bounced on the ground. Her forehead banged against a sharp rock. She rolled onto her back just as a demon closed on her. She managed to get her good leg up between them and kicked it off. She'd lost her sword. She yanked a knife from the sheath on her arm and slashed at the demon's throat as it launched itself at her again.

Hot blood splashed over her face, filling her eyes and spurting into her nose and mouth. It burned, and Max gagged and gasped. She twisted as the creature fell across her, knuckling at her eyes to clear them. She squirmed out from under it and staggered to her feet.

She turned just as another demon lunged for her. Before it could connect, two shots rang out, and its skull exploded. It dropped like a sack of onions. It twitched and convulsed and then went limp.

"Thanks," Max said into the microphone.

"Oorah," came the leader's gravelly voice in reply.

All of the demons were dead or incapacitated. For now. She wasn't sure if they were going to stay dead. Demons didn't die easy.

Tyler was on his hands and knees. He slowly clambered to his feet. Demon blood and gore drenched him from head to foot. It mixed with bright crimson ribbons that ran from his own flesh. His clothing hung in tattered shreds, and his entire body was a patchwork quilt of clawed skin.

He grinned at her raggedly. "That was fun."

"I thought I told you to go after that thing," she said, jerking her chin at the billowing sack. She kicked through the mist-covered debris on the ground, trying to find her sword.

He shrugged. "You couldn't take them alone. Besides, Alexander would've had my ass if I let anything happen to you," Tyler added. "He's almost as scary as you are."

"Right," Max said. "If that's what you think, I've been seriously slacking. So what do you want to do about the giant Hefty bag?"

"It's probably a birthing sac."

"Two points for Mr. Obvious."

He ignored her. "It's big enough to hold a couple of dozen of the bastards. The way they're kicking around, it looks like they're in a hurry to get out and get acquainted," Tyler said. "They'll be hungry. Babies always are. They're going to think we look pretty tasty."

She ran her fingers through her sticky, matted hair and made a face. Disgusting. "We could cut a hole in it and see if that forces them to come out one at a time."

"Might work." He stretched and cracked his back. "Only one way to find out."

"Would a grenade help?" came the rasping voice of the leader of the soldiers through the headphones.

"You've got grenades, Chief?" Max asked. "Any reason you didn't mention that ten or fifteen minutes ago?"

"I've got one left," he corrected. "We tried the others a little north of here, but they didn't take."

"Which means they aren't going to stay down," Max said to Tyler. "How long before they resurrect, Chief?"

"Maybe ten minutes, give or take."

Max grimaced and reached for her cell. She had to push the headphones aside, and her head instantly vibrated with the wailing cry. It was louder, if anything, and sharper. She lost her vision, and blood started to run out of her nose.

She punched in the speed dial, and Giselle answered on the first ring. "How bad is it?" she asked without preamble.

"Better get out here quick. We've got a demon infestation."

One thing about Giselle was that she didn't waste time asking a lot of stupid questions. "On my way."

The phone went dead. Max tucked it back into her vest and readjusted her headphones. It took longer for her vision to clear this time.

"It'll take her a little bit to get here. Couldn't hurt to blow them to bits before that. It would stop that noise, anyhow. Give our Blades a chance to recover and help once the demons start pulling themselves back together."

Max turned to scan the canyon behind them. The team of human hunters began sifting out of the trees. They were all wearing fatigues and carrying submachine guns slung over their shoulders. They wore camo paints and helmets, and they looked the worse for wear. Most were bandaged, and all had torn and bloody clothes.

Their leader marched out in front. He looked to be around thirty years old and was a bit more than six feet tall. Fox-colored stubble covered a stubborn jaw, and his eyes were blue, like glacier ice, and just as ruthless and cold. His skin was tanned, and he had white crow's feet around his eyes. He came to stand a few feet away from Max. His men hung back in a loose semicircle, the barrels of their guns pointing downward, but it would only take a flick of the wrist to raise them.

The leader looked Max up and down and then did the same to Tyler before turning back to Max.

"Name's Liam," he said by way of introduction.

"Max," she said. "This is Tyler."

He held out a grenade. "It's the last one. Know how to use it?"

"Pull the pin and get out of the way."

"That's about it."

She took it. "Thanks."

"I want these motherfuckers dead. If you can do it, I'll give you anything you want."

"Careful," Tyler said. "Shouldn't say things like that if you don't mean them. Magic is very literal."

The other man eyed him, his eyes narrowing. Finally, he nodded. "I'll keep that in mind. Do the two of you want some help?"

"We'll manage," Max said. She motioned for Tyler to join her, and they headed for the sac.

"Who did you just call?" Liam asked suddenly.

Max glanced back at him and grinned. "The Wicked Witch of the West. Who else?"

6

THE GRIMS WERE NOT EASY TO FOLLOW. IF NOT for Alexander's extended spirit senses, he and Thor would have lost them more than once. The snow deadened smells and covered tracks. Not that the truck could go where the Grims could. They were traveling across the mountains in a straight line toward—

Somewhere.

They could be going to New York or Florida for all Alexander knew. Or even Antarctica. He did not doubt that the beasts could easily travel across the ocean. Spike, however, might slow them down.

Colored flickers marking living creatures danced across the landscape, which spread out from Alexander in a ghostly overlay of reality. What he saw in his mindscape went miles farther than he could actually see with his eyes. He tried to distract himself with the play of colors, but he could not forget about Max.

"You want to talk about it?" Thor asked as they drove through Hamilton toward Salmon.

Alexander stilled his hands. He had been tapping his

fingers restlessly since they left Horngate. His Prime was on edge. "Talk about what?" he asked, feigning confusion.

His friend eyed him sideways. "You know, old son, it don't take a genius to spot a goat in a flock of sheep," he said. "What's going on with you and Max?"

Just like Thor to drive a blade right into the heart of the matter. Alexander went back to tapping. "Nothing a frontal lobotomy would not cure," he growled.

"That good, eh?" Thor shrugged. "Well, nothing worth having comes easy, and Max definitely ain't easy. Question is if you think she's worth the trouble."

"I am beginning to wonder," Alexander said, staring out the window. He felt Thor's startled stare like a slap.

"Are you shitting me?"

His lips curved slightly. "Maybe. Probably." He dragged his fingers over his scalp.

"What's wrong?"

"She keeps pushing me away. Only time she seems to want me around is in bed, and then it seems like all she is trying to do is forget about Niko and the angels. I could be anybody."

"But you aren't. She picked you." Thor was silent a moment. "She'll figure it out and come around. You just have to be patient and wait."

"For how long?"

"The way you feel about her, forever might be just long enough," Thor said.

Alexander rolled down the window and leaned his arm on the sill. The air was back to being unseasonably warm. Drizzle dampened his skin. Forever. That was a hell of a long time to wait.

*   *   *

JUST BEFORE CROSSING INTO IDAHO, THOR TURNED EAST toward the Big Hole, following the path of the Grims. They kept their lights off, and thanks to magic, they made no sound at all. The truck's engine had been replaced with a tangle of gold filaments wrapping a chunk of silver. The whole thing was no bigger than Alexander's fist. It was held suspended in the middle of the engine compartment by lengths of plastic twine. Its magic was strong enough to overcome the magic-smothering effect of the truck's steel body.

Driving silently kept them from the notice of human predators. It did not, however, keep them safe from rock trolls, as it turned out.

The road ribboned through a series of small valleys and meadows following a swift-flowing river. Although Alexander could see spirit flames for both animals and magical creatures, they were largely left alone. Right up until they started dropping down into the Big Hole—an enormous flat valley in the northern Rockies.

The road exploded in front of them. Concrete, black-top, and dirt spewed up into the air. Thor swerved and slammed on the brakes. They skidded and spun in a circle, stopping sideways on the road, road debris hailing down on them. The windshield shattered, raining down bits of safety glass. The roof dented inward as a massive chunk of concrete bounced off it.

There was now a crater more than twenty feet across where the road had been. Inside it stood a rock troll. It stood tall as a house at the shoulder, with great hulking shoulders and what appeared to be a boulder for a head. The beast looked as if it had been rudely molded out of still-warm rock and left to harden, and then someone had jabbed holes in its face for eyes and stuck bits of jagged quartz in its mouth for teeth. Its chest was bigger than their truck and each hand and foot could have crushed them with one blow.

"This could get ugly," Thor said, tipping his straw hat back on his head.

"It could," Alexander said, opening his door. "But maybe it will be fun."

"Now you sound like Max. Can't we go around it?"

"They are faster than they look. It can run more than eighty miles an hour for short bursts. We will not get far."

"And the news keeps getting better. Since you know so much, how do we kill it?"

"I have no idea. Explosives might work. Or they could just make it mad."

"It already looks plenty pissed."

"See what you can rig. I will distract it," Alexander said, moving away from the truck and down toward the open field and the river below. Maybe the rock troll would not like running water. He should be so lucky.

The troll swayed back and forth, its attention flickering between Thor and the truck and Alexander. At last, it made a decision. With one heaving motion, it vaulted out of its hole and galloped after Alexander on all fours, the ground shaking each time it planted those massive hands and feet.

It was far more nimble than it looked. Alexander swerved to the right around a stand of birch and aspen trees. The troll followed easily.

Alexander threaded through a series of rocky outcroppings. He was going for higher ground. The one thing besides explosives that might damage the rock troll was a fall.

The troll bounded up onto one of the massive boulders and leaped after Alexander. It sailed through the air and when it landed, the ground shuddered and bucked. It would not be a remotely good idea to get hit by that beast.

A rock the size of Alexander's head bounced on the ground beside him. Too damned close. He dodged into a knot of blue spruce and sprinted up through the trees. The rock troll bellowed, a deep, guttural sound that echoed down the valley. Branches snapped, and wood squealed and whined as the troll plowed through trees.

The moment's respite gave Alexander time to think. He had led the rock troll away from the truck to give Thor a chance to rig an explosion, but now he was too far away to get back before the beast overtook him. That left him with only one real choice: jump off the bluff into the river. The troll would likely follow. With luck, it would break apart. If not, Alexander was fairly certain the beast could not swim, which might give him a moment or two to get away. The river offered little safety if running water did not bother the creature. The troll could probably wade or run along the bank until it could snatch Alexander out.

He cleared the spruces and lunged up onto the top of a small escarpment, about ten feet up. Behind him, the troll swiped its stone paw through the air. It knocked into one of Alexander's ankles. He felt bone break, and his foot and leg went numb.

Alexander landed heavily on his stomach. The breath exploded from his lungs. He sucked in air as he dragged his knees up to lever himself upright. The rock troll was already clambering over the lip of the ledge. It gnashed its teeth together, and it sounded like stones in a metal grinder.

Alexander looked up. He had hoped for another forty or fifty feet of elevation. The drop to the river bottom was less than a hundred feet. He could survive that, which meant the odds were good the rock troll could, too. But he had little choice left. His foot dangled from his shattered ankle, useless. He would not heal in time to get any higher. His only route now was down.

He looked behind him. The rock troll was crouching down, shaking itself like a bull. It pawed at the chalky dirt with both massive hands, shoveling it up over its head. A cloud of dust filled the air. Alexander eased back slowly, searching for the edge. As fast as the beast could move, he needed to make sure he could leap out of reach before the troll snatched him out of the air.

More dust puffed upward. Taking the chance that the troll might have temporarily blinded itself, Alexander stepped backward. He landed just twenty feet below on a narrow ledge. He squelched a cry of pain as hot agony speared up his leg and spine. He made a staggering run to the end of the shelf and launched himself out over the river, just as the rock troll bellowed its fury at its prey's escape.

Alexander crashed into the river. It was like hitting a steel wall. Bones cracked, and his lungs pancaked. He slid under the icy water and bounced against several boulders. He spun and could not tell up from down. Seconds passed like minutes. Everything inside him demanded air. He kicked and clawed upward, only to find himself grabbing silt at the bottom of the river. He turned and shoved upward with all the power in his good leg. He broke through and dragged in a shallow breath. It was all he could manage.

He slewed around, searching for the rock troll. It had landed beside the river. One of it arms was twisted wrongside around, and it looked like its head had shifted to the right. The fact that it could be hurt offered some hope that the explosives would work. If Thor could get anywhere near it.

The troll heaved itself up and lumbered along the bank after Alexander, dragging its damaged arm. It uprooted a clump of desert sage and threw it, followed by chunks of wood and stone—whatever it could reach. Each time it threw something, it had to slow down. In the meantime, Alexander swam as fast as he could downstream. His body was sluggish, and he could barely kick. His arms were both broken, and it was all he could do to force them through the water.

But with the river's swift current and his own efforts, he was able to keep ahead of the troll, although avoiding the creature's missiles was much more difficult. One rock slammed into his shoulder. It crushed bone and opened up long gashes down his back.

Alexander had little idea where Thor and the truck were. He had lost all sense of direction. His head spun dizzily, and one eye was swollen shut. Every bit of concentration was going into staying afloat and avoiding the troll's projectiles.

The rock troll did not seem inclined to get into the water yet, but that could simply be because it was faster on land. Alexander did not dare to crawl out on the other side of the river. Either the troll would stone him to death from afar, or it would hop over the river and stomp him into the ground. Neither sounded enticing.

Before he was aware of it, he was nearly under a bridge crossing the river.

"Hold on, son," Thor called, and then explosions ripped through the night.

Alexander passed under the bridge. Rocks and dirt hailed down, and the stink of fire and explosives filled the air. Then there was silence.

He kicked, pushing himself over the bank. He scrabbled up so that his upper body was out of the water. He drew several breaths and forced himself to his hands and knees. A moment later, Thor joined him and helped him to his feet. Alexander swayed, and Thor put his arm around his waist.

"The rock troll?" Alexander rasped.

"No troll. Just rock, for now. And I don't think we ought to stick around to see if it pulls itself back together."

"Agreed."

Thor helped Alexander back to the truck, then helped to peel off his dripping jeans.

"Just cut the damned shirt off," Alexander said, unwilling to wrestle himself free of the wet fabric. He felt as if he might faint. Or vomit. Or maybe both.

"Now, this is friendship. I much prefer getting women naked," Thor said, then scowled as Alexander's body was revealed. He was a patchwork of bruises. His ribs lumped oddly, his right shoulder was caved in, his left ankle was a mushy black mess, and the side of his skull ached from when he had hit the water.

"That looks like it hurts," he said, then dug in Alexander's pack for a dry pair of jeans and a shirt. With Thor's help, Alexander was able to put on the jeans, but he did not try the shirt. He would wait until he healed some first.

Thor went to the back of the truck and returned with a jug of Ugly Juice. "Drink it. All of it, right now. Don't go making faces. You aren't two years old. Suck it up, and take your medicine. Be quick. I don't want to have another run-in with that thing. "

Thor yanked what was left of the windshield out and swept the safety glass off the seats. He then piled a selection of the food Magpie had sent with them into the front seat.

In the meantime, Alexander drained the jug of Ugly Juice. Almost immediately, he could feel his body putting the calories to work, fueling his healing spells. Whatever disgusting ingredients Magpie put into the syrupy juice, it had a lot of calories. And probably some magic, given that she was also a Circle-level witch.

Thor climbed into the driver's seat and examined Alexander. "You don't look so good."

"I expect I feel worse than I look. Cannot seem to catch my breath. My head feels like I fell on an anvil."

"It's looking a little dented, too. You going to be all right?"

"Sooner or later. Better get driving. The Grims are getting to the edge of my sensory range. We are going to lose them soon."

Thor drove around the crater left by the rock troll and cruised down toward the bridge.

"Fuck."

Alexander had leaned the seat back and closed his eyes. Now he sat up, sucking a pained breath through his teeth. "What?" But then he saw the slow-swirling cloud of red dust centered over the twitching pieces of the rock troll. The stones of its body started to roll together and take troll shape again.

"Floor it," Alexander said just as Thor jammed the gas pedal all the way down. The truck fishtailed and practically flew over the bridge and up the road. They hit a hundred miles an hour, and the speedometer pegged out. The truck still accelerated. Thank the witches for magic.

"That was the same red dust that attacked Max in the angel vault, wasn't it?" Thor asked, watching out his sideview mirror.

"Looked like it. But how did it get out here?" Alexander lifted his hand to rub his throbbing head and instantly regretted it. Pain enveloped him in a fiery cocoon. He dropped his hand back into his lap.

"Can only mean the preacher witch is after us. But why?" Thor mused.

"Why break into Horngate and burn five innocent people on our doorstep? Who knows what he's up to."

"Apparently he's nuttier than a squirrel's cheeks in October."

"Let us hope he is done with us," Alexander said, leaning back and closing his eyes.

"I don't know, son. That sort of crazy tends to stay focused. He seems to have a hate-on for witches. Maybe he figures we're just as bad. At least if he's after us, he's not likely to be harrassing anybody back at Horngate. That would take a lot more energy than he's likely to have."

"Thank goodness for that," Alexander murmured. He didn't like to think what could be happening to Max if she caught the preacher witch's attention. "How do you suppose a witch comes to want to burn up his own kind? I mean, fighting over territory I get. But he is anti-witch."

Thor shrugged. "How are there gay Republicans? Some people don't make a whole lot of sense."

They slowed down in Wisdom just enough to make the turn south toward Jackson before speeding up again. Lights flickered in a scattering of houses and the smell of woodsmoke drifted through the air. What looked like a dark, lush jungle swathed the foothills of the Pioneers for as far as Alexander could see. The trees were squat and broad, and . . .

"Thor," Alexander said warningly.

"I see 'em," the blond Blade said grimly, his hands flexing on the steering wheel.

The trees had begun crawling toward them. Their roots roped and twisted over the ground like giant knotty snakes. Streamers of red wreathed their branches.

"We left that rock troll in the dust. How the hell does the preacher know where we are?"

"Maybe he can scry us," Alexander said. "But that does not explain how he is casting spells over such distances. Unless he is a lot more powerful than we thought."

Thor glanced sharply at him. "Are you thinking he's a mage?"

"I am thinking we had better find out how he is managing to cast magic like this. But first, I think we should survive. I would sure like to know why he is so interested in what we are doing tonight."

The trees rippled over the ground with incredible speed. Thor swerved around reaching roots. "They don't seem to like the road," he said. "It's like it burns them."

That was all the notice he gave before driving off onto the shoulder to put the road between the truck and the attacking trees. They jolted hard over the clumps of grass, piled rocks, and rutted dirt.

Alexander bounced up against the roof as the truck flew into the air, then dropped back to the ground. Thor ran through the barbed-wire fence and out into the field beside the road.

"That did it," he said, slowing slightly. "They aren't crossing."

Alexander did not answer. He gripped the door handle with white-knuckled fingers. The plastic cracked under his grip. His skull had struck the roof in the same place he had smashed it previously. Blood dribbled down his forehead. His vision had gone snowy, like static on a TV.

"Oh, hell," Thor said, hitting the accelerator again. "They are burrowing under."

A moan rose in the night, a high-pitched sound drenched in fury and pain. The truck jolted and bounced over the uneven ground of the open field. Thor crashed through another fence, and metal screeched as the barbs scraped the body of the truck. They jolted through a ditch, over a dirt road, and back into a field. Thor swerved around sagebrush and out-croppings of rock.

Alexander was tossed and jolted, banging around in his seat. Once he almost bounced through the open front windshield. Thor grabbed him and yanked him back down. Then everything went black.

When he awoke, he was still in his seat. Thor had reclined it as far back as it would go and was smearing a cold healing salve on his head. Alexander batted him away and sat up with a groan.

"I am fine," he said. "I do not need a nurse."

"Right. I figured when your brain started oozing out of your ears that you were just having a quick nap."

Alexander gave a weak grin. His head was spinning, and his stomach was churning in response. "You are exaggerating."

"Not by much. I wasn't particularly sure you were going to wake up." Thor's jaw was tense, and behind the taut mask of his face, his Blade was in a frenzy. Before Alexander could speak, he shoved another jug of Ugly Juice at him. "Drink."

Alexander did not argue. He gulped down the noxious brew and then ate the food that Thor supplied. After about fifteen minutes, his vision settled, and he felt the bones in his skull hardening in place. The pain remained, but it was more bearable.

He pushed up out of the truck and glanced around. They were out in the middle of a field beside a wind-ing creek and surrounded by willows. The road and the predatory forest were nowhere to be seen. "What happened?"

"The road, mostly. The trees burrowed their roots

under, but they couldn't get that far. Eventually, they gave up. Or the preacher witch ran out of magic."

"I doubt that," Alexander said. "More likely, he got distracted."

"I don't want to think about what might have got his attention," Thor said darkly.

Alexander nodded. He could call Max and check in, but she already thought he was too possessive. He would let her tell him when she wanted him. *If* she wanted him. He could do little to help her right at the moment, if she needed help.

"All the same, the preacher witch seems a little too interested in us. What do you suppose we did to deserve that?" Thor asked.

Alexander deliberately turned his attention away from Max. "Maybe he does not want us following the Grims."

"Why not?"

Alexander shrugged. He had no answers to that question. He let his senses range outward and discovered the Grims much closer than he had expected. And not just them but other beings in brilliant shades of violet, scarlet, yellow, and orange. The salamanders? A wild flare of magic blossomed around them, sending out pulsing ripples of distorting energy.

Alexander took a few steps away from the truck. His legs were wobbly, but his ankle held. His ribs felt rubbery but whole. His rolled his shoulder to test it. It ached and made crackling noises. Good enough.

"We should go," he said to Thor.

The other man eyed him dubiously. "You aren't fit."

"Maybe not, but we only have a few hours before dawn. Who knows where they will disappear to if we wait out the day? Besides, the faster we get this over with and get back home, the less likely the preacher witch will remember to kill us."

"I hate being on his to-do list," Thor grumbled. "All right. But you're barely stitched up. One light blow, and you'll shatter. We'll go to the Grims, but we're not hopping into any unnecessary trouble."

"Is what we do ever unnecessary?" Alexander asked as he slid back into the truck and adjusted the seat back upright.

"You sound just like Max," Thor said, sliding in beside him. "Her attitude is catching. Just like a bad flu. Just remember, you're not in any better shape right now than an ordinary human. Maybe worse. So don't be stupid. I just hope stupidity isn't catching, too," he muttered under his breath.

Alexander smiled and shut his eyes, gripping the sides of the seat hard as the truck started rolling over the field. Thor went slowly enough to make the jouncing less painful, but it was still agonizing. Still, every passing moment provided healing to his body. But Thor was right. Even when they traversed the twenty miles or so to get to the Grims, he was not going to be in any shape to fight.

THOR KEPT TO THE FIELDS, SLOWLY ANGLING EAST BACK to the road and keeping a watchful eye on the unmoving forest.

The closer they got to Jackson and the Grims, the hotter it was getting. It had to be at least a hundred twenty degrees. Heat distorted the air, making everything in sight ripple.

Thor pulled to a stop on flat dirt just before the road. He got out and knelt down beside it, then leaned back through the window. "The tar is soft as taffy. We'll get stuck on it. I say we leave the truck here, or we chance having the rubber melt off the tires." He glanced down and back up. "We may be riding back on the rims at this point, anyway."

Alexander got out. He no longer felt as dizzy. His shoulder still crackled as the bones settled back together, but otherwise he felt whole. Fragile as glass but whole.

Shadowblades were made to tolerate extreme heat and cold—within reason. Fire would burn them, of course, and they would eventually freeze solid. Hopefully the heat coming out of Jackson would not be so significant that they would have to turn back.

They left their guns in the truck, as they both feared exploding ammunition. They followed the road, staying beside it. The terrain was mostly flat. Jackson nestled up against the foothills of the Pioneers in a long, narrow valley.

The heat increased as they approached the town. It was entirely deserted. The buildings were dried and cracked as if they'd been cooked in an oven. It felt like an oven. Alexander found it hard to breathe the hot, dry air. The magic there was dense. It was like pushing through molasses. Every step was increasingly difficult. The closer they came to the Grims and the source of the magic, the thicker the magic became.

He stopped as they came abreast of a barnlike building. Or what had once been a building. The roof had fallen in, and the walls sagged apart. Around it were little cabins that had collapsed into kindling. The trees were rusty and skeletal, their needles in dry piles on the ground. Next to the big building were the remains of what appeared to be a swimming pool. It was cracked and buckled, along with the ground around it.

"That way," Alexander said, pointing.

He and Thor jumped over the road and slogged past the pool. Beyond was a hillside of crisped grass and scrub. The ground crunched beneath their feet. Heat pulsed through the air and rose from the dirt. The soles of Alexander's boots grew sticky and soft and clumped with dirt and weeds.

They were close. The Grims were just beyond the crown of the hill, and so was the source of the magic and what Alexander assumed were salamanders. The Grims seemed to be arrayed along the hillside, watching. Spike was with them.

The two Blades staggered up the hill, fighting to breathe. Alexander's strength was quickly sapping. He straightened his spine, refusing to let Thor see his struggle.

They both stopped dead at the crown of the hill as a wall of heat slammed into them. Alexander could feel the moisture leaching from his body tissues like water from a sieve. He instantly felt parched as desert sand. He and Thor could only take a few minutes of that heat before they had to retreat.

The Grims sat watchfully in a semicircle just below the two Blades. Spike was nestled against Beyul, and she whimpered low in her throat. Beyul nuzzled her, and she subsided.

Below the Grims was a crack in the earth. It was a

hundred feet long and fifteen feet wide at its broadest point. Brilliant rainbow-colored flames rose out of it, and the rock on either side glowed orange. Within those flames, serpentine beasts crawled. Alexander counted nine of them. Each was a different jeweled color. They were six or seven feet long, with four short, stout legs. Their tails were as long as their bodies, and their snouts were narrow and toothy.

They crawled in and out of the crack, their stubby wings fluttering for balance. A green one snapped at a yellow one, and a snarling spat ensued, both losing their grip on the rock and plummeting down inside. A few moments later, they crawled back out.

"How far down do you think that crack goes?" Thor whispered, his voice dry as dust.

"Forever," Alexander replied, not altogether joking. "That is elemental fire, not center-of-the-earth fire. It will not only melt the flesh from your bones, but it will also destroy your essence."

"Good to know. As it is, I'm turning into jerky even as we speak. What do you want to do now?"

"I do not think the Grims are coming back until they are done watching or . . . whatevering."

"We can't wait with them. We'll mummify. Hell, you're already halfway there," Thor said, looking Alexander over. "C'mon. We're leaving. Now."

Alexander hesitated, then nodded. He sent a mind call out to Beyul, asking if the beast would come back to Horngate. The Grim neither answered nor looked at him. The animals were entirely independent; they went where they wanted when they wanted, and even the angels were wary of them. Nobody knew why they chose to do what they did—such as staying at Horngate for the past five or six weeks. Were they moving on now?

"Let's go," Thor said, grasping Alexander's forearm and pulling him away.

They barely went a step when something caught Alexander's attention.

"Look!"

A streamer of red dust had appeared above the gemlike flames. It swirled lazily a moment, then gathered into a tight ball.

"We should really get the fuck out of here," Thor said, stepping back and pulling Alexander with him.

But the other man refused to move. Suddenly he knew that *this* was what the preacher had not wanted them to see.

The ball dropped like it had been launched from a cannon. It disappeared inside the flames. For a long moment, nothing happened. Then the ground shuddered and power swelled and thickened in the air. Something terrible was about to happen.

"I don't think I want to wait to see what happens next," Thor said, and Alexander reluctantly agreed.

They started backing up the hill. Neither wanted to turn his back on whatever the preacher witch was up to. They reached the crown of the hill and were turning to launch themselves downward when fire flared up from the crack and the air shook with a rupture of magic. A much larger salamander clawed its way out of the crack. It was at least thirty feet long, nose to tail. It appeared to be made of green fire, its body shifting and flickering like flames. Its head darted to the little salamanders. Then, satisfied, she—Alexander was fairly certain the beast was the mother of the littler salamanders—looked up to examine the Grims.

Her eyes were the size of hubcaps, and they swirled carnelian red. Her head swung back and forth in a long arc in front of the Grims. She huffed, and yellow flames erupted from her mouth. They enveloped the Grims. Alexander and Thor staggered back from the heat, skidding down behind the top of the hill.

His skin blistering, Alexander crawled back up to the top. The Grims remained sitting, unfazed by the wash of elemental fire. Spike, however, was not so blasé. She cowered, whimpering. Her fur smoked, although she looked otherwise unharmed. Beyul must have protected her.

The salamander mother snapped at the air in front of the Grims. She snatched one of them but let go immediately, shaking her head furiously. A streamer of the red dust wreathed around her head. She paused as if listening, then her gaze fixed on Spike.

Oh, hell! The preacher was *directing* the salamander! He was going after to Spike, the only beast vulnerable to attack.

Alexander jumped to his feet, wanting to warn Spike, but Thor dragged him down just as the salamander belched another gout of fire and dove in again. This time, her jaws closed over the Calopus. An instant later she reared up in the air and spun with liquid ease and dove down into the crack. The young salamanders vanished after her. The crack started to zipper shut, the edges pulling together.

Beyul lost his casual demeanor. He roared and

plunged down after the salamanders. The other Grims stood watching a moment, then followed one after another, sliding through the narrowing crack like smudges of smoke. In just a few seconds, they were gone, and all that was left was a cooling scar on the ground.

Alexander rose and slowly walked down to the seam of melted rock and dirt. It still glowed orange. "They are gone," he said hollowly, disbelieving.

"Maybe they'll be back," Thor said, pacing to the end of the scar and back.

"I do not think that is their style," Alexander said. "They are curious. They go wherever their interest leads. Who knows where that crack really led to? Probably another world altogether." He hesitated. "I doubt Spike could survive the fire and the salamander." He thought of Max. She would be heartbroken. She had fallen in love with Spike, despite her unwillingness to care about anyone. To care about him. He shook his head. "That bastard preacher witch has a lot to answer for."

"That he does." Thor looked at Alexander, eyes like frozen diamonds. "Let's go start making him pay."

7

THE MOVEMENT INSIDE THE DEMON BIRTHING sac had become frenzied. The creatures inside jabbed and pushed in all directions. The membrane stretched beneath the onslaught, threads of blue and black worming through the sickly white expanse. Mist continued to billow off it.

"I don't think we've got a lot of time before the bastards hatch," Tyler said.

"Cut me a hole, and I'll toss the grenade inside," Max said. "Might take a lot more out that way."

"Sure, and then in the ten seconds it takes to explode, they'll rip their way out, and the grenade won't do anything at all."

"Okay, fine. I'll release the spoon and count to three. Then you make your cut, and I'll pop it in. After that, we'll run like hell."

Liam answered before Tyler could. "If the fuse lasts that long. Cooking off is risky and stupid. It's just as likely to blow up in your hand. And trust me, that pineapple will turn even something like you into cat food."

"Something like me?" Max's brows rose. "What do you think I am?"

"Not a fucking clue, but after watching you fight, I know you aren't human."

She grinned. "Don't forget it, Chief. Now, get out of the way before you get killed. And thanks for the advice."

"Like I said, I want these motherfuckers dead. Good luck." With that, he motioned at his men, and they hustled back toward the trees.

Max eyed Tyler. "I suppose you have an opinion."

"Damned right I do. We cut the hole and toss the grenade. Better to risk the demon spawn tearing out than having you blow up," Tyler said, his eyes narrowing to slits. He thrust his jaw out.

Max only nodded. He wasn't going to back down, and it wasn't worth the time to argue. The truth was that a few seconds probably wouldn't make a lot of difference. But sooner or later, she was going to have to take serious risks, and he was going to have to live with it. Neither one of them was made to sit on a shelf and look pretty. Shadowblades were built for war, and sometimes they died. Niko wasn't the first brother they'd lost, and he wouldn't be the last.

Inwardly, she sneered at herself. *Easy to say, harder to do.* Like she was handling her losses all that well. She wasn't doing any better than Tyler.

She grinned at him suddenly with a flash of her old bravado. "Let's do this."

He stared a minute, then smiled and shook his head. "That sac is dancing around like a carnival bounce house. It'll be easy to miss the cut once I make it," he warned.

"I never miss."

"Right. And I get laid every night. Come on, before your nose grows so long you can't walk."

She and Tyler approached the thrusting, squirming sac. Max wrinkled her nose. It smelled worse than the demons had. It was like a stew of hot garbage, rotten eggs, burned hair, and a flooded outhouse. It was enough to make her gag. She spit and wiped her mouth with the back of her hand.

"How can anything smell that bad?" Tyler muttered as he also spit.

"Natural predator deterrent," Max said, breathing through her mouth. "Everybody gets too sick walking up to it to actually try eating it."

As they approached, the movement inside the sac billowed and bulged toward them. They halted as the membrane stretched so thin they could see scraping claws and snapping teeth.

"They look hungry," Tyler said.

"Maybe they'll like pineapple," Max sad, turning the grenade in her fingers.

"Let's serve it up and see," Tyler said. "Ready?"

Max pulled the pin, holding the spoon down. She kept her sword ready in her other hand. "Do it."

Tyler stabbed downward. The point of his blade pushed inward, but the sac only stretched without piercing. Pointed claws scrabbled at it from within. "Houston, we may have a problem," he said. He lifted his knife and stabbed it harder. Still nothing. "Well, the good news is that they aren't going to be tearing out real soon."

"Which means they aren't ready to come out yet and

are probably vulnerable. That sac is protecting them as much as it's keeping them away from us."

"We could wait for Giselle to show up and let her deal with it."

"Now, what fun would that be?" Max asked. "Besides, who knows when the sac will mature? Could be seconds. Not to mention the other demons are starting to get lively." She surveyed the meadow of mist behind them. It was starting to bubble and churn with hidden currents.

"So we keep trying. Got ideas on how to cut it open? Maybe you have a cutting torch tucked in your pocket?"

"No, but maybe I've got the next best thing." Max dug one hand in her vest for a plastic tube of powder, the other hand still holding the spoon down on the grenade. "Hold out your knife."

He did as told. She unstoppered the tube with her teeth and poured a line of silvery powder along the edge of the knife. She carefully pushed the stopper back in, slid the tube back into her pocket, and withdrew a lighter.

She met Tyler's gaze. "This stuff will melt the knife. You need to go quick."

"You could have mentioned that sooner. It's my favorite knife."

"Time to get a new favorite."

"Aren't you helpful? Like rain in a flood. Or warts on a donkey's ass."

"I try to be. Ready?"

She didn't wait for an answer, flicking the lighter and holding the flame to the powder. It flared incandescent blue, its heat intense.

Tyler held the knife a moment until the entire blade was engulfed and then struck downward. This time, the blade slid easily through the tough sac. Thick yellow liquid burst outward, drenching the two of them in an acid shower. Immediately, Max's skin erupted in boils. The stuff dripped down her forehead, and she shook her head to clear it away from her eyes. Some of the acid goo dribbled into her left eye, blinding it. It felt like her eyes were boiling. They streamed tears, and she focused on what she was supposed to be doing.

The slit in the sac was only about a foot long. Goo-slicked demon arms and legs thrust out, scraping at the air. Unlike the adults, they had dark yellow skin that was almost runny, like melted wax. Their fingers were long and spidery and only slightly smaller than those of the adults. Clearly, they would be born ready to rampage.

A half dozen claws tore blindly at the hole, while several snouts thrust up between them, jaws snapping wildly. There had to be at least forty or fifty demon babies in there. They couldn't be allowed to live. They would end up infesting half the world.

Tyler jabbed at the hungry spawn with his incandescent blade. Demon flesh sizzled, and the stench of the open sac grew even worse. The demon babies wriggled back, and Max thrust her hand inside the sac. It was like reaching into a vat of jellied acid. Her hand burned and bubbled. Taloned fingers clawed her, and teeth ripped open her arm. The taste of her blood sent the demon spawn into a spasming craze. The entire sac exploded with frenzied movement.

Five or six mouths clamped down on her, one over

her fist, its tongue licking eagerly at her hand. *Perfect.* Max let go of the grenade, pushing it deep into the creature's throat. She jerked back, yanking her arm free of the hole and the hungry demons. It was nothing but hamburger. At least it was still attached. Not wasting any more time, she turned and fled toward the creek.

"Move your ass, Tyler!" she shouted before gulping a breath and jumping in. The water was only four feet deep. She pulled herself down to the bottom, wedging herself beneath a shelf of rocks. Tyler splashed down right beside her.

Three seconds later, the grenade exploded. The ground rocked, and the shock wave rolled through the water. Above, golden fire bloomed, and then rocks and debris splashed down all around them, a lot of it demon parts.

Max pulled her feet up under her, shoved herself up to the surface, and climbed back out of the creek. Her headphones had been knocked askew, and she was relieved to discover that the wailing had stopped. It had been replaced by the chuckle of the creek and mewling whimpers of whatever demon spawn still lived. She lurched up onto the bank, using her sword as a cane. Her left arm dangled uselessly. It flamed with agony, but she pushed the pain down inside her, ignoring it. She'd hurt worse before and would again.

Tyler climbed up onto the bank beside her. He glanced at her arm. "Exfoliation usually means leaving behind the muscle," he said. "I think you're doing it wrong."

"I'll let the spa know," Max replied wryly. The milky mist was thinning, revealing the twitching bits of hacked-up adult demons and the deflated birthing sac.

Slick acid mucus covered everything for a good hundred-foot radius. It was an inch thick at least and squelched under Max's feet. Her boots had been eaten away to nearly nothing, and the thick glop made her exposed skin bubble and burn. Her skin went from raw red to gray and black.

"This is just disgusting," Tyler said. His boots were nothing but shreds, and his feet looked as bad as hers.

"Probably shouldn't wade around in this stuff for long. Your feet might rot off," Max said.

"This stuff is everywhere. Unless you want me to stand on your shoulders . . ." He eyed her balefully.

"No chance. Your feet stink, even without that gunk."

The birthing sac puddled flat on the ground. The inside was scorched with burn holes that made it look like melted Swiss cheese. Bits of juvenile demon littered it and the surrounding area. There wasn't much left to say what else they looked like.

"Think the little ones will resurrect?" Tyler asked, watching the bits of the adults jiggling and wriggling across the ground.

Max skewered a chunk of one on the point of her sword. "No idea. But given our luck, I'd say it's likely."

She looked out across the clearing. Liam and his men were picking their way back in a loose scrimmage line. Behind them came Oak, Jody, and Steel. They wobbled uncertainly as if their vision was still recovering. On the north side of the creek, Nami, Simon, Flint, and one of Liam's soldiers emerged from the trees. The soldier staggered, streaks of blood running from his nose and ears. Flint pulled the man's arm around his neck and hoisted him along.

Max wandered around to examine the demon debris and started swearing.

"What?" Tyler said, coming to join her.

"They're fucking hydras," she said, pointing. The pieces of the adult creatures weren't drawing back together to make the original demons whole as she'd expected. Instead, they were bubbling and expanding. Fast. "Every little piece is going to grow into a new demon," she said. "We just exponentially increased the threat."

"Like I said, the grenades didn't take," Liam said, stopping a few feet away.

"You could have been more specific," Tyler said acidly.

The other man stared, his gaze stony. "Would it have made a difference?"

"Might have."

"You got rid of that sac, the noise, and the mist crap. I count that as a win. So what now?" Liam asked Max. His gaze dropped to her arm, and his face paled. "Shit. That looks bad."

"I'll be fine," she said with a shrug. She winced. "Eventually. Anyhow, we'll do the only thing we can do: keep fighting until Giselle gets here."

He tore his eyes from her mangled arm. "She's the Wicked Witch?"

"Yep."

Before he could say anything else, his men let out yelps of surprise, whipping their guns up as Oak, Jody, and Steel arrived. The three Blades approached so quietly no one had noticed them. Liam swung around, then looked at Max. "They're yours?"

She nodded. "I'd appreciate it if you had your men lower their guns."

"Do it," he barked, and his men obeyed, a few very reluctantly.

"What about Gates?" asked one with gray eyes and black hair. "Where is he?"

"That the one you took the headphones from?" Oak asked Max.

She glanced the question at Liam, and he nodded confirmation.

"He's going to need some healing," Oak said. "Fell out of the tree and sucked up some mist before I could find him." He tapped a finger near his eye. "I went pretty blind for a while."

"How bad?" Liam asked, scowling. It was the first bit of real expression Max had seen from him.

"He'll be dying before morning if he doesn't get help," Oak said in a careless voice.

Liam's lip curled in fury and disgust. His soldiers started railing at Oak, their voices ringing loudly. Worse, they lifted the muzzles of their guns.

Max glared at Oak.

He had the grace to look abashed. He held up his hands. "Sorry. Let me rephrase that. He'll be fine once our healers can get a look at him."

"Fine?" Liam demanded, but he was looking at Max. "Is that true?"

She shrugged. "If he doesn't die first, then he can probably be healed."

"That's not very reassuring."

"I'm not here to change your diapers, Chief. Soldiers die. You know it." But it hurt. He knew that, too, just as well as she did.

His cheeks turned red, and his nostrils flared white.

"He wouldn't be in danger if you hadn't taken his earphones."

"No? Seems to me you were awfully close to being demon dinner. How many people have you already lost?"

"We'd have handled it," he said, and his voice was flat and deadly cold.

"Sure. Right up until you ran out of bullets, and then they'd have made a tasty meal out of you," Tyler said.

"It's done now," Max said, deciding the recriminations had gone on long enough. "Now we have to stay alive until Giselle gets here."

Liam scraped his bottom lip with his teeth and nodded. "It isn't as bad as it looks. They won't all grow into new demons. Most will converge and combine until they're big enough to become a demon. But the numbers usually double, maybe triple."

"And they don't seem to like fire," Max said. She turned to her Blades. "Gather wood. We're going to hem them in against the river." They scattered instantly. She looked at Liam. "Have your men start gathering whatever's moving and pile it over there on the remnants of the sac. We'll see about getting them cooking."

She didn't wait to hear his reply. Her arm was starting to heal, but it still had no strength. She started skewering demon globs and piling them on the sac. Liam's men joined in with grim determination. Max quickly realized her mistake when the globs started merging like drops of mercury. Quickly, demons started to form. She hacked them apart with her sword. The only saving grace was that they didn't immediately start joining back together.

Her Blades hauled back entire trees and large limbs. They made an angular circle around the pile of demon scraps, with the heaviest fortification in a U shape away from the river. Max hoped that the combination of running water and a thin screen of fire on that side would be enough to keep them from escaping captivity. She wanted as big a fire on the other three sides as she could manage. Giselle didn't have far to come from Horngate, but this was rough country, and she also didn't have a good way to get there. It would probably be another hour or two before she arrived. That meant a couple of hours keeping the fire burning hot enough and high enough to keep the demons trapped. That was going to take a lot of wood.

Once the pile of logs was reasonably high, Max spread more of the incinerator powder around and lit it. It flared and became an inferno. It was burning through wood so fast the flames would likely die in less than ten minutes.

"Keep everyone gathering wood," she told Oak and Tyler. "We'll be in serious trouble if we run out."

"The fire won't kill them," Liam said as he tossed a hunk of squirming flesh into the flames. "All it does is slow 'em down."

"That's all we have to do," Max said, gingerly bending her injured arm. The flesh and skin had begun to regenerate, and it felt too tight. "We just have to keep the fire going till Giselle gets here. Don't suppose you have a couple of chain saws in your pockets, do you?"

"Nope." His head tilted. "Why are you doing this?"

"Seriously, Chief? Do *you* want to see these demons

going rampaging and killing a lot of people? I sure as hell don't."

His brows rose. "What do you care? Why would you risk your life for strangers?"

"Did I say they were strangers?"

"*I'm* saying it."

She shrugged, getting annoyed. "Maybe they are. But that doesn't mean I want to see them slaughtered."

"So you're letting yourself get torn to shreds in order protect a bunch of people you don't know. Just out of the goodness of your heart?" he asked incredulously.

She blew out an exasperated breath. "Why not? Besides, it protects us, too," Max said. "Don't go thinking it doesn't."

"But you could hang back and give up everybody else as easier targets. The demons would probably leave you alone," Liam insisted.

"Maybe," Max admitted. "Have you got a point?"

"I'm just wondering what you're really getting out of this. I don't buy you helping strangers for nothing. And we *are* strangers. Nobody goes through that"— he thrust his chin at her arm—"for people they don't know."

"Maybe some of us do," Max said. "I don't know what you want to hear, Chief. This is our job. That's all I can tell you. Is it really all that shocking? Firefighters, cops, soldiers—they all do selfless things that get them maimed and killed. Hell, what are you doing fighting out here? What makes you better than us?"

He gave her a long look, then shook his head. "I've seen a lot since things changed. Most of it isn't particularly benevolent. And if you were really interested in protecting Missoula, that bastard Benjamin Sterling wouldn't be taking over everything and killing and torturing people."

Max froze. "Benjamin Sterling," she repeated flatly, carving the name into her memory. "Reddish hair? Walks around dressed like Jesus and calls himself the right hand of God?"

"That's him. He's no hand of God, either. If anything, he's doing Satan's work. Has a whole following called Earth's Last Stand. They claim to want to root out everything unnatural. Like you, for instance. And anybody who doesn't buy what he's selling."

Max stood stock-still, letting the information sink in. Then she whirled as sudden certainty struck her. She strode back and forth, scouring the ground and trees, searching.

"What are you looking for?" Liam asked, following her.

"Dust," she said tensely. "Red dust."

"Like this?"

He held up his arm. A smear of red dust stained his shirtsleeve. Max stared at it, her teeth grinding.

"That's the stuff. Where did you find it?"

"It's been on the trail."

"What trail?" she demanded sharply.

"We had word that these demons were harassing folks up around Arlee. We went up to take a look and see if we could stop them before they came down and got us. We're out of Rattlesnake Canyon on the north side of Missoula. Anyhow, by the time we got there, most of Arlee was dead. Torn to shreds and eaten, mostly." He swallowed hard, his expression haunted. "This dust was all around, a trail we followed right here to them."

"Then these demons are here because he brought them," Max said slowly. "That dust is a mark of his magic. The question is why? What's he up to?"

"Magic?" Liam blinked in shock. "What do you mean?"

"The bastard is a witch. Strong one, too." She stomped a squirming piece of demon flesh flat before skewering it and carrying it back to the fire. Inside the flames, the rest of the demons were starting to take shape.

"I don't believe it," Liam said, but she could tell he wasn't all that sure.

"Believe it or not, it's up to you. You've been warned."

Her Blades piled more wood on the fire, but it wasn't enough. It needed to be hotter and higher. She and Liam worked awhile, the silence growing more tense. Finally Max broke it, wanting to explain Horngate to him.

"Most witches are selfish and power-hungry," Max said. "They want to build strong covensteads and grow their power. Or become some kind of cult king, like your Sterling."

"He's not mine," Liam denied quickly.

Max ignored him. "Horngate is . . . Giselle founded the covenstead as a refuge, a sanctuary. She saw the Change coming and wanted to make a place to save what she could of humanity. So we protect who we can. Strangers or not."

"How many witches are there?" Liam asked. He shoved a hand through his hair. "I can't believe I'm seriously asking that."

Max shrugged. "Until the Guardians unleashed the flood of magic back into the world, there was no reason you should know. Witches stayed under the radar. Everything Uncanny and Divine did."

"What does that mean? Who or what are these Guardians? Uncanny and Divine? You said before that the demons were Divine."

"The Guardians are, well, stupidly powerful beings that control our world. Or many worlds. I couldn't begin to tell you any more than that. Uncanny creatures are made out of magic but can't do magic. Divine things can."

He digested that a moment. "What makes these demons Divine?"

She shrugged. "No idea. I can smell it, though."

"Why didn't they fight back against us with magic?"

Max looked down at the scar on her palm. Hidden underneath was the tiny angel feather Tutresiel had given her. Her stomach clenched, and her eyes burned. She blinked away the tears. Angels were Divine not because of some God on high but because they had the ability to give their feathers away, and those feathers had magical properties. What made the demons Divine could be something like that. Surely, if they could cast spells, they would have.

"No clue," she said. "Sometimes magic isn't all that easy to use."

"I feel like I've wandered into a minefield on Mars." He growled in frustration. "How do I navigate if I don't even know what the threats are? How do I keep my people alive?"

"We'll help," Max found herself promising. She knew better than anyone what it felt like to lose people she was responsible for. If she could help him, she would.

Movement within the fire circle caught her attention. Demons. They were mostly full-grown and looking like they were ready for a fight. An unworldly chorus of cries erupted from their throats, sending goose bumps racing down Max's legs.

"Looks like things are about to get interesting again," Tyler said, tossing a heavy tree trunk onto the fire and coming to stand beside her.

"At least, this time, the rest of us will get a chance to play," Oak said as he dragged up another pile of tree limbs and heaved them onto the fire. They were dead and dry and burst quickly into flame. Sparks rose in a brilliant dance. "You guys hogged all the action last time."

"And here I thought you were just being lazy," Tyler said. "Making us do all the work. Maybe this time we should sit it out and watch."

"I don't think that's going to happen," Max said. "Spread out. Here they come."

White mist rose like a geyser. It spilled out over the fire circle and instantly doused the flames.

"Well, I guess we know at least one Divine thing they can do," Max said to Liam. "Better get your men out of here. This is going to get ugly."

He shook his head. "No, ma'am. This is our fight, too. Besides, there's no time."

The demons bounded out over the smoking pile of debris. Mist seeped from their skin, turning them into wraiths. Except that these wraiths had teeth and claws and were incredibly pissed off.

There were at least twice as many as before. Even with Liam's team, they were outnumbered by at least three to one. The eight Blades fanned out, keeping their new human allies behind them. Max found herself flanked by Simon and Nami.

"Watch the talons—they're poisonous. And the mist is a weapon, too," she warned. "Shot shells will slow them down. So will blowing off their heads."

Both nodded, faces intent. Gone was Simon's smartass attitude. He was all business. He was holding a .45. Nami's expression was predatory and ruthless. She had drawn her pistol-grip shotgun. Max's had been destroyed by the flood of acid goo when the birthing sac exploded.

Max slid her sword into her belt and pulled out her .45. As the demons landed outside the charred woodpile, she started shooting. She aimed quickly, snapping off shots with accuracy born from years of practice. Her .45 was loaded with hollow-points. Each bullet went through a demon's head, taking its brain and half its skull with it. Nami's shotgun took off entire heads. Behind her, Liam's men shot, and their aim was nearly as deadly.

But even so, the demons were hardly fazed. They staggered about for a few seconds as blobs of flesh oozed up from their bodies and repaired their wounds. Within a minute, they were coming again, and this time, shooting them did less damage. They became almost elastic, the bullets passing through their flesh with minimal effect. Anything that lodged within was soon squeezed out, along with more of the oozing puslike liquid that slicked their skin. Max wondered if their new regenerative ability had come from the addition of the baby demon bits.

The milky mist they were manufacturing didn't just hug the ground anymore, but it reached out in ghostly fingers and attacked the small group of defenders. Its potency had increased, too, and Max's skin bubbled and blistered the moment it touched her. Breathing it was like sucking in mustard gas. Instantly, her mouth, nose, throat, and lungs turned into raw hamburger. She fell back a few steps to get away from the tendrils reaching for her, but they followed tenaciously.

All around her, she heard wet, choking coughs. She retreated a few more steps. "Fall back!" she called, but it came out more like a whisper. Her Blades heard, though, and began a slow retreat. She kept slightly forward, chopping at the demons with her sword. The mist brushed her eyes. It felt like an army of fire ants was chewing at her eyeballs. They blistered, and her vision blurred into a gray haze.

Talons raked her scalp and then her hip and thigh. Poison burned in the wounds. She spun away and ran into one of Liam's men. She shoved him ahead of her. "Back!" she rasped.

He grabbed her vest and yanked her after him, all the while firing at the demons following behind.

The next few minutes were a nightmare. Max outdistanced the mist long enough to gain her vision back but then plunged back in to drag out Jody, who'd fallen. Simon stood protectively over her, jabbing blindly at the demons with a pair of combat knives.

Holding her breath, Max hoisted Jody by her collar and grabbed Simon's bloody shirt. "C'mon," she said, and hauled them both back.

"Get to the creek!" she hollered, and then leaped to

head off a trio of demons who'd homed in on one of Liam's soldiers. She slashed at their legs and kicked at their chests. They careened together. A split second later, they sorted themselves out and lunged at Max. Swinging with short, hard chops, she hacked them apart with brutal efficiency, just in time for the mist to steal her vision again.

She dropped back to heal her eyes and then dove in again. It became a kind of odd rhythm, with her Blades tag-teaming as they all slowly worked their way to the relative safety of the creek.

Once there, Max halted on the bank. Four of Liam's men stood in the middle, firing back the way they'd come. Jody lay on the far side, her body twitching uncontrollably. Simon stood over her, hands on his knees as he panted raggedly. Blood streamed from his wounds and ran down his nose and chin.

A wedge of demons had cut between them and the rest of her Blades, blocking them from the safety of the creek. Liam and one of his men stood with him. The other two of his men sprawled a dozen yards away, demons ripping hungrily at their flesh.

There was no way the small group was going to get through the demons without losing someone else. They were nearly surrounded. Liam and his man were a liability. Without them to protect, her Blades might fight free. Max didn't think. She jammed her sword into its sheath. Using the angel feather embedded in her palm, she leaped into the air, vaulting over the swarming mass of demons.

She landed behind Liam and his remaining soldier. "I'm taking them," she told Tyler, and then grabbed each of them by the arm. "Get the hell over to the creek."

With that, she dove deep inside herself and into the abyss between worlds. It wasn't easy. She was exhausted, and her body screamed with agony. Her healing spells were working overtime, and she didn't have the energy to spare to haul herself through the abyss, much less two passengers. Still, there was no choice. She wasn't going to let them become demon food.

Traveling through the abyss was one of her unique talents. She wasn't sure there was anybody else in the world who could do it, and she had no idea why she could. It wasn't easy. It was like putting herself through a meat grinder. It was agony. She ignored it. Pain was just motivation.

Then, suddenly, in the blink of an eye, they left the demon battle behind and entered the chill silence of the abyss. The ebony night stretched out forever, broken only by swirling flashes of jewel-colored magic and thin strands of rainbow light.

Her companions looked terrified. They both sported scrapes and gouges, and Liam's left hand hung limp and useless. They opened their mouths to speak, and nothing came out. There was no sound in the abyss. Max shook her head at them and took a breath. Then she reached for her destination. All it required was a thought—where did she want to be? And she would go there.

Pulling them with her, she dove out of the abyss. The pain this time was doubled. She had few reserves left, and the demands on her ravaged body were excruciating. Still, she had no choice. She had a feeling the demons weren't going to let the water stop them for long. If Benjamin Sterling was helping them, they'd find a way across all too quickly. If she didn't bring help, everybody was going to die.

She dropped out of the abyss onto a snow-covered dirt road. She crashed to her knees, and her companions sprawled beside her.

She staggered to her feet, turning to look around her. Snow fell thick and heavy, shrouding the world in white and silence. Where was Giselle? The witch-bitch was the only one who could stop the demons at this point. Max had homed in on her location, but where the hell was she?

She turned in a circle. The road cut through the mountains following a narrow, twisting course. To either side, the jagged slopes rose sharply, trees towering high up into the sky. Just then, she heard the roar of a four-wheeler engine revving to life.

She followed the sound to a fire road on the other side of a rock jut. Giselle was straddling a four-wheeler in the back of a pickup truck. The tailgate was down, and wheel ramps were clamped into place to allow her to ride the four-wheeler to the ground.

The witch looked up as Max came into sight. She cut the engine, slid off the four-wheeler, and stood. She wore jeans and a jacket, with hiking boots and thick gloves. Snow caught in her hair and eyelashes. A heavy backpack lumped on her back.

"Max! What happened? Where is everyone?"

"You came alone?" Max demanded, fury churning in her stomach. As powerful as Giselle was, would she be enough?

The witch's chin jutted. "I didn't want to leave Horngate unguarded. Where is everyone? Where are the demons?"

Max gritted her teeth and then let it go. "We'll go through the abyss," she said, holding a hand out to help the witch down.

Giselle ignored her, leaping lightly to the ground. She scanned Max from head to foot. "Can you do it? You look like you're about to pass out."

"Do I have a choice? Give me your hand. There's not a lot of time."

Just then, Liam found them. To his credit, he didn't ask what had happened or how they'd gotten there. He glanced at Max and then Giselle. "This is the Wicked Witch?" he asked, his brows rising in obvious skepticism that anyone as small and delicate-looking as Giselle could be a threat.

"Yes," Max said at the same moment Giselle repeated, "Wicked Witch?"

"I call it like I see it," Max told her.

Giselle glared. "Since when do I have green skin?"

Max stared a moment and then smiled despite herself. Lately, Giselle had rediscovered her sense of humor. She was still ruthless, vicious, and extraordinarily dangerous, but she was also learning to embrace her human side—the side that had once made her and Max best friends. Of course, that didn't mean they'd be friends again, especially with Giselle willing to harvest angel parts to fuel her magic.

Max's smile slid away as her anger returned.

"Who are you?" Giselle asked Liam.

"Name's Liam. Liam O'Ryan," he clarified when she just waited.

"Chief and his men have been tracking the demons," Max said. "Looks like the preacher witch—Benjamin Sterling is his name—is behind the attack."

Black magic twisted around Giselle's hands and turned her eyes to pits of smoke. She was pissed. *Good*. "Where are they?" she asked.

"Through the abyss. Ready?" Max held out her hand, and this time, Giselle took it. Max drew her gore-covered sword. "You'll have to stay here," she told Liam.

He started to protest, but she didn't bother to wait. Max dropped into the abyss.

She pushed hard, dragging herself and Giselle into the infinite blackness. Her body throbbed, and her heart ratcheted in her chest like a jackhammer. Her head spun drunkenly, and she felt bitterly cold. Temperatures had no effect on Shadowblades, but now she felt like she'd been trapped in a freezer. She shuddered, and her teeth chattered.

Grasping Giselle's hand tighter, she focused on the demon canyon. She pictured the opposite side of the stream and hoped the demons hadn't crossed.

A few seconds later, Max hauled them through. They dropped out of thin air onto the rocky bank. Max collapsed in a boneless heap. The sword clattered onto the rock, and she let go, unable to hold it any longer. Her muscles cramped, seizing into tight knots. It took all she had just to lever up on one elbow. She continued to shiver convulsively. She clamped her jaws together to keep her teeth from clacking.

Giselle had landed on her feet. She took in the scene quickly. Max felt her drawing in magic. It was a powerful surge. It came from the air and the ground and the water—Giselle was an elemental witch, taking her power from the natural world. Power spun around her like a black whirlwind. Dark green lightning forked through the air around her.

The whirling magic condensed into a tight knot. The air in the canyon went still. Even the yelps and howling cries of the demons seemed muted. Max could hear Giselle muttering a chant. Her voice was harsh with fury.

Power erupted from her. It rolled across the creek and through the demons like a nuclear shock wave. Rocks exploded into powder. Across the clearing, trees snapped and flattened. The sound of the destruction roared and echoed. After several minutes, silence descended, broken only by the sound of rushing water.

The cloud of magic surrounding Giselle settled over her like a cloak of smoke. She strode forward, splashing through the creek. She slipped, and Steel caught her arm, holding her erect. On the other side, Flint took her other arm and helped her across.

The only three men Liam had left knelt on the ground near Jody, who now lay all too still. Her chest rose and fell, and relief sluiced through Max. One of the men had tucked his vest under her head and was stroking a hand over her hair, talking to her all the while. The others stared at the destruction on the other side in awe or horror or maybe both.

Tyler, Oak, and Nami lurched up out of the water like bloody rag dolls. Max swiveled her head, looking for Simon, the only Blade left unaccounted for. He was nowhere to be seen. She struggled to her feet and instantly sagged. She caught herself against a rock and scanned the canyon again. No sign of him.

No.

Her chest hurt like someone had impaled her on a chain saw.

Not again not again not again.

She found herself whispering the words over and over like a prayer.

Giselle slipped her backpack off her shoulders and unzipped it. She withdrew a silver knife. Without any ceremony at all, she slid it across her wrist. Blood dripped to the ground. She started walking around the outside of the battlefield, chanting all the while.

The ward circle she was creating was enormous. She was going to lose a lot of blood. All the same, when she came back around and closed the circle, she didn't seem to be any worse for wear. The witch stopped, and her voice rose as she finished casting her spell. The circle flared with orange light. Max looked away, blinking, but orange splotches swam across her vision even after the light faded to a dull glow. It startled her. Witchlight didn't usually affect her vision.

Max felt magic collecting again. It prickled all over her body, and scraped along the underside of her skin. It warmed her slightly, although she continued to shiver uncontrollably.

Magic wound tighter, making it hard to breathe. The pressure increased for another minute and then popped like a champagne cork releasing. The night turned dull green, as all across the interior of the spell circle, worms of green magic wove back and forth. They burrowed into the ground and knotted together, forming a thick tapestry of pure magic. When it was done, Giselle spoke again, and the weaving began to glow, turning a clear emerald color.

For a second, Max could see darkness beneath it—black blotches and trails of demon blood. There was no sign of any actual bodies.

Slowly, the emerald color sank into the ground. It limned the rubble and pulled any demon remains down with it. A few minutes later, the emerald light faded. As it did, a swirl of red dust rose in the air and disappeared. A moment later, snow began to fall over the canyon.

8

GISELLE BENT AND RELEASED THE WARD CIR-
cle. Magic continued to surround her as
she turned to face the five Blades who had
flanked her throughout the ritual. One by one, she set
a hand on them. Black magic wrapped them and slid
away, leaving them healed.

Once they were done, Tyler sent Oak and Steel
to the opposite side of the clearing, no doubt to see
if they could find the soldier Max had left there. It
wasn't likely he could have survived the burst of magic
and the flattening of the trees. Gates was his name,
Max remembered.

Tyler helped Giselle across the river. A look of relief
filled his face when he saw Max. He led Giselle over,
but Max waved her away.

"Jody needs you more. I can wait," she said, trying to
quiet her shivers.

"Occasionally, you could go first," Giselle said sourly,
but she went.

Tyler glanced at Max as if he wanted to say something, but then he went with Giselle. Max resisted the

urge to call him back and ask about Simon. Instead, she forced herself to stand and wobbled slowly down to the edge of the creek. Dropping to her knees, she scooped up some of the icy water and drank it. She scowled at the taste and realized her hands were covered with blood and demon gore. She rinsed them and washed her mouth out before drinking again.

Tyler returned, leading Liam's three men. One of them, the black-haired man who'd spoken up about Gates before, limped over and stopped in front of Max, his legs braced wide, as if he might tip over at any moment. He was wet, and blood trickled from a dozen cuts on his head and arms. His clothes were torn and ragged. He carried his gun propped on his shoulder. The other two men were in similar condition. He scowled at her, his gray eyes tense.

"What did you do with O'Ryan and Cruz?"

Max looked up at him, not bothering to stand. She wasn't sure she could at the moment. Her body was quaking, and her voice, when she spoke, shook almost unintelligibly. "They're safe."

"Where are they?"

She shook her head and waved vaguely westward. "Over there, I think."

"You think?" he demanded, and Tyler made a warning sound.

"That's right, Bambi. I think."

Hands closed on Max's shoulders. Giselle. She'd heard the witch coming, of course. Magic coursed downward, filling her. Warmth followed hard on its heels. A moment later, she shook off Giselle and stood. It wasn't a full healing, but her body could do the rest.

Giselle had already used up too much of herself, and she wasn't done. The soldiers needed help, too.

Wordlessly, Giselle healed each of the three. Oak and Steel returned carrying a battered man. He looked as if he'd been beaten with a dozen baseball bats. His helmet had an orange-sized dent in it. Blood seeped down his neck and stained his shoulders. His right ribs were caved in, and ends of bone thrust through the flesh of his legs and one arm. His nose was mashed, and his mouth was a pulpy mess.

"Oh, my God," one of the other soldiers whispered, and then vomited.

Bambi's face went white and blank. He swallowed hard. "Gates," he grated, and said nothing else.

"Is he breathing?" Max asked.

"Barely," Oak replied as he settled him on the ground. "And not for long."

"Get out of my way," Giselle said. She knelt down. Taking a breath, she drew power from around her. She held her hands out above him, and magic snaked from her palms. It wormed into his body. She began to mutter beneath her breath, and magic swelled thickly in the air. Soon it was impossible to see her or Gates.

Max pulled Tyler aside. "Where's Simon?"

He looked down. "I don't know. You jumped out with the two men, and we fought our way to the creek. I thought he made it, but then we haven't seen him. There's been no time to look . . ."

She nodded, her throat knotting. Turning to her other Blades, she said, "Simon's missing. Find him. Check downstream. He might have washed down."

They scattered. Max glanced down at Giselle. She

ought to stay. The three soldiers might not take it well if their companion died. They might decide to get a little revenge.

"Yates and Talsky, you're with me. We don't leave anybody behind," Bambi told Max by way of explanation, and he started off with the other two to search for Simon.

She hesitated a moment and then set off after them.

THE WIND HAD STARTED TO PICK UP, BLOWING AWAY much of the demon stench. For that, Max was grateful. Giselle's binding spell had destroyed all of their physical remnants, but the smell wanted to linger.

Flint and Steel had followed the creek south, while everyone else had begun a systematic search of the canyon. There was still no sign of him. With every passing minute, Max's chest grew more hollow. Refusing to give up hope, she searched through the flattened trees. A holler brought her running. Oak had found him at last.

His body had wedged between two boulders in an eddy of the creek. Oak pulled him out, laid him on the bank, and pumped his chest. Simon's eyes were staring and lifeless. His wounds had been washed clean. The ugly red hashes contrasted sharply with his pale, wet skin.

"C'mon," Oak muttered as he compressed Simon's chest.

It was too late. There was no life left in him. No small ember to blow back into flame.

"He's gone," Max said in a soft, toneless voice.

Tyler made a strangled sound and spun around. He strode away, his body rigid with emotion.

Oak balled his fists, his head hanging down. "Dammit!"

Max brushed her fingers over his head and bent to pick up Simon's dripping body. Tears ran silently down her cheeks. She didn't try to stop them; she couldn't if she wanted to. She carried him back to where Giselle had just finished healing the injured man.

Giselle watched as they approached, her arms wrapped around herself. Her eyes were sunken and shadowed, her shoulders hunched with exhaustion. Max came to a stop in front of her. The witch looked at Simon and closed her eyes. A moment later, she opened them.

"Let's take him home."

Flint hoisted the healed Gates, and they started up out of the canyon. Max sent Nami and Jody ahead to find the truck.

They went silently, passing the sleeping soldier among them, lifting him over the fallen trees. Max refused to let go of Simon, using her angel's feather to take long leaps up to the rim of the canyon. Bambi and the other two soldiers clambered over the mess of fallen wood. Despite their exhaustion, they remained alert and watchful. Tyler made his own solitary way, although he didn't go far. He wouldn't. Just in case something else attacked.

They slogged westward through the dense curtain of snow. A foot had already fallen, smothering the mountains and trees in heavy silence. Despite her grief, Max kept an eye out for any sign of the red dust. Where it went, nothing good followed.

Nami and Jody returned and led the way to the

truck. It was a three-mile trek. By the time they arrived, they were all soaked to the skin, and all four of the soldiers were shivering.

Liam met them. His gaze settled on his injured man in Oak's arms. He scowled.

"He's going to be fine," Giselle said. "He'll wake when he's ready."

"What happened?" he asked.

Bambi answered. "A shit storm," he said tersely.

Liam took the hint and asked nothing else. He eyed Simon and gave Max a nod of sympathy.

He and his companion had kept the back of the truck clean of snow, and now the group loaded up. Oak took the wheel, with Giselle riding shotgun. Gates sat in the backseat with two of his companions, while everyone else sat in the bed. Everybody but Tyler, who claimed the four-wheeler.

The return to Horngate was made in silence. Max sat with Simon across her lap and her back against the cab. She brushed the snow away from his face, not ready to see him shrouded in death.

They went north to Highway 90, then down back through Missoula. There was no traffic. Their truck was dead silent, and Oak needed no lights to see by. They were a ghost.

As they started down Reserve Street, Max came out of her grief enough to realize that maybe Liam and his men might want to go back to their own homes instead of to Horngate.

"Do you want us to drop you off somewhere?" she asked. "We'll take you wherever you want to go."

Liam rubbed his jaw, considering the question. "Are

you saying you don't want us to see where you're from? Or maybe you want to know where we're from?"

Max shook her head, too tired in her body and soul to spar with him. "I'm saying you might want a ride home. If you don't want us to know where you live, you can get out here and walk to wherever you're going. If you want to see Horngate, we'll bring you back into town whenever you want. I don't much care. Just make up your mind."

He exchanged a look with Bambi, who shrugged, and then he said, "We'll go with you."

"Fine," Max said, and went back to brooding.

THANKS TO THE EXTRA HELP OF MAGIC, THE TRUCK WAS able to plow through the snow with relative ease. When they returned to Horngate, everything was covered in a thick layer of white. They pulled into the parking cavern. Everyone piled out in slow silence. Max came last, Simon's body cold and stiff in her arms.

She said nothing to anyone but strode inside, carrying him through the fortress to the angel vault. She stood in the middle, facing the fountain. There were only the two slabs for the angels. Her chest hurt with the emotion building up inside. She couldn't stop crying, and her nose was running. She sniffed and went around to the other side of the fountain. The ground was covered in gray ash. She scraped it away with her foot. A few seconds later, Tyler joined her, peeling off his tattered shirt and swiping the floor clean.

When he was through, Max knelt and laid Simon down, straightening his limbs and smoothing the hair away from his face. The pressure in her chest grew, churning unbearably. Her skin felt tight, like it would split from the building strain.

Suddenly, she lunged to her feet. Tyler stood behind her. His hands hung at his sides, and his face was empty. She wanted to say something to him, but she didn't know how to comfort him. She didn't know how to comfort herself. Instead, she slid past him and back out into the corridor.

Giselle was there, along with her other Blades and most of the Sunspears—Max's daylight counterparts. She ignored them all, striding past as if wolves were chasing her.

She should have gone to eat and replenish her energy stores. Instead, she went to her apartment. She needed to be alone. Inside, the wards prevented her Prime power from leaking out onto everybody else. She'd asked Giselle to install them when people started complaining about the torrent of power that spun out of control when she and Alexander were together. It was now the one place of real privacy she had, where she could hide and let her emotions get away from her.

The door shut behind her. She leaned back against it, closing her eyes. Instantly, she opened them again. She didn't really want to be alone. She didn't want to think. She ached for Alexander more than she could say.

She almost reached for her phone to call him, but it was gone, along with her vest. Not that she would have actually called. After the way he'd walked away from her, after the way she'd driven him off, what would she say? *Sorry I was a bitch, but I need you now, so do you mind pretending I'm sane and you still want me? At least, until the next time I freak out again and push you away?* That would go over well.

She went to the bathroom and peeled off her stinking clothing and scrubbed away the blood, dirt, and demon goo. She stayed in the shower for more than an hour. Eventually, the sobs came, tearing at her with wrenching violence. She held them back as long as she could, but they wouldn't be contained forever. She stood in the steam, leaning against the wall as her grief and guilt for Simon, Niko, and the angels poured out of her.

When the storm was over, she was drained. Like a robot, she went to her bedroom and dressed in a pair of sweats and a T-shirt. That left her with nothing to do but think, the thing she wanted to do least of all.

She sat on the edge of her bed. It was still rumpled and smelled of Alexander and sex. She rested her elbows on her knees and pressed her forehead against her knotted hands. It wasn't until then that she realized her floor was covered in a layer of red dust.

She straightened and tried to pick her feet off the floor. They didn't move. She could do nothing but watch as the dust collected into two long snakes. They wound around her legs and slid up over her thighs and stomach, circling her body until the dust covered her like a second skin from head to toe.

When she was completely enshrouded, she found herself being gently bent back onto the bed.

Darkness dragged her down.

9

THOR AND ALEXANDER ELECTED TO GO NORTH TO Divide, then up through Butte and west on 90 for the return trip home. Somewhere between Anaconda and Deer Lodge, Alexander gave a guttural noise and flung open his door.

"What the hell?"

Thor jammed on the brakes and skidded to a stop. Alexander launched from the truck, ran a few feet, and then stopped and turned in a circle. His Prime was frenzied. Every muscle was corded. There was no enemy. It was far away, and it was not threatening him at all.

"Max!" he shouted up to the sky, as if she could hear him, as if he could help her.

He pushed his senses out, but it was too far to see her spirit flame. He swallowed and tasted her pain on the back of his tongue. He got lost in it, feeling with her. Instinct drove him. He started running along the road, drawn by her need. Then it turned. The physical pain was gone, but something far deeper and more profound was overwhelming her.

The air went out of him, and he sagged to the ground, his head bowing. He felt the wash of her grief and guilt. So heavy, so deep. Like falling into a bottomless pit of tar. It pulled him down, trapping him in thick, inescapable glue. He could not breathe. Loss smothered him, pushing the air out of his lungs and stopping his heart.

"Alexander." Thor shook his shoulder. "Alexander! What's going on? Talk to me."

Slowly, Alexander swam up out of Max's emotions. He sucked in a heavy breath and then another, then clambered to his feet. He felt a thousand years old. This was the weight she carried. No wonder she had no room for him. The burden of death, loss, and guilt was already too heavy.

He shook away the thought. It did not have to be that way. She could choose him. He smiled humorlessly. When pigs flew.

"What the hell is going on?" Thor demanded again.

Alexander wiped a hand over his face. "Someone has died."

"Not Max?"

Alexander shook his head. "No. Someone else."

"You gonna call her? Find out what happened?"

"Not now. I do not want to distract her." Nor did she want to hear from him. She did not want a reminder that she had given another piece of her heart away. That at any moment it could be broken, too.

"We should go," he said curtly, and returned to the truck, turning his head to the window, silence pooling around him.

They only got as far as Drummond before dawn struck and they had to pull off the road.

Things there remained relatively ordinary. No rock trolls leaped out to smash them to smithereens, and no forests crawled over the ground to get them. Everything looked a lot as it had before the Change: trees, grass, rivers, rocks, and hills. Nothing looked all that menacing.

Still, neither Blade liked the idea of spending the night away from Horngate trapped in a light-sealed box in the back of the truck. It left them vulnerable to attacks, and Alexander doubted that the preacher witch cared whether it was day or night. Nor did anyone else. The box was entirely sealed from light in ordinary human ways, then reinforced and armored with magic. Still, Alexander doubted it would hold up to one of the preacher witch's determined attacks.

They pulled off the highway and drove up into the hills, following a forest-service road. Thor parked under a copse of trees, and they got out and pulled limbs down to cover the truck. They climbed into the box in the back and slid the locking bars into place before activating the wards. The box filled most of the bed of the truck and was long enough to allow both Blades to lie down, so long as they were slightly propped at one end.

They ate, finishing off the supplies Magpie had packed for them. Max still had not called when Alexander drifted off. His body was craving healing sleep, although his mind stewed over the possibilities of what had happened.

The dream began almost instantly, as if it had been lying in wait for him.

It was daylight. The sun was high overhead, yet he

did not burn. He seemed to be floating above Missoula. He could see the fork in the river at Kelly Island, the highway stretching east and west, the airport, Rattlesnake Canyon, Mount Sentinel, and Pattee Canyon. Suddenly, he was hurtling downward. He felt himself flinching and tried to pull back, but he was helpless to stop himself.

He plunged down, the world blurring into shades of green and gray. He smashed into the ground and was pulled upright like a puppet, none the worse for wear. He found himself dangling from a string knotted through the top of his skull, his feet inches from the ground.

He was in a clear area surrounded by makeshift sheds, tents, and booths. Snow domed up on top of the buildings, and the tents sagged beneath the weight. Some had collapsed where they were not reinforced. The snow on the ground was trampled and gray. People wandered up and down among the booths in heavy jackets, eyeing one another suspiciously. Everybody went armed.

That much Alexander took in as he was twitched around into place. He found himself facing an open space just beyond the line of booths. He was not alone. All of Horngate seemed to have been pulled there, at least judging from those he could see. Every Shadowblade and Sunspear, every witch, every ordinary human. Even the children. All of them were semitransparent and dangled from red strings. Alexander was really beginning to hate that color.

They hung in a circle several people deep. He tried to shift his eyes from side to side to search for Max, to see who was absent and therefore dead, but he was frozen in place. Then his attention was stolen by the tableau in the center of the circle.

Snow had ceased to fall, and in its place, red dust sifted from the leaden sky. It covered the snow in the center of the circle, turning it scarlet. A moment later, it stopped.

Seconds ticked past as nothing happened. Then Alexander heard shouts behind him.

"Run!" screamed a familiar voice. "Run, Carrie!" It was Max's niece, Tory.

Carrie Lydman staggered into the circle. She was crying. Her cheek was sliced open, and her mouth was swollen and purple. She obviously could not see the specters from Horngate. She fell, and Tory raced up and grabbed her arm and jerked her upright.

"Come on, Carrie!"

Tory dragged her friend forward. She had scratches along one side of her face, and her nose was bleeding and swollen. Someone had ripped her shirt open, and her right tennis shoe was gone.

The two girls barely made another three steps before people swarmed them. The attackers carried pitchforks and baseball bats. They circled the girls, prodding at them and smacking at their legs to make them fall. Carrie went down on her stomach with a shriek. She rolled to her back and sat up. She was splotched with red from the dust. She looked like she was drenched in blood.

Tory grabbed for the weapons, swearing and kicking. She wrestled a bat from someone and started swinging it. Wood cracked loudly. She ducked and swung and tripped over Carrie. She fell headlong. Instantly, she was grabbed. A burly man with yellow hair got her in a choke hold, while a woman duct-taped her arms to her sides. Someone else bound her legs. All the while, Tory was spitting and twisting.

"You fuckers are going to pay for this! My aunt will grind you into dog food. She'll tie your dicks in knots and make you eat your own balls!"

If he could, Alexander would have smiled at her nerve. She certainly had Max's blood running through her veins.

The man choking her let her go, and someone else slapped her hard enough to twist her head around. Her lip split. Before she could say anything, someone else planted a hand on her chest and shoved her into the snow. Meanwhile, Carrie lay on her stomach. She had also been bound and was sobbing wildly as she lifted her head out of the snow.

Alexander struggled to get away from his bonds to help her, but he was nothing more than a ghost audience at this spectacle.

The attackers backed up and left the girls alone.

"That one is a hellcat," said the burly man with the yellow hair as he pointed at Tory. "Little bitch bit me." He shook his hand.

"Reverend Sterling will take care of her," said another man with a potbelly and a beard. He leered at the girls. "Know what's going to happen to you, pretty things? The Reverend is gonna cleanse your soul, and after that, he'll put buns in your ovens so you can be mothers to the new earth. The Godly earth. That is, if he don't burn you for witches first. Better hope you pass his tests, or you'll find yourself at your own barbecue."

He chortled, and several of his companions laughed along with him. One of the women gave him a disapproving look, crossing her arms as the captive girls squirmed against their bonds.

"Elijah, you better shut up. Reverend Sterling is a great man. He's the right hand of God. He's not going to dirty himself on the likes of these filthy whores. If they aren't witches, they're consorting with 'em. They're devils. Their wombs are rotten. They couldn't give birth to anything good."

The man called Elijah gave her a startled look, then looked down, shuffling his feet. "Yes, Mary," he said. "I just figured if anyone could make them holy enough to carry his seed, the Reverend could."

She stared and clearly had no good response to this. If she argued, she was denigrating her master. If she agreed, then she was tacitly saying that her master could rape and impregnate the girls.

Alexander wanted to spit. He doubted that Mary cared for the health of Carrie or Tory. She was simply jealous of any woman Sterling might want to climb on top of. Alexander wondered if her name was really Mary, or if it had been given to her by Sterling. The same with Elijah. The biblical theme was highly coincidental.

He got his answer when Mary turned to the woman beside her. "Mary, go tell the Reverend we've caught the girls."

The mousey Mary ran off. Her coat flapped open to reveal a slightly rounded belly. She was pregnant. The bearded man's threat was real.

Nobody spoke as they waited. Tory continued to struggle on the ground, but Carrie lay still on her stomach, tears rolling down her face as she whimpered. Alexander could hear her saying "Please" and "Oh, God," but mostly her words were unintelligible.

At last, he heard the sounds of many tramping feet. A brilliant light grew up behind him, casting harsh shadows on the ground. The clearing flooded with people. They strode through the transparent collection of Horngate people and formed a circle around the two girls. Then Benjamin Sterling arrived.

He floated in on a swirl of the red dust. He was surrounded by a brilliant yellow corona, so bright it was hard to look at. He came to hover over the girls, and silence fell as everyone waited for him to speak.

Alexander stared in dismay. Witches could not fly, float, or hover. It took too much power. For Sterling to make such a casual show of it meant he was far more powerful than a mere witch. He could be a full mage or even a sorcerer. No wonder he could permeate Horngate's wards with his dust. No wonder he could manipulate the rock troll, the forest, and the salamanders, not to mention pulling all of Horngate into this nightmare, which was all too real.

Sterling folded his hands over his chest as he examined the two captives.

"You poor sinners," he said softly, his voice warm and rich. "Look what the devil has brought you to. I ache for you, for the evil you have harbored in your hearts."

"Evil?" Tory shouted, managing to sit up. "You're the fucking evil asshole. You're a murderer, burning people at the stake. Where's my uncle, you son of a bitch? What did you do to him?"

"Your uncle?" He shook his head regretfully. "That is unfortunate. That means you have no soul. I'm sorry to hear that. God cannot help those birthed from the womb of evil. I had dearly hoped you could be saved."

He shook his head and bowed it as if praying, then straightened.

"Bring them," he ordered. "We will bestow God's mercy on them."

"Both are rotten?" muttered Elijah. "Seems a waste."

Sterling overheard. "It is no waste if we rid the earth of this tide of corruption. Would you lie with them? Would you risk implanting your seed where it can only grow into something wicked and malignant to God?" He swung his hand out, pointing at the now-cowering man. "You are no sinner, Elijah, but you must repent. Whip him."

Elijah's coat and shirt were stripped away, and he was dragged to a nearby steel signpost. His hands were duct-taped above his head. Someone produced a whip, and the crowd counted as the stripes were laid down. Fifteen in all. Elijah's back was a bloody mess at the end of it, and he had slid down to his knees.

Sterling drew closer, and the duct tape fell away.

"Rise, my son. Be embraced by your sisters and brothers. Share in God's love. You have paid your debt to Him, and you are cleansed. You see? The red dust does not touch you. It touches none of you," he said, opening his arms wide. "It falls only on sinners. All of you stand proud before me, an army for the King on High. God wants you to know He believes in you, and

He knows that you will tear out the devil's roots on this earth. He has sent me to you to prepare this world for His coming. Together we will destroy the evil that has washed across our hallowed shores. We are the Last Stand of Earth!"

His voice rang out, and his audience stared, rapt. As he ended, they shouted, and someone broke into "Onward, Christian Soldiers." Every voice picked it up until it drowned out every other sound. Even Elijah stood and sang as others handed him his clothing.

Sterling let it go on for a while, then raised his hands. An instant hush descended.

"Now, my friends, we have hard work to do. The people here in the River Market have knowingly consorted with witches." He crooked his fingers, and several men carried Kyle in. He was fastened with red magic bands to a wood rail. The bands circled his chest, hips, and feet. His hands and head dangled. His face was covered in blood and bruises, and he was unconscious.

"This one sought to trade his witch hexes and curses."

Shock coursed through Alexander. Kyle did *what*?

Sterling continued. "We have no choice now but to obliterate this market and kill the vermin within. They may once have been your friends, they may even be your family, but they are the tools of Mephistopheles, and in this war, we cannot show them mercy. You must show them that God is to be feared; you must teach them that the devil and his ways are not welcome here. It is a lesson that can only be learned with blood and suffering. Gird yourselves for the battle you must fight. Now, go forth. Teach them well, my children. Teach them well."

With that, he rose into the air, pointing dramatically toward the market. His followers surged forward. Soon Alexander heard screams and the smashing of wood and glass. Billows of smoke rose in the air, and fire roared as it burned through the market.

Sterling watched the mayhem with a smile. Occasionally, he pointed out fleeing people or launched a fireball from his palm. Alexander could only watch. The men holding Kyle dropped him onto the ground and found two more poles for Carrie and Tory.

Tory was talking to her father, begging him to wake up, to no avail. Sterling's followers silently roped her to a post and did the same to Carrie. Then they waited, watching the carnage behind Alexander with obvious delight, occasionally calling out encouragement.

Eventually, Sterling was satisfied. He summoned his people back to him.

"Children, you have done well. These people will be an example for all of God's rage and glory. Soon others will see what we have done, and they will turn to God and join our crusade. Then we will eradicate the devil from this valley. We will gather our army of the exalted and march out to cleanse the world. If you stay strong, if you believe in me—the right hand of God—then we cannot fail. We will not fail," he said, his voice rising and his yellow corona brightening.

"Now, bring these others. We will make an example of them. Evil must be taught to crawl back into hell where it came from. We will flay the skin from their flesh and stake them out where all can see and hear their torment and know that God's will has been done."

They began singing again as they lifted Kyle, Tory,

and Carrie and carried them out of sight, leaving behind the churned-up, blood-colored snow.

For a moment, nothing happened. Then the dust rose in a liquid cloud, leaving the snow pristine. The cloud turned in a slow circle, currents within it eddying and coiling. It hung between the dreamers before slowly expanding to encompass them. Inside it, a multitude of voices whispered. Alexander could not make sense of them. They spun away from him, leaving only fragments of words.

He concentrated. After a few minutes, bits of sound started to slide together like the teeth of a thousand gears, all spinning together to make one message.

"I am waiting, children of the damned. Come to me and fight. Or bow down, and I will rip your spines from your bodies. Choose and die." This was followed by slow laughter that built in mirth.

The world exploded. Alexander was fragmented into a thousand bits. The next moment, he fell back into his body. He lay there paralyzed. Slowly, the pieces of himself fit back together, the echoing laughter still ringing in his ears.

HOURS PASSED BEFORE HE WAS ABLE TO BLINK AND flick the tips of his fingers. It was another two hours before he was able to force his body to obey him. He sat up and turned to Thor, who was staring wildly at him, his body practically humming with the tension of his attempts to move.

Alexander reached over and propped him upright before grabbing his phone. His dream had been no dream.

He hit the speed dial for Max. The phone rang and

rang, but she did not pick up. His heart clenched, but he would have known if she had died. He would have felt her spirit flame die.

He punched Tyler's number into his phone and got no answer. Could they all be paralyzed still? Surely, Max would have come to herself if he had?

He tried Giselle, then Magpie and a dozen others. No one answered. He looked down at his phone and wondered if it was even working. It worked on magic and communicated only with other magically enabled phones. Maybe Sterling had disabled them.

He tossed his cell onto the floor and stretched and flexed to work off the last of the numbness

"Was . . . that . . . for real?" Thor gasped out.

"Depends," Alexander said. "If you had a dream about watching Sterling take out Kyle, Tory, and Carrie Lydman, then I would give it good odds."

"Was afraid . . . of that." Thor's face looked as if he had been Botoxed. Nothing moved. "Feel like a corpse."

"It will get better soon."

"Good. Sterling needs killing. Sooner the better."

"You got that right."

Unfortunately, the preacher witch was not going to go down easily. If at all.

10

MAX CAME OUT OF THE DREAM WITH THE sound of Sterling's laughter chasing after her. She wanted to scream and swear, but she was frozen solid. It took long hours for her body to respond. When it finally did, she dragged herself off the bed and crashed to the floor. She crawled out to her front door and into the corridor. Nami lay at the foot of the stairs, her legs twisted. She was breathing.

Flint's door was open, and Max could see his feet, as if he'd tumbled flat on his face as soon as he walked in. She crawled to the steps and around Nami, straightening the other woman's legs. Nami stared at her, a streak of red running over her eyebrow. "It'll wear off soon," Max told her. "In the meantime, I've got to borrow your phone," she said, fishing it out of Nami's pocket.

She clumsily punched in Giselle's number and waited. It rang, but there was no answer. She tried Tyler and Oz, then Gregory, Judith, and Magpie. No one picked up. They were probably still defrosting. At least, she hoped so.

Max crawled up the stairs. She'd left almost everyone back at the angel vault. They might still be there.

She'd managed to climb to her feet and made her way through the fortress by leaning on the walls. She felt like rubber. Her body was clumsy and uncoordinated. Not that many people littered the halls. It had been near dawn when Sterling had struck. Most had still been in bed.

A sudden thought struck her, and she turned. She broke into a stumbling run as she headed for the dining commons and the kitchen. Magpie was already up early cooking. If she'd fallen onto a grill or a knife, she could be dead or close to it.

The water was running in the kitchen, and smoke billowed from the oven and the pots on the stove. Magpie lay facedown in a pond of milk on the floor by the refrigerator. Her kitchen help were sprawled in the aisles. None seem particularly injured, although they were still unconscious.

Max turned Magpie over. The Circle witch's eyes were open and sparking with fury. She blinked at Max but was otherwise stiff as a board. Milk crusted her face and gummed in her hair, but she looked no worse for wear. A streak of red ran along her cheek like war paint. Max picked her up and laid her on the wide prep table running down the center of the kitchen.

"I'm going to find Giselle," Max told her. "You'll be fine."

She turned off the stove and the oven and checked all of the kitchen aides before hustling away. Each one was marked with a splash of red. She grabbed a pot and examined her own face in the distorted reflection on the side. A smear of red ran from her forehead to her cheek.

Max tossed the pot aside with an echoing clatter and rammed out of the swinging doors. Fury boiled inside her. She was going to kill Sterling. Tear his heart out and feed it to him.

Her body was becoming hers again. She broke into a jog, not yet trusting her balance to go faster. The corridor outside the angel vault was empty. Max went inside. Tyler was slumped over on the floor near Simon's body, which was covered in a white sheet. Tyler was starting to kick and twitch. Giselle was leaning heavily against Xaphan's table. Her cheek and chin were bruised. The red streak ran across her lips and curled down under her jaw.

"You saw it all?" she asked, bracing her arms on the stone table. "We have to go find them. Get them back. I didn't know they were gone. When did they go? How?"

"I don't know. Tory was pissed at me for telling her our little trip was postponed. Maybe she talked Kyle into going anyway."

"That girl needs a cage."

"She'd pick the lock."

"I hope she plays this smart and waits for us," Giselle said, but she didn't sound very optimistic.

Max snorted. *Unlikely.* Tory had gone down fighting Sterling's minions with every fiber of her being. She'd rather fight and die than wait for anybody to rescue her. Max could sympathize. Her niece might be a giant pain in the ass, but she was tough. Max had to respect her for that, even while she wanted to strangle her.

"Everybody's down," she said, changing the subject. She couldn't let herself think about Tory, Carrie, and Kyle. She had to stay focused on rescuing them. Emotion would only get in the way. "It will be at least a few hours until everyone recovers."

"That's too long. We need to get going after them now. Before—"

Before Sterling follows through on his bloodthirsty promises.

"I won't let him get that far," Max said, although whether she was trying to convince Giselle or herself, she wasn't sure.

"This isn't right," the witch said, rubbing her forehead. "Tyler and I came into the vault for Simon. . . . The next thing I know, I'm yanked out of my body and down into the River Market with the rest of Horngate. But that was at dawn, and the business down there was later, well after the sun was up. What happened to us all in between?" She frowned, then dismissed the question with a wave of her hand. "It's not important right now. Did you call Alexander to check on him?"

Max shook her head. She'd been avoiding him. She was really good at it. "He and Thor should be fine. They'd call us if there was a problem."

"You didn't see them?" Giselle asked in surprise. "They were at the market, too."

"What?"

"They weren't far from you, along the same side of the circle. We should find out if they are all right. If they weren't in the light-sealed box when Sterling took them . . ." She trailed off.

Max felt her face go white. Her hand clenched

around Nami's phone, but she didn't try to call. She didn't want any witnesses when she did. "They might still be waking up and not able to get in touch. I'll try in a little while."

Giselle gave her a sharp look that Max ignored.

"Once Tyler is awake, he and I can go into town and see what we can find out," Max said. "The two of us ought to be able to avoid attention."

"Fine," Giselle said. "You can take Gregory, too."

"No. Horngate needs every one of its witches here defending the covenstead."

"I doubt it would matter. You heard Sterling—he means for us to die. He's got power, Max. A lot of it. I'm not sure we can stop him."

Max's mouth fell open. She had never before heard Giselle speak of defeat. Even when she took on the Guardians and a pair of angels. "We have the Fury Seed. That should be plenty to smash him flat," she said.

"Before today, I'd have agreed. But that trick with pulling all of us out of our bodies was extraordinary all by itself. Then he was levitating at the same time. Either one is beyond anything I can do. Together—" She shook her head slowly. "I don't have any idea what he's capable of. He has powers far greater than even a mage or a sorcerer. I still don't know how he got inside Horngate without tripping the wards."

"You sound like you're giving up," Max said in surprise and no little anger.

Giselle's head jerked up, her cheeks flushing. "Give up? Never. No fucking way. I'm just saying we are going to need to finesse this. We don't have the brute force to win; Sterling does. So we have to find his Achilles' heel. To do that, we can't hold anybody back here. We have to take the fight to him. We can't waste any time."

Max considered that and nodded. "All right. I'll take Tyler and Gregory. When everyone else stirs, you can bring backup. You can decide what witches you think will be useful. Make sure my Blades and the Spears calorie-load. They'll need it."

"I will." Giselle started to say something else but then frowned and started scratching her right arm. Then her left and her legs, torso, and head.

"What's wrong?"

"I feel like I've suddenly developed a bad case of poison ivy." She scratched harder, her nails raising red welts on her skin. She shimmied and twisted, then stumbled as her still-clumsy body gave way. She landed on her shoulder, still scrabbling at her calf and then clawing up under her shirt.

Max bent and lifted her back to her feet. "What can I do?"

Giselle jerked her head. "I don't know . . ." She scratched her cheeks and scraped her fingers roughly back and forth over her scalp. "It's like acid on my nerves."

At that moment, the light in the vault took on a red cast, and the trickling fall of water turned milky instead of clear. Max squatted down to get a closer look. It still smelled like water. She reached out and dipped her hand in it. Usually frigid, the liquid was warm now, and there was a faint oily slickness to it. She touched it to her tongue. It stung, like licking a nine-volt battery.

The taste was sweet like syrup but with a bite. It made her lips numb. There was no feel of magic from it.

So what the hell is it?

"Could it be natural?" she asked, knowing already what the answer would be.

Giselle's movements were growing more frenzied, and the welts hashing her skin were starting to turn bloody. "Like what? A milk truck dumped its load and leaked down into the mountain?" The witch snorted. "It's definitely not natural. You can bet Sterling is behind it, and whatever it is, it's giving me fucking hives."

"It's not magic. Not a hex or anything like that?"

"Not any kind I've encountered."

"Then how is it doing this to you?"

"I don't fucking know," Giselle snapped, and she gave a little scream of fury as she clawed her stomach and rubbed her hip against the stone table. "It's getting worse."

Max watched her for a long moment. At the rate Giselle's torment was increasing, it wouldn't be long before she tore her own skin off. Part of Max—the old part that still hated Giselle for betraying her and for suggesting that the angels were fodder for harvest— was eager to watch it happen. The new Max was working on forgiveness.

"Can you fight it?"

"I can't—I can't think." Giselle growled and clawed at her legs, jumping up and down and scraping her back against the rough wall. Her teeth ground together, and she made a sound of frustration. "Maybe if I could concentrate for half a second, I could do something." She began jerking at her hair. "It feels like

I'm being eaten alive by termites." She caught a hard breath, and her body spasmed. "Oh, shit. Make that rats. Or maybe feral cats."

She moaned and gouged herself harder. Blood rose along the scrapes and trickled down her arms. Max grabbed Giselle's wrists, easily keeping her from jerking away.

"Let go of me!" Giselle wailed as she twisted, fury and desperation flickering through her eyes.

"And have you rip your own face off? As entertaining as that sounds, I think everybody is better off if you keep whole. You've got to give the pain to me," she told Giselle. "Do it now before you shred yourself to pieces."

"I—no."

"Why not?"

"Because. It isn't—"

"Isn't what?" Max demanded in exasperation. "Just give me your pain, and you'll be able to concentrate on kicking Sterling's ass. You designed me for this."

Giselle's face contorted, and she wrenched backward. Max didn't give an inch. Threads of magic curled over the witch's flushed skin. Ordinarily, it flowed in a graceful embroidery of danger and threat. But this time, it was knotted and tangled, matting together in flat patches that stuck like tar.

"Quit wasting time," Max said. "Give me your pain now before you take a permanent ride on the loony bus."

"I—"

For a moment, Max thought she was going to have to pull Giselle into the abyss, far away from any attack. Then, suddenly, an ugly grinding sensation flowed through her wrists, followed by a sadistic, unholy itching. It chewed its way up her arms and sank into her bones. The feeling was relentless. It gnawed in places she couldn't reach. Her fingers curled, her nails digging hard into Giselle's wrists. Giselle made a high-pitched sound that instantly cut off. It was all Max could do not to let go and scrape at the merciless sensations enveloping her. But if she did, Giselle wouldn't be able to concentrate.

"Fix this," Max hissed. She'd suffered plenty before—pain of every kind. But this was different. It found places she'd not realized existed, and it inflamed them with a violent itch. She want to rip herself apart to get at it.

Giselle's face hardened into a mask of cold fury. Her magic lost its tangled, matted look and became elegant, roping around her in muscular vines. She wrenched one hand free and gripped Max's wrist with the other. Giselle towed her to the wall with sharp, determined strides and slapped one hand flat to the stone.

"Get the fuck out of my house!"

Magic forked across the vault. The mountain trembled and shook. The floor bucked, and cracks spread across it.

Max staggered sideways and crashed hard to her knees. Giselle's hold on her wrist slipped. Max's hand twisted and clamped down on Giselle's forearm. She knew she was holding too hard. She felt Giselle's bones compressing and bending beneath her fingers. But the demonic itch had burrowed deeper inside and intensified. She could barely think anymore. It was worse than pain; she didn't know how long she could continue to endure it without clawing herself to pieces. Sterling could teach Giselle a thing or two about torture, and the witch-bitch was an expert.

Magic cascaded over her like wet cement. Unfriendly magic. Red magic. She struggled to stand but couldn't move.

She heard Giselle swearing, a flat string of words running from her lips like an incantation. Maybe it was.

Max couldn't breathe. She couldn't blink. Her heart stopped, and her body went numb. For that, she was grateful. With the numbness came relief from the raging itch.

Roaring filled her ears, and she couldn't tell if the sound was in her head or something she was actually hearing. Her body began to ache. It was a dull pain, as if her muscles were starving for air. Globs of yellow and orange and red spotted her vision. She was going to pass out.

Before she could, she pushed down inside herself, searching for her fortress and the door into the abyss. She fumbled blindly, unable to find it. She was lost inside her own body.

Her consciousness ebbed, and she felt the edges of herself curling up like an autumn leaf. *No!*

Unexpectedly, Alexander's face filled her mindscape. His eyes were piercing, his expression coldly accusing. "So you'd run away from me again?" Max thought she heard him say, and the condemnation and pain in his voice made her cringe. "Always running. Why can't you just choose to stay? Why can't you choose me?"

She wanted to answer. She *had* chosen him. She just

hadn't figured out what that meant yet. And this, now, wasn't a choice. She was fighting as hard as she could.

"Fight harder."

The implacable words cut like a falling ax. Then his face faded to gray, and her mind was full of pearly mist. Gradually, it, too, faded, until there was almost total darkness.

She was dying.

It wasn't the first time, but it could be her last.

GISELLE'S VOICE SIFTED THROUGH THE DARKNESS FIRST. Her words were scattered and jumbled, but then Max grinned as she realized the witch was still swearing.

Feeling prickled over her body and then sank in like pins pushed slowly into a corkboard. Fire followed. Max sucked in a breath as her body twitched and contracted. She became aware that she was still holding on to Giselle. She told herself to relax and let go, but her knuckles refused to unlock. She blinked, opening her eyes.

She was lying on the floor of the vault. Giselle knelt beside her, her free hand pressed flat against Max's heart. Black strands of magic spooled and looped around her. Her hair flowed with it, turning her into a wraith. Her face was white, and her lips were clamped tight as she continued her litany. She fell silent when she saw that Max was awake.

"About time," she said, pulling her hand away. It shook. "Can you let me go now? I think my arm is broken. I'm at least going to have serious bruises."

Max followed her look down to where her fingers coiled around the witch's arm. She was white-knuckled, and Giselle's skin was already purpling beneath her grip. All the same—

"I don't think I can let go at this point," she said, and her voice was disgustingly weak. "Did you get rid of Sterling?"

"For now," Giselle said. "But we have to put him down soon. I used the Fury Seed, but I'm pretty sure that only slapped his hand. I'm hoping he's tired from the energy he already expended today. If we're lucky, it will take him a day or two to collect himself."

Max lifted her head. It was probably the heaviest thing she'd ever lifted. "Luck is a fickle bitch." Her head fell back against the floor. She told herself to sit up. She didn't listen. Even breathing was exhausting.

"So," she mused sardonically. "Sterling has Kyle, Carrie, and Tory and seemingly endless power. We have two mostly dead angels, no Grims, a bunch of semiparalyzed people, and let's see—one territory witch, two Triangle witches, a Circle witch, one untrained Star-level witch, and one hedge witch who is next to useless. Oh, and we have the Fury Seed."

"That about sums it up. Except for me having a broken arm and you being somewhat dead as well," Giselle said.

"I guess it's pretty much business as usual, then."

"Pretty much. Can you move yet?"

Max had been trying to relax her hand, and it finally gave a fraction. Her brow furrowing, she concentrated. Finally, her fingers spasmed open and then curled into a claw. Giselle jerked away, cradling her arm against her stomach.

"That hurts a bit," she said. Her face was pale, and

sweat sheened her skin. She smelled rank, and now Max noticed that her shirt was drenched. Scratches hashed her skin, and blood trickled from many of the welts.

"Attack by itching. That's a new one on me," Max said.

"I'll have to remember it," Giselle said. "It's very effective."

"So something good came of all this," Max said as she finally persuaded her stomach muscles to sit her up. "A new torture technique to add to your inventory. How nice for you."

Giselle's phone rang suddenly. It was a low trill of clarinet notes. She dug it awkwardly out of her pocket, having to use her opposite hand. She glanced at the screen and lifted her brows at Max, then answered. "Alexander. I was going to call you."

"Is she all right?" he demanded without preamble. "I tried calling her. She is not answering."

With her supernatural hearing, Max heard every word clearly. She frowned. How did he know something was wrong? But then, he'd gone feral for a while and come back from it, which was unheard of. After he'd come back from the other side, he had abilities he'd never had before. Maybe this was one of them.

"She'll live," Giselle said. "But I want you back here."

"We are just west of Deer Lodge. We will get to the River Market an hour after sundown."

"You had the dream, too?"

He laughed harshly. "That was no dream, and you know it."

Giselle grimaced. "What about the Grims? Are they with you?"

Silence. "I would not expect them soon."

"What happened?"

"They went . . . elsewhere."

She waited for him to elaborate, but he said nothing more. "All right. Do you want to talk to Max? She's right here."

More silence. Thick and hot. "I think not."

Giselle's brows rose as she looked at Max. "Okaaaay," she said. "Then we're done. Get here fast."

"We will. Do try to stay out of further trouble until we return. I would rather not scrape your ass up off the floor." The phone went dead.

Giselle lifted it from her ear and glared at it. "Just who the hell does he think he's talking to?"

"You," Max said.

Giselle scowled at her. "You and I both know the message was for both of us. He was perfectly aware that you were listening in."

Max shrugged. "Maybe. But it's still funny."

"I may have to teach him some manners soon," Giselle said.

"I'd like a front-row seat when you do. And popcorn. For the record, I'll put my money on him for the win."

The witch arched a brow. "Then you'll be broke. I've taken both of you to the woodshed before, and I can do it again."

Max shook her head, a slow smile curving her lips. "I don't think so." She heaved herself to her feet. "Besides, for once, we're on the same side. You don't want to fuck that up. Making enemies out of us would really ruin your day. Sterling already has too much going for him."

"Got any idea why Alexander didn't want to talk to

you?" Giselle shot back. "Did he find himself a new girlfriend? Maybe one who doesn't chew his ass and treat him like he's got leprosy?"

Max recoiled from the barb. It was too close to the truth. If she didn't get her shit together, Alexander wasn't going to hang around. He would find someone else, someone who acted like she wanted him. The question was, how long before he had a bellyful and gave up on her?

She straightened and glanced around the chamber. Tyler had managed to push himself up onto his elbows. He gave her a searching look. She turned away, feeling exposed. Her gaze hooked on the continuing gleams shining on Tutresiel's wings, then flicked to Xaphan. Tiny blue and purple flames flickered around the edges of his iridescent feathers.

Max blinked. The flames didn't go away.

"Holy Mother of fuck," she whispered, and treacherous hope started to thud heavily in her chest.

I T WAS AFTER NIGHTFALL WHEN TYLER HAD RECOVERED. He and Max had eaten all they could, and both had drunk a gallon or more of the disgusting Ugly Juice.

"Ready?" Max asked as she shoved herself away from the table.

Tyler stood, giving her a pirate smile. "As I'll ever be."

A brambly recklessness had grown up around him in the last few hours. It was prickly and unpredictable, with an edge of wildness. It was also catching.

Max found herself grinning back at him. "Let's go raise some hell."

"Please don't," Giselle said, walking in through the door. She looked haggard. "I came to tell you to be careful."

Max just stared at her.

The witch rolled her eyes. "I'm serious. Your job is to find Sterling and then bring us to him. No more." She glared at Tyler. "Keep an eye on her."

"Don't I always?" he asked innocently.

"You're just as likely to follow her into her insanity," Giselle said.

"But I watch her the whole time," he said with a grin. "Most times with both eyes."

"I can't believe I'm sending you out together. Neither of you has the sense the Spirits gave rocks. Where's Gregory?"

"We were just going to get him," Max said.

"No need. I'm ready." The dark-haired witch strode in. His black hair fell over his eyes. His lips were set in a flat line, and Max could feel his magic like a trapped thunderstorm. He wore a lightweight jacket with a lot of bulging pockets. Max didn't bother asking if he would be warm enough. His clothing was no doubt magically warm and protected against weather.

The gaunt witch glanced around at the others eating in the dining commons, and then his sunken gaze settled on Max. He looked prepared to kill. That was a change. Gregory was a natural healer. "What are we waiting for?"

"Not a thing, Tiger," Max said. "Give me your hand."

She reached out to both Tyler and Gregory, but before they could move, her younger sister, Tris, barged in between them. The other woman looked older than her hard-earned forty-six years, while Max's body would be stalled at twenty-one until the day she was killed. The perks of no longer being human.

Tris flipped her graying hair over her shoulder, worry cutting deep furrows between her brows. She was beginning to get that plastic look of fury and panic that she seemed to wear a lot lately. It was hard dealing with a world turned inside out with magic, a father and a brother who were witches, and a suddenly not-dead sister who wasn't human any longer. That was on top of nearly getting eaten by a horde of hungry fairies and losing her home and everything she owned. Stir in the fact that she'd watched Tory and Kyle get dragged off by a crazy preacher witch with a taste for blood and torture, and she had a right to her panic and anger.

"What are you doing to get Kyle and the kids back?" she demanded, her jaw thrusting out.

"If you get out of the way, Tyler, Gregory, and I will be off to look for them right now," Max said, annoyed at the accusation in her sister's voice. She had told Tory and Kyle to stay put. It wasn't her fault they'd ignored her.

"Look for them? Just the three of you? And then what? They could be already——" Her voice broke. She swallowed, and her eyes glittered with unshed tears. "We wouldn't be here if it wasn't for you. You find them and bring them back. This is your fault."

"Hold on a motherfucking minute," Tyler said, stepping around to face Tris. His fury crackled like a bonfire around him.

Tris scooted back, glaring at him.

"How is this Max's fault?" he demanded, following her until he had her trapped against the wall. "She saved you and your family from certain death. Sure, your idiot daughter and brother wouldn't be in this mess if Max had left you to die weeks ago. She probably should have, given what an ungrateful bitch you've turned out to be. As for your kid and your brother, they were told to stay here and to not go into Missoula. But they chose to be stupid. Not that it was a surprise. They usually do. I don't know what the hell kind of parents you and your husband are. When is it your turn to take responsibility for that juvenile delinquent you raised? I swear, if you all weren't Max's blood, I'm betting Giselle would have booted your asses to the curb a long time ago."

He didn't wait for an answer. Instead, he spun around to get in Max's face. "Do not say a word," he said. He was shaking with fury. "Take us out of here before someone gets my fist in her face."

Without a word, Max grasped him and Gregory and dropped through her fortress and into the abyss. She was more than a little shocked at the vehemence of Tyler's tirade. It warmed a part of her that had been frozen since Niko's death. She hated having hostages to fortune in the shape of her friends and family, but this reminded her why it was worth it. To have someone who would take her side no matter what, who would follow her on a one-way ticket to hell and never complain, who would make her laugh and piss her off and make her love him forever.

Which made her think of Alexander. Tyler was safer. He didn't demand so much. He didn't cost as much. And she didn't love him the same way.

Love.

She loved Alexander. How the hell had that happened?

Refusing to consider the idea, she shoved it into the back of her mind and pulled them out of the abyss and into the devastation of the River Market.

"Holy mother . . ." Tyler breathed as he turned around.

"Nothing holy about what happened here," Max said tightly.

The stench of burned bodies and wood turned her stomach. Worse was that a thin sliver of it was almost pleasant, like barbecue, only this was the kind served in hell. The ground was frozen, a hardened churn of mud and blood. Snow was beginning to fall again. Gregory sucked in a harsh breath, but before he could speak, a shot rang out. Tyler jerked with the impact and grunted. Max grabbed him and Gregory and took a running jump into the air. Her leap took them soaring. More gunshots followed, bullets whistling through the air around them. None hit its mark.

They landed several hundred yards west, dropping down onto the roof of a store in a downtown strip. The snow was a good couple of feet deep. Gregory sprawled across it while Max set Tyler on his feet. He groaned.

"Where are you hit?"

"In the side." He lifted his shirt and vest. A hole the size of a quarter bored through flesh a few inches below his ribs on his right side. It was a through-and-through. Max took up two handfuls of snow and flattened them over the holes to stanch the blood until his spells fixed him.

"Good thing they can't see at night," she said, more shaken than she wanted to let on. That was too close. "I'm not liking the shoot-first-and-ask-questions-later attitude, though."

"They *are* trigger-happy," Tyler said, wincing as she pressed against the wounds. "With good reason. I get a feeling we're not going to be making a lot of friends around here."

"I'm sure that Sterling planned that. Divide-and-conquer works best for him."

"Let me see him," Gregory said, pushing her aside. His hands replaced hers on Tyler's side, and green magic flared. A moment later, he pulled away. All that was left of the holes were little fading puckers.

Max swallowed around the knot in her throat and turned to go crouch on the edge of the roof. The river was south. "I think we're up on the old Macy's," she said over her shoulder. Tyler hunkered down beside her as Gregory stood behind.

"The River Market is, or was, over there." She pointed to where smoke still rose. "We should be able to pick up Sterling's trail and follow him back to his hideout. Not that he's hiding."

"Let's do it."

She gave Tyler an assessing look and then glanced up at Gregory. He gave a little nod. She stood, slipped her arm around their waists, and jumped down to the ground, the feather in her hand making them float rather than fall.

They started working their way back. Max went first, with Gregory behind and Tyler bringing up the rear.

There were far more people about than Max had expected. Too many of them for her, Tyler, and Gregory to go unnoticed for long. They needed a better plan.

She stopped in the mouth of an alley just a block from the River Market. Piles of shopping carts littered the road, along with other stinking garbage and debris. There were dozens of burned-out cars and an abandoned garbage truck. Feral cats flittered off like shadows.

Ahead, she could see a crowd of people gathering near the market. More than a crowd—a good hundred or more. They appeared to be arguing. She could hear the rise and fall of angry voices but couldn't make out the words.

Then gunshots rang out again, and a handful of people crumpled to the snow. There were screams and chaos as a ragged line of attackers moved up out of the trees by the river. They were firing rapidly into the panicked crowd. A few people collected themselves to fire back but not enough to do any real damage.

"They have to be Sterling's people," Tyler said. "They're fucking slaughtering them."

"Not again," Gregory said, and he started muttering to himself as he stepped out of the alley and flung his hands out. A streak of green magic shot across the open field. It dropped down in front of the line of shooters and disappeared. Ten seconds later, tentacles of green shot up out of the ground like massive jungle vines. They roped and squirmed over the ground, finding the attackers and coiling around them.

In less than a minute, all of them were caught in Gregory's snare.

"Time to die," he said, and the vines sucked back down into the ground and vanished, along with their prisoners.

Max and Tyler were silent a moment, then Tyler slapped Gregory on the shoulder. "Elegant. Capture and burial in one fell swoop. I didn't know you had it in you."

The witch shook off his hand, staring at the field of people, who had gone silent except for the moans and screams of the wounded. "I'm done watching innocent people die," he said meaningfully and then walked away, right toward the field.

Max overtook him, stepping in front of him as a shield. "Just because you helped them doesn't mean they aren't going to try and kill you," she said.

"I'll take my chances."

Tyler came abreast of Max. "You're taking our chances, too," he pointed out.

"Walk away, then. I won't tell."

"Yeah, that's not going to happen," Tyler said. "Even if I was willing to leave you, Max wouldn't, and I won't leave her. We're like those cousins who show up at holidays to eat all the food and never leave. You're stuck with us."

"Your choice."

"Not really," Max said. "But I would be really disappointed in you if you walked away."

Gregory gave a short laugh and said nothing.

"Stop right there!" someone shouted.

The trio did as ordered.

"We're here to help," Max called. "We can help with your wounded."

"We don't need help."

"Yes, you do," Gregory said as he tried to push between Max and Tyler. They didn't move. He went to go around, but Max caught him and shoved him back. He made a growling sound and then sighed. "I took care of your enemies, and now I can heal your people. I'm the best chance they have for survival. Do you want them to die?"

That was met with silence and whispers. More than a few guns were leveled at them. Those that weren't already aimed in their direction.

"Who's to say you won't kill 'em?"

"Don't they know I could force them to let me help them?" Gregory muttered in frustration.

"People don't like to be made to do things, even for their own good," Max said.

"Besides, you won't be able to contain them all. Others are going to come along and see what's happening and start shooting," Tyler added.

"I can put up shields."

"Whatever you decide, we'll back your play," Max said.

That startled him into silence. Then, "Thanks."

"What do you want to do?"

"Start walking," he said grimly. He set his hands on their shoulders, and a green bubble enveloped them.

"Are we going to be screwed when you let go of us?" Tyler asked as he and Max paced forward.

"Maybe. Maybe not."

"Is that a joke?" Max asked.

"Couldn't be," Tyler said. "Gregory has no sense of humor. Had it removed as a child."

"Funny," Gregory said from behind them. "It would be even funnier if I let you get shot."

"I'd take that threat more seriously if you didn't make a habit of giving mouth-to-mouth to dying flies," Tyler said.

"I just killed sixty-three people," the witch said, his voice strained. "That should definitely make you worry."

"Not really," Max said. "They were monsters. Killing was the only solution."

"Do you think so?" he asked quietly.

"Can't save a rabid dog, Gregory," Max said softly. "Innocent people are living because you killed the bad guys. It's ugly, but it's true."

"Thank you. I . . . I never want to be like Sterling."

Max flicked a glance at him over her shoulder. "Not even possible. You don't have the DNA for that kind of megalomaniac crazy."

"I hope not."

"We'll plant you in the ground long before we let you go that route, if it makes you feel better," Tyler added.

"That makes me feel a lot better," Gregory said, and Max didn't think he was joking.

"You need to stop right there!" a man shouted. "Do you want to get shot?"

"Been there, done that once tonight," Tyler muttered. They kept walking.

A shot rang out. The bullet bounced off Gregory's shield. Someone else fired. Then several more.

"You're wasting your bullets," Max called out.

Apparently, they'd figured that out, because now some had started to retreat, while others stood defensively over the fallen.

Max veered toward the first body she saw that was still breathing. It was a woman. Her chest jerked, and blood bubbled from her lips. Two men and another woman stood guard over her. One of the men was barely that. He might have been eighteen, but Max guessed he was probably closer to sixteen. The other man was in his early twenties, with curly brown hair and five o'clock shadow. The woman was masculine-looking and was in her early thirties. She had a jutting nose and chin and dark sunken eyes. She was dressed in heavy canvas jeans and a thick coat. As with the others, snow topped her hair in a white cap.

"Who are you?" she demanded.

"I'll tell you," Max said, "but get out of the way so Gregory can work. Your friend doesn't have long to live."

"My *wife*," the older of the two men said loudly.

"Then you want her to live," Tyler said, and grabbed

his arm and pulled him aside. "Trust me. Gregory will save her."

"Oh, God, please, I'll do anything you want," the man begged, his shoulders jerking as he began to sob. "Anything."

Tyler stared at him, then drew a breath and put his arm around him. "Easy," he said. "She'll be okay."

"And the baby?"

Oh, shit. Max put a hand on Gregory's shoulder. His hands rested on the woman's chest, and green roped around her, burrowing inside.

"I heard," he said before she spoke.

"All right, tell me who you are," the woman said again. Her feet were set wide, and although she looked wary, she didn't look afraid. Points for her.

"Short version: I'm Max, and he's Tyler. We're Shadowblades," Max said, pointing to Tyler, "and Gregory there is a witch."

The younger boy gasped and clutched his rifle tighter at the last word.

"What's a Shadowblade?" the woman asked.

"We used to be human. Then a witch wrapped us up in spells and made us warriors. We're stronger and faster than you are," Max said. They didn't need to know what else she and Tyler could do. Or couldn't do. Such as survive sunlight.

Others had gathered around, and several voices repeated the word "witch." The atmosphere instantly became more tense and more frightened.

"Witches are servants of the devil," someone said loudly behind Max. There was an instant murmur of agreement.

"The Bible says we shouldn't suffer a witch to live,"

someone else said, and the murmuring got louder and more approving. "That includes their demon servants like you."

The woman whirled around at that. "If you think that, then maybe you think Benjamin Sterling really is the right hand of God. Maybe you think he's doing good works. Just who the hell torched the River Market and slaughtered everybody? Who shot at us tonight? The Last Standers, that's who. And who's healing us? Not Sterling. A witch. So why don't you do us all a favor and shut your piehole until you have something worth hearing to say?"

She turned back to Max. "What exactly are you doing here tonight?"

"We're looking for Benjamin Sterling."

The woman's face went white, and her lips pulled back from her teeth. "Why?"

"We're going to kill him."

She relaxed slightly. "I wish you the best of luck. We've tried. He's a slippery bastard. Did you see what he did here at the market?"

Max nodded. "We'll get him."

"He's got himself an army. I hope there are a lot more of you."

"Enough."

The green light of Gregory's magic died, and Max bent and helped him up.

"She'll live. Baby, too," he said tersely. "Let her sleep for a while. Who else?"

The husband stared at Gregory and then dove to the ground to gather his wife in his arms and lift her out of the snow, whispering words of endearment against her throat.

Gregory moved to the next person. This one was a man, shot in the leg. Someone had bandaged it with a shirt.

"Go on," he said as they approached. "I can wait. Others need you more."

There were three people dead, and the rest weren't as bad off as the first woman. It took Gregory another twenty minutes to heal them.

"Now what?" asked the woman, who'd told them her name was Kara.

"Can you tell us where to find Sterling?"

Kara shook her head. "He's got several places. We're never sure where he is. He's made himself some sort of temple up above Mansion Heights and a kind of a commune. The Walmart out on Reserve is his, too. Lot of his people stay there. Costco, too. And the mall. Several other places. It's hard to say where he lays his head at night."

"Then I guess we'd better get to finding him," Max said. "Take care of yourselves."

"Why now?" Kara asked suddenly.

"Why now what?"

"Sterling. Why are you coming after him now? He's been killing people and taking over Missoula since the Change began. So why are you suddenly interested?"

"We just found out about him," Max said. There was no point in lying. "The people he took today at the market are ours."

"I'm sorry to hear it."

"He won't have them long."

"I hope not. It won't end well if he does. Good luck, Max. I hope I see you again."

Max nodded, and she and Tyler and Gregory headed back toward what was left of the River Market. They'd only gone a few steps when Max's cell phone rang with a high-pitched sound humans couldn't hear.

"What now?" she asked, punching the speaker button so her companions could hear.

"Tris took off to go look for Kyle and the kids," came Giselle's exasperated voice. "Doris Lydman, and Geoff Brewer went with them. I'd loaned Liam and his men a vehicle to get back into town, and apparently those three idiots hitched a ride with them."

"When?" Max asked, cold settling around her like armor. Somewhere inside her, she was screaming her fear and frustration. *How could they be so fucking stupid?* She locked it away along with all of her other emotions. She couldn't afford to give in to them.

"Not long after you left. We're heading out now. We should overtake them before they get far," Giselle said. "Snow's deep, though. I'm not sure what kind of time we'll make. What have you found out?"

"Not a lot. Sterling's people came back to finish the job at the market. Gregory planted them in the ground. We're going to hunt down Sterling's trail now. Call as soon as you find Tris and the others."

"Don't worry about her." As if saying that would make any difference at all. "Just find Sterling," Giselle said, and then hung up.

Max put her cell phone back into her vest pocket and wordlessly stalked away.

They picked the trail up at the bridge. They followed Higgins south, Max and Tyler breaking the trail for Gregory, who had a harder time in the deepening snow. It was already knee-deep and drifting deeper in some places.

Sterling and his mob had stuck to Higgins until Brooks, and then they had exploded in a dozen different directions. Sterling's scent vanished, along with any hint of Kyle, Tory, or Carrie.

"What now?" Gregory asked. "Wait," he said, wheeling around. "Something's going on, over there." He pointed northwest.

Max felt it, too, a burst of Divine magic.

She hoisted Gregory up in her arms and started into a long, loping run. He clutched her around the neck.

"Is this necessary? It's embarrassing, not to mention uncomfortable."

"You're too slow," Max said. "Now, sit still and shut up."

"Careful, or I'll seal your lips shut," he said with a dark look.

"I hate to say it, but I wish we had the angels," Tyler said beside her. "Even Tutresiel, the bastard. Be nice to have flyovers."

"If only Princess Charming would show up and kiss them awake," Max said.

"You could always try it."

"I'm neither charming nor a princess."

"True," Gregory said.

"You don't have to be insulting," Max said.

"Is it an insult if it's the truth?" Tyler asked. "Though you're apparently charming enough for Alexander. But then, he does have questionable taste."

"At least I'm getting laid. Your bed is in deep freeze."

"I'm holding out for Magpie," Tyler said. "Or maybe even Giselle."

"You must like blue balls."

Gregory snorted, and Tyler laughed. "Okay, you win."

"You thought I wouldn't?"

They cut through the neighborhood, going in a diagonal. The houses were mostly deserted. Others had metal- and plywood-covered windows. Woodsmoke curled from a few chimneys. Almost everywhere was dark. Cars were parked every which way, some burned out, while others had been torn apart. At one house, they were pulled around in a kind of a fence. Smart, given how much most Uncanny creatures hated iron.

They hit the railroad tracks after Walnut Street and followed them back toward the river. The entwined smells of animal manure, sewage, and diesel washed over them first. That was followed by the stench of too many people living too close together. Coronas of light lit up the snow, and generators grumbled loudly.

The trio passed next to what had formerly been a large open industrial area. Now it was fenced with a patchwork wall of cars, sheet steel, logs, and whatever else they'd been able to find. Max could smell livestock and hear various farm sounds from within. Generators throbbed and lights glared inside. Along the top of the wall were tangles of barbed wire and grim-faced guards with rifles.

Max set Gregory on his feet, and the three of them slid through the shadows below the guards, silent as death. On the other side, they approached McCormick Park. A baseball field on the left side of the railroad tracks was stacked with logs. Much of the timber along the river had been cut down, along with a lot of residential trees. Armed men and women stood guard over it.

On the right side of the tracks was a living compound. More generators rumbled in the night, and lights glared brightly. Big commercial floodlights illuminated the makeshift camp. Like the livestock pens, it had been turned into a fort with high walls and concertina wire and metal spikes along the top. More guards paced along catwalks just inside the wire. A dry moat containing everything from tangles of barbed wire and rusty saw blades to sharpened sticks and steel fence posts circled it. The moat was about twelve feet deep and twenty feet across. A drawbridge was pulled up on the inside.

From their vantage point, the three could see inside. There was a mishmash of buildings made of hay bales, logs, rock, and brick, mixed together with tents, camp trailers, and RVs. Porta-potties ran along the south side. Fire pits helped keep those in tents warm. A pump station chugged loudly along the riverside, putting out clouds of black smoke.

"I hope they're remembering to boil the water," Tyler said softly. "Lots of parasites in that stuff."

"At this point, that may be the least of their worries," Max said as the snow suddenly turned thicker and heavier. "They have to survive winter first. Hell, they have to survive tonight."

Divine magic filled the air, and Max couldn't get a sense of its source. It was swelling and felt like a balloon about to burst. Instinct told her this place was the target. But why?

Near the middle of the compound was a steel hut with guards patrolling around it.

"That's gotta be their supplies," Tyler said.

Max nodded. Undoubtedly, that was where they kept food, clothing, medicines, and anything else of value they had scrounged. Maybe that was what Sterling was coming after. Or the animals. If it had been her, she wouldn't have segregated the livestock. She'd have built one big compound and put everything inside together. Those animals were going to feed these people this winter, but separated as they were, it would be a lot easier to hit the livestock and get away. If everything was together, the livestock could be kept at the center with the other valuables, and raiders would have to fight through to get to them and fight to get back out. Of course, with Sterling's magic and numbers, she doubted there was much these people could do to protect themselves.

"What do you want to do now?" Tyler asked.

"These people are in serious trouble, and they don't even know it," Gregory said. "We need to help them."

"The best way to help them is to kill Sterling," Max said. "The sooner the better."

"In the meantime, they'll die. We could at least warn them, give them a chance to escape."

She ran her fingers through her snow-dampened hair. "It's time we don't have," she said, but she'd already made up her mind. "Probably won't matter, anyway."

"So we'll make time. Dammit, what are we here for if not to save people? If we kill Sterling and everybody else is dead, what's the point?"

Magic curled between Gregory's clenched fingers. He was in a towering rage. Green sparks roved over his skin, and the air around him quivered.

"Easy, now, Gregory," she said. "I didn't say we

weren't going to do something. I'll go inside and tell them to get ready for a fight."

"That's it? I'm coming in with you to help."

"I won't risk you."

"It's not up to you, now, is it?"

She gave him a long, steady look. "Actually, it is. I can drop you like a sack of sugar before you can do anything about it. And just so you know, that's exactly what I'll do if you don't promise to stay put."

He looked away, scraping his lower lip with his teeth. "Fine. I'll behave. Just go."

She pointed to a small shack next to the railroad. "Wait there. If anyone but us comes for you, fry them."

His jaw knotted, and he walked down to the shack and pulled its door open. He stepped inside. "Good enough?"

"Shut the door."

He pulled it closed except for a thin crack.

Max sighed. "I can't believe I'm going to do this," she said.

"Really?" Tyler asked. "I knew we were doing it before Gregory opened his mouth."

"You're saying I'm predictable."

"As a straight man at a stripper club. How do you want to handle this? Are they going to believe that Sterling's about to attack?"

"They'll probably figure we're the advance team. They'll likely shoot us where we stand before we ever get a word out," Max said.

"Which brings us back to the question—how do you want to handle this?"

"We could just jump over the fence."

"Yeah, because that won't scream attack. These people are going to be paranoid, and with good reason. We jump in without an invitation, and they'll kill us for sure."

"Then I guess we go the front-door route," Max said, a thin smile curving her lips. She felt reckless and free. It was good to be doing something.

"Who wants to live forever?" he asked, grinning back at her, and warmth dribbled into the frozen husk of her heart.

The swirling snow was thick enough to hide their approach until they were at the lip of the moat. Snow mounded in the bottom and hid many of the dangers within.

On the other side, sheets of corrugated steel formed the gates. It looked as if they'd been layered together with massive bolts to form impenetrable slabs more than seventeen feet tall. Max nodded appreciation. It would take a bomb to blow them open. Or a couple of good blasts of magic.

"Hey! Who's out there? What do you want?"

At the shout, Max could hear the instant boil of movement within. There was a crackle of radio static as word went around, and several rifles zeroed in on her and Tyler. She expected every one of them was a marksman. In Montana, almost everyone hunted for food and used big-bore rifles to do it. One wrong move, and she and Tyler would be dropped. This was going well already.

"We came to tell you that you're about to get attacked," Max shouted back. "We're pretty sure it's Sterling's people."

That was met with silence.

"Well, this is going well," Tyler murmured.

"Get lost," the man on the wall shouted. "You've got five seconds, and then we're going to shoot."

"Even better," Tyler said.

Max glared at him, then sighed. "Plan B, I guess," she said.

"What is that?"

"Time to get face-to-face," Max murmured as she tensed to jump. "You stay here and guard Gregory," she said.

"I don't think so, my pretty," he said, hooking a hand tightly into her waistband.

"My pretty?" she echoed. "Don't tell me you've been watching *The Wizard of Oz* again."

"What can I say? I've got a crush on Dorothy."

"Really? I thought you'd have been all over the Wicked Witch. All that green skin? Just your type. Hold on tight," Max added, and then leaped into the air.

The angel feather embedded in her palm gave her far more loft, and Tyler had added his spring to hers. She launched them at an angle to avoid drifting in the air too long and making big targets of themselves. Instead, they bulleted over the wall and landed in the middle of a tent, crushing it. Max staggered and fell over something like a cot and rammed into a table or a dresser.

She bounced back to her feet and spun around to locate Tyler. He'd let go of her and dropped down a few feet away, landing on an open patch of ground. *Show-off.* Shouts sounded behind them, and a couple of shots rang out, although what they were aiming at, Max didn't know. The bullets didn't hit anywhere near them. She hoped the idiots hadn't put bullets in their own people. She could smell them all around—unwashed and scared.

"Move and you're dead," came a cold voice from just ahead. A man emerged from the swirl of snow. He wore a camo balaclava and insulated coveralls. Typical Montana winter wear. He held a gun out before him and had sighted in on Tyler. Also typical. Men always assumed other men were more of a threat.

Tyler spun his knife in his hand. He could put it in the man's throat before he could squeeze off a shot.

Others closed in around them, all pointing weapons. Max sighed quietly.

"Lower your weapons," called a woman's strong voice. "They're friends." Kara stepped forward. "Quite an entrance. Trying to get yourself killed?" She looked past them. "Where's the witch?"

"We left him somewhere safe," Max said.

Kara's brows rose, and Max shrugged.

"Safe enough. He can handle himself." *I hope.*

"So what do you want?"

"Like I told the men at the gate, we think there's an attack coming your way. Tonight. Sterling's people, if I had to guess."

She stiffened. "How long do we have?"

"No idea. Could be minutes. Could be hours. But it'll be soon. We can smell the magic."

"All right, then." Kara wheeled around. "Allison, go hit the alarm. Everybody else, get into position. You know what to do. This is not a drill. Where's Ham? Get the nonfighting personnel into the cellar. Move it!"

Max was impressed with their organization. Immediately, they started to move.

Too late.

Canisters hailed down and bounced across the

ground. They hissed with escaping gas. They were almost instantly followed by Molotov cocktails. Bottles shattered, and fire spattered throughout the shantytown. People screamed, and guns fired. Max dropped to her stomach, pulling Tyler down with her. Bullets flew over their heads, and the chemical smell of the tear gas permeated the compound.

"This is getting exciting," Tyler said. He coughed, and tears and snot ran down his face.

The caustic gas burned like acid in Max's eyes, and her nose and mouth were on fire. She swiped at her eyes, trying to see.

All around them, people ran. Some had gas masks, and she couldn't tell if they were good guys or bad guys. It was chaos.

Max got to her feet just in time to snatch a teenage girl by the collar and whirl her out of the way of a falling Molotov cocktail. It exploded, splattering Max with gasoline and fire. Tyler shoved her down into the muddy snow, and she rolled as he slapped at the flames.

When she stood, her clothing was filthy, and her skin stung. Her burns weren't all that significant, and her healing spells kicked in and smoothed them away in a matter of seconds.

"I'm starting to get irritated," she said.

"What do you want to do?"

"Kill whoever tossed that cocktail. But first we'd better see if we can help."

Just then, a series of blasts shook the walls, and scarlet flames rose to towering heights. Chunks of shrapnel whirled through the air. Screams erupted again, and Max smelled blood and the acrid-sweet odor of magic.

In wordless agreement, she and Tyler ran toward the explosions, leaping over fallen people and crushed tents and shacks. A gap had appeared next to the gates. Beyond it, a bridge had been pushed down over the moat, and people were pouring over it. Most of them were wearing camo, with masks and green bandannas tied around various parts of their bodies—necks, arms, wrists, ankles. So they'd know one another in the fight, Max guessed.

They carried guns and were disciplined. They came across the bridge in twos. The first intruders formed a protective perimeter as the others reached the compound. All thirty-five of them made it safely. As soon as they were clear of the bridge, they formed a skirmish line five wide and seven deep.

It was clear that they knew exactly where they were going, and shockingly, their goal wasn't the hut of supplies. Instead, they marched toward the water system.

"What are they up to?" Max muttered.

"The pump setup, maybe? Or if these people have a purification system, that would be pretty damned valuable," Tyler said. "'Course, Sterling has magic to burn, so what does he need it for?"

"Maybe he just doesn't want them to have it. Give them parasites, and they won't be strong enough to fight him. Or they'll come begging for help."

"Do we let them take it?" he asked. "Giselle did say to keep you out of trouble."

"Screw Giselle."

"Sounds good to me," Tyler said with a cold grin. "Let's go get in the way, shall we?"

She tripped on something and looked down. She'd

run into a boy with a ragged gash in his head. He was no more than eleven years old, and he was dead.

Up to this point, Max had been mostly irritated. Faced with this broken child, her annoyance flashed into rage. Children were not supposed to be casualties of war. It was a concrete line she refused ever to cross, and she didn't tolerate it from anybody else, either.

Her Prime smothered every other part of her. Her fury was savage. She skimmed through the veil of snow, snatching the invaders, snapping their necks, and tossing them aside. She wanted them all dead. They continued to shoot and clash with the compounders, and bullets whined through the air. One grazed Max's shoulder, and another whistled past her right ear.

The screams continued mixed with wailing cries and shouts. Smoke thickened the snow until it was nearly impossible to see. Max relied on her nose. Tyler leaped eagerly forward. She felt his emotions, wild and anguished, as if in this fight, he could redeem himself for letting Niko die. As if anything could ever make the weight of guilt lighter.

She wasn't sure how many she'd killed or even if the bodies she'd tossed aside had all been invaders. She smelled blood in the smoke. The invaders began to realize that their numbers had dwindled. They bunched together, circling, backs to one another, guns pointed outward.

They shifted uneasily, unsure where they should go.

"Truce!" called one, and he was instantly cuffed across the mouth by one of his companions.

"Truce? For murdering bastards like you? We'll send you to hell first!" someone called back. Furious shouts echoed the sentiment.

"Good idea," Max muttered. She picked up a chunk of brick and threw it. It was like a missile. It smashed one of the invaders in the forehead. He dropped to the ground. His companions flinched away from him and then surged back together to close the circle again.

Tyler lobbed a rock. Another man crumpled. Max winged another one. The grouped invaders panicked as another one of them fell. They lost cohesion and started shooting into the veil of smoke and snow as they skittered backward.

But there was no escaping.

The compounders had begun to sling whatever debris came to hand. It was a vicious punishment straight out of the Bible. The invaders quickly ran out of bullets, but there was no end to the hail of stones and rubble that descended upon them. They tried to run but were hemmed in on every side.

It was not long before they fell, begging for their lives. But the compounders had no mercy to give.

It was over within minutes.

After the mob took over, Max found the fury draining out of her. She stepped back, letting them do what they would. She found Tyler beside her. Blood ran down the side of his face, and he'd been shot in the ribs. The wounds had closed, but he was still breathing heavily, one of his lungs punctured. He hunched over with his hands on his knees.

"Are you going to live?" Max asked, nudging him on the shoulder.

"Afraid so. You aren't getting rid of me that easily." He straightened with a groan.

"Get rid of you?" she asked. "Who would keep me

out of trouble then?" Despite her light words, her throat was tight. She thought of Simon's pale, limp body. Death was hunting them this night, and it wasn't done yet.

"I thought you gave that job to Alexander," Tyler said slyly.

Max couldn't help the little smile that curved the corner of her lips. "It is fun staying out of trouble with him."

Tyler rolled his eyes. "You know it makes me want to puke when you go all doughy over him, don't you?"

"Doughy?" she repeated in disbelief. "Say that again, and I might have to kick your teeth down your throat."

"It's true. I say his name, and you get that look in your eyes like a kid at Christmas."

She grinned. "I'll give you that, as long as he's under the tree wearing nothing but a bow."

Tyler made a face. "Give me some brain bleach. Not the image I needed in my head."

"Really? It's working for me," Max said, her smile widening at his discomfort. "He's really good in the sack. And I like getting laid regularly." She stared. "Are you blushing?"

"No," he said with a grimace, his cheeks blotching brick red. "What do you want to do now?" he asked, shifting the subject quickly.

Max scanned the surrounding damage. "We've got to get moving. I don't want Gregory in here. We'll never pry him out. They have too many wounds to lick, and we're running out of time."

"So start a war and run? Sounds like a plan to me."

"We didn't start anything."

He snorted. "Right."

"Sterling's people were coming whether we were here or not," she reminded him.

"Semantics."

They started for the gap the bomb had made in the outer wall. The people they passed watched them warily but did not challenge them. Within the compound, someone screamed and others wept. Max hardened her heart against them as Tyler skirted a man who was staggering dazedly in a circle, blood streaking his face. They'd come back and help once they took Sterling down.

"This shouldn't have happened," Tyler said darkly, turning to survey the destruction. There was little enough to see. The smoke and snow made ghosts of everyone. "We should have protected these people."

"We didn't know." It was a lousy excuse, and she knew it. They should have known. This was their territory, and this was their job.

They were starting through the gap when Kara caught up with them.

"Hey!" She was splattered with mud, and blood smeared one of her thighs and the sleeve of her shirt.

"Yeah?" Max was having a hard time mustering anything like manners. The feeling that she should stay and help was like a nail in her heel.

"Thank you," the other woman said unexpectedly. "If not for the two of you, I'm not sure we'd have fended them off." She hesitated. "Could you help us? With . . . magic?" She said the last word like she couldn't quite believe what was coming out of her mouth. Max admired her. Faced with reality, Kara was learning quickly who made a good ally.

Max rubbed a hand over the back of her neck. "Maybe." Kara's face remained stoic. Max liked her all the more for it. She blew out a breath. "First we have to take down Sterling."

"If you need help, send word. We'll come. Not just us. There's a group up in Rattlesnake Canyon and another at the university. We can pull together a couple thousand people or more between us. All armed and willing to go after the Last Standers."

"Impressive," Max said.

"It's nothing compared with how many followers Sterling has. He's got upward of twenty thousand. Maybe more. He'll field them all, kids to grandparents. He doesn't care who dies in his name. All the same, this may be our best chance to beat him. We won't back down. Send for us, and we'll come."

"We will," Max said, and stretched out her hand. Kara shook it firmly. Then Max and Tyler headed out of the gap in the wall, only to find themselves face-to-face with Alexander and Thor.

12

SHE IS ALIVE. SHE IS ALIVE.

Alexander silently chanted the words like a spell. They were all that was keeping him contained while Thor drove slowly through the night.

"We'll have to talk to Giselle about adding a snow-plow to this truck," the other man muttered with a sidelong view at Alexander.

Alexander did not answer, his fingers drumming his thighs.

"Giselle said she was okay," Thor tried again. "You'd know different. Wouldn't you?"

Alexander jerked his head in a nod. "Yes." But it was not enough to know. He needed more than that. He needed to touch her, to wrap himself around her and feel her heart beat against his. He needed to feel her breath move her ribs and taste her fire on his lips.

"Well, okay, then. You can let the whole beast-outta-hell act slide now," Thor said. The words were careful, questioning. One did not mess around with Alexander in this mood.

His jaw knotted. He drew in a deep breath, letting it out slowly. "I am trying," he grated.

Thor sucked his teeth, then spit out the open window. "Driving with you is like driving with a family of pissed-off porcupines," he said mournfully. "Wish I could get drunk. Hell, I wish *you* could get drunk."

That won him a smile. "I wish you would stop driving like a blue-haired old lady going to Sunday church," Alexander shot back.

"If I go any faster, I'm going to drive us into a fairy circle or take us off a cliff. Slow and steady keeps us all alive and in our own skins. Got any idea what Max would do to me if I got you hurt or killed because I was driving too fast?" He whistled low and shook his head, pushing his battered cowboy hat back on his head. "That's one horror movie I have no intention of starring in, boss," he drawled.

"I might just have a role for you in mine," Alexander growled back.

Thor just grinned. "You're scary, but you've got nothing on Max. She's in a class of terrifying all her own."

Alexander grunted and said no more. Instead, he eyed his phone on the dash. She had not called him. She had nearly died twice and had not bothered to call him either time.

Thor took the Orange Street exit. It was coming up on nine, nearly an hour later than they had planned to get back to Missoula. Alexander was opening and closing his fists, impatience spurring him mercilessly. He could see Max's spirit flame and those of Tyler and Gregory. They had gone south of the river and were now angling back to the northwest. They must have picked up Sterling's trail. Knowing Max, she would confront the bastard and get herself killed for her trouble.

He made a sound deep in his throat, his teeth grinding together.

"Almost there," Thor said soothingly.

The truck nosed down under the freeway, and Thor pulled off on the side. "Snow's too deep," he said at Alexander's questioning glare. "Gonna have to go on foot."

Alexander shoved open his door. The snow came up nearly to his knee. He waited impatiently for Thor to get out and set the wards on the truck, and then they set off down the street. It was mostly deserted, with several cars and trucks sitting in the middle of the road as if they had run out of gas and their owners had abandoned them where they sat. The smell of woodsmoke drifted through the falling snow, along with the stink of sewage and rotting garbage.

They had just come to a narrow underpass large enough for only two vehicles to pass when a voice stopped them. "Wait just a second there. Where you boys going? Don'tcha know there's a toll to walk on my streets?"

Alexander shook himself. He had been so intent on finding Max that he had not been paying attention to anything around him. The snow and other powerful smells covered the scent of their attackers, who stank as much like garbage and raw sewage as the real thing.

There were two groups of three men on either side of the road and several more inside the tunnel. Those on the sides were on the raised walkway about five feet above the level of the road.

"This is interesting," Thor drawled softly.

Alexander cracked his knuckles. "I'll take the right, you take the left."

"Wait a bit," Thor said, then raised his voice. "You know boys, I don't often offer advice. I figure everybody's got a right to be stupid now and again. But since we're in a hurry and I'm sure you don't really want to die tonight, I tell you this: you don't know it, but you've dug yourself down into a deep hole. Best cut your losses now and stop digging. And by that I mean turn around and run before you get yourselves dead."

"Fuck off!" came a voice from within the tunnel.

Alexander growled and he unleashed his Prime. Thor's Blade rose, and the air turned thick with the ferocity of their threat.

"Holy shit," one of the attackers said, and fear shook his voice. "What the hell was that?"

"I don't know, but I ain't hanging around to find out." One of the men on the right fled, leaping up the bank through the snow and disappearing. His companions hesitated, then followed him.

"Williams?" someone in the tunnel yelled. "Williams! Royce! Garcia! Get your asses back here!"

Alexander lost patience. He lunged up over the rail onto the sidewalk on the left. Before the three men there could react, he slammed into them. He tore a shotgun from one and jammed the butt into his stomach before bashing it against the second one's skull. He kicked the last one in the thigh. The man shrieked as his leg broke, and he dropped to the ground in a whimpering ball.

Alexander started prowling forward.

"Run now, boys, if you want to live!" Thor yelled. He was at the other end of the tunnel, having vaulted up to the top of the pass and dropped down on the other side. Now the tunnel insiders were trapped between him and Alexander.

A shotgun blast struck the wall near Alexander's head, showering him with bits of cement. He launched himself. Thor struck from behind. In just a few seconds, the two waiting men lay still on the ground. Alexander did not wait to see if they were still breathing. Instead, he set off again. Thor fell in behind.

Suddenly, an explosion of Divine magic shook the air, and red flames shot high in the air. It blinded Alexander's spirit sight. Max had been headed in that direction. He started to run.

He and Thor came to the river and raced along it. The tall red flames vanished, and they followed the sounds of gunshots, screams, and more explosions. Less than a mile down, they came abreast of a walled compound on the south side in McCormick Park. Along one side was a smoking gap. Fires burned within the camp, but the gunshots were dwindling. The falling snow made it impossible to see anything distinctly.

"Over there," Thor called, pointing to a railroad bridge.

The two Blades skimmed across, over the invaders' bridge and up over the rubble in the gap just as Max and Tyler appeared at the top. Both were plastered in mud and blood.

Alexander did not think. He snatched Max up against him, one arm snaking hard around her waist, the other holding the back of her head. He kissed her with all his pent-up need, fury, and fear. It was brutally hard. His teeth ground against hers, and he thrust his tongue inside her mouth, tasting her, devouring her. He squeezed his eyes tightly shut at the almost unbearable wave of relief and joy that swept over him at having her in his arms again.

The kiss went on, and he dimly became aware that she was holding him just as hard, her fingers digging into his flesh like grappling hooks. She pressed hungrily against him, her body taut and shaking. He felt her moan deep in her chest, and his arms spasmed tighter.

"This is all romantic and all, but don't you two think we ought to get Gregory and get a move on?" Tyler asked.

Max stiffened and pushed herself away. Alexander forced himself to let her go. Her lips were swollen, he noticed with supreme satisfaction. She was *his*, whether she liked it or not.

"Good to see you, too," she said, but her voice lacked the warmth he ached for. He found himself recoiling, his emotions snapping back like a broken rubber band. It sent him spiraling. He felt unmoored, like a ship adrift in a hurricane, and he had no means to bring himself to shore.

"Where is Gregory?" he asked, stepping back, his expression shuttering. He could not rein in his Prime.

Max's eyes narrowed at his reaction. "Back at the signal shack." She pointed.

The four of them crossed back over the moat.

"So," Thor said, breaking the tense silence. "Anything new happening here?"

"Well," Tyler said, "not really. There was the demon attack. Oh, and then Sterling got into Horngate again with his dust and nearly killed Max and Giselle. Both Xaphan and Tutresiel seem to be showing signs of life. So hardly anything, really. How about you? Anything interesting happen to you two?"

"Pretty much the same as you. Had a bit of an episode with a rock troll. It nearly killed Alexander. Isn't that a coincidence? Then we were chased by a very fast enchanted forest, after which we got introduced to a family of salamanders. One of them snatched up Spike and disappeared into a fiery hole. The Grims followed, and the ground snapped shut. Really, just another boring night."

"You were almost killed?" Max asked Alexander in a strangled voice.

"Thor exaggerates."

"Thor does not exaggerate," the man in question said.

"Shut up," Alexander said.

"See what I have been putting up with?" Thor asked Tyler. "He's worse than a grizzly bear with a sore paw."

"Maybe he needs a little honey," Tyler said suggestively.

"Shut up, Tyler," Max said.

"I think she needs a little honey, too," he whispered loudly.

Alexander tossed a blistering look over his shoulder. They came to a small shack beside the railroad tracks. Max opened the door.

"All over, Gregory. Come on out."

Nothing.

She looked inside, then wrenched back. "He's not here."

"Where the hell did he go?" Tyler asked.

"Damned witches," Max said. She looked at Alexander. "Can you see his flame?"

He pushed his senses outward but could see only gray. "That explosion of magic seems to have fried my circuits for the moment," he said.

"This way," called Thor. He had found tracks leading away along the front of the livestock enclosure. The four of them broke into a jog.

"Tris, Geoff Brewer, and Doris Lydman jacked a ride with the guys we picked up in the demon attack. They're going hunting for Kyle, Tory, and Carrie," Max said. She ran shoulder-to-shoulder with Alexander.

He stopped, scowling. "Guys you picked up?"

She nodded. "Ex-soldiers, it looked like. They'd been tracking the demons that killed Simon. We joined them."

That killed Simon. So that was who had died. He wanted to offer her comfort, but she clearly did not want it. Instead, he focused on what she was saying. "Do you trust them?"

She shrugged. "Maybe. They handled themselves well enough. But who knows what they're about to run into, or if they'll have Tris's back when the shit hits the fan? What the fuck was she thinking?"

"She wants to protect her daughter, and she does not like sitting and waiting. She is your sister, after all," he said, his mouth twisting in a sardonic smile.

"Giselle thinks they won't make it into town with the snow. I think they're probably already here. Tris is too stubborn not to get her way, and Liam and his crew are motivated. They witnessed the thing at the River Market, too. They wanted to get back to their families."

"So they might leave Tris, Geoff, and Doris high and dry once they get here."

"They could. I don't think it's their style, though."

He nodded and then spun around and started following the tracks again. Thor and Tyler had outdistanced them. Suddenly, Alexander stopped and confronted Max, unable to stop himself.

"You did not call me," he said, his voice full of rusty nails.

She recoiled, then her shoulders squared, her expression turning stubborn. "No. Was I supposed to?"

"You almost died." His voice went flat. If he let his emotions out, he would not be able to control himself. He would pick her up and shake her. Or kiss her. Or maybe fall on his knees and beg.

"I almost die a lot. It's not exactly breaking news."

"I do not like it."

She snorted. "It's not like I enjoy it. I'd rather be in Tahiti."

"You could have fooled me," he ground out.

"If it bothers you so much, why don't you just hop a ride on a different roller coaster?" Her head tilted as if she was genuinely curious.

I would if I could. "Maybe I should."

"My, but you're in a crap mood, Slick. Did you get your period or something?"

"I do not know who I want to kill more right now—you or me," he growled.

"Sounds very healthy. Maybe you should call a shrink. I hear Dr. Phil is available."

He opened his mouth and then snapped it shut, giving a frustrated shake of his head. There was no point to this. He turned and started off again.

"I missed you," she said.

The words sounded small, as if they hurt to say. For

Max, it was a big step. She did not often reveal her real feelings. For Alexander, it was not nearly enough.

"You miss Ben and Jerry's," he said in disgust. "Not to mention avocados, chocolate, and Taco Bell. I am pretty sure I'm down on the bottom of the list of things you miss."

She ground her teeth. *Good*.

"Mother of fuck, Slick. What crawled up your ass and died?"

"Let us just say I got slapped with reality," he said, and jogged away. Inwardly, he sighed. What had possessed him to fall in love with such a stubborn, annoying woman?

Gregory had found a bridge and crossed back over the river, winding through a dark neighborhood.

"Is it me, or is there a path cleared for him?" Tyler wondered out loud.

"It's not you," Thor answered.

"So he was lured," Max said. "Sterling has to be behind this. We need to hurry."

Magic swelled in the air like a storm. Alexander broke into a fast run, with Max at his shoulder and Thor and Tyler hard on their heels. They passed the cemetery, the magic thickening around them. The hair on Alexander's body prickled like a wire brush. A growl reverberated deep in his chest.

The world went still. The snow hung motionless as a photograph.

Alexander drew a breath. The air was molasses.

"This is not good," Max said, her voice elongated and slow.

"What else is new?" Alexander's voice was distorted as well.

They could still move. The snow was a curtain that clung to them like thick cobwebs. Alexander dashed it from his eyes. It felt sticky and strange. They wandered through it, searching for Gregory.

Alexander's spirit sight began to return. Ahead, Gregory's spirit flame was cream and green. It burned incandescent, as did his magic, which lit up the night like a small star. Near him was something else. It oozed along the ground in thick blue vines, winding and twisting in a mystical weaving. It circled the witch, trapping him in place.

"What is it?" Thor asked as the four stopped outside the curls and twists of the thing on the ground. "Is it a spell, or is it alive?"

Alexander had no answer. Max knelt and flipped out a knife. She prodded a gleaming tendril, and magic exploded. She flew backward, landing a good twenty feet away. She hoisted herself to her feet and returned.

"Well, whatever it is, it didn't like that," she said, dusting herself off. Blood trickled from the corner of her mouth, and her breathing was wet, as if she'd broken a rib and it had punctured a lung.

"Got any ideas?" Alexander asked.

"I think we should get Gregory out of there before it kills him and us. And hope we all don't die, anyway," she said, cracking her knuckles absently.

"We could call Giselle."

"She's already on her way into town, but she'll never get here in time to help him. Gregory's giving all he's got. He's not going to last long. I doubt I could get into the abyss and back with her in time."

In fact, the gaunt witch was caught up in an intense

struggle. From his expression, it was clear he was fighting for his life. His magic flared white, creating a thin shell around him. Veins of green magic flickered within it, coalescing into knots and then spreading like roots. It held the twisting blue vines away from him, but the pattern on the ground was growing more dense and condensing. Its edges were starting to lift, as if it intended to close around Gregory and swallow him.

"So we go get him," Alexander said, his body tensing.

"Are we going in with a plan?" Tyler asked. "Or are we just going balls to the wall and hope it works out?"

The corner of Max's mouth crooked up, and she shook her head, her gaze locked on the tableau in front of them. "We're going to wing it. I'll jump over to Gregory—my unlocking spells should drop me through his shields without damaging them. Then I'll jump him out. You three try to distract the creature or spell or whatever the fuck it is."

She did not wait for a response but launched instantly into the air. Alexander drew two of his knives and followed, slicing the blades through the dirt and dragging them through the writhing ropes of blue as he went. He did not get far. Magic seared him. It was like stepping on a land mine. He was thrust backward like he had been shot from a cannon, landing on his back. The air exploded from his chest, and his vision went black as his head slammed against the ground.

Luckily, the snow cushioned his fall enough that his skull did not shatter. He rolled to his stomach and lunged to his feet. He raced back. Tyler and Thor had done better. Thor was flinging a salt, herb, and metal mixture over the vine pattern, while Tyler jabbed at it with his knives. The pattern twitched and rippled in response, then snapped upward, knotting into a ball where Gregory had been standing just a few moments before.

Max and the witch were a hundred yards north and heading east as fast as she could run. The other three Blades followed. The snow was falling again, but magic swelled livid and angry behind them.

"Faster," Alexander called sharply.

They overtook Max. Her body was a mass of scarlet burns. Most of her clothes had been charred away. She was carrying Gregory in her arms, but it was a struggle. The witch was awake, though clearly exhausted and weak. He was arguing with her to put him down.

Alexander slowed long enough to snatch the witch and toss him over his shoulder. Tyler had already swung Max up piggyback, and they ran as fast as they could.

They found themselves in an open area. The ground was tumbled and scrubby with sage and weeds poking up through the snow. The place had been used as a gravel pit, for dirt-bike riding, and likely for dumping trash and getting high. Thor led the way toward a tall mound of dirt and gravel, now covered with snow. He circled around to the other side and dropped down into a steep trench. The others jumped down beside him.

Alexander kicked aside snow until he found dirt and lowered Gregory down. Instantly, he turned to Max. She was on her knees, pulling snow up over her melted flesh. He made a harsh whining sound, stretching out for her, stopping when she flashed a look at him. Her eyelids were gone and most of her nose. Her hair was a matted black cap plastered to her skull. Her fingers were blackened stubs, and her skin looked like melted wax.

His hands dropped, and he swallowed bile. His Prime raged, clawing, shredding at his insides.

Thor had turned and was quietly retching. Tyler was swearing, his face white. Gregory was struggling to stand.

"Let me—" he began, and got no further.

A scouring blast of magic swept across them like the shock wave of a nuclear bomb. It brought with it a wind that rushed past with all the fury of a superheated tornado. Alexander pushed Max down into the snow and huddled over her to protect her. Tyler added his bulk to shielding her.

Alexander felt her body quivering. Helplessness strangled him, and he struggled to keep his Prime from overwhelming his mind. He was constantly fighting for dominance, to keep from sliding over the edge and disappearing entirely into his beast. He had thought he had gained mastery, or at least equilibrium, but when it came to his feelings for Max, all bets were off.

The snow in the trench melted instantly, leaving them in pools of tepid water and squelching mud. Gravel pelted them in a stinging hail. Then, just as quickly, the wind stopped, and the air dropped to well below zero. The water skimmed with a skin of ice. The temperature continued to drop. Thor wrapped Gregory in a hug, pulling the witch tightly against him to keep him warm.

Alexander hesitated. Ordinarily, Max's spells protected her body from the temperature. But she'd been badly hurt, and all of her energy was going into healing. He did not know if she could handle the still-dropping cold. She made his mind up for him when her teeth chattered and then stopped suddenly, as if she had clamped her jaws tight.

He pushed Tyler away and sat down on the ice, pulling Max's ruined body onto his lap. He did his best to ignore her soft mewls of pain, although the sounds raked his Prime and sent his mind spinning with torment and rage. Sterling was going to pay dearly for doing this to her.

He tore off his vest and held her against the warmth of his chest.

"Easy," he whispered against her crisp, melted hair. "I have you. Easy."

He reached out and fumbled inside one of the pockets of his vest, pulling out his silver emergency sack. He pulled it around her. It acted as a blanket, reflecting heat back onto her. Tyler crouched on the other side of her, his arms wrapped around his stomach as he could only watch helplessly.

She quivered. The temperature continued to drop, and the snow swallowed the world again. The stench of the Divine penetrated everywhere: a caustic, sweet miasma that filled Alexander's lungs like cold oil. Once again, the magical blast had burned out his ability to sense far. Only this time, it was worse. It was like the brilliant splotches left behind after staring into a bright light. Odd blurs and smears of ghostly magic swam across the landscape, and he could not tell real from false. He might as well be wearing a burlap sack on his head.

He listened intently, but the snow muffled all sounds. He shifted Max, trying to get his feet under him in case they were attacked, but she made a mewling sound that cut through him like a sword, and he stopped dead.

"Give me some power bars."

Tyler grappled in his vest and fished out a couple of bars. He tore one open with his teeth, and Alexander took it and put it to Max's mouth. "Eat," he ordered.

She forced her jaws to open and bit down, chewing slowly. She swallowed hard and took another bite. He fed her both bars. Before he could take the next from Tyler, the cold snapped.

It was an audible sound, like the crack of a whip. It echoed from the mountains. Instantly, the bitter cold lifted, and warmth flowed down into the trench.

"About time," Thor said, and then Alexander heard him and Gregory moving. The witch staggered over. He was crusted in ice. He knelt down beside Alexander and pushed his hands under the silver emergency sack.

Magic seeped into the air. This time, Alexander recognized it as belonging to Gregory: a green flavor with hints of cayenne, honey, and hemlock.

A warm white glow like moonlight on water streamed down his arms. Max made a gasping sound, her body jerking. Alexander's arms clamped down, and she whimpered. He forced himself to loosen his grip. His vision went entirely gray, as if the world was a landscape of the dead. His Prime was scrabbling at the bindings of his control.

No, he told himself. *No.* Gregory would heal Max. She would be all right.

But how long before she is not? How long before death finds her? It would, he knew. Her life was a never-ending war, and she was always at the forefront of every battle. She would never be safe; she would never hold back. He could never keep her from harm.

Bile flooded his throat as his stomach twisted sharply. He felt a mixture of self-disgust and utter impotence. They clawed at him like twin lions, shredding him from within, ripping at the seams of his fragile control. If they kept up, one day soon, he would simply vanish, and all that would be left was the beast within. That beast was bloodthirsty, ruthless, and brutal. The only way to stop him would be to kill him.

A feral Prime was not easy to kill.

His mouth twisted in a bitter smile. He had foolishly thought he had found a balance. But every time something like this happened, he felt his human side thinning as the Shadowblade Prime took greater control of his divided soul. This time, Alexander would win. But next time—

13

HEALING MAGIC SUFFUSED MAX WITH STUNNING heat. It flowed through her body and wrapped her skin in a silken cocoon. It soothed her nerves, and the pain slowly melted into something more bearable.

She let it go on longer than she should have, reveling in the combination of being in Alexander's embrace and the nearly orgasmic pleasure of evaporating pain. But Gregory was wasting himself. She pushed him away. "Save your strength," she rasped. "I'm okay."

"It's my fault," he muttered, grasping her again. "This shouldn't have happened. I don't know where I was going. One minute I was in the shack, and then I needed to go, to follow the path."

"It wasn't your fault," she said. "It was Sterling. Don't worry about it. I'll be fine. So back off, already."

Thor pulled him back and put his emergency silver sack around the witch's shoulders. "She's crabby," he pointed out reassuringly. "It's a sure sign she's going to be fine. Come on over here, and squat down for a minute and get yourself defrosted. Let's see if I can find us the makings for a fire."

"I'll go, too," Tyler said, and leaped out of the trench.

Thor settled Gregory and then followed. The two returned a few minutes later, and before long, they had a small fire going. In the meantime, Max found herself relaxing against Alexander's chest. His heart beat fast beneath his ribs, and his body was coiled tightly, although his arms were slack around her hips.

She pushed herself away slightly so that she could look at him. He stared past her, his face carved in an iron mask. His eyes were pearl white. A snake of ice wriggled down her spine.

"Alexander?" she asked carefully.

His gaze flicked to her, quick as a cobra strike.

"You okay?" she asked. If he was really feral, if he had really lost his mind to his Blade, he wasn't acting like it.

He blinked. "I am fine," he said, and then heaved himself up, lifting Max with him. He set her on her feet before stepping back. "I am fine," he repeated, and then jumped out of the trench and vanished into the snow.

Max stared after him, then forced herself to turn away. She bit down hard on the inside of her cheek, tasting blood. How was she going to fix this?

The silver sack crinkled as she turned, and she looked down at herself. Her clothes were charred scraps of nothing. The soles of her boots had melted to her feet; the rest of her boots were gone. Her skin was still puckered and red, with a few shrinking blistered and black patches. Why was it she kept ending up naked? And never having any fun getting that way? It was damned unfair.

She bent and peeled away the remnants of her boots and brushed off what was left of her clothes. She examined her arms ruefully. Her favorite knives were gone. She had a feeling only Tyler would sympathize with that.

Alexander had left his vest. She picked it up and fished out his supply of power bars and ate them. Next, she took out his cell phone. Hers was gone with all the rest of her stuff. She flipped it open and punched in Giselle's number. Nothing. It wasn't working. She wasn't all that surprised. The magical blast had been extraordinary. She would have been more surprised if the phone was still working.

She slid the phone back into its pocket and turned to her companions. Gregory was hunched over the small fire, Thor's silver sack around his shoulders collecting and reflecting the heat back on him. His head hung low.

Max tightened her silver sack around herself, so that Gregory wouldn't have to blush when he looked at her, and crouched down opposite him. "What exactly happened back there?"

He lifted his head. His eyes were red-rimmed and bloodshot. His shaggy hair clung wetly to his forehead. He didn't speak right away. That was Gregory. He liked to collect his thoughts first. Probably figuring out the fewest words possible to say what he had to. Max waited, fighting for patience.

Finally, he spoke. "It was a trap, of sorts."

"What do you mean, of sorts? Either it was a trap or it wasn't."

He sighed and scratched his cheek. "It was a trap, but only for witches, and it wasn't the sort of thing designed to kill me or capture me. It wanted to eat me."

"Eat you?"

"Eat my magic." He shook his head. "It's hard to explain." Again that grim smile. "Don't get me wrong. It would have killed me. But only as a by-product and not quickly. Maybe not for years."

"What do you mean, eat your magic?" Thor asked.

Gregory tipped his head, thinking. "Think of it as milking a snake for venom," he said finally. "The snake keeps living, keeps giving up its prize. Just like a milk cow. Until the milk runs out, and eventually it does."

He stopped, his attention turning inward. His gaunt face turned bleak. Max was about to prompt him again when he continued.

"Every witch is connected to his or her specific element. It's like we have roots digging down into, well, magical soil, for lack of a better explanation. Anyhow, witches have those roots. The deeper they go, the stronger we are, and the stronger we are, the deeper and broader their reach. This trap wanted to pull me up by the roots, but more than that, it wanted to pull the magic with it. Eventually, the roots die, but not for a long time. A long, painful time."

He stopped abruptly, as if disconcerted at how much he'd been talking. He looked at Max. "If you hadn't—" He grimaced. "Anyway, I shouldn't have left. I walked right into it, and I didn't deserve what you did for me. I don't know if I'll ever be able to pay you back."

She stared at him. "You are a fucking idiot. You don't

owe me anything. I was just in the right place at the right time."

He shrugged. "Still."

There was no talking him out of it, so Max didn't bother to try. It was surprising to discover a witch with a sense of morality. It was sort of like finding the holy grail. A singular event. Mythical, even. Maybe miraculous.

"What now?" Gregory asked.

"What made you leave the shack?"

He rubbed his forehead. "I'm not entirely sure. I felt compelled, like I was needed, like someone was ill and calling for me. I knew I should stay, but I kept following the path in front of me." He grimaced. "I really can't remember very well."

"We have got to get on with killing Sterling."

"You make it sound easy. He's got power to burn."

"Then we'll burn him."

His lips quirked in a gallows smile. "I'd like to light the match."

"Get in line," Tyler said through stiff lips.

Max looked up at him. He was visibly struggling with what had happened to her. This was the second time she'd come close to dying in less than twelve hours. She didn't know how to help him. How to reassure him. Her habit of dealing with loss and fear was to isolate herself. But the two of them were too close for that. They had to figure out a new way.

She looked down.

"Before we go off hunting Sterling, we'll want to scavenge you up some clothes," Thor said, breaking the tension. "Not that I object to the Lady Godiva look, but it could call more attention to us than we want."

He cast a looked at the falling snow. Max knew what he was thinking: where was Alexander? She was wondering the same thing.

She felt him returning long before he dropped back down into the trench. He was layered with snow, and the white ringing his eyes had thinned. He dropped a fat gym bag at Max's feet.

"Clothes and weapons," he said tersely. "I will get more wood."

He snatched up his vest and was gone again. Max bit back her annoyance and unzipped the bag. She found a pair of blue jeans, a long-sleeved navy shirt, and a pair of black boxer briefs. They smelled of Alexander.

Max put them on. The scent of Alexander wrapped her. She closed her eyes a moment, just breathing him in. The pants were too big, but there was a belt to keep them up. The shirt was also baggy, but comfortable. She dug in the bag to find out what else he had brought back from the truck. She found another tactical vest and a .45. She put on the vest and tucked the gun into her rear waistband. At the bottom of the bag were a combat knife and a bag of pepper sticks. She offered them to Thor, Tyler, and Gregory. All three refused.

"You need the calories," Gregory said with a stern look. "Eat all of it."

"Getting pushy, aren't you?"

"Apparently, it takes an entire coven to keep you out of trouble."

"You think that one coven would be enough?" Tyler asked, his voice brittle.

"No," Alexander said before leaping down beside

her. His gaze slid over her, his nostrils flaring. "I had no extra shoes."

Max shrugged. "Won't be a problem. Thanks for going to get this stuff for me."

His brows rose, and he gave her a distant look. "Someone had to," was all he said. He bent and built up the fire until it roared.

"That should help you warm up," he told Gregory.

The witch stood, rubbing his hands against his thighs. "We don't have time for me to warm up. We need to get going."

"Sure," Tyler said. "Tell us where to start."

"I had an idea about that," Max said. "Maybe we could track the people who attacked the compound."

"Probably a long shot," Thor said.

"If you've got other ideas, I'm all ears."

No one offered any.

"All right, then. Gregory, you got hit pretty hard. Are you sure you don't need more rest?" Max asked.

"Do you?" he returned, his gaze running down to her hands. They were red now, the new skin smooth and tight, her fingernails growing back in.

"Then let's go," Max said. She climbed up out of the trench with Tyler right behind. Thor helped Gregory up, and Alexander came last. He continued to simmer with hard-held emotions. She decided to ignore him, to give him space until he was ready to talk to her. His presence grated against her, and right or wrong, her temper was rising by the minute.

Max figured she'd find a pair of shoes at the compound, along with a trail to follow. Being barefoot didn't bother her, but she didn't like leaving her blood around if she cut herself. Sterling might be able to make serious trouble for her with it.

She led the way, going slowly to let Gregory keep up. Alexander brushed past her to walk a few steps ahead. Max scowled at his back but didn't try to overtake him.

They edged east through the quiet neighborhoods. It looked like a bomb had hit. Many houses had collapsed, and the rest were leaning drunkenly, with caved-in roofs and walls. Everything was eerily quiet, like a grave. Maybe it was one mass grave. Who knew how many people had been tucked into bed or hiding in the basements?

Max ran her tongue along the sharp edge of her teeth. One way or another, Sterling was going to die.

The burst of heat and subsequent cold had melted the heavy blanket of snow and refrozen it into sheets of thick ice, sleeking everything inside a brittle shroud. Thor held on to Gregory to help him walk, but all five of them had a hard time keeping their feet. With the thickly falling snow, it took them nearly an hour to reach the bridge.

It had not suffered the same damage, although it sagged to the left. The river had absorbed the brunt of the magic. They carefully crossed and slogged back up the river path to the compound.

Crews were working on repairing the outer skin of the wall with a patchwork of metal and wood. Welding torches flashed blue-white through the heavy snow. Others were carrying bodies to a spot near the river. Max tore her eyes away from the sight, her throat knotting. Too much death.

"We should not stay here long," Alexander said. "We might have trouble pulling Gregory away from the wounded."

"Oh, so you talk, do you?" Max responded sourly. "And here I thought you'd lost your voice. Or maybe you're just the strong, silent type."

He made a growling sound low in his throat. "I speak when I have something to say."

She stopped, turning to look at him. "I get a feeling you've got a lot to say, Slick. In fact, I get the feeling you're choking on it. So why don't you stop pouting like a five-year-old and get it off your chest, already?"

He spun, grasping her arms, the tendons in his neck taut as wire.

Max's chin jutted. "I guess I hit a nerve there."

"You. Hit. All. My. Nerves," he said, each word spaced out and bitten off. He punctuated each one with a small shake.

"Sounds painful. Maybe you should see a doctor for that."

Thor snorted softly and pulled Gregory back a few steps. "Can't be too careful," he told the witch. "You don't want to be too close when the shit hits the fan."

"There's no place on earth far enough," Tyler replied sardonically. "I might have to strip down with all the heat coming off them. If only they'd kiss and make up, already. Time's a-ticking."

Max's lips twitched despite herself. She caught a glint of humor in Alexander's eyes, then it vanished. His gaze bored through her as if he was searching for something.

He didn't find it.

His hands dropped, and it was like watching a dozen barred doors slam shut. It was almost like watching him fade back into the distance, even though he was standing right in front of her. But his expression was closed, sealed as tight as Fort Knox.

"No need for doctors. I believe I am cured of whatever ailed me." His voice was offhand. "It is quite a miracle."

He turned away. Max stared after him. Panic erupted inside her, and she felt cold and brittle, as if she'd been dunked in liquid nitrogen. *What just happened? What did he mean, cured? Cured of me?*

Her throat filled with boulders, and her eyes burned with tears. They did nothing to break the grip of the cold that held her like a statue. Until—

"Well?" he said, looking at her. "Shall we get moving, boss?"

The question shattered her. His demeanor was impersonal. He wasn't even angry. It was like he felt nothing.

She'd been waiting for it to happen. It was inevitable. Why would he keep chasing her when she acted like she didn't want to be caught?

Max blinked. Then she stretched her lips into a grin. It felt like a grimace. She wanted to scream. To cry. To punch him in the stomach. Break his jaw. Make him react. Instead, she headed for the bridge into the compound.

As they walked, Max fought to get a handle on her emotions. Or, rather, she grappled at them, trying to ball them up and stuff them down inside. She'd deal with them later.

Maybe in a hundred years.

Her stomach lurched, and she swallowed her nausea. Every single cell of her body was attuned to Alexander. She had given in to feeling things she had never been willing to feel before, and she didn't know how she was going to survive them shattering. They would. He was done. He had made that much clear.

A flame of anger flickered to life in her chest. It was cold and cut like a scalpel with every flicker. If he had ever really cared for her, he wouldn't have been able to shut down so completely. Which meant the real problem was that his ego was bruised. She didn't let herself think through her logic. Instead, she embraced the pain and the anger. It was armor. With it, she wouldn't have room to feel anything else.

She focused on it, letting the razor edges of the cleansing flame fill her. It whirled, slashing and chopping. Beneath the onslaught, her fear and hurt shrank into a hard kernel deep within. Now she could function. Now she didn't have to listen for Alexander's breath and heartbeat. Now she could go back to being just herself. It was better this way, anyhow. Losing Niko and Simon had proven the truth of that. Being alone meant not getting gutted when people you cared about died or stopped being—

Whatever it was Alexander was to her.

Everything, a soft voice whispered in her mind. She strangled it. Nothing. He was nothing.

14

THIS TIME, WHEN THEY ARRIVED AT THE COMpound, they identified themselves and were allowed in. On the other side, a semicircle of people met them. Most guns were not pointed at them, although soon another thirty or forty armed people closed the circle, each one ready to fight if the need arose. So much for gratitude.

Kara shoved through to the front of the group. Her shoulders were damp with melting snow. Her straight, dark hair clung to her forehead, cheeks, and neck.

"Back already?"

"We ran into a little trouble," Max said.

"That thing across the river? What happened?"

"It was a trap. For our kind," Max said.

Kara's cheek twitched. She still wasn't happy about the idea of real magic actually existing. Other compounders made the sign of the cross or clutched at a necklace. More than a few hammers cocked back.

Kara heard them. She glanced around sharply. "Get back to work. These people aren't here to hurt us." To Max, she jerked her chin. "Follow me."

She turned and threaded her way through the encampment. A few of the gathered people continued with them, unwilling to trust the visitors.

Gregory muttered beneath his breath at the sight of the thin, pale inhabitants of the compound. The sounds of crying, coughing, and moaning carried through the night. The fight had left many hurt, and it sounded like plenty of others were sick. These days, colds could kill.

"They shouldn't be living like this," he said.

"Nope," Thor said, his voice bland. But Max could feel his Blade raging.

"We should do something. What's power for if not to help?"

"Some might say it is to conquer and dominate," Alexander said, his voice equally bland.

"Some would be fucking wrong," Gregory shot back.

"Yep," Max said quietly. "That's why you belong with us."

He stopped. "I need to help them."

She turned. His sunken eyes were burning with feverish heat. His body resonated with magic, despite his exhaustion from fighting the trap and healing her.

"You can't. We need to go after Sterling. Otherwise, healing these people won't do any good in the long run."

"I don't care. In the short run, some might die, and that's unacceptable."

She sighed. "I know, Buttercup. That's one of the reasons I like you. That doesn't mean I'm going to let you be stupid."

He drew a breath to say something, but she looked away to Alexander. She kept her expression neutral. "Watch him. Keep him safe, and don't let him overdo it." She glanced at Thor and Tyler. "Thor, go with them. Tyler, you go see if you can pick up a trail."

"What about you?" he asked with a frown.

Max noticed that Alexander didn't seem all that concerned about her. It made his change feel more real than anything else had. "I can handle myself. Go," she said, hurt stabbing through her gut.

Their local guardians eyed her and then followed the three men. Because, of course, a lone woman wasn't nearly as dangerous as three men. *Little do they know,* she thought sourly.

She joined Kara again, not looking back. She didn't want to see Alexander's indifference. Her mouth twisted in a mocking smile. All that time she'd run from him, and now that she'd figured out she was caught, he was done chasing. Done wanting. Fine. It was smarter this way. She'd scratch her sexual itch with men she didn't care about, and things at Horngate would get back to normal. No more personal drama.

"In here," Kara said, drawing Max after her into a small shed made of stone, plywood, bricks, and mud. The roof was rusty corrugated steel, and the door was two-by-fours nailed together, with hinges made of wire. They screeched as the door opened and shut.

It was decently warm inside. A small woodstove with a kettle on top sat in the far left corner. A queen-size bed ran along the other wall, with a dresser at the foot of it. Several plastic trunks held who knew what and doubled as benches around a round wood table. Another table with a metal tub on top served as the kitchen sink. An orange tabby leaped up from its spot in front of the stove and disappeared under the bed.

"Sit," Kara said. "Want some hot cider? We've been having to do something with the apples before they spoil." She reached for the kettle on the stove.

"I can't stay. I just need some shoes. And I'm wondering what else you can tell me about Sterling and the Last Standers."

Kara shrugged out of her coat and set it in front of the stove to dry. She poured two mugs and handed one to Max.

It smelled heavenly, with a hint of clove and cinnamon. There wasn't a lot of either left to go around. "Thanks," Max said, sipping. She lifted her head and eyed Kara through the steam. "What do you know?"

Kara pushed her hair back from her face, and Max revised her estimation of the woman's age. Maybe mid-twenties. Kara carried herself with such careful control and confidence that Max had pegged her for five to ten years older.

"How much do you know about what's been happening in Missoula since fairy-tale time started up again?" Kara asked.

"Not nearly enough. We've had some troubles we've had to deal with," Max said, not wanting Kara to think Horngate was ignoring the city.

Kara snorted. "Haven't we all? We didn't know what was going on at first. Some stuff stopped working. Phones. TV and cable. The Internet. Then we stopped getting deliveries. No food, no fuel, nothing. That's when panic set in. Only took a couple of weeks. Everyone started going into survival mode. Some grouped up and took over stores and made strongholds there, selling off the products. Did that at Saint Pat's and Community Hospital, too. All the drugs, you know."

She shook her head. "Anyhow, pretty quick, regular people were going hungry and getting robbed, raped, killed. So some of us started organizing. We gave up our houses—weren't safe enough, and we couldn't protect ourselves—and set up this camp."

"What about Sterling?"

"Did you know that the Unabomber lived in Montana? We get a lot of lunatics around here. A lot of religious and patriot types who want to live off the grid without the government nosing into their business. We get the whole range: Church Universal and Triumphant, Montana Militia, the Montana Freemen, polygamists, Cal Greenup and his militia, Hutterites, World Church of the Creator, a bunch of neo-Nazis, and oh, yeah, word is that some of the Ruby Ridge folks moved up by the Flathead."

"So you're saying Sterling is one of these lunatics."

Kara gusted a sigh. "He seemed harmless at first. Started standing on stumps and shouting on and on about fire and brimstone and Satan and hell. People started flocking to him when he started curing cancer and diabetes and whatever other diseases they might have. All they have to do is promise to worship at his feet. He's been picking up followers left and right.

"He showed up around here just after the changes started. Heard he came from somewhere up by Great Falls. Claims God sent him to bring his light to the people here. He says if you're not with him, you're the enemy—children of the devil—and he's going to wipe

God's enemies off the face of the earth. That's about all I know. Not all that helpful, I know."

Max stared up at the roof, folding in on herself and thinking hard. Options unfolded, and she considered them.

"If someone like me happened to join these Last Standers, would they take me to Sterling?"

Kara stared. "You can't be serious."

"Would they?"

"Probably. Word is he checks out all the new followers for the taint of evil. Lays hands on them or something. But you can't do that. You don't know what he'll do to you. It's worse than you can possibly imagine." She looked haunted.

Max rubbed her hand hard over her mouth and came to a decision. It was risky, but at least it was a plan, which was more than they had now. She just had to convince the others. Alexander probably wouldn't argue, but Tyler . . . he was going to go ballistic.

She smiled at Kara. "I'll be fine," she said. "I'm tough to kill."

"Has anyone told you you're a bad liar?"

"Frequently," Max said. "But I have no intention of letting Sterling do anything permanent to me."

"You know what they say about the road to hell and good intentions," the other woman said. She raised her mug. "Here's to stupidity and bravery and killing the bad guys," she said.

Max chinked her mug against Kara's and drained the last of the cider.

"Can I borrow a pair of shoes?" she asked.

15

SOMETHING HAD HAPPENED. SOMETHING VERY strange. Alexander did not know if it was bad or good. All he knew for sure was that he felt more in control of himself than he had in a long time. Since he had met Max.

It felt amazing.

He had been so wild, so angry, and then he had looked into her eyes, and something within him had released. Just—let go. He did not know what. He had not had a chance to think about it and was not sure that he even wanted to. All he knew for sure was that when Max walked away with Kara, he had not felt the usual surge of fear or the urge to go with her and protect her. In fact, he felt nothing. It was as if all his emotions had frozen solid and he could no longer touch them.

The relief of not having to feel was breathtaking. He felt free. Really free, for the first time in almost a hundred years. It was intoxicating.

As they turned to follow Gregory, Thor cocked an eyebrow at him. At some point, his battered straw cowboy hat had vanished.

"That's okay with you?" he asked, tipping his head at Max's retreating back.

"She can handle herself."

"Usually," Thor agreed, his gaze narrowing.

"Then why should I object?" Alexander asked matter-of-factly.

He looked at Gregory, who was already making a beeline for a woman coughing raggedly as she stirred a pot over a fire. More coughing and weak childish crying came from within the tent behind her. Snow settled on top. It would not be long before it collapsed.

When Gregory approached, flanked by Alexander, Thor, and the four self-appointed compound guards, the woman stumbled to her feet, shrinking back.

"What's going on? What do you want?" she demanded. Her words were thick and full of snot. Her nose and upper lip were red and chapped, and her body shook with chills. Suddenly, she turned and vomited, heaving until she had emptied her guts.

At last, she straightened, wiping her mouth. Before anyone could move, Gregory brushed his hand over her forehead.

"You're burning up."

"So?" she said, knocking him away. "I'm sick. What's it to you?"

"Sit," he ordered, pointing back to the upended bucket she'd been using for a chair.

She scowled. "I don't take orders from you. Just who the hell are you, anyhow?"

"Today I'm the doctor," Gregory said with a thin smile. "This is a house call. So sit."

Her entire demeanor changed from fear to hope.

"A doctor? Oh, thank God! Come in. My kids—" She reached for the tent zipper, but Gregory's hand closed around her wrist.

"You first."

The four guards started forward, but Thor and Alexander turned deadly looks on them.

"Let the sawbones work," Thor drawled, falling heavily into his Texas accent.

"He's not a doctor, he's a fucking sorcerer," one growled.

"Actually, I'm a witch," Gregory said mildly, not letting go of his new patient. His eyes had taken on a silvery sheen, a little like an animal caught in the light at night. "Sorcerers are much more powerful than I'll ever be, and frequently, they are mentally impaired. You really don't want to mess around with the likes of them."

"We don't want to mess around with the likes of *you*," sneered another guard, the muzzle of his gun rising to fix on Gregory's chest.

Alexander made a hissing noise. "Do not even think about it."

"Or what? I'll kill you, too? Sounds like a pretty good plan to me."

Alexander smiled a slow crocodile smile. "Would you like to try?"

The other man blanched and took a step back.

"All of you, shut up," Gregory snapped. "It's okay," he told the woman gently. She looked scared half to death, like a wild deer trussed in ropes. "I'll fix you up. Your kids, too. You don't have to be afraid."

Gregory was good with people. His entire demeanor was calming. After a few moments, his patient gave in and sat back down.

"What are you going to do?" she asked, twisting her fingers together.

"Cure you. It won't hurt."

With that, he went to stand behind her, setting his hands on her shoulders. She jumped and stiffened. The sheen in his eyes intensified, turning them to silvery disks. Green magic swirled around his hands and wound around her chest in long streamers. It sank in. She jerked as if she was going to stand up and then went still, her eyes widening as her mouth fell open in a silent "oh." Slowly, she relaxed, leaning back against him like a kitten cuddling up against its mother's stomach.

A minute or two later, Gregory lifted his hands, his magic whispering away like mist. The woman sat very still, then stood up and drew a deep breath and let it out. She turned to look at him. The red chapping on her face was gone, as were her fever and her cough.

"I'm better. I—" She bit her lips. "Thank you. You said you can help my boys, too? They aren't doing very good." She looked down, flushing. "I don't have much to pay with. Some jewelry, maybe. Spices and some blankets I might be able to spare." She shook her head sharply and looked back up at him, her jaw firm. "Doesn't matter. Anything I've got, you can have if you can help them. They're really sick."

The witch curled his lip and waved away her words. "I didn't ask for payment. Let's have a look at them."

She went to the tent and took a push broom to shove the snow off the top before unzipping the flap and ducking inside. Gregory went with her. She zipped the flap closed again. Thor exchanged a look with Alexander, but neither moved to join them. Instead, the two Blades turned to keep an eye on the four guards, who looked as if they did not entirely know what they should be doing.

Magic flared inside the tent, once and then twice. A few minutes later, Gregory and his companion emerged. "Who else needs help?" he rasped.

"Hold up a minute," Thor said. "You've already been through a nasty fight tonight. You have to conserve your energy."

Gregory's expression was incendiary. "I can take care of myself. It's not your business."

"But it is," Alexander said. "We need you to go after Sterling."

"These people are in trouble. Half of them are going to die if I don't help them."

"What the hell are you talking about?" said one of the four guards, and fear turned his voice high. "It's just a bad cold. Happens."

Gregory shook his head. "It's not just a cold. It's strep, too. And very likely the flu. The way you're living, half your population could be wiped out. One of the boys actually had rheumatic fever."

Alexander cocked his head. "You are sure? I thought that was cured in the 1800s."

"I am sure. Once upon a time, I really was a doctor. And rheumatic fever has not been cured. Outbreaks happen still, and we're probably looking at one. It happens when strep goes untreated. The only way to cure it without magic is plenty of antibiotics over several months. I don't think these people have nearly enough." He looked at the men. "We're looking for swollen, painful joints, skin rash, fever, nosebleeds, shortness of breath, and maybe a lack of coordination. Sound familiar?"

They exchanged looks. Then one wearing a John Deere cap and a gray down jacket nodded. "Maybe."

The man in stained Carhartt overalls beside him chimed in. "Yeah, okay, me, too. A few. It's not that bad."

"Oh? Are you willing to bet your life on it? And your family's lives?" Gregory demanded. "Once it sets in, rheumatic fever can destroy a person's heart and cripple them forever. Plus, even with a long-term course of antibiotics—months and maybe years—the fever is quite likely to return." He glared at Alexander. "Which means they need me."

"They do. But so do we. You had better deal with that fact right up front," Alexander said. He shifted, gathering the woman and the four men in his gaze. "You need to triage. Find out who is sickest. That is, if you want help from the likes of us."

The four men stared at Alexander and then at one another. Indecision bound them.

"Oh, for crying out loud," the woman exclaimed. "Warren, Larry, and Carl, you go start checking on folks and making a list. Jerry, you go tell Kara what's going on and start pulling together the Board. We're going to need a plan."

They hesitated, eyeing the two Shadowblades and the witch, clearly not wanting to leave them alone.

The woman made a disgusted sound and stomped forward. She poked her finger sharply into the Carhartt overalls. "Understand me right now. No one here is going to die because the help is coming from a witch, not if I have anything to say about it. And there's no mother, no father, who's going to let their child die because they don't like magic." She stepped back, putting her fists on her hips. "What are you waiting for? Get on with it. Now."

The men turned away reluctantly.

The woman swung back around to examine Gregory. Her mouth pursed. "You look wrung out. You need something to eat and drink. I have a stew going. It's not much, but it's filling."

"It'll be perfect," Thor said, even as Gregory started to shake his head. "And he thanks you for it."

With a frown, Gregory brushed away the snow from a log and sat on it.

"I'm perfectly fine."

"Right," Max said as she joined them. "You look it, too, all scarecrowy and anorexic. You could be voted Missoula's most handsomest zombie."

The witch scowled at her but accepted the bowl and spoon that his patient handed him. "Isn't it a little late to be cooking?" he asked with ill grace.

"You're welcome," the woman said as she returned to her pot, giving it a sharp stir before poking at the fire. "You try being sick and having two sick boys. Time might get away from you, too. The fire went out with the snow, and then Cody started crying, and there wasn't anything I could do but hold him—"

Her mouth pinched shut. Gregory looked as if she had just spanked his nose with a rolled-up newspaper. He scooped up a mouthful and gulped it down. His eyes bulged, and he gasped.

"Don't you like it?" the woman snapped.

"It's good. Just hot."

"You might have noticed that it *did* just come off the fire," she pointed out.

Thor snickered, and Max grinned at Alexander. He only stared. A moment later, her expression turned troubled, and she looked away. It left Alexander feeling . . . nothing. It was like looking at a stranger.

What has happened?

This sudden cessation of feeling could not be real. Could it? Was it magic? Was he under a spell?

His brows winged downward. Would he know if he was? And then—would he want it broken? Would he want to go back to the torment that was loving Max?

He could be done with that dreadful, shredding, gnawing desperation that tore incessantly at him with rusty claws. Every moment of every day, he felt as if he was caught up in a storm that left him seasick and drowning. The need for her was crushing, ugly, inescapable. All of that could be over forever.

Did he want it back? Perhaps more important, if this was a spell, what else had been done to him? The thought was more than unsettling. He did not feel, smell, or taste foreign magic on himself. But would he even know?

His musing was interrupted by Max.

"I need to talk to you," she said, looking first at Gregory and then at Thor and Alexander. "Is Tyler back yet?"

"Why do I get the feeling I am not going to like this one bit?" Thor asked.

Gregory looked up at her and then back down. He had finished his stew and scuffed the snow away from the dirt

beneath his feet. He took the spoon and dug an *anneau*—
a circle enclosing a five-pointed star enclosing a triangle.
At the center was a small dot. He dug it deep into the
hard soil. The spoon handle bent, and he straightened
it again. When he was satisfied, he touched the center
of the *anneau* with his forefinger and whispered a chant.
The *anneau* glowed bright green and then faded away.
But instantly, a bubble seemed to grow around the camp-
site. It was probably twenty feet in diameter and contained the tent and the fire pit, along with parts of the
hovels on either side. Within, the snow ceased to fall. Instead, it dusted the top of the invisible dome. Heat from
the fire stopped vanishing into the cold night and instead
began to warm the now-enclosed space.

Gregory gave Max a defiant look and stood, handing
his bowl back to the woman. "The stew was delicious."
He turned to Max. "I'll listen, but I plan to stay and
help these people before they die of an epidemic."

Max gave him a long look and nodded. "Everybody
has choices to make," she said, and Alexander's mouth
dropped open and then snapped shut.

Was she under some sort of spell, too? They needed
Gregory to fight Sterling.

"Did you bump your head?" Thor asked, clearly
thinking the same thing. "Or maybe someone gave you
a frontal lobotomy?"

Her mouth quirked, but the smile did not reach her
eyes. "Not that I noticed. Let's talk. Somewhere a little
bit private."

"You can use my house," Kara said, having now
joined them. "No one will bother you there. Help
yourself to the cider."

"Thanks."

"I'm going to go pull the Board together." Kara looked up at the snow collecting on top of the protective bubble and then at the woman Gregory had helped. "Okay if we meet here, Lena?"

Lena nodded. "Of course."

"Good deal. I'll be back shortly."

Max silently led the way back to Kara's shed. Tyler joined them just outside the door. The five of them could barely fit inside. Thor and Tyler sat on the bed, and Alexander stood at the foot. Max poured cider for everyone and sat down at the table. Gregory had found a knife and was carving an *anneau* symbol into the floor. Soon Kara would also have a magic bubble protecting her home.

"I take it you've got a plan?" asked Thor. The orange striped cat had appeared on his lap and was nuzzling furiously against his knuckles as he pet her.

"I do."

"We're going to hate this, aren't we?" Tyler asked, his lips pinching tight.

"A lot. But it is a plan, and it could work."

"Let's hear it," Thor said, casting Alexander a worried look.

Alexander merely leaned against the wall, listening.

"Thor and Alexander, you two go find Tris. Tyler's going to go get Giselle."

"And you?" Alexander asked, rubbing his finger over his upper lip. "What are you going to do?"

"I'm going to go become Benjamin Sterling's newest follower."

16

"ARE YOU FUCKING NUTS?" THOR EXCLAIMED, jumping to his feet. The cat squalled and dove under the bed. "You can't hide what you are. He'll kill you for sure, if the sun doesn't get to you first."

"He won't kill me fast. I should have enough time to find Kyle and the kids and then take them out through the abyss. As for the sun, I'm going to take the Amengohr amulet with me," Max said. "Takes the sun out of the equation."

The amulet made a Shadowblade invisible at night and allowed her to walk in the daylight without getting cooked extra-crispy.

"You will require far more food than usual to sustain it. You will not get anything like what you need from Sterling, if you get any food at all," Alexander pointed out.

He was bizarrely calm. A few hours ago, her announcement would have sent him into a raving frenzy. Max's heart spasmed, and tears burned in her eyes. She blinked them away as she tried to swallow the rock that rose in her throat. Tyler still hadn't said anything. His silence was unnerving.

"I don't intend to take long."

"And what if he prevents you from stepping into the abyss?" Gregory pointed out.

Max shrugged. "It's a chance I'm willing to take."

"You're nuttier than squirrel shit," Thor said, his Texan drawl becoming more pronounced. "He could swat you like a fly. It's suicide. Tell her," he said to Alexander, his blue eyes sharp with accusation. That Alexander should care more, that he should want to stop her.

Instead, Alexander said, "Is that the whole plan? You go in alone and do an abyss rescue?"

"I can't risk any other Blades and Spears," she said, matching his even tone. "I'll be the only one with the amulet."

"Giselle will not go for this at all," Gregory said.

"It's not like she's around to object. Phones stopped working. We don't have time to waste waiting to track her down."

"Waiting for her to spank your ass and tell you no, you mean." Tyler spoke at last.

Max smiled and cocked her head. "So we don't need to ask her. We already know what she'll say."

Tyler made a frustrated sound, then swung around and punched his fist through the wall.

"I'm not sure Kara was looking for a window," Max said.

"Fuck you," he said, his back to her. He pulled his hand back in. Blood streaked his arm from where the wood and metal had cut deep gouges. He turned to glare at Alexander. "Why aren't you trying to stop her? You know this is crazy, even if you have suddenly gone mental and forgotten how you feel about her. What's your fucking problem?"

Frustration sent Tyler's Blade to the killing edge. He was strong. Nearing to Prime, really. Max looked at Alexander, waiting for his reply.

"There is no use in trying to stop her," he pointed out. "She is going to do it with or without us. May as well try to figure out how to help her. Maybe she will not die." He said it offhandedly, like he was talking about a flat tire.

It was like a kick to the chest. The breath went out of Max, and it was all she could do not to fall onto the floor and curl up around the hurt. But then anger rescued her. So he was done with her. So what? It had to happen sooner or later. She'd known that all along. *Pull up your big girl panties, and deal with it,* she told herself.

"I would prefer that we had Spike or one of the Grims," Alexander added after a thoughtful moment.

"Well, we don't," Max said tartly. "What we have is a guy with too much power who hates witches and isn't afraid to torture people."

"It's a lousy plan," Thor said, but without force. He had already given in. "What are you going to do if he pulls magic on you? Or locks you up in a dungeon and you can't get out?"

"If I get into trouble I can't get out of, I expect you guys will get me out of it." She pushed her hair behind her ears. "I'm not crazy," she said quietly. "This is the best way to find Sterling before he kills Kyle and the kids. If I can't kill him, you will."

"Your cheese done slid off your cracker," Thor said.

He wiped a hand over his mouth, then nodded. "All right. I'm done arguing." He glanced at Alexander. "You going to say anything that doesn't sound like you've been possessed?"

Max noticed that Alexander twitched and stiffened, but then he shrugged and slid his gaze to her. "Be careful. Do not get killed."

"Yeah, because that would bother you a whole bunch," Max said. *Damn.* She wished she could pull the words back. She didn't want him knowing how much she hurt.

"Anything else you want to say, Tyler?" she asked.

"No," he said, not looking at her.

She stood. "All right. I'm out of here."

"Wait!"

Tyler grappled her close, wrapping her tightly in his arms. His throat worked, but no words came out. The tears she'd been holding slid down her cheeks. She wanted to promise him that she'd be back, that she wouldn't die. But she couldn't lie to him. Instead, she settled for, "See you when I see you."

With that, she plunged down through her inner fortress and out into the abyss.

THE AMULET WAS IN ALEXANDER'S APARTMENT. SHE dropped just inside the door and stood. Everything within was neat. The bed was made, and there were no decorations anywhere. It looked like he'd never lived there at all. Maybe that was the way he liked it. Once he moved on, he moved on all the way.

Still, he'd left the amulet there instead of bringing it to her apartment. She'd never questioned that choice, assuming that he'd get around to it eventually. But maybe it was a sign that he'd been holding something back against the time when he'd be done with her. She couldn't imagine ever being done with him.

Pain rolled through her like thunder across the great plains. It shook her, and she leaned back against the wall, her hands on her knees. She drew a harsh breath. How was she going to survive this pain?

Stupid, she told herself. It wasn't deadly. People didn't really die of broken hearts.

She forced herself to straighten and went to the closet. A few clothes hung inside, but there was little else there. Alexander had brought nothing from his previous covenstead and had little time to accumulate more. What he did have was in Max's apartment. She'd have to move it back. She'd do it now if she had the time, just to keep from having to watch him do it later.

Despite the fact that his room was warded so that it only opened to him, Alexander had made an effort to hide the amulet. Giselle had created the wards and could walk in anytime, and locks didn't hold Max. On top of that, Magpie occasionally had the power to walk through locked doors, whenever a true prophecy was riding her. Plus there was always the possibility that someone could break into Horngate and find it, someone like Sterling.

The amulet was hidden in the wall in the back corner beneath a shoe shelf. The shelf was screwed in, and Max resisted the urge to yank it out with brute force. Instead, she lay on her stomach and reached under. There was nothing to indicate that anything was hidden there. The magic that hid the compartment was gypsy smoke magic, and it left little trace of itself to be noticed. The spell had been laid by Alexander's sister Valery when she'd visited Horngate.

Max snorted to herself. *Visited.* As if it had been social and not a life-and-death fight against a rising Fury. The same fight that had ended with Niko's death and the two angels lying in the vault in magical comas.

She gritted her teeth against the memories and shoved them down.

Her fingers prodded into the corner, meeting dry, roughly finished stone. She felt along the corner, looking for the right spot. It was small. A keyhole, really. It took Max nearly a minute to find it. She poked her finger through the magic guarding it, clamping her teeth against the sudden surge of pain. It was like sticking her finger into an electric pencil sharpener. She could feel it shredding her skin and nipping at her bone.

Undaunted, she shoved deeper until her finger was completely inserted. The lock was a test of endurance. Even Alexander had to endure this particular annoyance when he wanted the amulet.

That was the point, he'd told Max when Valery had set it up. Even though the amulet provided Shadowblades with the miracle of walking safely during the day and invisibility at night, it took as much as it gave, quickly sapping the wearer's strength. It would be easy to wear it to death. Thus, it was necessary to make even him think twice before using it.

Several long minutes passed. Max held herself still, letting the locking spell have its way with her. Finally, the pain stopped, and there was a give. The stone around her finger melted away to reveal a hollow in the rock. She scooted forward, turning her hand up awkwardly beneath the shelf. The tips of her fingers brushed against soft cloth. She pinched it and twitched her hand, pulling it off the little shelf it rested on.

The bag fell into her hand, the amulet a heavy weight inside.

Max blew out a relieved breath and waited for the next part of the lock. It didn't disappoint. Something clasped her wrist, and she knew she wouldn't be able to wrestle free without destroying the amulet in the process.

Fire engulfed her hand. She could feel her skin bubbling and charring. Illusion. Maybe. Alexander had only pulled out the amulet once when Valery set the locks, and Max hadn't been there to see it. But she could smell her flesh cooking. It *could* be illusion, her mind insisted. But the pain was all too real.

She rested her head on the cool stone of the floor, closing her eyes and enduring. Finally, the flames stopped, but the tightness banding her wrist remained. Valery wasn't done. *Sadistic bitch.* Max smiled despite herself. The smoke witch was just following orders. Alexander had wanted something that was tough even for Max. He knew her ability to open locks and wanted to be sure that when she did, she really meant it.

Max steeled herself for whatever came next.

Nothing happened.

She frowned and jerked her arm. The bands holding her wrist compressed, and she felt her bones bending.

"Holy Mother of fuck," she muttered. "Are you going to pull my hand entirely off?"

But she knew that the last test was to get her hand

out. So she pulled, turning onto her side and bracing her feet against the wall. With every ounce of increased pressure, the banding on her hand tightened. Bones cracked, and her hand went numb. She couldn't even tell anymore if she was still holding the amulet.

Max gritted her teeth and yanked with all her might. Her shoulder popped out of its socket, and the magic band tightened more.

She yelped and relaxed for a second, trying to think. Brute force wasn't getting her out. Dropping the amulet might, but that wasn't an option.

Still, she'd never met a lock she couldn't break. Alexander wouldn't have let her come to get this if he didn't think she could figure it out.

So what should she do? And then it suddenly hit her. It was devious and perfect for protecting the amulet, and if Max was wrong, she was going to have to go through the whole process all over again.

One by one, she forced her fingers to uncurl from the amulet until it was lying flat on her palm. Then she slowly turned her hand over and pulled it out of the hole. It came easily. And so did the amulet. It remained in her palm, defying gravity.

Max stared at the soft gray felt bag, then collapsed back onto the floor, her eyes closing in relief.

A few seconds later, she sat up and examined her hand. None of it had been illusion. Her fingers were mangled, her wrist collapsed down to an inch diameter. And why not? Valery knew that she and Alexander healed quickly. And Alexander knew enough about the lock to minimize the damage to his bones getting the amulet out.

"Fucker could have warned me," Max murmured out loud, startling herself.

She heaved to her feet, shoving the amulet back in her pocket. She carried her arm against her stomach and left his room, crossing the hall to her own. Inside, she found socks and boots. She pulled on the socks awkwardly, using only one hand, then stuffed her feet into the boots without lacing them.

Max glanced down at her wrist. It was pushing outward, regaining its shape. Her mangled hand was also repairing itself. But she needed a good calorie boost to optimize her healing and to prepare herself for wearing the amulet. Which meant bearding Magpie in her kitchen den. And the witch was probably going to give her an earful.

She sighed. Better get it over with. She didn't have time to waste.

LUCKILY, THERE WEREN'T A LOT OF PEOPLE RUNNING around in the middle of the night. The Sunspears had gone to Missoula with Giselle, and everyone else was asleep. Magpie never seemed to sleep, though.

Max walked into the dining commons and found it empty, but the scent of cooking food permeated out into the hallway and made her stomach growl.

She went first to the pitcher of milk sitting on the buffet. It was magicked to keep it cold. The milk came straight from the cows and was thick with cream. Max poured a glass and drank it down, following it with two more. She felt the coolness spread through her stomach and chest. After pouring another, she went to push open one of the swinging doors into the kitchen.

She didn't go in. Except in the case of emergencies, one needed an invitation to Magpie's domain, or one paid the price in inedible food.

The witch stood at one of the stoves, her back to Max. Her hair fell down her back in a blue-black raven's wing, except for two streaks of white at her temples, which gave her the nickname of Magpie.

She turned and looked over her shoulder at Max, her sharp gaze taking in her wounded arm, before traveling back up to linger on her face.

"You look like shit."

"Feel like it. I need to calorie-load."

The witch's eyes narrowed. "What's going on?"

"If you don't mind, I'm in a hurry. I'll tell you, but I'd like to get started eating, and," Max said, lifting her arm, "I'm having a little trouble getting things one-handed."

Magpie pointed to a table with two chairs in the corner to the left of the door. "Sit there."

Max stared and then slowly pushed inside and sat gingerly. Magpie went to the refrigerator—now powered by magic, as was everything else in Horngate—and brought Max an entire bread pudding loaded with bourbon sauce. She gave her silverware and some more milk, then headed back to the stove, where she started cracking eggs for an omelet and tossed on four T-bone steaks.

"All right, tell me."

Max dug in and, between bites, told her everything that happened, even Alexander's sudden change. It was hard to keep secrets from Magpie, and there was no one else to tell.

Magpie listened without offering any judgment or advice, bringing more food as it was ready. It wasn't long before Max could use her hand again, albeit painfully. Her fingers were covered with new skin, and although they looked skeletal, the muscles were starting to bulk them up again. Her wrist was back to full size but weak. In another hour or so, it would be back to normal.

She forced herself to eat past the point of comfort. Her earlier healing had taken a lot out of her, even with Gregory's help, and she not only had to replenish herself, she also had to prepare to wear the amulet. It ate energy like a giant tapeworm.

"As plans go, it's not a good one," Magpie said, coming to sit opposite Max, her arms crossed, her pale brow furrowed.

"No, but it's the only one I've got. Unless you've got a suggestion?"

The witch shook her head. "Wish I did." She hesitated, then shook her head again. "I tried calling Giselle. Phones aren't working."

"Whatever blasted us in that trench must have shorted hers out, too." She shoved back from the table and stood up; her stomach bulged. "Thanks for the food. I'm going to check the angels before I go. Wish me luck."

Max started to push through the doors and stopped when Magpie spoke.

"How long can you wear that amulet before you die?"

"Longer than I'll need to," she said, and pushed on out of the kitchen.

Seeing the angels wouldn't take but a minute. It

might be the last time she had the chance, and she had some last words to tell them, just in case. Even if they didn't remember.

She stopped and turned back and swung the door open. Magpie was stacking dishes. She looked up. "Something else?"

"Just . . . thanks."

Magpie's brows rose. "For what?"

"For the food." Today and yesterday and the last thirty years' worth.

The witch frowned and put her hands on her hips. "What's that supposed to mean?"

"Don't get your panties in a wad," Max said, wishing she'd suppressed the urge to say anything. "It was a simple thank-you."

"No, it wasn't," Magpie snapped. "I'm not a fool, and I'll thank you not to treat me like one. Now, what exactly are you trying to say to me? Spit it out."

Max gave a little shake of her head. She should have known better. Soft. She was going soft, that was the trouble. Too much teenage-girl angst over Alexander. She needed to get hold of herself. She straightened her spine and rolled her head to crack her neck. Coolly, she met Magpie's exasperated gaze.

"You're right. I meant thanks. And good-bye."

With that, she spun about and jogged off to the angel vault.

17

"WHAT THE FUCK'S WRONG WITH YOU?" THOR demanded, staring at Alexander. "Three hours ago you were all over Max like a sixteen-year-old boy with his first hooker. Now you let her go off and put herself in Sterling's hands without batting an eyelash. Are you possessed?"

Alexander rubbed a finger over his lips. Then he shrugged, deciding the question deserved an honest answer. No, his *friend* deserved an honest answer. "I have considered the possibility."

Thor jerked back. "What?"

"It is a fact that my feelings for Max have changed startlingly, and I do not know why. It is well within the realm of possibility that I could have been bespelled without knowing it."

Thor dragged his fingers through his hair and then spun to look at Gregory. "What do you think?"

The witch stared at Alexander for a long moment, then shook his head. "I don't see anything. I can look more deeply, but I might not be able to detect it." He looked at Thor. Do you smell anything out of place on him?

Thor glared at Alexander and strode forward, sniffing around his neck and down his chest. He circled around him, then stepped back and shook his head. "Nothing out of the ordinary. You could use a shower," he added.

"I am not the only one," Alexander retorted. He cocked his head at Gregory. "Check me out."

"Turn around."

Alexander turned to face the stove. The witch put his hands on Alexander's shoulders, and green magic flared brightly. It slid into his flesh like curling scalpels. He stiffened, and his Prime roared awake, the tiny shack swelling with his power.

"Easy," Gregory muttered, his fingers clenching tighter.

"I did not know you were going to try to kill me," Alexander said through clenched teeth, his body rigid.

"It's just a perk," the witch said dryly. "Besides, you're a big boy. You can handle it."

"Remember that when I drop-kick your ass across the city."

The magic progressed from the top of Alexander's head to his feet, slicing him thin as it searched for some sort of geas. His breath came short, and he braced his legs wide, forcing himself to hold still. Finally, Gregory stepped back, his magic fading. He staggered, and Tyler caught him and helped him into a chair.

"Get me some of the cider, would you?" Gregory asked. Thor complied, and Gregory sipped gratefully.

"What did you find?" Alexander asked.

"Nothing that shouldn't be there."

"But there could be something you don't see, right?" Thor pushed.

"That's what I said." He scratched the stubble on his jaw. "Though something that powerful would take some time to develop and set. It's pretty specific to you—making you not care about Max. Plus, it came on you pretty sudden."

"But it's not impossible," Thor said. "He went to get Max clothes from the truck. He was alone then. Somebody could have gotten to him then, right?"

Or maybe when Sterling had ripped him from his body and dangled him at the River Market. Alexander mentioned the possibility.

"Maybe. But why go after your bond with Max?" Gregory shook his head. "It's just as likely that this is your own doing. You could very well be shutting yourself down to protect yourself. But Thor and Tyler should keep an eye on you anyway. If this is a spell, who knows what else was done to you?"

"Maybe he'll grow horns and a tail and baa like a goat," Thor said darkly.

"Shut up," Alexander said. His Prime was still on edge, and so was he. Part of him liked not feeling anything for Max, but part of him missed that intensity, the joy of being with her, and even the fury and pain of fearing for her life. Had he shut those feelings down himself? If so, could he bring them back? Or did he want to keep his newfound freedom?

"Whatever has happened to me, it does not change the fact that we have a job to do," he said, giving himself a little shake to clear the vestiges of pain from his body.

Thor stared broodingly at him, his arms folded, and then nodded. "All right. We can shelve it for now, but something's not right with you."

Alexander shrugged. "We have our orders. Max wants us to find Tris."

"I'm going to find Giselle now," Tyler announced. He had been watching Alexander's testing in brooding silence. "I'll let her know what Max has planned."

He slipped out the door before anyone could reply.

"You know, the big hole in Max's plan is how everyone is going to find her once she finds Sterling," Gregory said slowly.

His two companions stared at him; then realization slowly dawned.

"She wouldn't," Thor said.

"She would," Alexander replied. "She would make sure we were all going to be safe, and then she would go after Sterling herself." That should have made him feel . . . something.

"I can't believe we didn't see this coming." Thor's glare spoke volumes. The old Alexander, the one who cared about Max, *would have* seen it.

"Nothing we can do about it now. We should do what she told us to."

"That's it? That's all you've got? You ought to be going ballistic."

Alexander ignored that. "We need to find Tris and make sure she, Doris, and Geoff are safe."

Thor blew out an exasperated breath. "Fine. How are we going to do that?"

"We go look."

"Oh. Brilliant. Why didn't I think of that?"

"I'm staying here," Gregory declared, swigging down the rest of his cider and standing. His eyes were bloodshot and sunken. He was clearly running on fumes.

Alexander scowled at him. He did not want to leave Thor to watchdog Gregory, but the witch was likely to kill himself trying to heal everyone. That could not be allowed.

He took a breath, but before he could speak, Gregory interrupted. "No, Thor is going with you. People are in trouble, and even if I went with you, I'd only slow you down. I'm not stupid. I'm not going to kill myself. I'll make sure they don't have anyone in immediate danger, and then I'll rest and start again when I'm fresher. I'll stay until things are handled. You know where to find me if you really need me."

"And if they decide they don't want a witch in their midst?" Alexander asked, tapping his fingers against his thigh.

"I'll protect myself."

Thor snorted. "You'll get to work, and they'll bash you in the head. Or shoot you. Slit your throat. Strangle you . . ."

"Enough," Gregory said with a dry chuckle. "I'll set up a ward circle, and I'm sure Kara will assign me guards if you ask nicely. Lena will likely do it no matter how you ask. She seems fond of me."

"I don't like it," Thor said.

"Got anything better?" Alexander said. "We cannot haul him out of here against his will. You either come with me or stay here and guard Gregory. Besides, Max said it herself—everybody has choices to make. She knew what Gregory planned and was not going to fight him on it."

"That's because she was planning to commit suicide," Thor said. He scraped his teeth over his lower lip, leaving white tracks against his skin. Finally, he nodded. "Let's talk to Kara, then." He eyed Gregory balefully. "You even try to die, I'll come back and rip your guts out myself. And if you do die, I swear I'll drag you out of whatever hell you've fallen into and make you suffer so much more than you can ever imagine."

Gregory was taken aback. "I didn't know you cared so much."

"I don't," Thor snapped. "But this covenstead means a lot to me. We can't afford to lose you."

"Then let us get going," Alexander said. He brought up the rear, setting a hand on Thor's shoulder and squeezing. The other man shrugged him away and stalked out of the shed.

Alexander understood Thor's feelings all too well. They had both been turned into Shadowblades by Selange. She was short-tempered, vicious, ruthless, and capricious. She had not cared about the health or safety of anyone within her covenstead, except as their illness or loss might lessen her power and prestige. Because of Max, both he and Thor had escaped her covenstead and been claimed by Giselle and Horngate. Both Blades would fight until death to protect their new home.

They soon found Kara at Lena's tent. A group of people had gathered within the magical bubble that Gregory had created. Snow rested on top of it like frosting on a cupcake. Within, the ground was turning soggy with the increasing warmth. Many had stripped off their heavy coats.

The group fell silent as the three Horngaters approached. The few who'd been sitting stood. About two-thirds of them were men, the rest women. They ranged from young to grizzled, and none of them looked all that happy. Lena was downright furious. Her cheeks were flagged red, and the muscle in her jaw was throbbing with fury.

The three stepped through the bubble into the warm air. Thor and Alexander flanked Gregory, slightly in front of him. The others fell back a step at the palpable threat that radiated from them. Everyone except for Lena and Kara. Lena smiled at them, her gaze fixing on Gregory with real warmth. Alexander approved. She might not trust magic, but she knew goodness when she saw it, and she did not let his being a witch interfere with her gratitude.

"Thanks for coming back," she said, then looked around the circle. "*We* appreciate your willingness to help us."

One of Gregory's brows quirked up, but he did not challenge the obvious lie. Before he could speak, Alexander interrupted.

"Gregory is willing to stay and heal your people," he said, eyes gliding around the circle, meeting each person's gaze in turn. "But you must guarantee his safety. You must give him a place to sleep and feed him. He will not have the strength to take care of everyone at once." He narrowed his attention on Lena and Kara. "You must make sure he does not overdo it. He is an idiot and will give all he has."

Lena frowned at Gregory and nodded. Alexander almost felt sorry for the witch. Lena was tough as rusty nails, and it was clear she was going to take personal charge of Gregory. Gratitude was a double-edged sword.

"I still don't like this," rumbled a barrel-chested man with a thick blond beard. His eyes were steel-blue, and he carried a shotgun in the crook of his arm.

"Don't have to like it, Marty," said another man. He was short, with a round belly, a thick mustache, and thinning hair. "You've been outvoted, so shut up, do what you're asked, and don't cause trouble."

"Witches are evil," someone muttered. Alexander couldn't tell who.

"I don't know that witches are any more evil than anybody else," Kara said. "What I do know is that so far, these folks have done nothing but help us, and I for one am not going to look a gift horse in the mouth. We've got sick people, and this man—this witch—can help them. Any of you want to count on God for curing your families, you go on and keep praying. But I think God has sent us our help, and he's standing right in front of us. Your other choice is Benjamin Sterling, and I sure as hell don't want any part of him."

Clearly, Kara had already raised this point before, and it was having its intended effect. No one answered, and her mouth tightened in a flat grin. She looked at Alexander. "We'll take care of him. You have my word."

He nodded. He would have to trust her. "Then we will leave him in your hands. Do not let him do much more before he rests."

Gregory made a disgusted sound. "I am not four years old."

"Doesn't mean you don't need a keeper," Thor said from his other side.

"You two be careful, whatever you're up to," Kara said.

"That word is not actually in our vocabulary," Alexander said dryly, and Thor snorted.

"Then I wish you luck," she said, and reached out to shake their hands. "Gregory will be here when you get back."

"Then we will be on our way." Alexander glanced at the witch. "Do not be stupid."

"You're one to talk," the witch retorted, then held out his hand. "May the Spirits guard you and bring you safely home."

"See you when we see you," Alexander said after shaking hands. "Watch your back."

With that, he and Thor started off on the hunt.

"HOW CAN YOU FEEL NOTHING?" THOR ASKED, FINALLY breaking the silence of the last twenty minutes. He had spent a good fifteen minutes before that trying to dig more out of Alexander than the fact that his feelings for Max had just suddenly shut down.

The snow was falling in a thick curtain, making it almost impossible to see more than a few feet ahead. It piled up to mid-thigh, deeper where it had drifted. It brought with it a muffling silence that seemed to go on forever.

Thor and Alexander slogged through it in bounding leaps. They had decided to head down to Highway 93 where it entered town and try to pick up the trail there.

"You've been insane about Max practically since you met her. No one stops feeling that kind of emotion just like that—" He snapped his fingers. "So what is really going on? And this time, the truth, if you can manage it."

"I told you. Something snapped, and I felt nothing. I looked into her eyes and realized nothing with her would ever change. It is self-preservation. If I do not cut her off, I will certainly go rabid."

"Bullcrap. That's the most chickenshit thing I've ever heard in my life, and if there's one thing I know for sure, you aren't a coward. There must be something else."

Alexander rubbed a hand across the top of his head, knocking away the snow that had accumulated. This conversation was getting old, and he had no good answers. "I told you I thought it could be a spell."

"But it isn't."

"Maybe. But Gregory said himself he might not be able to detect it. You should be careful. If something changed how I feel about Max, it could affect me in other ways, too. Watch your back with me."

Thor stopped dead in the middle of the street and stared at him. "You are taking this awfully well. The Alexander I know would be pissed to find out he might be under a spell. He'd be chewing up the scenery looking for answers."

Alexander rubbed a hand over his head again. "I should be angry, I know. But right now, the sheer relief from all that torture is . . . amazing."

"Torture?" Thor repeated skeptically. "You've been happier than a fox in a henhouse since you've been with Max."

"Have I? There have certainly been some happy moments, but—" He shook his head. "The rest has been nothing but fear and worry and desperation."

"So? You aren't willing to suffer a little bit for the love of your life? Your soul mate?"

Alexander laughed. "You sound as naive as a sixteen-year-old girl."

Thor snarled. "That doesn't make me wrong. And I notice you don't deny you love her."

"Maybe I do. Or did. But if so, it is gone," Alexander said. "Now, can we get back to work? We still have a ways to go, and the trail is buried under a couple feet of snow."

"Fine. But this isn't over. I'm not going to watch my best friend throw away something this good without a fight. Women like Max only come along once in a lifetime."

Alexander merely shrugged and started off again. He felt whole and alive. Thor might think he had lost something important, but the truth was, he felt strong and focused in ways he had not for a long time, and he liked it.

THEY PICKED UP THE TRAIL NOT FAR FROM WHERE HIGH-way 93 crossed the river. The Suburban was turned sideways in the road. The windows were shattered, and the doors were riddled with bullet holes. Snow was piled on the seats and floorboards. There were no bodies or blood.

"What the hell happened?" Thor asked, swiping his hand over the side of the truck to clear the snow. He examined the bullet holes.

Alexander dug down to the front passenger tire. The rubber was shredded. The same on the driver's side. "They were ambushed. Someone set up a spike strip, and they ran right over it."

"How did they know they were even coming?"

"Probably did not matter. Anybody driving was worth going after. The question is, did our people get away, or were they taken?"

Both Blades dug inside the truck to get a clear scent of the five people who had been inside. Tris, Doris Lydman, and Geoff Brewer were familiar. The last two—the ones Max had called Liam and Bambi—smelled like sweat, gun oil, and the outdoors.

The truck had been torn apart, and everything possibly valuable had been taken. The glove compartment hung open. The seats had been shredded, and the backseat had been ripped out. Underneath it, the weapons locker was empty. It took someone from Horngate to open the wards, which meant that Tris and her companions were well armed. According to Max, Liam and Bambi would know what to do with the weapons. At least some of them. The magical items would likely confuse them. But at least they had taken everything.

"So where did they go?" Alexander pondered aloud, turning to examine the terrain, although the thick snow made that nearly impossible. He was not that familiar with Missoula. Neither was Thor. They had only moved to Horngate a few months ago, and they had had little reason to come to Missoula during that time.

He remembered that there was a Walmart just up on the right, and on the left was a country club with a golf course and some stores. Farther south behind the truck was a storage place. It perched right on the riverbank. Across Highway 93 from it was a residential area.

He immediately discounted the latter. Anybody still

living in the houses would not be interested in this kind of ambush. They would be loners just working on survival, and this had taken some organization. Just getting the spike strip would call for a police connection, not to mention the amount of guns and ammunition. Anyone living in that residential area would be saving their ammo to protect themselves and hunt food.

But the other three places could house groups of people, particularly the Walmart. Most of the bullet holes were on that side of the truck, which could mean that was where the attackers had come from. Either way, the Horngate group would not have run into the hail of fire. Which meant they had headed for the storage unit, the country club, or the strip mall.

The soldiers would have taken charge, which meant they would have likely headed out to the golf course and turned north. There was a better chance of losing pursuers that way.

"I figure the golf course is the best bet," Alexander told Thor.

"Agreed. But finding them is going to be a bitch. I wish we had one of the Grims. I bet they could sniff out a mouse in a blizzard."

"Maybe we will get lucky. The question is, where is Giselle? She and the other Blades were coming in after Tris. They could not have missed seeing the truck. So what happened to them?"

18

MAX ENTERED THE ANGEL VAULT. XAPHAN'S IRI-descent black wings continued to burn with blue and purple flames. They had scorched the rock slab he lay on, and little stalactites hung down around the edges where the heat had melted the stone. The sheet that had covered him was gone, and he was dusted with a layer of fine ash from its destruction. She touched his ankle. He felt warm. She touched Tutresiel. He did, too.

She went to the top of the table by Xaphan's head. His wings were folded around his sides, the feathers extending nearly to his heels. The tops of his wings curved up nearly as high as his head on either side.

Max hesitated. Why was she doing this? It wasn't like either of them could hear or would care what she said. She ought to be saying things to her Blades. But they weren't there, and somehow she needed to talk to the angels.

"So stop wasting time, already," she muttered to herself. She leaned over Xaphan, and the flames from his wings heated her skin. Blisters bubbled on her cheek and forehead. She ignored them, leaning as close as she could to his ear.

"If it weren't for me, you wouldn't be half dead right now. I'm sorry. I owe you big-time, and I don't think I'm going to be able to pay you back. If I don't make it back, know that I'll miss you."

She pressed a kiss to his forehead and straightened up. It wasn't much. It didn't begin to capture what she really wanted to say. But she needed to say it all the same.

She went to stand beside Tutresiel. Her heart hurt looking at him. He was rude, capricious, acerbic, and sometimes vicious. He was also her friend. She didn't know why. But somehow he had decided he liked her, and he didn't like anybody. One thing was certain: he knew her. He understood her and didn't get irritated because she was herself. Not like just about everyone else in her life. Especially Alexander. She had no doubt that that was why he'd given up on her. Too much hurt. But Tutresiel would never give up on her. And she wasn't about to give up on him.

She bent close to his ear, her hand splaying across the hard muscles of his too-cold chest.

"Wake up, you bastard," she whispered. And waited for a few seconds. Nothing. She hadn't really thought anything would happen. But hope springs eternal and all that crap. Her hand curled into a ball on his chest.

"I'm in some trouble again. Might not make it back. I know I don't have to tell you to take care of yourself. I just wanted to tell you one last thing, Kitten. I know how much you hate hearing it, but I like you. I consider you a friend. I even trust you. Remember that, would you?"

She shifted and brushed her lips against his, then

straightened. "Well, you must be far gone, because if anything would make you open your mouth and tell me to shove it up my ass, that would have done it." Sadness coiled around her. She would miss him. She *did* miss him.

Now for just one more thing. She closed her eyes and reached out for Spike. She could never tell if the Calopus could hear her or if Spike could just pluck thoughts from Max's mind whenever she felt like it. It didn't hurt to try to send a message.

There were no words. Just the feelings she'd developed for the animal. Affection, joy, love, trust, loneliness. She missed the beast. They had formed a bond as close as she had with Tyler or Thor or Tutresiel. Even Niko.

Max shook away the thought. It was time to go. She glanced once more at the angels. *Will I ever see them again?*

She couldn't shake the feeling that she might not be coming back. Maybe it was that everything seemed to be falling apart, crumbling away beneath her feet. Everyone she cared about seemed to be vanishing, and every time she grabbed for them, she ended up clawing through smoke.

"Enough," she told herself, the word echoing loudly in the small chamber. She was feeling sorry for herself. She needed to get her shit together and get going.

She was just starting to drop into her fortress and step through the abyss when a curl of red smoke rose from the basin of milky water.

It flowed through the air, sketching out a shape. First eyes, then a head with a nose and a mouth, then a body. Behind it formed wings in a parody of the two angels. Max's body tightened with fury.

"Show your face, Sterling," she demanded. "What do you want?"

The eyes were vacant-looking, lacking irises. They were merely the outer oval shape. Still, Max didn't think for a second that the thing was blind.

It darted forward, and Max leaped back. It stopped where she had been, its mouth smiling. It had no teeth or tongue.

"I am Justice," it said in a low, musical voice that sent prickles along Max's skin.

"Justice? For what? For who? You're delusional, Sterling. You're more evil than I could ever hope to be."

The face shifted into Benjamin Sterling's, then melted back into the stick-figure look. It smiled, savage and pitiless.

"I will make you pay. This den of witches, but most of all you. I know what you did. I came for you, for all of you. You will pay for your hubris."

Max frowned. "I'm afraid I don't know what you're talking about," she said. "Hubris? That's a little melodramatic, don't you think?"

Sterling's little doll gave a shrug, and the red lines of its body shivered and hardened again. "Call it what you like. Arrogance. Insolence. Impudence. You have committed your crime, and I will have justice."

"So what am I supposed to have done to you?"

"You broke the law. *You* are not allowed."

The emphasis on "you" made Max wonder. This didn't seem like Sterling. The words were wrong. He was more fire and brimstone. This seemed different. "You aren't Sterling, are you?" she asked cautiously.

"He is my puppet. Or perhaps I am his." The creature smiled.

"I don't understand."

"You will." Its arm jetted out faster than her eye could follow. Red smoke wound around her, and pain cut into her stomach, between her breasts, and up to her neck. She felt blood soaking into her shirt, and bits of it fell to the floor in rags, the rest of the cloth hanging in shreds from her shoulders.

She looked down at herself. A complex pattern had been carved on her skin. There were strange letters and symbols overlapping in what looked like an Egyptian cartouche, although the writing was nothing like Egyptian hieroglyphics. It was flowing and snaky and jagged and harsh. The design bled and did not heal.

When the thing spoke again, it was only inches from her face. Max jerked her head up, forcing herself not to fall back.

"That is my seal. When you come, they will know you, and you may pass without question. Do not take long, or I will kill the ones you seek."

"I'll be coming," Max said, finding her voice. "But you aren't going to win."

The creature tipped its head. "And who will stop me?" It spread its red wings. "Not the angels," it whispered, sweeping up into the air to hover over first Tutresiel and then Xaphan. "For you have laid them low, and even I cannot easily wake them."

It focused on her again, its body and wings pulling inward until all that was left was the face surrounded by a red nimbus of smoke. Its hatred boiled in the room.

"Know this: when I am done, you and every spirit

you care for will be destroyed. Their souls will be torn to shreds and scattered across worlds and time." With that, the face collapsed. The air continued to resonate, and dust sifted down from the ceiling. The cloud of red smoke continued to hover, then started to expand. It smelled like Divine magic. But there was something not quite right about it, as if it was mixed with something else. Max frowned. She needed to know what that creature was.

The smoke started to seethe and roil, like a bloody storm caught in a cauldron. It pushed outward until it swallowed the fountain, the angels, and Simon. Max stepped back against the door. It didn't budge. The fucker had locked it somehow.

The cloud was only a few feet away and closing fast on the walls. Before Max could even blink, it sprang outward, filling the entire vault. Something like a Taser blast zapped through her body. Every hair on her body stood on end, and she shook violently, her head snapping back and forth. But unlike a Taser blast, it didn't stop, and Max was pretty sure it wouldn't before she dropped dead.

The only way out was the abyss. If she could concentrate enough to pull herself through.

She dove down inside herself, focusing hard on the pain. She let it fill her, offering it no resistance. As the pain took her, her mind separated. It was a trick she'd learned at Giselle's hands, during years of torture. Let the pain be. Accept it. Let your mind go wherever it has to in order to stay sane. Only Max didn't let herself go too far. Once she could think, she dropped into the fortress like a stone off a cliff and pulled herself into the abyss.

She collected herself inside the crystal darkness. Ribbons of magic glowed far away, and bursts of wild magic drifted in swarms and schools. She glanced again at the creature's seal. It continued to bleed. She bit her lip. That wasn't good. She was going to need a constant supply of calories to keep herself going if it didn't stop. Adding the Amengohr amulet on top of that meant she would have precious little time to find Kyle and the kids.

Not that the creature planned to let her. It had Kyle. Somehow it was tied up with Benjamin Sterling. Was it the power behind the throne? A demon that Sterling had harnessed? If so, what was Sterling? A sorcerer? He would have to be incredibly strong to control a demon as powerful as this creature. It had slipped through Horngate's wards like they weren't there. Several times. Giselle had barely been able to beat it off using the nearly unlimited power of the Fury Seed. And it had relit Xaphan's wings. It was powerful, so Sterling had to be even more so. Unless Sterling was its puppet.

Either way, how the hell was Max going to defeat the two of them together?

The key was to figure out just what this creature thought she had done and then figure out how to appease it. Maybe she could persuade it to take its mood out on her and leave Horngate and the rest of her family alone.

If she couldn't figure out how to kill it first. Or disable it somehow.

She grimaced. It would probably be easier to drink the ocean. All the same, it wasn't like she had a choice. Or time to spare.

Collecting herself, she picked her destination and stepped out of the abyss.

19

THOR AND ALEXANDER TRUDGED SLOWLY IN A broad zigzagging pattern across the golf course. They had begun at the country-club parking lot, hoping that they would cross Tris's trail. The snow was blinding, and the dips and hills of the course made for fifteen-foot snowdrifts, sometimes even deeper.

They were having precious little luck. There simply was nothing to smell. Suddenly, Thor gave a shout. Alexander slogged through the snow toward Thor's voice. He dropped down into a sand trap, the snow coming up to his waist. He swore and pushed forward. Strong as he was, the soft snow was as close to quicksand as Montana could make, and the going was very slow. How had Tris and her companions made it? The snow wouldn't have been quite as deep, but it would still have been treacherous.

"Over here!" Thor called again, and Alexander closed the distance between them.

The blond Blade was soaking wet, and snow clung to him like cotton candy. He stood in a copse where the snow was only knee-deep. His cheeks were flushed rosy, and he was smiling.

"They blazed a trail for us. Tris must've figured some-one would come bird-dogging her and didn't want us getting lost."

Alexander caught the scent now. Blood. There was a patch of it on the tree about shoulder height. It was not much bigger than a quarter, as if someone had cut a finger and purposefully smeared it there.

"Look for more," he ordered.

The two men found three more patches leading in a line. They pointed back toward Reserve Street.

They hiked across the golf course, following the di-rection of the blood. In each copse they passed, they found another set of blood patches. There were two different donors. Alexander did not recognize either one. They had to be the soldiers, Liam and Bambi. At least they weren't stupid.

They crossed Post Siding Road into the other half of the golf course. The small company of Horngaters had angled east. They kept to the golf course, no doubt figuring it was safer than encountering the people who might be inhabiting the strip mall that ran beside it.

"They can't have gotten much farther," Thor said. "There are five of them. Two are middle-aged women and one a middle-aged man. They can't have passed here that long ago. They only had a few hours' head start on us, and I know we covered that ground a hell of a lot faster than they could have."

Alexander nodded. He had come to the same conclu-sion. "I wish this damned snow would stop," he said.

"No, you don't," Thor said. "Snow works more for us than against us. The enemy can't see us or smell us. They're likely hunkered down and don't think we'll come for them until this lets up."

It made sense.

"So where would they go?" Thor mused.

"If it were me, I would head for somewhere quiet. A house, maybe. A lot of them are deserted, but with two armed and trained men, they could take someplace where people were living. They could get information, dry clothes, and whatever else they needed."

Thor nodded. "So which house?"

"There is not much on this side of Reserve for a while, but across the street behind the businesses is a big neighborhood. That is the most likely place."

They crossed Reserve near a gutted jewelry store. Its windows were broken out, and a lot of its wood had been peeled away before someone set fire to it. Now it was just a shell. Alexander could smell cooking meat, and his mouth watered. He reached into his vest pocket and took out a power bar. He tore it open and ate it, then two more in quick succession. That was all he had. Max had eaten the rest. Thor followed suit. Slogging through the snow on the golf course had taken a lot of energy out of both of them.

The neighborhood was a long triangular wedge between Reserve Street and the mall. The two Blades started at the closest point and methodically zigzagged along the streets, looking for the blood trail or some other sign that the Horngate group was nearby.

"Wait," Alexander said, putting a hand up. It was the faintest whiff of the two soldiers. Faint, but he had no doubts. "This way."

He followed the scent for a block along the street.

He turned through a yard and tripped. He turned his fall into a roll.

"Tree stump," Thor said in a low voice. "Cut recently."

"Easy firewood," Alexander said, turning back to find the scent trail. He did not bother brushing himself off. The snow stuck to him, lending him camouflage in the ghost night.

They passed between two houses. On the other side was the one they were looking for. It was neatly tucked away, with a long driveway leading out to the road. A large yard surrounded it on three sides, giving it an air of privacy. Smoke came from its chimney, and with it the delicious scent of cooking meat.

"Do we knock?" Thor asked.

"It is probably a good way to get shot," Alexander said. "I would rather go in quietly. Check the perimeter, and see if you can find a good way inside."

Thor went left, and Alexander went right. There was a porch along the front of the house, but all of the windows on the bottom floor were covered with corrugated steel. Another piece had been hung over the front door as extra protection. Alexander continued around to the back. There was a deck on the upper floor. Thor stood beneath it.

"The place is sealed tight. Best chance is up there. It's at the back of the house. They might not hear us breaking the lock."

The little house backed up on a two-story duplex. The place looked deserted. Alexander climbed up to the second floor across from the deck and jumped over. The heavy blanket of snow on the deck muffled his landing. A moment later, Thor joined him.

A corrugated-steel door covered the sliding glass doors. There was no latch on the outside, and the metal door was fastened tightly. Even the hinges were inside, out of reach. There was no room for so much as a fingertip between the wall of the house and the steel.

"Right about now, it would be handy to have Max here. She could use that lockpicking voodoo of hers and just walk on in, no fuss, no muss," Thor mused.

Alexander knew his friend said it to needle him. It worked. He might not feel emotionally connected with her anymore, but he *was* worried. Where was she? Had she gotten herself captured yet?

"I guess we will have to do it the old-fashioned way," Alexander said to Thor.

"Which would be?"

"Brute strength and ingenuity." He took out a knife and wedged the tip under the steel. He hammered the pommel with the palm of his hand, driving it under with a screech of metal that made him wince. He did the same lower down, giving them two levers to pry open the door.

"Careful not to break the knives," he cautioned as Thor readied himself to pull up on the two hilts. "We only need enough room to get a grip underneath."

A moment later, Alexander was able to slide his fingers beneath the steel. He pulled it back. It was anchored in place by three sliding locks, the kind found in horse stalls. He tugged, and the first one broke away from the wood where it was fastened. He moved his hands down and repeated the process on the next two. The door swung free at last, exposing another door, this one made of wood with insulation stapled to it.

It did not take much to push it open, the wood splintering away from the lock. Inside was the master bedroom. The bed was mounded with blankets to keep out the cold. Homemade oil lamps in canning jars sat on the nightstands and the dresser. A bathroom connected to the room on one side. The door was closed, but Alexander could smell the stench of waste. No doubt they had to collect it and dump it. Plumbing had failed when the electricity did.

Thor swung the two panels shut behind them. The inner door wanted to hang open. He hooked his foot around the bench at the foot of the bed and pulled it over to hold it closed.

Alexander resheathed one of the knives, keeping the other in his hand. The two padded softly out into the hallway. Alexander could smell the five Horngate folks and three others.

They edged to the top of the stairs. The vantage point showed them the front door and a few feet of tiled hallway off to the right. Thor lifted a questioning brow at Alexander. He understood the question. Try a silent approach down the stairs and hope they were not immediately seen or heard, or jump down into the foyer and go for a blitz attack, hoping they could take out any enemies before they could react?

Alexander put a finger across his lips and pointed down the stairs. With any luck, the Horngaters had control of the situation. If not, he did not want to get them shot.

He went down first, testing each step to avoid squeaking. Midway down, he crouched behind the banister. Opposite him was a broad archway into a living room. A fire was roaring in the fireplace, and a number of people were gathered around it. Tris was standing beside Geoff and looking down at someone in an overstuffed chair. Doris was sitting in a corner of the couch. It had been pulled close to the fire. She was wrapped up in a heavy comforter and drinking some sort of soup, by the smell of it.

Alexander could not see the two soldiers. They were out of sight behind the wall or in another room.

"Where would this Sterling take them?" Tris was asking. "Please," she added, her voice choking. Geoff Brewer put an arm around her shoulder. Both stared intently down into the chair.

A man's weary voice replied. "I just don't know. Things have really split apart. It's been all I can do to keep the kids safe and fed and warm. Please. Don't hurt them."

Tris threw up her hands in exasperation. "I told you. We aren't here to hurt you or your family. We just need some clothes, a place to warm up, a little food, and some information."

Thor crept down to join Alexander.

"Well?" he whispered, so softly that nobody but Alexander might hear him.

Alexander jerked his head and went to the bottom of the stairs, crossing to stand just outside the door. He crouched down and peered into the room. One of the soldiers was within. He looked to be in his mid-thirties, with short copper-colored hair and a ruddy face. He was standing by a window, the interior wood-and-insulation door wide open. He alternated between watching the group by the fire and looking outside through a peephole drilled into the steel. He held a .45 at the ready.

Alexander looked over his shoulder at Thor. He held up one finger and pointed through the wall at the window.

Thor's brows went up in a silent question. *Where's the other one?*

Alexander shrugged, then straightened. There was no point wasting any more time. The two soldiers were on Horngate's side. Hopefully they would not shoot first and ask questions later.

Alexander edged to the doorway and knocked on the wall. Everyone jerked and stared. The soldier at the window brought his gun level, sighting in on Alexander's chest. Thor stepped around him to fill up the rest of the doorway.

"It's okay, Liam," Tris said, staring at the two Blades with a combination of relief and nervousness. "They belong to us. The dark one is Alexander, and the other is Thor," she said. "They are Shadowblades like Max."

The soldier came forward, extending a hand. "Name's Liam."

The two Blades shook.

"Max mentioned you," Alexander said.

"Is she here, too?" Tris asked, trying to see behind them.

Alexander shook his head. "No."

Something in the way he said it made her frown. She stared hard at him. She did not look that much like Max, except for that tough-as-nails attitude. Her hair was long, the gold-blond strands graying. She wore it in a braid down her back. She was in her forties now; her slender body had turned soft around the middle, and her dark eyes were bracketed with crow's feet.

"Have you found Kyle and the kids?" she asked.

Alexander shook his head. "Not yet."

She scowled. "Then what are you doing *here*?"

"Finding you," he said mildly, his gaze skewering her. "It seems Max had some concerns about your safety."

She flushed. "I wasn't going to sit on my hands waiting. That bastard is going to kill them. He said he would torture them. We all saw what he was capable of."

Alexander did not answer. His gaze darted behind her, where another door had swung quietly open. The man standing there could only be Bambi. His black hair was cut short, and stubble darkened his jaw. His gray eyes were flat as they flicked across the scene. His .45 was half raised.

"What's going on?" he asked Liam.

"Max sent some company," came the gravelly reply.

Bambi lowered his gun. "So the blood trail worked."

Thor nodded. "Thanks for that. We would've wasted a lot more time without it." He looked at Tris, who flushed again.

"What now?" Geoff asked. He still had his arm around Tris.

"Now we have to get you safe and then get back to finding your kids."

Doris Lydman made a sniffling sound, then swallowed, and when she spoke, her voice was surprisingly strong and stubborn. "We aren't going back. We're going to keep looking until we find them."

Alexander left the doorway and went to stand beside the couch. "You are not equipped to deal with what you will find," he told them all flatly. "You are a handicap to us. If we have to worry about you, we will not be able to do all that we could to find your kids."

"Should listen to him," said the man in the chair. "Benjamin Sterling is bad news."

Alexander examined him. He looked to be around fifty years old. A bald spot formed a small island in his shaggy brown hair. He had a thick beard, and his hands were scabbed and scarred. He was well used to using them.

"What do you know about him?" Alexander asked. "And what do we call you?"

"Name's Powell," he said, shoving to his feet. He went to stare down at the fire, one hand on the mantel, the other fisting at his side. His throat worked, and after a few moments, he spoke.

"They're a cult, plain and simple. They showed up about the time the electricity failed. One day they didn't exist, and the next it seemed they were everywhere. Benjamin Sterling claimed to be the hand of God. He was going around healing people and telling them he was the only way to find salvation. A lot of people believed him. And why not? He didn't give 'em much of a choice. Follow him, and get food, shelter, clothes, and a key to heaven. Don't, and he might just kill you or take everything you've got."

"But you didn't join."

He laughed without humor. "Not me. I don't cotton to herd thinking. I figure I'll find my own way into heaven or hell without any help from some slick preacher. If either one even exists." He grimaced. "Mind you, my wife had other ideas. She was too scared to stick it out here with me. Couldn't convince her we could make it, either. She tried taking the kids, but they—"

He broke off, glancing at Bambi, who remained in

the doorway. The soldier nodded assurance. The older man turned to look at Alexander.

"My kids had more faith in me. In us. I told Christina she could go, and fine, but if she tried to get them to come back and take us, we'd disappear, and she'd never see us again. She loves us. She's just scared, like I said. So she left, and them Standers haven't been back. For now."

He straightened, turning his back on the fire to continue his story. "I made sure this house was as tight as I could make it. I laid in a supply of wood, and I've been out hunting and putting away all the meat I can for winter. I've got some canned vegetables and beans and the like, and I've been scavenging what I can from houses, but most of them are picked over. I don't have much, but we should get through winter, and after that, maybe we'll head somewhere warmer, where we can grow things, and where we won't have to deal with them Standers.

"I warn you, now, Sterling may call himself the hand of God, but he's got devil power. He don't mind killing. If he's the one that's got hold of your kids, then I'm sorry for you. I'd put a bullet in my kids before I'd let him take them."

Doris gasped, staring.

"That's a hell of a thing to say," Geoff said.

"It is what it is. I'd call it a mercy killing, and I'd be right. If you didn't want to know what I thought, you shouldn't have broke into my house and started asking questions."

"But you have a plan to get them, don't you?" Tris asked Alexander. "Don't you?"

Thor snorted and coughed, turning away. Alexander eyed him acidly before answering.

"Max is going to join the Last Standers," he said bluntly.

"She's going to what?"

"She is going to join them," Alexander repeated, once again wondering at his lack of emotion at the risk she was taking. "She figures it is the best way to find Kyle and the kids. When she does, she will haul them out of there."

"Nobody escapes from them," Powell said. "Get yourself a headstone, and forget about her."

"You don't know Max," Thor growled.

He glared at Alexander as if waiting for him to respond to Powell's casual dismissal, but Alexander just shrugged. Max would live or die, and arguing about it made no difference.

"Do you have some food?" Alexander asked instead. "We could eat."

Powell nodded. "This way," he said, guiding them toward the door where Bambi still stood. He stepped back and let them through. Inside was a dining room. Or it had been. Built into the walls were china cabinets and a hutch. The dining table was gone, and in its place was a pair of twin beds. In them were Powell's children. He stopped by each bed to check the sleepers and pull the quilts higher over their shoulders, then led the way through another swinging door into the kitchen.

He had modified it considerably. Where the oven had been was now a woodstove. He'd cut a hole in the wall to vent it. On it was a big pot of stew. Down at the end of the counter, he'd build a brick oven. Several loaves of bread sat on the counter.

"Don't have much flour left," he said. "Had a feeling

things weren't right when the Change started. Went to the grocery store and got everything I could."

"We might be able to help you out," Alexander said.

Powell sucked his teeth and grabbed a couple of bowls out of the cupboard. "Whatever you're selling, I probably can't afford to buy," he said flatly.

"Maybe," Alexander said. "We can talk about it."

"That's what them Standers said. But they weren't interested in talking. Just taking. Can't say I see much of a difference between you."

"That's because you don't know us yet," Thor said.

Powell scooped a hearty stew into the bowls. "Stew is what we eat most around here. Kids are getting sick of it."

Alexander tasted it. "It is good."

He polished it off in a couple of minutes, as did Thor. Wordlessly, Powell filled the bowls again and then a third time.

"You boys are hungry."

"We need a lot of calories to do what we do," Alexander replied.

Powell propped his hip against the cabinet, folding his arms. "And just what is that?"

Thor smiled. It was a dangerous, vicious look. "We kill things. Especially vermin, like the Standers."

Powell held his ground, but his fingers dug hard into his arms, maybe to keep them from shaking. "Exactly where are you from?"

"Place called Horngate," Alexander said, pointing his spoon in the general direction. "Up in the mountains about twenty or thirty miles from here."

"That organic farm with the greenhouses?"

"Yes, we do that, too."

Powell scratched his beard. His fingers were thick and heavy, as if he worked with his hands for a living. "So let me see if I understand this. You're organic farmers and vermin killers. Do you own the place?"

Alexander shook his head. "Giselle owns it. She is a witch."

Thor coughed hard, setting his bowl down with a clatter. Finally, he straightened, wiping his mouth with the back of his hand.

"You going to live?" Alexander asked.

"No thanks to you," Thor said. "You're just going to announce she's a witch to everyone you meet now?"

"Not a lot of point in hiding it anymore," Alexander said, scraping at his bowl. "The compounders already know. Word is going to spread one way or another."

During this exchange, Powell had been swiveling his head back and forth at them, his mouth open. He finally closed it and paced away to the back door, which had three dead bolts and a steel-covered window. He marched back.

"What the hell do you mean, a witch? Like pointy hat and flies on a broom?"

"Giselle does not fly," Alexander said. "Not on a broom or anything else. I have never seen her even wear a hat. Have you, Thor?"

"Nope," the other man said. "Heard she has a pair of ruby slippers somewhere, though. And some do call her the Wicked Witch of the West. Though not where she can hear them, of course."

"Not entirely true," came a gravelly voice from the doorway leading back to the foyer. It was Liam. "Max introduced her to me as the Wicked Witch."

"Did she, now?" Alexander said, his gaze running over the other man.

"Is Max really going to join the Last Standers?" Liam asked.

Alexander nodded, and Liam frowned. Just then, Bambi pushed in from the other room.

"If you are Liam," Alexander said to the copper-haired man, "then you must be Bambi," he said to the black-haired soldier.

The other man looked startled and shook his head ruefully. "Tell me that is not going to stick forever."

"Probably not," Thor drawled. "Most of us don't live forever."

"That's very comforting," said Bambi. "The name is Radnor. Jack Radnor, if it matters."

Thor shook his head. "Can't see that it does, Bambi."

"So what happens now?" Liam asked. "And how can we help?"

"First we need to find Giselle," Alexander said. "And we had better hurry. Max is walking into hell, and she will not last long." Even as the words left his mouth, he wondered at the chill around his heart. She could very well die.

Inwardly, he laughed. As if that was the first time or the second time or even the third. She was always walking the razor edge of life and death. She had nearly died three times in the last twelve hours alone. Maybe he had simply gotten used to it.

Or something was very, very wrong with him.

He needed to find Giselle.

20

MAX DIDN'T BOTHER GOING IN SEARCH OF A new shirt. It would just waste time and strength, and she had to conserve all she had of both. Before going to eat, she'd tied the Amengohr amulet around her waist with a leather cord and tucked it inside her pants pocket. She wasn't sure if her red visitor had noticed it or not, but there was no point in advertising it. The creature knew what she was, so it might be all that stood between her and a sunlit death.

The creature's words slithered through her mind, poisonous and festering: *When I am done, you and every spirit you care for will be destroyed. Their souls will be torn to shreds and scattered across worlds and time.*

She was sure the creature had Kyle and the kids. But what about Tris and Giselle? What about Tyler and Alexander and Thor? There were so many she cared about. She could not let this creature beat her. But it had all the power. More than Giselle. More than Max could hope to defeat.

There had to be a way.

In the end, there was only one place for Max to go next.

She stepped through the abyss and landed on a hard-wood floor inside a broad space. She fell awkwardly and rolled up into a crouch, sliding her gun from her waistband and swinging it back and forth.

"You ruined my spell," Giselle said, sitting cross-legged in the middle of a chalk ward circle. As Max turned to face her, she leaped to her feet. "What happened to you?"

Without waiting for an answer, she bent and released the circle before coming to stand in front of Max.

"What's that on your chest and stomach?" She reached out her hand but didn't touch, for which Max was grateful. The cuts on her stomach ached like they'd been carved with acid.

"Benjamin Sterling isn't working alone. He's got himself a demon of some kind, or it's got him. It said this mark was its seal and that it wanted me to come visit it." Max glanced around again. "Where are we? Where is everybody?"

"I sent them scouting. We're going to use this place as a base until we find them. We can make a light-safe room in the basement. Oz is going to bring the Sunspears when it's light. Come on. Let me get a better look at that," Giselle said, pulling Max nearer to the candles. "Lie down."

Max did as ordered, feeling drained. Giselle picked up a candle and held it close. As usual, her hair was pulled back from her face. Shadows hollowed at her eyes and cheeks, giving her an austere look.

Giselle frowned, her eyes becoming unfocused. She murmured some words and touched one of the designs with her finger. Fire flared up, scorching Max's stom-ach. Giselle dropped the candle and skittered back on her hands and heels as the fire rose in a scarlet column nearly to the ceiling.

The flames roared for nearly half a minute before they died away. Max couldn't move, couldn't roll over to try to douse them. Her body was paralyzed. All she could do was feel. In her mind, she thought she heard a triumphant chuckle.

When the impromptu fire died and she could move again, Max sat up gingerly, looking down at herself. Her skin remained white and bloody. The flames had been illusion. Painful illusion.

"Let's not do that again soon," she said to Giselle, breathing deeply.

"I want to hear everything," the witch said, standing up. "I'll be right back."

She left through a door at the end of the empty hall. It was like a banquet hall or something, minus chairs, tables, or much of anything else besides air and floor. There was a fireplace at either end, one of which had a fire burning in it.

A few minutes later, Giselle returned with a black men's polo shirt and some jars of canned peaches.

"We found these in a pantry in the basement. Whoever used to live here either forgot about them or didn't get a chance to come back."

Max slid the shirt on. It was loose and baggy. "Where are we?" she asked, unscrewing a cap and prying off the lid seal with her knife. She drank the syrup and then stabbed the peaches with the blade. She went through all three at high speed. "Got more?"

"Come on. Might as well take you to the stash. You can tell me everything you know."

"We'll have to make it quick. I've got to go join the Last Standers or get captured by them before light."

"You what?"

"I'll fill you in. But I need all the calories I can get. This seal is costing me more than just blood. It's eating up my energy."

They went through the door into a huge kitchen. It looked big enough to run a restaurant.

"What is this place?"

"Best as I can tell, it was a house. There are eight bedrooms upstairs and another two in the basement. That room you dropped into was probably the dining room, and of course, this is the kitchen."

"Who lived here, the Waltons?"

"Who knows? The place can't have been empty that long, but most of the furniture's gone, except some stuff they didn't seem to want anymore. And some clothes—that shirt you're wearing, for one. Not a lot of dust, either, and no vandalism. How anybody would haul away as much stuff as must've filled this house without a half dozen U-Hauls, I don't know. But I am pretty sure they left post-Change."

"How did you find it?"

"We got attacked coming over the river and managed to steer off onto a side road. We meandered around, then I started scrying for Kyle. It led me in this direction. The snow was getting pretty deep, and we found this place. There's a barn, so we parked inside. I sent the others off to see what they could find and was about to cast a larger scry when you so rudely interrupted me."

Grasping a candle, she opened a door leading into the basement. Along one side of the rectangular basement were the two bedrooms, and another large room filled the far end. It held a pool table and an air-hockey table. To the left was a utility room containing the heater, washing machines, and two chest freezers. Next to it was an enormous room full of empty shelves. Giselle went right into a smaller storage room. This contained jars of pickles, fruit, meat, vegetables, jellies, dried beans, rice, flour, and dozens of other staples.

"Were they expecting the apocalypse?" Max asked.

Giselle shrugged. "Probably. There are a lot of end-of-the-world types living in Montana. Now, start talking. What's going on?"

Max told her everything that had happened. She left out as many details as she could, but it still took more than a half hour. Of course, eating slowed her down.

"So Alexander and Thor are looking for Tris. Tyler's looking for you. Gregory is at the compound. Is Judith with you?" Max set aside the jar of sweet pickles she'd just eaten and reached for a sack of raisins.

"She's back at Horngate with Magpie. We had an idea to try to channel the power of the Fury Seed through them to me. It may be too far. Tell me more about Alexander."

"What's there to tell? Whatever he felt for me, he's done with it. I might as well be a stranger, for all he seems to care." Her throat hurt with suppressed emotion.

"That's odd," Giselle said, her brows furrowing. She was sitting on the floor across from Max, leaning against the shelves. "In the space of a couple of minutes, he falls out of love with you? That's really . . . strange. Unbelievable, even. I wonder if he had help with that."

Love? The word sliced deep. Max's lungs hurt as she drew a shallow breath. "What do you mean, help?"

"It's possible he got himself hexed or cursed or bespelled. This might not have anything to do with him."

That rocked Max back. She hadn't considered the possibility of magic. But then she remembered the way he'd looked into her eyes and the sudden shift, as if he'd made up his mind. That hadn't been a spell.

She cleared her throat. "Whatever. It's not really important at the moment. I need to get going. With luck, I can get close enough to kill Sterling and maybe haul Kyle and the kids out through the abyss. But this creature is going to come after Horngate in full force. You need to collect everybody and get back to Horngate. If you can pull on the power of the Fury Seed, you might be able to hold it off."

"What if you can't get them out?" Giselle leaned forward, her hands on her knees. "It's a stupid plan. We can do better."

"Maybe, if we had time. But we don't. This thing is killing me. Between that and the Amengohr amulet, I'll be lucky to survive to tomorrow night." Max scraped her hands through her hair and stared at Giselle. Her nemesis. Her witch. Her friend. "I'm all ears if you've got other ideas."

"I could go in with you."

Startled laughter exploded from Max. "You can't be serious. That thing almost took you down inside your own wards. You only fended it off because I took your pain and you had the Fury Seed to draw on. On its home turf, it'll eat you alive."

"Not if Judith and Magpie can channel the power

of the Fury Seed to me." Flickers of black magic shadowed her eyes. "Two of us are more likely to survive
than you alone."

"No. You'll just be walking into the same trap I am. I
have to," Max said, pointing down at her bleeding stomach. "You don't." She shook her head. "There's no other
way around this one. I'll do all I can to weaken Sterling
and his demon. You hit them hard with whatever you
can. Kill them. No one will be safe until they're dead."

Giselle stood and paced up and down, threads of
black magic sliding over her skin. Finally, she stopped
and nodded. "You'd better get out of here before the
others show up. They won't want to let you go, either."

They went up the stairs to the kitchen. Max turned toward the door and then stopped, turning around. Giselle
was watching her, black magic wreathing around her,
sparks flashing angrily. She looked like an avenging spirit.

Max's mouth opened. No words came. She closed
her lips and gave an apologetic shrug. A moment later,
she stepped out through the door into a world of white.

Snow lay deep over everything. Feet of it. Her shirt
started freezing up instantly, the blood-soaked mate-
rial stiffening in the cold.

Above her, dark, pointed shadows loomed out of the
thick-falling flakes, signaling trees. Below, everything
was hidden. She had some idea where they were. If
Mansion Heights was east and north, and if there was
a tree line on the slope above and behind her, then
downslope were gentle swells of fields that dammed
up at the edge of the city.

She turned up toward the trees, where the snow was
lighter, and started east.

She had gone only a few feet when the snow turned scarlet before her. A shape detached itself. It was her creature, no more substantial than before. Snow fell through the red outlines of its body and wings.

It bent forward and touched her stomach. Her shirt turned to ash and fell away.

"That's better," it said smugly. "I do not wish you to cover yourself. Everybody must know you belong to me and only me."

"Fuck you," Max said.

The creature smiled. *Demon.* It had to be a demon, Max thought.

"Is that an invitation?" A curl of smoke unwound from its ankle and feathered up Max's pants leg. It burned like acid where it touched. She stepped back, but it only followed, the demon chuckling.

"Don't fight it. You asked, remember?"

The smoke went higher until it slipped under her underwear. The feeling was agonizing. Max swiped her foot through the red tendril connecting them, but her boot merely passed through without affecting the torment in her crotch.

The smoke found her entrance and thickened, pushing against her bluntly. Max stepped back, the snow making progress hard. The demon didn't move, and the assault didn't stop. The pain was intimate, excruciating.

"Careful what you ask for," it said, and a long red tongue slipped out of its mouth. "I will do with you what I want. You will be punished. You will scream, and you will beg for death. But if you are polite, perhaps it will end sooner rather than later."

The smoke thrust up inside her, hard. Max doubled

over and dropped to her knees as pain radiated out through her gut. The smoke dissolved, leaving her flesh throbbing with the acid burns and the humiliation of having it inside her, raping her.

"Did you get off, you fucking bastard?" she asked, clambering to her feet. "Is that what you are? A rapist?"

Its expression turned vicious, and it flicked forward so that its face was less than an inch away from hers. "I am *Justice*," it hissed. "You are condemned. You are nothing. You are *meat*. Do you understand? What I do to you, you deserve."

"That's what all rapists say," she spit. "And every single one of them is evil. You're not Justice. You prey on the weak. You're a flat-out coward."

The demon straightened, staring down at her. "You need a muzzle," it said, then waved its hand.

Fire stitched through Max's lips. She tried to open them, but they were fastened shut. Panic struck her. It was primal. She gouged at her lips, trying to pry them apart, but they were sealed.

"Don't worry," the demon said. "Eventually, I will allow you to scream. Never say I am without mercy." It turned to look behind her at the building. "I have business."

He brushed past her. Red smoke spun around the farmhouse. The door opened, and Giselle came out. Her arms were fastened at her side. She walked stiffly, like a wood soldier whose knees won't bend. She walked straight to the demon, never glancing away.

Max leaped to her feet, her shouts bottling up in her mouth. She ran forward, planning to pick up Giselle and jump away, using the angel feather embedded in her palm. She never made it. The demon's arm came up and smashed her in the chest. Pain exploded in her body, and she flew into the air. She crashed through the limbs of the trees before crumpling to the ground.

Instantly, she was back on her feet. Blood ran down over her eyes, and she knuckled it away. Giselle was only a few feet from the demon now. Max launched herself again. This time, she was prepared for the demon's move. Or she thought she was. She dodged around the reach of its arm and wings, but it suddenly turned into Stretch Armstrong and smashed her back again.

This time, she lost consciousness. It last only a minute or two. Probably. When she crawled to her feet, the demon had its arm around Giselle. She stood within its grasp, not fighting.

"You care for her," it said, running a red finger down Giselle's cheek. "Good. Another soul will die for your sins. It is not yet enough, but the balance grows more even. You may tell her good-bye if you wish."

Suddenly Max could speak. "I swear I will kill you," she rasped.

"You will try. You will fail." With that, it spread its wings and leaped into the air, the doll-like Giselle clasped under one arm. "I will be waiting," it said, hovering for a moment before it winged away toward Mansion Heights.

Max stared after it, fury and frustration choking her. Slowly, she sank to her knees, watching as the demon grew smaller. What the hell was she going to do now? There didn't seem to be any way out of the hole she was in. It just kept getting deeper.

21

ALEXANDER AND THOR POLISHED OFF ALL OF the stew Powell had made. The man grumbled but did not protest. Clearly, he just wanted them out of his house. The fact that his visitors had not threatened him or his children made him more cooperative. That and their shared animosity toward the Last Standers.

Suddenly, Thor froze, dropping the glass of water he had been drinking. The glass shattered.

"Oh, fucking hell," he muttered as he sagged back against the wall, his hands clamping over his head.

"What is it? What is wrong?" Alexander demanded.

"Shit shit shit shit," Thor muttered, rocking forward.

"What's happening to him?" Doris said, fingers digging hard into the couch. Everyone had gathered back in the living-room area.

"Shhh," Tris told her. "Leave him be. This is magic."

Geoff had leaped forward to grip Thor's elbow and was pulling him toward a chair. "C'mon. Sit down before you fall down."

To Alexander's amazement, Thor obeyed, collapsing

into the chair, his head between his knees. He panted as if he couldn't catch his breath.

Finally, he collected himself enough to sit up. His gaze went immediately to Alexander.

"Something's happened to Giselle. I can feel her, but the bond hurts. Like acid eating through my skull." He scowled. "Damn. I'm not fully bound to her. I can't imagine what the others are feeling. It probably knocked them ass over teakettle."

"Can you tell what has happened? She *is* still alive?" Alexander asked.

Thor nodded. "The bond would break if she was dead. But something's happened."

Alexander rubbed at his forehead. There was a dull ache there. It had been coming on for a few hours. "We need to get Gregory," he said.

"And do what?"

Alexander tried his spirit sense. It was still patchy but clear enough that he could make things out. He pushed outward. He found Gregory's spirit flame, green with cream streaks. He pushed further. He ran across other Blades. They were scattered through the city, although now they seemed to be moving south. One by one, he ticked them off. Tyler, Nami, Oak, Flint, Steel, Ivy, Jody—

No Max.

He pushed further. And found her.

Her spirit flame was a rich mix of orange and blue, like a hot fire. Except that now it flickered unsteadily, and there was a tattered quality to it.

She was hurt.

The ache in his head intensified. He shook himself.

"I know where Max is," he said. "We will get Gregory and meet her." Alexander looked at Liam and Bambi. "You will stay and guard everyone?"

He did not wait for an answer but headed out the door. Thor flanked him, asking no more questions. They had not gone more than a dozen yards when a demand spiked through Alexander. It was Max, summoning her Blades. It stopped him cold.

Thor jerked around like he was yanked on a string. Alexander caught his arm. "We have to get Gregory first," he said. Something had happened to Giselle. Now Max was summoning them, and her spirit flame was damaged. Whatever was going on, they would need Gregory. He was sure of it.

"Let's go," Thor said, not arguing.

As one, they turned and began bounding through the deep snow. Suddenly, Alexander veered, turning west, away from the compound.

"What are you doing?" Thor demanded.

"Flint and Steel are just ahead."

The twins were ruddy-faced and crusted with snow. Both were wiry, with short blond hair, blue eyes, and a knack for always knowing where the other was.

Alexander barely stopped. "Tell Max we found Tris. We are bringing Gregory."

He and Thor resumed their trek to the compound. Once there, Alexander pounded on the gate.

"Who's there?" A voice demanded.

Alexander's teeth ground together. "I am Alexander. I am here for the witch."

No one answered. Frustration mounted. Alexander

punched the heavy steel door, making a deep dent the shape of his fist.

"Let us in, or I swear I will tear your legs off!"

Still nothing but murmurs and shuffling feet. The snow muffled everything beyond his ability to hear it.

"They say you catch more flies with sugar," Thor said, finally catching up.

Alexander growled deep in his throat. "I will remember that the next time I am catching flies." He stood back, looking up. The top was invisible in the snow. It was about twenty feet high, if he recalled correctly. He could jump that.

"I am going in," he said, and crouched. Just then, he heard a jangle of chains and the clank of metal on metal. Then a chain ladder dropped.

"Come up. Gate won't open. Too much snow." It was Kara.

Alexander did not wait for a second invitation. He leaped up, grasping a crossbar on the ladder and pulling himself up hand over hand. He tugged himself over the top. Thor followed a moment later. The people on top fell back along the decking. Two roused Blades were enough to make some people piss their pants.

"We need Gregory," Alexander told Kara.

"He's in my shack," she said, reading their urgency and not asking questions.

The compounders had dug out a system of paths throughout the little city. They were fast filling up again, and Alexander brushed past a number of men and women shoveling.

Protective domes rose here and there where Gregory had worked his magic. Snow pillowed on top, and ice slicked the sides where the heat within had melted the snow. Alexander hoped to hell that the witch had not exhausted himself to uselessness.

Alexander threaded his way through the snow maze to Kara's house. Within the dome, it was warm and moist as the heat from her woodstove melted the snow on the ground. Inside Kara's shack, Gregory sprawled across the bed. His coat, shirt, pants, and socks hung by the fire to dry. Alexander shook his shoulder.

"Wake up."

The witch blinked, slowly registering his visitors. He sat up. "What's going on? What time is it?"

"It is about two hours to dawn. We have to go."

Gregory rose and pulled on his clothing. He glanced up and flushed when Kara walked in, then turned back to lacing up his boots. He yawned and shook his head to clear the muzziness. "What's going on?"

"Something happened to Giselle. Max summoned the Blades."

The witch froze, looking up. "Something happened to Giselle?" he repeated hoarsely. "She's not . . . dead?"

Giselle was the heart of Horngate. If she died, the *anneau*—the magical heart of the covenstead—would unwind. Alexander was not all that sure what that meant, but it was clear that Gregory feared it.

"No," Thor answered. "I can still feel her. But she's not good."

"Can we help?" Kara asked quietly.

Alexander considered her. "You are welcome to come join our fight."

"Where?"

"South. I am not sure where, but just outside the city."

She nodded. "Mansion Heights. Sterling has built himself a temple there."

"We plan to attack at nightfall," he said, although he had no idea if that was true. "We have got to go now."

He shouldered his way out of the shack. Gregory, Thor, and Kara followed. He strode quickly, too fast for Gregory, who was hampered by the snow and exhaustion. Alexander spun around and wordlessly tossed the witch over his shoulder.

"Hey!" Gregory yelped. "Put me down!"

"No."

Alexander found the wall and a set of steps leading upward. He took them five at a time. "I need a rope," he told Kara, setting Gregory back on his feet.

"This way," Kara said, leading them along the decking. They passed several guards hunched over barrels full of burning wood. The snow was doing everything it could to douse the flames.

Kara stopped near the gate and shoved the snow off the top of a steel box. Inside were tools and several coils of rope. She pulled one out and handed it to Alexander.

"Thanks," he forced himself to say. Then he tied one end, casting the rest over the side.

He motioned for Thor to go first. The blond Blade grabbed the rope and swung over the side, lowering himself.

"Your turn," Alexander told Gregory. "Piggyback."

The witch scowled. "The caveman routine is already getting old," he said.

Alexander smiled. "But faster." He turned and squatted down to allow Gregory to hop on his back. The witch hesitated, then jumped. Alexander caught him easily, hoisting him higher. "Put your arms around my neck. Tighter. Tighter. You are not going to choke me. Better. Do not let go."

Following Thor, he grabbed the rope and leaped over the side, dangling with one hand as he got himself turned to face the wall. Gregory made no sound, but his heart pounded furiously. Alexander lowered them hand over hand. Thor grabbed Gregory and lifted him away at the bottom.

"The snow is deep," the witch said in surprise. It came halfway up his chest.

"And getting deeper every second," Thor said.

"I can't walk in this."

"Which is why we will carry you," Alexander said, dropping down beside them.

"Piggyback? There has to be another way."

"We are open to suggestions. But make it fast. We are in a hurry."

"Snowmobiles."

Thor slapped his pockets. "I'm fresh out."

"Someone has to have them around here."

"If they do, they are buried under several feet of snow or tucked into a garage somewhere," Thor said. "We don't have time to look."

Gregory's lips pinched together, then he gave in. "Fine. Just keep your eyes peeled."

"Sure," Thor replied, glancing at the thick snow still falling. "Maybe it will let up soon."

"And pigs might fly," Alexander said. "Jump on," he told Gregory, and when the witch was firmly situated, they started off again.

They went about a quarter of a mile before they had to give up. Gregory could not maintain his hold. Alexander's jumps were too violent.

"What about a sled of some kind?" Thor asked. "We could make one with some rope and a sheet of plywood or some siding off a house and pull him behind us."

They were in an older neighborhood not far from Brooks Street. Or so he thought. It was hard to tell. The houses here were largely deserted, although a few had smoke coming from the chimneys. They chose the closest one, a Craftsman bungalow with a front porch and thick brick pillars. The door was locked but broke easily when Alexander kicked it in.

Inside, the house was cold. The rooms were a mixture of order and chaos, as if the owners had abandoned the place quickly. The furniture was mostly in place, but the cupboards and cabinets were open, the contents scattered across the floor. It appeared that the owners had taken what they wanted and left the rest.

"See if you can find something in here we can use," Alexander told the other two. "I will check the garage."

He went through the kitchen and out into the attached garage. There were no vehicles inside. Golf clubs, bats, skis, and other sports equipment filled the vertical cupboards in the front, along with garden tools. A lawn mower was parked off to the side with several bicycles. Lawn chemicals and blocks of toilet paper and paper towels lined the shelves above.

Alexander's eye caught on the overhead rack. On it were two kayaks and a canoe. He leaped up and grabbed the rack, pulling a kayak down with his other hand. It clattered to the floor. He dug through the rack of tools and equipment on the workbench just outside the door and found a roll of heavy twine. It would do.

He hauled the kayak into the house. Thor looked up from the kitchen table. He had turned it over and was taking the pedestal base off it. Seeing Alexander, he leaped to his feet.

"That'll do it," he said, straightening up. "I'll get Gregory."

"Meet me out front," Alexander said.

Once outside, he unrolled about fifty feet of the twine, then repeated that, doubling it over several times until he had eight strands. By the time he did, Thor and Gregory joined him.

The witch had found a stocking cap and some heavy gloves. Alexander stopped what he was doing and looked at him. "You can spell your clothes to keep them dry and warm, can you not?"

Gregory grimaced and nodded. Alexander knew the other man did not like wasting magic on himself.

"Do it," he said. He wanted Gregory to conserve his magic as much as possible, but he did not want him to get sick or be too frozen to move.

He and Thor tied the hank of twine to the T-bar at the front of the kayak. Then they made knots down the length of it about eighteen inches apart to hold the strands together. Then they tied lasso loops at the ends and put them over their heads and across their chests.

Gregory tried to crawl into the kayak, but the snow was too soft and deep, and he could not get himself high enough. The light craft kept turning over. Finally, Thor held it in place while Alexander hoisted Gregory inside.

A moment later, the two Blades launched themselves through the snow again. The kayak bounced and whisked behind them, but it remained upright.

The cool calm of the earlier night was giving way to foreboding. Horngate was Alexander's home now, and if Giselle had been taken, they were in serious trouble.

Beyul! He needed the Grim now. Horngate needed him. Alexander did not know what had happened to Giselle or how badly Max was hurt, but the Last Standers had Kyle, and one tired Triangle-level witch and a handful of Shadowblades weren't going to be able to do much. Beyul did not answer.

They came to the southern edge of town, where a small gulf of open fields was bracketed by housing developments. Max's summons tugged on them. They followed. Both Blades had grown tired and needed calories. Powell's stew had not been nearly enough to replenish them.

"Where the hell is she?" Thor muttered as they climbed up a long hill.

"Not far," Alexander said.

The farmhouse appeared out of nowhere. Suddenly, it was in front of them, looming out of the snow. Someone had entered recently. There were several trails leading up the steps. Alexander already knew who was inside. Their spirit flames told him.

He did not wait for Thor to help Gregory out of the kayak. He flipped the twine rope over his head and went to the door. He yanked it open and strode inside.

Some of the Blades were upstairs. He could hear clomping about, dragging furniture. A twin mattress bounced over the upstairs railing and landed at his feet. He stepped across it. His prey was ahead.

He went through a pair of pocket doors into a broad living room. It, too, was empty, except for some candles. Max had spilled blood there. On the other side of the room was a doorway into a kitchen. Max was there, talking to Tyler. He was bare-chested. She was wearing his shirt. It was yellow, and blood soaked the front of it. For a moment, Alexander's entire focus narrowed until that blood was all he could see. The smell of it was coppery, Uncanny, pungent. The pain in his head throbbed harder.

Both Tyler and Max had looked up when Alexander entered. He tore his gaze from the blood, looking at Max's face. Her expression was shuttered and distant. Pain and other emotions made tight brackets around her mouth and nose.

After a moment, Max spoke. "Good you're here, Slick. I wanted to tell you good-bye."

22

"I HAVE A PLAN," MAX SAID, HAVING GATHERED ALL OF the Shadowblades and Gregory.

She explained all she knew about the creature that had attacked her. "I'm going to go do what it told me to do. I'll put on the Amengohr amulet and surrender myself. If I'm lucky, I'll get a chance to grab the creature and take it into the abyss. I hope that breaks the spell on Giselle, and she can deal with Sterling. The rest of you will help her. Without his demon creature, I'm hoping Sterling is just an ordinary witch."

"That's a lot of hoping," Thor said sourly.

"Where will you be?" Tyler demanded. He had taken a knife out and was carving gouges into the wall. Better than in her flesh, she supposed.

"I hope to be alive, but I figure I'll be useless about then."

"Explain," Alexander said. He had been listening silently. His expression was bland, almost indifferent.

"My plan is to take the fucker into the abyss and dump its ass there," she said. "If I can get ahold of it, I can drag it through. Then I'll come back out. But with the drain of this mark on my chest, the amulet, and actually going into the abyss, I figure I'll pretty much be wasted once I get out."

"What if the abyss doesn't hold him?" asked Tyler, voicing the fear she hadn't wanted to contemplate.

"I don't know," she said. If the demon could walk the abyss the way she could—which was a talent more than just rare—then there was no place that could hold it.

Or was there?

An idea sparked in her mind. There was one place she knew of designed to trap someone with just that talent. If it still existed. The only trouble was, if she took the demon there, she'd be caught, too. The last time she'd got stuck in that prison, Spike had rescued her. But Spike was gone, and she didn't know if the Calopus was ever coming back. And if she did, it might not be before Max died of thirst and hunger.

She looked at her Blades, one by one. Should she tell them? Her gaze settled on Alexander.

"There is one place," she said slowly. "It was designed to capture a demigod with the ability to walk through the abyss. I could take the bastard there."

Silence descended, smothering sound. Five seconds. Ten.

"Correct me if I am wrong," Alexander said, "but is that not where you were trapped? Where you could not move, even to blink? Spike had to save you, or you would still be there."

"That's the place." She nodded. It didn't escape her that he didn't sound particularly upset by the notion. Her gaze flicked to Tyler. He turned away so she couldn't see his face. His muscles roped beneath his skin as he spun the knife in his fingers. He hadn't found a shirt to replace the one he'd given her. She looked back at Alexander. He was staring at the wall. She had no idea what he was thinking.

"I don't see a choice," she said finally. "If I don't go after the demon, we're all dead. If I have to pull it into that trap to stop him—if the trap even still exists—then I'm stranded. Spike can find me, if she comes back. If not . . ." She shrugged.

"Everybody else still lives. It's a price I'm willing to pay. It's a price I *have* to pay, and you know it. This is not me being impulsive and stupid. I just don't see any other way." She was talking mostly to Tyler, but the others shifted uneasily, their Blades rumbling with helplessness and anger.

She was their Prime. She didn't need their agreement or permission. And yet she wanted it. If they didn't give it, she'd still have to go. Unless someone came up with a better plan. But if Giselle hadn't been able to stop the creature, then Gregory wasn't going to have a snowball's chance in hell. The creature would slaughter her Blades with magic, long before they ever got close enough to even try to touch it. She couldn't let that happen. It wanted her. It wanted to torture her. Which meant she could get close enough to pull it into the abyss. There really was no other choice.

"What do you want us to do?" Tyler asked finally.

"As soon as it's dark, I want you to follow me into the cult headquarters and tear it apart. Find Kyle and Giselle, and put Sterling down."

Max stood as her throat knotted with emotion. She

was wasting time, and if she stayed much longer, she was going to start bawling. Not exactly the most inspiring image for her Blades. "I'd better get started."

Wordlessly, Tyler pulled her against him. His arms wrapped her tightly. She hugged him back. He kissed her cheek and abruptly stepped away. Then Thor grabbed her. One by one, each of her Blades hugged her in a silent ceremony of farewell. Even Gregory locked her in a bony embrace.

Finally, she was face-to-face again with Alexander. He did not hug her. He did not even touch her. "Be careful," he said softly.

"Now, Slick, you'll make me think you care what happens to me," she said. She didn't wait for an answer. She didn't want one. She felt numb.

She fished in her pocket for the amulet. One side was polished gold, with a round, faceted black diamond set in the center. The rock was the size of a walnut. Arrows rayed away from it, each interspersed with a circle of orange opals. Around the thick edge were archaic words that spilled over onto the back of the amulet, spiraling down into a small eye at the center.

Gripping it tightly, she rubbed it against the blood soaking her shirt. Instantly, she felt a tingling, and then power washed over her. She slipped the chain over her head.

"I guess that's it," she said. She hesitated, then went to the door. She opened it and slid through, not looking back.

As she had planned before, Max worked uphill into the tree line where the snow wasn't quite as deep. She also appreciated the shade of the trees. The amulet made her safe from the sun, but she couldn't help feeling like she was about to explode into flames at any moment.

The calories she'd eaten had given her a boost, but she still felt sluggish. The mark on her stomach did more than just bleed her, she was pretty sure. It was pulling away her strength. Slogging through the waist-deep snow beneath the trees wasn't helping. She had to be quick if she wanted to get the demon into the abyss and still hope to get back out herself.

It took her almost an hour to work her way to a point just above Mansion Heights. It was a housing development of expensive homes just south of the university. It rose up the side of the valley on a pair of broad, zigzagging roads that wove together in the center before meeting at the top. A few streets ending in courts filled the space between them. The development was incomplete, and there were only a few houses at the very top.

Looking down on it from a thin wedge of trees that arrowed down a wash to the development, Max saw that the place was teeming. She smelled enormous numbers of unwashed bodies. Buildings humped out of the snow. They were made of a patchwork of materials, as were the compounder shacks, but these were barnlike. Max guessed each could probably house a couple of hundred people, more if they squeezed in. She couldn't tell how many there were. All she knew for certain was that the place stank of Divine magic.

Suddenly, the smell swelled. Flakes of crimson dropped down, mixing with the white. They gathered in a bloody pile, slowly taking shape. Max reached out, snatching at the still-forming demon. Her hand passed through it like it wasn't there. *Shit.* How could she get the fucker into the abyss if she couldn't grab hold of it?

Its eyes were the last things to settle into place. It stared at her with undisguised glee. Then its eyes boiled with rage. It reached out and traced a red outline finger over her stomach. Instantly, the bloody yellow shirt vanished. "I told you not to cover up."

"You can't always get what you want."

"I *always* get what I want," it told her. "Come." It gestured toward the buildings below. As it did, the falling snow cleared, and the sun suddenly beamed down through an ever-widening opening. Max flinched back before she remembered the amulet. She wondered if the demon could see it.

"Do you have a name?" she said suddenly, tired of calling it the "creature" or the "demon."

"I do." It didn't tell her what it was.

"All right, if that's the way you want it, Daffy, then it's all good for me. Do you want to clear the road for me, too? After all, you don't want me passing out before you get to kill me."

"As you wish," it said with a smile, and snow moved away from in front of her. An arrow-straight path cut down to the ground, beckoning her forward. It was wide enough for them to walk abreast, even with Daffy's wings. Grief speared through Max's chest. It was so much like walking beside Xaphan or Tutresiel, except that Daffy's wings weren't likely to burn her to a crisp or slice her to the bone.

"I have a surprise for you."

Max's stomach turned. "What?"

"I can't tell you. It would ruin it, and I have worked so hard to surprise you." Daffy's voice was larded with glee.

The demon said no more. Max strode forward quickly. "Where are we going?"

"Follow the path. It will take you exactly where you need to be."

With that, the thing faded to nothing. For a split second, Max caught a whiff of that sweet battery-acid flavor she'd tasted in the angel-vault pool, and then it was gone.

A low hum vibrated through the air. It grew louder and turned into a full-on buzzing, like a planet-sized angry bee. She turned in a circle, searching for the source, but the sound came from everywhere. Then, suddenly, the doors of all the big barn structures opened up. At the same time, the level of the snow dropped until it was no higher than Max's knees. As people poured out of the barns, they couldn't help but see her, her upper body bare and bloody. They gathered around, staring.

Max continued to follow the path. It seemed to lead nowhere in particular. It meandered down to the bottom of the cult enclave, then back up, looping around to display Max better.

At first, the observers only watched groggily. They were dressed much like the compounders. They all carried weapons, most of them with three or four. As they caught sight of Max, they began to murmur to one another. The murmuring swelled into mutters and then to an onslaught of name-calling and accusations.

"Slut!"

"Whore of Satan!"

"Daughter of hell!"

"Delilah!"

"Jezebel!"

"Hell spawn!"

A lot of them held up crosses and Bibles, and some made signs of the cross over their chests, while others spit at her. A few picked up rocks and flung them, but they veered wide, never touching her. Daffy had marked her and wasn't going to let anybody else have fun torturing her. The demon did, however, want everyone to see her.

A parade formed on either side of the path as Last Standers followed her. She neared the top of the hill again. She found herself on a paved court surrounded by dirt. The path ended. There were no buildings near.

The spectators gathered around her, not stepping onto the pavement. She waited, but nothing happened. At last, she started walking again, heading for the place where the court melded into the street. She ran into an invisible wall and fell back, rubbing her head. A smear of blood hung chest-high where she'd hit. She reached out and touched it. The air was hard as rock and smooth. She circled, ignoring the bystanders and returning back where she started. She was sealed in.

She looked upward. She could jump. With Tutresiel's feather in her palm, she might clear it, if it didn't have a roof. But chances were it did. Besides, she didn't want to escape. She just needed to find a way to grab hold of the bastard.

She went to the middle of the court and sat cross-legged. Daffy wanted to punish her and wanted people to see her suffer. The demon wasn't going to waste a lot of time before it got started. It was already impatient. All she could do was wait for it to get on with the show.

It was noon before anything happened. The sun was golden, and Max reveled in its soft touch. It had been thirty years since she'd last seen it. The spectators continued to rail at her, preaching scripture and even praying, although whether they wanted to save her soul or damn her to hell, she wasn't entirely sure. Some sang hymns, and the children—there were so many children—eyed her with fear and sadness. As if they hadn't yet been so brainwashed that they couldn't feel sorry for her.

Suddenly, the crowd at the mouth of the road shifted and split. A man was approaching. Benjamin Sterling appeared, wearing his usual Jesus uniform. He passed through the invisible wall as if it was nothing more than air. He approached Max, stopping a few feet away.

He stared down at her. His face was ruddy, and his hair stood up straight. He'd need a lot of hair gel to get it to lie down flat. An anvil to his brainpan would solve the problem nicely. He was shorter than she was, maybe five foot six or seven.

"You have come before me for crimes against God. You bear the mark of Judgment on your chest, and you must face God's wrath. Let it be known that you will be punished. You cannot escape the price of your evil. But now you must decide. Will you confess your sins before this congregation and beg the Almighty's forgiveness? Will you bow down that you may be lifted to heaven? Or will you deny your guilt and burn in everlasting flames, the plaything of the devil? Choose!"

His voice rolled like thunder, and there was magic in it. All around, people clutched one another and started weeping. Max was untouched. Sterling's spell was designed to create awe and worship, but it did little more than annoy her. She'd seen far more things that were bigger, scarier, and more awe-inspiring. Daffy, his sidekick, was one.

She didn't bother to answer. She just sat there and waited to see what he would do next.

Behind her, something like fingers ruffled through her hair, and lips whispered at her ear. "Repent or not. The punishment will be the same."

Max stiffened. How could Daffy touch her without her being able to do the same? Her fingers curled into fists. Why was the demon hiding? Didn't the Last Standers know about it? Did Sterling?

"Do you repent? Do you call on our Lord God to save your soul? Do you beg forgiveness of the Son of God? This is your last chance." Sterling bent slightly, his blue eyes brilliant in the sunshine. His fingers were rough and calloused, and his bottom lip was chapped and split. A handful of freckles dashed across his nose and cheeks.

"God forgives, my child," he said, and still his voice carried to his followers. "Ask for his blessing. Receive your penance, and rise to heaven to live eternity unsoiled at his feet."

Max shifted so she was closer. "Do these people know you're a witch? A blood witch, if I had to guess. That's where you get your power, right? Blood rites?"

He scowled, his cheeks flushing. His hand whipped out, and he slapped her cheek with enough force to knock her to the ground—if she hadn't been a Shadowblade. As it was, she didn't move, didn't look away.

"What's the matter? Does the truth hurt? That power of yours is witch magic, and I ought to know."

His hand rose again. Max smiled.

"Does that make you feel better? Does it make you feel strong and tough? Go ahead. Do it again. I can take all you dish out."

His flush turned mottled as rage suffused him. He straightened. He pointed down at her. "You will die slowly. You will scream. You will beg for mercy, and none will be granted. You are filth. You are a deceiver, a succubus, a demon seed." He turned, raising his hands to the gathered congregation.

"Let it be known that the sinner is stubborn and will not repent! She revels in her demon ways. She is sick with Satan's poison. We must save her for our Lord Almighty on High. We must help her cast out the evil she carries inside her; we must destroy the root and branch of Satan. If God wills, she will live among us, a symbol of His strength and glory. Pray for her, my friends. Get on your knees and beg for the safety of her soul. We must ask our Lord to have mercy, to lay His hand on her and rip away the evil that stains her soul. We must be strong. We are soldiers for God, the Last Stand for Earth. We must put aside our finer feelings, and though this sinner may suffer, we must hold fast to the one true path. We must look ahead to the light of God and know that if we bear the burden of her suffering, she will be welcomed in His embrace.

Can you be strong, my brothers? Can you be strong, my sisters? Can you be strong for God?"

His voice rose, and shouts answered him. Someone broke into "Onward, Christian Soldiers," and the rest of the crowd picked it up. Soon everyone was shouting the words at the top of their lungs. They stamped their feet and pumped their fists in the air. Some shot guns into the air.

Sterling looked back at Max and smiled. His eyes were lit like a child's at Christmas. He rubbed his hands together. "You will not like being purified," he said so that only she could hear. "But I will. I will enjoy it very, very much."

He was a sociopath, a serial killer with a love of torture, and he'd found the perfect outlet for his lust for blood and pain. Max could read it in the eager anticipation on his face and the way he licked his lips. He probably had a hard-on just thinking about it.

She doubted there was anything he could do to her that Giselle hadn't already done. Except maybe kill her. But Sterling had the look of a man who'd tortured a lot of people in his line of work, and he was undoubtedly an expert at keeping his victims alive and squeezing out all the pain and suffering they were capable of. That was good for her. It would give her time. Time for the day to pass and for her to snag Daffy. Time also for the sun to go down and her Blades to come.

"Screw off," Max said. "If there's a god giving you the power to torture, maim, and kill, then he's a son of a whore and deserves to be hung up by his balls and whipped until his skin falls off."

She was hoping to piss Sterling off, force him to reveal more of what he was. It didn't work.

He tapped a finger against his lips. "That is an idea I might have to use," he said thoughtfully. "But you may not insult the Holiest of Holies, God Almighty." He pointed an imperious finger at her and shouted, "Silence, Whore of Babylon!"

Once again, his voice carried as if he'd shouted into a microphone. Magic wriggled across Max's mouth like maggots. She shook her head. The feeling continued. She opened her mouth to scrape her lips with her teeth—but once again her lips were sealed shut. She dug her fingernails into the seam of her mouth. She could not separate them. Sterling and his demon clearly didn't like people talking back.

"Don't worry," Sterling said quietly, watching her, his eyes glowing with rapt pleasure at her struggles. "I will let you scream. I want to hear you. First I may cut your tongue. Fillet it inside your mouth so you learn not to speak ill of the Lord. He is great and merciful. But a tide of evil has washed across this land, and there can be no mercy for unrepentant evil." He smiled, licking at the corner of his mouth as if to catch a driblet of drool. "I serve the Lord God with all my heart and soul. I will never fail Him by being too squeamish to do the work He calls on me to do. You will repent, or you will die."

She was going to die, anyway, if Daffy had anything to do with it. The demon didn't care if she repented or not. She doubted Sterling did, either.

Sterling's smile widened into unsuppressed glee, before vanishing into holy sternness. "I will give you the chance to repent again, but first you must learn the cost of defying the Lord and defiling this earth with your evil."

Max made a sound, her throat swelling with the effort. Sterling watched her and then turned away.

"Bring her to the temple," he said to no one in particular, and suddenly, the invisible walls vanished, and the crowd rushed at Max.

Hands grabbed her, bruising her as the fingers gouged deep into her flesh. Her bare breasts were pinched, and the bloody cuts on her stomach and chest were prodded. She kicked and slammed her fists into her captors. Several fell, but others quickly replaced them. They lifted her above their heads, all the while continuing to sing.

Max stopped fighting. This was what she wanted. She forced herself to remain still as the hands hoisted her along.

The journey to the temple wasn't short. They marched uphill toward the mountains. That surprised her. Kara had told her that Sterling liked an audience for his punishments. Max had half expected him to take her down into the center of Missoula. At least she could be grateful that she wasn't nailed to a cross. Yet.

The stink of rotting flesh permeated the cold air. Max's head was on the downhill side, and even lifting it up, she couldn't see where the stench came from. But a new feeling washed through the mob. It was angry and violent. They had been content just to carry her along the path, but now they returned to twisting fingers into her flesh, pinching, gouging, and scraping. They yanked her hair and punched at her. Max didn't react. They weren't her real enemy. Daffy was. But where was the demon? Would it show up to the party soon? If it didn't . . .

Finally, they jolted to a halt.

"Lower the sinner," Sterling ordered. "She must face God's wrath. Let her see what He has wrought."

They didn't so much lower her as drop her like a hot potato. She landed on unexpectedly muddy ground. Apparently Sterling had melted away the snow.

Her mass of attendants sifted slowly away but not before stepping on her and pummeling her with sharp kicks. Finally, she was alone on the ground. She staggered up, covered in blood and mud. Instantly, her mouth filled with bile. She couldn't spit it out and was forced to swallow it back down. She stared around her in horror.

Sterling wasn't just a sociopath. He was pure evil. He was the devil himself.

23

DOWN IN THE BASEMENT OF THE OLD HOUSE
where the Shadowblades hid from the sun, the
pain in Alexander's head sharpened. It matched
an ache growing in his chest, just below his sternum.

He lay on a discarded mattress and stared up at the
ceiling. He could not stop thinking about Max.

Thor came and sat beside him, his back against the
wall. "Are you really as cold-blodded about this as you
look?" he asked.

Alexander rolled onto his side. "You think I should
be in a rage."

"I think it would be *normal* if you were. *This* is not
normal." He gestured, taking Alexander in from head
to foot.

Alexander did not reply.

"Do you know what I think?" Thor pushed.

"I am guessing you will tell me."

"I think you're going to hate yourself a whole lot
when you wake up and realize you let the woman you
love go to her death without fighting for her. I think
you're going to want to kill yourself when that hap-

pens, which means Sterling or his little demon buddy win on both ends. If you ask me, you ought to be fighting harder to get back what's yours and not letting them take it away because it seems easier. The Alexander I know is too damned tough for that and too much in love with Max to let them get away with stealing his soul." He stood up. "Think about it."

Thor left Alexander to ponder his words. They circled in his head, snapping at one another. The trouble was, he knew something was missing, and Thor was right; he had been content to let it go without a fight because it was easier. But the *wrongness* of it was beginning to wear on him.

The day dribbled past as Alexander wrestled with himself. He knew with iron certainty that the key to breaking the spell on his emotions, whether it had been imposed by Sterling and his demon or whether he had done it to himself, was simply to want them back. It meant inviting pain back. That soul-devouring, heart-grinding pain. It meant letting go of his control and giving in to his emotions—emotions that Max did not fully share. Why would he want to do that to himself?

He remembered that first moment of glorious freedom when he had ceased to feel the torment.

He remembered the ecstasy of her touch and the taste of her on his lips.

He remembered the devastation when he thought she had died.

He could not feel that again. He could not.

Pain drilled through his head, and pressure built in his chest.

24

MAX STOOD AT THE BOTTOM OF A ROCKY KNOB. At the top was something that looked like a Greek temple. It was made of magic and glowed with gold light. It was breathtaking. Leading downward from it was a wide triangular path, its point arrowing into the doorway of the temple. Lining it were stakes with bodies in various levels of death and decay. They were naked. The stakes had been sharpened and greased. The victims had been sat on top. Gravity and their weight had impaled them slowly, the stakes sliding up into their bodies, killing them slowly.

Too many were still alive. They moaned and keened with marrow-chilling desperation. They reached out with shaking hands, begging for rescue, for death, for relief. Others were rotting, birds picking at their flesh. Max panicked, searching for Kyle, Tory, Carrie, and Giselle. Relief rolled through her. They weren't there.

Not yet.

But her relief was short-lived.

"Did you see? Look carefully," Daffy whispered, the demon's breath warm against her skin.

Max groped the air for it, but it just laughed.

Sterling stood at the base of a long set of steps leading up into the temple. She couldn't see much else. The glow was too bright. She squinted. There were shapes—

Fury and fear ribboned through her, twisting together into a tangle of knots.

Standing up in a line like statues were Kyle, Giselle, Tris, Bambi, Liam, Geoff Brewer, Doris Lydman, Tory, and Carrie Lydman. They were all glassy-eyed and stiff. Max wasn't even sure they were aware of where they were or what was going on. How had Daffy found Tris? Alexander and Thor had hidden them.

All of them were bruised and bloody, like they had put up a fight. Only Giselle was without a mark. But then, Max had watched Daffy steal her, and the demon had used magic. It looked as if the others had been taken by Sterling's minions.

"I told you I would get those you loved. I will let Sterling kill them all. He does enjoy it so. You will watch. And then I will open your stomach and spill your guts on the ground and let the birds eat you alive." Daffy stroked an invisible hand down her back. "This is the price."

For what? Max desperately wanted to ask just what her crime was. But her mouth remained sealed.

Her fear and panic tightened as she gathered herself. Everything narrowed down into one single need: get Daffy into the abyss. She turned, trying to find the demon. There was nothing behind her. It wasn't there. Except that it was. She could smell it.

"Don't turn your back on Sterling," the demon whispered, and it had moved around behind her again. "He doesn't like it. He will make you pay for insults."

What happened to no one but Daffy touching her? She wanted to ask, to prod at the demon until it took solid form. Her mouth worked, but she still couldn't get her lips open. She screamed, her neck tenting with the effort.

Laughter.

Then a sharp shove in her back. She fell onto her stomach in the mud. The gathered cultists roared with appreciation.

"Show Sterling some respect," Daffy said. "He is the hand of God, after all." More laughter.

Daffy knew full well that Sterling was a witch. If there was a god and Sterling was his instrument, then the world was pretty fucked.

She started to climb to her feet, but a force struck her in the back, driving her down again.

"Call your dogs, why don't you?" Daffy asked next to her ear, almost as if the demon was lying beside her. "Why don't they come to help you? Maybe they found something more interesting, like salamanders. Clever trick, that. Don't you think? Now you are all alone."

Another laugh. It wanted to brag. It wanted her to know what it had done, how it was beating her.

She started pushing herself up again, and once more the demon struck her down. Max squirmed across the ground on her belly, the burn of Daffy's mark flaming along her chest.

She came to the steps. Sterling stood just above her, watching her. She lifted her head to look at him.

"Beg for mercy," he told her, and suddenly her mouth could open. "Beg me," he said with oily eagerness.

"Please have mercy," Max said, deciding the better

part of valor was to hurry things along. The faster she dealt with Sterling, the faster she might be able to grab Daffy and take its magic out of the equation.

"You can do better." He put a foot on her head and shoved. "Try again."

"Please," Max said. "Please have mercy on me. I beg you." The words came sideways out of her mouth.

"Not good enough."

"It's all you're getting," she said, leaping to her feet before Daffy could knock her down again. "If you want more, you're going to have to make me."

She swung around, talking to the emptiness where Daffy might have been. "As for you, why don't you tell me just what it is you think I've done? I'd like to know why you're trying to kill me and my covenstead."

"Who are you talking to?" Sterling demanded.

But it was Daffy who answered. The demon's shape uncurled out of thin air. Gasps ran around among the watchers, and Max stepped to the side so she could see both the demon and Sterling. The cult leader watched with a kind of awe and pride. Which meant that he did know about Daffy and had, or thought he had, control over the demon.

She wasn't expecting Sterling to drop to his knees. "Oh, Lord Almighty! Thank you! Thank you for sending one of your own angels to us. You bless us with your generosity and goodness! In this time when Satan floods the earth with minions of evil, you send us a beacon in the darkness. Praise your name! Hallelujah!"

"Hallelujahs" echoed around the gathered crowd, growing stronger with each person. Max hardly heard. She was caught up in staring at Daffy. An angel? Was it possible? It had wings, but so did birds, dragons, and bats. Wings didn't make it angelic. She knew better than to think that angels were creatures of goodness and light. Tutresiel and Xaphan were neither. What were the odds that another would show up? The Guardians had sent Xaphan and Tutresiel to destroy Horngate, and through a trick of death and logic, they had bound themselves to Horngate and freed themselves from their Guardian masters. Both seemed to prefer the trade-off.

But Daffy?

The creature looked at her, nothing more than a cartoon outline of what an angel might look like. Then, slowly, color filtered down, shading it—him—in. Hair sprouted from his head. It was gold. His eyes were crimson, the same as Xaphan's and Tutresiel's. His wings were crimson edged in gold. The feathers were unsettlingly unformed, like smoke. His body was white as bone, and he was dressed in white pants and a white blousy shirt with lace at the cuffs and neck. It was open to his waist. He was barefoot.

Just like the other two angels, he was beautiful and deadly.

Max let out a slow breath. She felt stupid. Daffy had a lot of powers that Xaphan and Tutresiel didn't have—or hadn't shown her—but she should still have seen what he was.

He leaped into the air, gliding to the top of the steps. He turned, his wings stretching wide. His hair gleamed in the gold light of the temple.

"I am Shoftiel," he declared, and the air shook. It rattled against Max's eardrums and thrummed in her chest. All around, the Last Standers fell to their knees, weeping. "I am Judgment. I have come to see that justice is done."

He rose in the air. His wings boiled like smoke, but he did not flap them. Neat trick. He pointed at Max.

"You stand here before me, a servant of witches. You are accused of enslaving angels, of trying to kill them and harvest their bodies. You are accused, and you are judged. Now you will be punished."

Max could only stare. This was all about Xaphan and Tutresiel? She hadn't enslaved them. They had willingly joined Horngate to escape the chains of the Guardians. As for trying to kill them, they had done that to themselves. It had been a sacrifice. In an effort to save Horngate, they had folded themselves around the Fury after her birth and prevented her from destroying not just the covenstead but Missoula and everything else in about a hundred-mile radius.

She didn't think Daffy—Shoftiel—was going to believe her. She wouldn't have. Angels weren't the benevolent beings that people hoped they were. They were bloody, vengeful, angry, and merciless. In sacrificing themselves, Tutresiel and Xaphan had shown a side of themselves that Max hadn't thought even existed. A human side.

"You're full of shit," she told Shoftiel.

Hisses of fury rose from the crowd, and more rocks were thrown at her. This time, they hit her. She stood firm.

"You need to get your facts straight. Why don't you ask them for yourself?"

"How can I? Thanks to you, they lie on the verge of death." With that, he gestured downward. Gold light flared and faded. Hovering over the steps were Tutresiel and Xaphan. The fire angel's wings burned brilliantly. Tutresiel's wings had gained back their brilliant silver shine. His long black hair hung down between his wings. Both were naked, their bodies white as marble.

A knot rose in Max's throat. She fought past it. She wondered what they would think of Shoftiel. If they would be glad of his vengeance or not.

Somehow she doubted they would, if only because neither liked anyone else butting into his business. Just because they were angels didn't mean they automatically liked each other. In fact, Xaphan and Tutresiel had spent a lot of time trying to kill each other on first meeting.

Sterling had come to stand between the two comatose angels. He leaned over Xaphan and then Tutresiel. He fell to his knees before Shoftiel, tipping back his head, his arms falling wide.

"Command me, angel of God. Let me serve you. Let me do the Almighty's work. Let me distribute the justice of His judgment."

Shoftiel dropped down, settling on the steps above Sterling. "You shall," he told the cult leader. "You will write my punishment in her flesh and bones. But first—"

He lifted his hands high in the air. Magic seared downward in the shape of two golden lightning bolts. They fastened to his hands. The power was enough to knock Sterling down the stairs to sprawl beside Max. He remained where he'd fallen, staring in awe. Max stood her ground, but the heat and the force of the magic battering at her were immense. She could not hold out long.

She took a step forward. It was like walking through a cement wall. Still, she managed a couple of inches. If she could reach Shoftiel, she could grab him. She hoped. He had taken on his real form. Hopefully that meant her hands wouldn't pass through him. This was her chance.

She managed another sliding step up to the bottom of the stairs.

Shoftiel's hands snapped downward, unleashing the bolts of magic into both angels. Watery light surrounded them. It grew brighter and brighter until Max was forced to look away. What was he doing?

The flow of magic from the heavens continued for more than a minute. Max took advantage to lift a foot up onto the bottom step. She leaned her weight hard into it and tugged up her other leg. Her strength was dwindling rapidly. Her heart pounded with the effort, and she could feel the magic of the amulet sending roots down inside her, pulling on the spells that had created her. If she took it off, she'd fry. If she didn't, it would kill her, and soon. She had to get to Shoftiel and get him into the abyss quickly, or she wouldn't be able to do it at all.

Suddenly, the brilliant bolts of magic vanished. Max blinked, trying to clear the streaks of white from her vision.

Shoftiel was panting. His breaths were deep and rasping. He stood between the two prone angels. He glanced from one to the other as if waiting.

Nobody else moved. Even Sterling seemed to be holding his breath.

Xaphan's chest fluttered. It moved up and down as he breathed in and out. Max let out a startled cry and jerked forward. Her feet refused to move. She looked at Tutresiel. His fingers twitched and then curled and flexed. His chest rose.

Joy danced through her. She looked back at Shoftiel, wondering if he had any idea that the two angels would not appreciate his attacks on her or Giselle.

Tutresiel's eyes opened first. He blinked and turned his head.

"Shoftiel," he said. The word was blank, without any feeling whatsoever. He turned his head to look on the other side of himself and then lifted it slightly to look down past his feet. Finally, he saw Max.

His eyes narrowed at the blood and mud plastering her skin. His gaze hooked on Shoftiel's still-bleeding mark.

"What the fuck is going on?" he asked her.

"I will tell you what's going on," Shoftiel said, stepping down between Tutresiel and Xaphan, turning to face the silver-winged angel. "I have brought you back from Ledrel. You have been kept prisoners of witches, no doubt in order to harvest the magic from your bodies. I have set you free. I have judged the guilty. I have pulled you out of Ledrel that you may witness the punishment of those who wronged you."

The way he said it was accusing and disgusted, as if Tutresiel and Xaphan had allowed themselves to be enslaved and used. As if no self-respecting angel would be caught dead bound to a covenstead. And maybe they had. They had actively helped Horngate. They had sacrificed themselves to protect the covenstead from the Fury, although Max was fairly certain Shoftiel didn't know what had happened to put them in their comas.

"Why can't I move?" Tutresiel demanded.

"The sleep leaves slowly. It will pass."

"What's going on?" Xaphan said groggily.

Max's heart leaped. Shoftiel was blocking her view of the fire angel, but he was definitely alive and awake.

"Shoftiel? What are you doing here? Where are we?" Arctic cold underlined his words. He did not like the red-winged angel. Max didn't know if it was ordinary angel antagonism or something more personal.

Shoftiel gave his speech again.

"Who's wronged us?" Xaphan asked, and Shoftiel's wings flared wide.

"The witches of this *anneau*," Shoftiel said. "But more than them, this one is responsible for your chains." His wings folded, and he turned, pointing an accusing finger at Max.

Xaphan took in Max. "What have you done to her?" he asked Shoftiel in a dead voice. The flames on his wings flashed from orange to blue-white. It was the color of his rage.

"Little, so far," said Shoftiel. "But now that you are awake to bear witness, it is time to begin."

He glanced up at the sky. It was November, and the days were pretty short. Max figured it was about an hour before sunset.

"No," said Tutresiel. "I cannot move. I want to make her bleed myself."

Max's eyes widened, but he was watching Shoftiel.

"As do I," Xaphan said. He had managed to wrench himself up a few inches. "I demand the right to punish her myself."

Shoftiel stared back and forth between them. Max

couldn't see his face, but the smoky red of his wings was agitated. Finally, he nodded. "I will wait for one hour for you to recover. Justice waits for no one."

He started up the steps. At the top, he turned. His gaze locked with Max's, and his expression was no longer amused. It was cruel and promised pain beyond comprehension.

Sterling rose and bowed low to each of the angels. All three ignored him, which clearly pissed him off. Good. Maybe he'd get into it with Shoftiel and make a distraction.

The magic holding Max in place had vanished. But if she made a run at Shoftiel, he'd dodge. Or drop her before she got anywhere near him. But maybe she could make him come after her . . .

"So all of this is about two winged mutants who call themselves angels?" she asked. "Please. If you three were really angels, you wouldn't be down here on earth answering to witches. Even you, Daffy. You're at Sterling's beck and call, aren't you? Might as well be a dog that fetches. Do you sit and heel, too? I bet you aren't even housebroken."

The angel bristled. Tutresiel made a sound like suppressed laughter. Max darted a look at him. He gave a faint shake of his head. *Don't fuck with Shoftiel.* But she had to. She didn't know if Tutresiel and Xaphan could handle the other angel, and even if they could, she couldn't risk that it would be too late before they finished defrosting.

"I serve no one," Shoftiel hissed.

"Wow. Really? Seems like you're all about the Last Standers."

"They serve me," he said haughtily, gesturing at Sterling, who fell to his knees, bending until his forehead rested on the angel's feet. Max couldn't tell if it was the cult leader's idea or if Shoftiel had used magic to drag him down.

"I thought they served God," Max said. "You're just another of his servants, right? Doing whatever he tells you. A slave, really."

The gold in his wings sparked, casting gleaming showers down around him. Sterling yelped as charred spots speckled his robes and face where they landed, but the man didn't—or couldn't—move out of the way.

Max smiled. "What's the matter? Did I strike a nerve? Maybe you want to glue my mouth shut again. Truth hurts and all that."

"My kind are not slaves. For you to have put your paltry bindings on these two, you must pay. You must be an example to any who think to follow in your footsteps," he told her. "You have never felt pain like the kind I will inflict upon you."

"I don't know," she said thoughtfully. "You might be surprised. I'm better at getting tortured than anybody I know. It's my own special talent. You'll have to think hard to come up with something that hasn't already been done to me."

His lips peeled from his teeth in a scornful smile. "You underestimate me." He gestured, and a gob of red smoke flew from his fingers. It grew into a cloud and wrapped around Max. Instantly, she began to itch, just as she had in the angel vault—how many nights ago now? Only two? It seemed impossible.

Max didn't let herself react. "Now, that's what I call a lack of imagination. What are you, a one-trick pony?

Besides, I didn't bind Tutresiel and Xaphan. They bound themselves. This was their choice."

His upper lip curled. "No angel would ever willingly submit to a witch."

"And yet there they are. You really are stupid," Max said, trying to provoke him. He wasn't getting riled up the way she needed him to. She had to find a way to push his buttons. But the itching was getting to her. She was already weak. If this kept up more than a few minutes, it might be the end. She couldn't let herself fall apart. "I said they bound themselves. Giselle had nothing to do with it. 'Course, I *did* talk them into it."

It occurred to her then to wonder why Shoftiel had chosen her for the target of his ire.

Shoftiel stiffened, and his wings ruffled and lifted, the smoky red feathers trailing crimson. She was getting to him. She walked up the steps until she was between Tutresiel and Xaphan. Both angels watched her. Tutresiel's eyes were mere slits, and he looked like he wanted to strangle her. Xaphan flicked his fingers at her. The message was clear from both: don't piss off Shoftiel. Wait until they recovered.

Message received and ignored.

Max reached out and trailed her fingers up each of their thighs and hips. She felt them twitching, their muscles hardening beneath her touch. It wouldn't be long before they could move. But she couldn't be sure that they could take Shoftiel out. Her plan was still the best chance of success.

"They are lovely, aren't they?" she purred, as well as she could purr, given that termites were chewing every inch of her skin and her vision was starting to haze over with the drain of the amulet and her bleeding chest. The last time he'd hit her with this particular torture, she'd almost died. She would have if Giselle hadn't saved her. She had to get him to come after her *now*, if she was going to succeed in taking him into the abyss.

"You know what I just can't get enough of? I love telling them what to do, knowing they have to obey. Like little puppets. I pull the strings, and they dance for me. I can't tell you how many times I've made them crawl on the ground at my feet to lick my boots. I can make them eat shit." She forced a laugh. "It just never gets old."

Shoftiel made a low sound in his throat that quickly grew into a roar. His wings snapped wide, and red smoke swirled up from his feet, circling him in a slow cyclone. His body tensed, his fingers curling into claws. The air shivered with heat and electricity.

That did it. He was pissed now.

The Last Standers backed away, some of them starting to break and run. Sterling looked sickly. He was not at all in control of the situation or of Shoftiel, and he clearly knew it. Max wondered whether it was fear or magic that kept him frozen in place.

"On your knees," Shoftiel said, and with every word, a swarm of black insects emerged from his mouth. They multiplied until there had to be millions of them. They bunched and ribboned in the air, then the three swarms dove at Max with a buzzing whine.

They dropped over her like a wriggling, creeping cloth. They crawled into her ears and eyes, up her nose, and inside her open wounds. She shuddered.

Bugs. They bit her, and between them and the itching, she wanted to tear her skin off. But she forced herself to remain still and upright. She wouldn't give Shoftiel the satisfaction of watching her squirm.

"I said, on your knees!" he shouted, and the sound echoed across the valley. Max's eardrums ruptured, and she could only hear watery, muffled sounds. She shook her head. Pressure slammed down on her. Her legs wobbled. She locked her knees, leaning on Tutresiel and Xaphan. The latter's wings scorched her. She almost didn't mind. The heat cooked the bugs, too, and distracted her from the incessant itching.

She drew a breath, sucking insects into her mouth. "Come here and make me," she said hoarsely, then spit and snapped her lips shut. There were still bugs in her mouth. She swallowed them, her stomach lurching. Disgusting.

The next thing she knew, she was flying through the air. A moment after that, she felt the blow. Shoftiel had punched her in the chest. She landed in snow. She gasped as the air burst out of her. She couldn't catch her breath. Her ribs were caved in, and her lungs were sprinklers. Her heart felt as if there was a knife driving through it, and it sent pain radiating down her arms and legs. The only good thing was that the bugs and itching had vanished. It was almost worth it.

She closed her eyes for a second, then opened them again and started to push herself up. But before she could move, Shoftiel was in front of her. He stood between her splayed legs, his foot on her stomach. In his hand was a spear made of red smoke magic. It had two pointed prongs.

"You are not worthy even to look upon us."

"Right, because you are so fucking special," Max said. "Like herpes and Alzheimer's. So tell me, what made you get your panties all wadded up about me? I'm no witch. I can't bind anyone to anything. If you're all pissy about Tutresiel and Xaphan being bound to Horngate, why come after me? Why not Giselle?"

He stared down at her, his jaw jutting, his wings gilded smoke. Her hands inched toward his foot on her stomach. She didn't want him turning into smoke or evaporating before she got a good grip on him. She gathered herself to take him into the abyss.

Shoftiel bent lower, as if he wanted to share a secret. The scent of him was strong: syrupy-sweet and sharp, like über-hot peppers.

"They stink of you," he said. "Like you rubbed yourself all over them."

Max blinked. *Not* the answer she expected. "So you've got some jealousy issues?" she asked, her fingers working closer to his foot. She had spent a lot of time with the two angels. She'd leaned on them, hugged them, yelled at them, hit them, begged them to come back. "You got a secret hard on for Xaphan? Or maybe Tutresiel? I gotta say, I don't see it. Neither one of them would give you the time of day. I think they're way out of your league, Daffy. Maybe you should find yourself a nice sheep or a goat. They wouldn't give you much trouble."

He thrust down with his leg, and she gasped, tears running down the sides of her face into her hair. Her breath gurgled in her throat, and her stomach was tight. She was bleeding out inside. She wasn't going to last much longer.

"You have been judged. You have been found guilty. This is your punishment," he said, biting off every word. He drew back the spear.

"Just like that? A quickie? And here I thought you wanted me to suffer and die a thousand deaths and all that kind of crap. Oh, wait. You can't keep it up, can you? You've got a premature-ejaculation problem, don't you? You can't hold your vengeance? You've got to spurt it all out in one shot?"

She laughed. The sound was wet and weak, and it felt as if a lawn-mower blade was spinning inside her chest. "I thought you'd have more stamina than that."

The muscles in the angel's arms and chest bulged as his hands tightened convulsively on the spear. It might look like smoke, but it was solid. He was past pissed off. His mouth opened, but only inarticulate sound came out. He lifted his arm so that he could stab her through with force.

In that moment, several things happened at once.

Behind him, light flashed as if a nuclear bomb had gone off. Tutresiel rose in the air, streaming white fire from his feathers. He held an enormous sword in his hands. It glowed with such brilliant witchlight that the sun seemed to dim. His face was a study of rage. His attention was fixed on Shoftiel.

Good, thought Max dizzily. Once she took out Shoftiel, he'd be able to keep Sterling under control.

Then Xaphan rose on the other side of Shoftiel. His wings burned with blue-white flames. Max could feel the heat from them. The snow around her softened and melted into water.

"Let her go, Shoftiel," Xaphan ordered.

"She requires punishment. I have judged. I will have justice."

"You judged wrong," Tutresiel said in that soft voice that should have made Shoftiel's innards turn to Jell-O. "Let her go."

Shoftiel turned his head, disbelief written on his face. "You want to *protect* her?"

"She belongs to us," Xaphan said, not quite answering the question.

"I brought you back from Ledrel," Shoftiel said. "I want her. That is the price."

"No," Tutresiel said. "We do not agree."

"I brought you out of there, and I can send you back," Shoftiel warned. "You have no choice."

Could he really? Max gritted her teeth. Not while she could still do something about it. She'd been caught up in their exchange, but now she started dropping into her fortress.

She channeled all of her pain into strength, drawing on the spells that had created her. It was enough. Barely. As she started the plunge inside, she clamped her hands around Shoftiel's ankle and dragged him into the abyss.

Except that she didn't. She was too damned tired.

He looked down at her. "Pathetic."

"Get your foot off her," Tutresiel said, dropping to the ground. He raised his sword, pointing it at the base of Shoftiel's neck.

In that moment, Max knew exactly what she had to do. She sat up, forcing her body to obey. She had little strength. She weighed a thousand pounds. If she was lucky, she'd get one shot at this. She just had to time it right.

"You *threaten* me?" Shoftiel said. "You should be on your knees thanking me for pulling you out of Ledrel. You could have been stuck there for thousands of years. And for what? *Her?*"

He grabbed Max and jerked her to him. *Perfect.*

"She is more valuable to me than I can say," Tutresiel said softly. "Take your hands off her."

Shoftiel made a sound of pure fury and shoved Max away, releasing a bolt of fiery magic. Tutresiel knocked it away with his sword. The two turned in a circle, Shoftiel launching more bolts and Tutresiel batting them away.

Xaphan pulled Max back against him, enfolding her in his wings and pouring healing energy into her.

"What were you trying to do?" he whispered against her ear.

"What I'm still trying to do," she said. "Get rid of your buddy out there."

"There is no way. Shoftiel is powerful. Even together, Tutresiel and I can't beat him."

"There has to be something that will hurt him," Max said. Shoftiel wouldn't give up on killing her and wiping away Horngate. He was determined before, but now he was humiliated. He would bear that grudge till the end of days.

Xaphan shook his head, then gave a shrug. "If there is something, then I don't know what it is."

"What happens if Tutresiel skewers Shoftiel on his sword?"

"I don't know." He fell silent a long moment. Max looked up at him. "There's something you aren't saying. What is it?"

"It is a legend from long ago," he said reluctantly.

"What legend?"

"That once, many hundreds of years ago, Shoftiel visited his judgment on a pure soul. The woman's child forged a blade of blood and bone and drove it through Shoftiel's heart. He was banished to the Mistlands for five hundred years."

"A blade of blood and bone?" she repeated.

"That is the story."

"It's . . ." An idea was beginning to bloom in Max's brain. A crazy idea, but if the story was true—"It's a good story. If you don't take it too literally."

"I don't understand."

"That's okay, I do. Let me go now. It's time to finish this."

Xaphan lifted his wings away. Max felt much stronger, although Shoftiel's brand still bled on her chest and stomach. Apparently Xaphan's healing had limits.

Tutresiel and Shoftiel were still sparring. Max took a breath and marched up beside Tutresiel, putting her hand on his corded forearm. "I got this," she said, never taking her eyes off Shoftiel. She strode toward him.

"Let's be done with this," Max said, coming to stand a few feet away.

He raised his brows. "I will say this. You are no coward," he said. "I admit that it will give me some pain to kill you."

"Ain't that sweet?" she said. "Like a Hallmark card from Charles Manson. Before we go any further, I'd like to know something," she said, inching forward a little.

"What is that?"

"According to you, my crime was to enslave angels

and to contemplate harvesting their parts for my depraved and nefarious purposes. Is that about right?"

"It is."

"But now you know I didn't enslave anyone, and I didn't put them in comas, and I didn't play the farmer card, either. So why are you still out to kill me?"

His expression stilled. "Are you saying you are innocent?"

"What do you think?"

He lifted his chin arrogantly. "Your kind is never innocent," he said. "Perhaps you did not do this thing, but you are not innocent."

"Any more than you are, oh, angel of righteousness and justice," Max said dryly. "But in this case, Daffy, you are wrong."

Throughout their conversation, she'd been inching closer, so that by the time she spoke those last words, there was less than a foot between them. She gave no warning of her intention. Quick as a cobra strike, she jerked back her arm, flattening her hand and jabbing it into his chest as hard as she could. Her arm slid through his flesh, a blade of blood and bone.

In the blink of an eye, the world vanished.

25

THE DAY PASSED AGONIZINGLY SLOWLY. ALEXANder lost track of Max inside the haze of magic surrounding the cult compound. He paced the length of the basement, the pain in his head unrelenting.

Tyler watched him, sitting cross-legged at the foot of the basement steps. He pinwheeled his knives in his hands, his eyes hooded. He paused every now and again to cut a slice across his palm and watch it heal up. Alexander should have told him not to waste his energy, but Tyler needed an outlet for his boiling emotions. It was that or go chasing after Max in the sun. Cutting was less fatal.

Thor squatted against the wall, his gaze turned inward. His hands clenched and unclenched, as if he wanted to strangle someone.

Gregory had fallen into a hard sleep, and the other Blades snatched what rest they could. Oak sat on the steps above Tyler, watching Alexander pace.

"Waiting sucks," Nami announced in the silence of the afternoon.

"Amen," Tyler said softly. He set his hands on his knees and looked up at the ceiling, then sighed and looked back down again. "She's got to be okay," he said to no on in particular. "She has to."

No one answered. She *did not* actually have to be okay, and that was the problem.

Alexander shied from the thought. It made his head hurt. Max was resilient, smart, stubborn, and strong. She could take care of herself.

The question was, would she?

As dusk began to fall, he roused Gregory and ordered everybody to eat all they could from the pantry shelves. Finally, they opened the door and spilled out of the farmhouse. The snow had stopped falling at last. Alexander closed his eyes, pushing his senses outward.

"Holy Mother of fuck," he said slowly, using one of Max's favorite sayings.

"What?" Tyler said.

"Tutresiel and Xaphan are awake," Alexander said, then broke into a run, heading for a knob of ground well above Mansion Heights. Tyler and Thor fell in beside him. Behind them, the others strung out. Steel and Flint trailed farther behind, having loaded Gregory into his kayak sled.

"Awake?" Thor echoed. He shook his head. "Awake?" he repeated again. "What the hell are they doing here? How did they know?"

"I could not say. But I am absolutely sure it is them." He could not mistake their spirit flames—silver fire. "There is also a witch I do not recognize. Probably Sterling. Giselle, Kyle—oh, damn. They have got Tris,

Geoff Brewer, Doris Lydman, Liam, and Bambi. How did they get caught?"

"Are they alive? What about Max?" Tyler said.

"They are alive. No Max."

A crowd of people circled the area where the angels and the witches had collected. There were several thousand of them. Max was not among them.

"That means she made it into the abyss," Tyler said, his voice denying any other possibility.

Alexander did not answer. A shaft of fire burned through his head. His left eye felt as if it was going to pop out of his skull, and his chest felt as if it was going to explode.

"You don't see any sign of that demon she was talking about, do you?" asked Tyler.

"No." Alexander leaped through the snow. Why was she not back yet? Depositing the demon should not take so long. Unless she had been forced to take him into the trap. He shied from the thought, the pain in his head spiking.

A gleaming building rose up on a knoll. It was still more than a mile away. The place was lit up like a gaudy Las Vegas casino.

Suddenly, an angel rose in the air. His wings glinted silver. Tutresiel. He streaked through the darkness, heading straight for the group of Shadowblades. He dropped down in front of Alexander, landing in the deep snow. He held his sword. It lit the night with a beacon of white witchlight.

"Where did she take him?" he demanded before anybody else could speak.

"Take who?" Alexander shot back. Although he had

to admit to being glad the angel was alive and ready to fight, he still did not like the bastard.

Tutresiel bared his teeth. "Shoftiel. Where did Max take him?"

"Into the abyss. She thought she could dump him there," Tyler answered.

Tutresiel tipped his head back, closing his eyes. "Fuck, no," he murmured. He straightened. "Where are the Grims? They can follow her into the abyss, right?"

"Gone," Alexander said tonelessly. One thing was certain, Tutresiel liked Max. He was worried for her, and that scared the shit out of Alexander.

"Gone? Where?"

"They followed a family of salamanders through a crack in the world," Thor said. "All of them just left. So did Spike, Max's Calopus."

"Max had a Calopus?" Tutresiel asked, startled. "When did she find one of those?" He ran a hand through his hair in an uncharacteristic show of agitation. "Just how long were we in Ledrel?"

"If by Ledrel you mean mostly dead, four or five weeks," Tyler answered

Tutresiel's gaze ran across the Blades, searching for who was not there. "Niko," he said. "And Simon. Where are they?"

That he knew who was missing startled Alexander. "Dead," he said.

Something passed over Tutresiel's cold face and vanished.

"What exactly is going on?" Alexander asked. "Who is Shoftiel?"

Tutresiel gave him a long stare. Alexander glared back, not backing down. He had fought the angel before, and while he knew he could not kill him, Tutresiel clearly could be brought to the edge of death. Alexander was willing to make the effort to bring him there again.

"He is one of the angels of punishment—the Malake Habbalah."

"He's an *angel*?" Tyler said. "How many of you are there? And why are you so fixated on Horngate?"

"There are thousands of us," he said. "We all have varying powers and abilities, much like witches or Shadowblades. Shoftiel, however, is special."

"Of course he is," Thor said. "How special is he, exactly?"

"There are seven angels of punishment. Each one has dominion over a region of hell, which is not in any way hell as your religious books envision it. Each presiding angel has unusually strong powers."

He stopped a moment, his teeth gritting together. "Shoftiel has always thought himself superior. Religious documents have named him the angel of God's judgment, and he loves the role. He believes angels should be ruling the world, with every human and nonhuman enslaved to service. While undoubtedly many other angels agree, we don't tend to trust one another. Nor do we take orders well. It takes a lot to get us to join together. Shoftiel hasn't been able to gather the forces he needs. Somehow he learned that Xaphan and I were in Ledrel in Horngate."

"Ledrel?" Alexander interrupted.

"Between life and death. He assumed that the coven

was keeping us in order to harvest parts of our wings and bodies to fuel their spells. So he came to rescue us, no doubt expecting us to join his cause and serve him as payment."

"So why all this other with Sterling? And why go after Max?"

"Sterling? What is that?"

"Not what—who. A witch. He has formed a cult called Earth's Last Stand and has been hunting down witches and killing them. Your friend Shoftiel has been helping him. Why would he do that?"

Tutresiel shook his head. "Shoftiel is no friend of mine. He is mad and, at the same time, brilliant. He likes to spoil and ruin. It would suit him well to be worshipped and to destroy witches and corrupt humans in the bargain. As for Max—" He drew a breath and blew it out, turning away. "He said he smelled her on us. She'd touched us. That was enough to punish her."

"That's because she was in that stupid vault every free moment, talking to you and trying to wake you up," Tyler said hotly.

The angel nodded, saying nothing.

"So what now? Max was going to take Shoftiel into the abyss to lose him. Are you saying he can walk the abyss like she can?" Alexander asked.

"She didn't go to the abyss," Xaphan said, dropping silently down beside them.

Tutresiel scowled. "Of course she did. Where else could she go?"

Xaphan gave him a long look. "Blade of blood and bone," he said at last.

Tutresiel stared, nonplussed. "That's—" He broke

off, a smile playing around his lips. "She beat him. Max beat him at his own game."

"What does that mean?" Tyler demanded. "What are you talking about?"

"I told Max an old story about someone getting vengeance on Shoftiel and sending him to the Mistlands. When an innocent woman was wrongly killed by Shoftiel, her son forged a sword of blood and bone and used it to banish Shoftiel to the Mistlands for five hundred years," Xaphan explained.

"What does that have to do with Max?" Alexander asked.

"At the end, she thrust her arm through his heart. A blade of blood and bone. They vanished," Tutresiel said. "I had forgotten the story and assumed she took him into the abyss. But that's not where they went at all."

"Where *did* they go?"

"The Mistlands."

"Where's that?" Tyler pushed. "How do we get her back?"

"I don't know, and I don't know," Xaphan answered.

Alexander stood apart, no longer hearing anything they said. A roaring sound filled his ears, and the pressure in his chest swelled so tightly his heart thudded unevenly.

Inside him, something gave. Armor cracked like spring ice splintering apart on a frozen river. A torrent of emotions washed through him, and he rocked back and forth as if struck.

"Alexander?"

He could barely hear Thor ask his name. He turned, eyeing his friend. "What did I do?" he whispered hoarsely. And all of the fear, loss, and pain he thought he could avoid came crashing in on him like a tsunami. It crushed him under its rushing weight. He struggled against the raging cataract, then gave in, letting himself be carried away.

His Prime rose, smothering all vestiges of his humanity. But he was not out of control. He was brutal, precise, and focused. Max would want him to see the rest of this through. She was not gone. She was not dead. He had given up on her before; he would not do it again.

He became aware of the sudden wariness of the Blades around him. They had fallen back, watching him carefully. He ignored them, turning back to Tutresiel.

"How is everyone else? Is Giselle all right?"

"They are bound in Shoftiel's magic. Xaphan and I cannot break it without hurting them. A witch might." He glanced at Gregory.

"Take him," Alexander ordered. "We will follow."

Without another word, Tutresiel launched off the ground, swooping back down to pluck Gregory out of the kayak and fly him back to where the others were imprisoned. Xaphan leaped into the air after him.

"You're eyes have gone white," Thor told Alexander as they ran after the angels.

"Have they?"

"But you're okay? Not going to rip any throats out?"

"The night is young yet," Alexander said with a toothy grin. "And we have a lot of enemies left to kill."

The glowing yellow building reminded Alexander of a Greek temple. It had columns all around, with broad steps leading up the front. Everything was made from gold light.

Sterling and his people had retreated, harried away by Xaphan. They had not gone far, just down to Mansion Heights, and it looked as if they were forming up in a mob. They were going to be back before long.

Alexander's stomach tightened. It would be a bloodbath, with Sterling's followers doing most of the bleeding. They could not hope to stand against Tutresiel and Xaphan, even with a powerful witch like Sterling helping them. Stir in Giselle, Gregory, Kyle, and the Shadowblades, and those people did not have a chance. They did not deserve such a death. They were stupid and gullible but not evil. He could not allow it to happen. Max would not want him to.

Gregory was at the top of the steps. All of the Horngate prisoners were locked inside columns of power. Although their eyes were open, they seemed unconscious and unaware of their surroundings. Gregory was working on releasing Giselle.

Alexander grappled with his emotions. The pain was raw, as if every nerve he had was being scraped by rusty razors. He was suffocating. Drowning in molten lead. His head pounded, his body throbbing as his hurt grew and grew. His Prime was growing more agitated, and despite his outward demeanor, the boundary between reason and going feral was as thin as gauze. The wildness filled him and overflowed. He gripped a spur of exposed granite, trying to hold himself down to sanity.

A hand fell on his shoulder. He looked up. Tyler's face was carved ice. His eyes had begun to show a ring of feralness. His fingers dug into Alexander's shoulder, pinching bone. The other hand gripped a knife, his knuckles white.

"I can't—" He gritted through clenched teeth.

Alexander did not think. Instinct guided him. He pulled Tyler against him, wrapping his arms around him and letting his Prime loose. Tyler did not need reassurance. There was none to give. What he needed was his sense of place. He needed a leader, a Prime, to help him pull himself back together. Or push him back together.

The power of Alexander's Prime washed out, wrapping around the other Blades. He felt their relief as they leaned into his strength. Tyler made a harsh sound and tried to shove himself away. Alexander did not let him go.

His aura surrounded Tyler and smothered the feralness. He pushed the wildness back down inside the other Blade, feeling the moment when Tyler took control. Next, Alexander reached out to the others. Through sheer dominance, he settled them back down, helping them channel their panic, grief, and anger back into focus.

The worst of it was that every bit of their emotions only mounded on top of his own, making it that much more difficult to keep himself reined in. At the same time, helping them reminded him of what he was and his responsibilities as Prime. In the end, that gave him the strength he needed.

He let Tyler go.

The other man shook himself, not meeting his gaze. "Thanks."

"Anytime," Alexander said dryly.

He turned, and the other Blades drifted toward him, like metal to a magnet. None knew quite what to do. They needed action.

"Go check on Sterling," Alexander told Tyler. "Take everyone with you. Watch out. The Last Standers are armed to the teeth, and even without Shoftiel helping him, Sterling is a powerful witch."

Tyler nodded and gestured for the others to follow him.

Alexander trotted up the temple steps to check on Gregory. The witch was sweating and pale. He circled around the pillar holding Giselle, glancing up as Alexander joined him.

"These bonds are like nothing I've ever seen," Gregory said. "I haven't been able to put even a dent in them. I need Judith, but to tell the truth, I'm not sure she and I are going to be able to do much better."

Alexander chewed his lips, thinking. Then he strode back down the stairs to where the angels stood talking together.

"Gregory cannot get them out alone. He thinks Judith's help will not be enough." He turned and pointed to Liam and Bambi. "Those two are new friends of Max's. They just volunteered to be guinea pigs. I want you two to see if you can crack the magic. You have got Tutresiel's sword and Xaphan's magic. Between the two of you, you ought to be able to break open the spells."

"They might not survive," Xaphan pointed out.

"They might not," Alexander agreed. "Do it anyhow."

Both angels nodded and skimmed up the steps. Gregory drew back, watching. Tutresiel went first. He pulled his sword from the pocket universe he kept it stored in. It appeared flaming white in his upraised hands. He swung. The blade smashed against the golden column and bounced back. Magic exploded. The force shoved Alexander backward and widened the ring of melted snow surrounding the temple.

Tutresiel bent and looked at his handiwork. He shook his head and drew back to try again. This time, the white witchlight surrounding the blade seemed to sharpen, like a diamond lit by the sun. He swung straight down. The sword stuck in the column. The two magics crackled, sending bolts of sizzling gold and white streaking through the air. All around, the night grew hot as a blast furnace.

The muscles in Tutresiel's arms, back, and legs bulged as he struggled to pull his sword free. Finally, it came loose. He spun with the force of the release. He was panting.

He turned back to face the column. It no longer stood straight and round. Instead, it looked a little bit like melted taffy. It had bubbled and melted, and the top was blackened.

Tutresiel stood back a moment, and then his sword vanished. Before Alexander could ask what he was up to, he rose into the air until he was a good two hundred feet up. Then he turned and dove. He held his wings close and, at the last moment, spread them with a loud metallic ringing sound. Then he crashed into the column with the leading edge of one wing. The force flipped him around and sent him rolling down the steps and into the mud.

A moment later, the column simply shattered, the

chunks of it dissolving as they fell. Liam slumped to the floor. Xaphan bent and checked him.

"Alive," he said. He slapped the man's face. "Wake up."

Alexander bent and offered Tutresiel a hand. The angel eyed him disdainfully and stood on his own. His body was caked with mud.

They went up the stairs, where Liam was starting to come to. He blinked, his eyes widening at Xaphan. His attention moved to Tutresiel and then Alexander.

"Am I nuts?" he asked. "Or do the two guys standing next to you have wings?"

"They are angels," Alexander said.

Liam's gaze flicked back and forth between the two. "You have got to be shitting me. This is heaven? How come I hurt so fucking much? Where's all the white light?"

"You are not in heaven," Alexander said, reaching down to pull him up. Liam leaned against him heavily. "This is still Montana, and these angels, well, I would not call them particularly angelic. Come on, you need to get out of the way."

He pulled Liam down the steps and onto an outcropping of rock, before returning to Tutresiel and Xaphan. "Can you do that again? For Giselle?"

"I have to rest first," Tutresiel said. "I am still weak from being in Ledrel."

"You try, then," Alexander told Xaphan, not letting his frustration show. He pointed at Bambi. "See if you can get him out."

Xaphan gave a thin smile and extended his wings. Flames erupted along every single feather. The fire stretched high into the air. The flames were orange, blue, and yellow. Heat flashed through the air, drying the mud clinging to Tutresiel. Xaphan stepped up to the pillar and embraced it, folding his wings down around it.

Nothing happened.

Then the fire shifted into the white-blue of a welding torch. The stench of burning hair and ozone swelled in the air. The ground dried under the heat, and Alexander's lips and eyes turned parched. He backed away until he stood beside Liam, who was staring, his eyes wide.

"Is Jack going to be okay?" he asked in his rough voice.

"Hard to say." Alexander's mouth twitched with gallows humor. "If I recall the movie, Bambi survived the forest fire, if it makes you feel any better."

Liam snorted. "I feel like I've wandered into a horror flick," he said. "Afghanistan seems almost normal compared to this."

"Welcome to the new world," Alexander said. "Where your dreams and nightmares come true and everything you read in the fairy tales is real. Get used to it."

Just then, there was a sound of shattering glass, and Xaphan tumbled through the air, landing fifty feet from the temple. He sank through the snow, and the ground lit on fire, his wings igniting dirt and rock alike. He rolled to his feet and knelt down, setting his hand onto the burning earth. A moment later, the flames died, leaving a scorched spot a full twenty feet in diameter.

Alexander approached the temple, with Liam hard on his heels. Tutresiel got to Bambi before them. He picked him up like a rag doll. The unconscious man's head lolled, his hands and legs dangling lifelessly. Liam squeezed in and lifted his jaw. "Jack! C'mon, Jack! Wake up!" He gave Bambi a little shake.

The other man coughed suddenly. Tutresiel let him go, and he dropped like a bag of onions. Liam swore and crouched beside his friend. Alexander turned to Xaphan. The angel was practically translucent. *Dammit*.

"How long before you two might be able to release Giselle?" he asked.

"A couple of hours. Maybe more," Tutresiel said.

Gunshots rang out down in Mansion Heights. Alexander spun around and ran to get a better view. The Last Standers had gathered inside their barns and houses and spread out into bunkers all along the crown of the hill. Below, a mob of people were flowing out of Missoula. They rode on snowmobiles, skis, and snowshoes. They carried torches, but as the shots rang out, they doused the fires.

Kara had brought the cavalry, and a war was about to erupt. He had to stop it. Max would want him to stop it.

He turned to look at Tutresiel and Xaphan. "Get Sterling. Whatever it takes. Take him out. I will handle the rest."

He did not wait for a reply but launched himself down the hill. Even with Sterling gone, he did not know how nine Shadowblades were going to stop a war. Each side had at least a couple of thousand people and a lot of weaponry. It was going to take a miracle, and he was fresh out.

26

THE WORLD WAS WHITE. THERE WAS NO DEPTH to it. No shadows, no shapes. Just misty whiteness. Everything, that is, besides the red angel and Max. He was looking around him in patent disbelief. She watched him, part of her wanting to gloat at his defeat, the other part of her wondering just how she was going to get out of the place.

"You've been here before," she said, and her voice sounded washed-out and gray.

"Unfortunately," Shoftiel answered with a grimace. "I spent five hundred years here."

"Looks like you've got another five hundred to look forward to."

"Yes. Thanks for that."

"Nothing you didn't deserve."

"I did believe you were enslaving and harvesting my brothers."

"Well, that makes all your torture and murder all right, then," Max snapped. She looked down at herself. She was still naked from the waist up. Her right arm was smeared with his blood. His sigil on her stomach and chest was gone. "I stopped bleeding."

"My hold on you broke when you stabbed me. That was clever, by the way. Painful but clever."

"I don't suppose you know how to get out of here," she asked.

"No. Otherwise, I would not have waited five hundred years for the curse of the blood-and-bone blade to wear off."

"Of course, you could be lying. You probably are."

"I could be. I could want your delightful company for the next five centuries."

"No thanks." Max stretched and turned. "I think I'll have a look around."

"I will accompany you."

Max scowled. "I don't want your company."

"I didn't ask."

"Are you planning to try to kill me again, Daffy? Finish the job?"

"I would, but no one can die in the Mistlands."

"That's too bad. You could use a little killing." She started away and stopped when he fell in beside her. "What's your damage?"

He frowned. "My damage?"

"Why are you following me? We've established that you hate me and want to kill me. That pretty much means we're not going to be besties. So shove off."

"Afraid not. I'm not ready to say good-bye just yet, and once you disappear into the mists, chances are we will not see each other again."

"How big is this place?"

"Who knows? There are no landmarks, nothing to

measure by. You can walk forever, but who knows if you go in a straight line? It does tend to get monotonous. I once flew for what I believe was four days. I got nowhere."

At that point, it occurred to Max that she might be able to escape through the abyss. Gathering herself, she dropped into her fortress, and—nothing.

"No exit that way, I'm afraid," Shoftiel said, almost sympathetically. "I must have tried that a thousand times my first day and at least once every day after."

"What about food? Water?" Max was trying very hard not to sound as panicky as she was beginning to feel.

"Don't need them."

They wandered together through the endless mist. She was glad of Shoftiel's company, despite herself, and despite the insanity of strolling half-naked with the asshole who'd spent most of the last couple of days trying to kill her. The monotony was suffocating. Max bent to touch the ground. It was soft, like velvet, and slightly moist. There were no rocks, no trees, no landmarks of any kind.

She couldn't stay there. There had to be a way out.

"I take it your magic doesn't work?"

He shook his head. "I'm toothless in this realm."

Max put her head down, thinking. Maybe she should clack her heels together three times and say, "There's no place like home. There's no place like home. There's no place like home." Too bad she didn't have a pair of magic ruby slippers.

There had to be a way. She paced a circle around Shoftiel, then another and another. Around and around she went. He watched with a disdainful smirk.

Clearly, he thought that if he hadn't figured a way out in five hundred years, she wasn't going to, either.

What did you do when you were in a prison with no doors, no walls, no locks? But of course, there was a lock. The inability to leave. That was the lock.

Max stopped. She was a walking key. No lock could hold her. All she had to do was figure out how to leave.

And then she knew. There were no doors because the realm itself was a door. And if she was the key . . .

She grinned at Shoftiel. "Time for me to go home. Enjoy your stay. I look forward to never seeing you again."

With that, she closed her eyes and fell backward. In her mind, she pictured herself falling through the mist and out of it.

Falling, falling, falling, falling.

She bounced on hard-packed dirt, and her eyes popped open. She half expected to see Shoftiel laughing down at her. But he and the mist were gone.

27

ALEXANDER FLUNG HIMSELF HEADLONG DOWN the hill. The snow had turned to a glop of slush, ice, and mud. It was not until he had reached the top of Mansion Heights that he realized he had left Gregory up at the temple. Just then, a streak of fire erupted along the base of the hill in the field between the bottom of the Heights and the nearest neighborhood. It ran from right to left and grew into a wall of flame, separating the two motley armies.

Xaphan.

The flames rose more than forty feet in the air and showed no sign of diminishing. *Effective,* Alexander thought. Now to figure out how to contain Sterling and his minions before this thing turned into a massacre.

Both sides were well armed, but he had no doubts that the Last Standers had stockpiled ammunition. They had the high ground, bunkers, and Sterling. Not to mention a T-shaped killing field. The attackers would have to cross the open field along the bottom of the Heights where Xaphan's walls burned, then they would filter up the center in a long wash between the houses. The Last Standers would be able to pick off their enemies with little risk to themselves.

His senses spread wide and picked up on the Blades. They had infiltrated the Heights and were working their way inward toward Sterling's stronghold. Alexander could see the witch's spirit flame. It was dark pink with overlays of blue and yellow. The angels were circling above. There was no one who could not see the brilliant spread of Tutresiel's silver wings and his sword. He was limned in white light. Xaphan's wings trailed fire, and flames crackled around his body in lurid contrast to Tutresiel.

As the Last Standers caught sight of them, they emerged from their bunkers and houses, pointing upward, their faces a mixture of awe, fear, and joy. Alexander slipped in among them. Jody silently slid up beside him. Then, one by one, the other Blades sifted out of the crowd. Only Tyler, Oak, and Thor were absent. Alexander pulled them off to the side of one of the big barns. "Go look in the bunkers and the houses," he whispered. "Look for explosives. This is not the kind of group that will go quietly when they lose. They will have a backup plan. I am guessing it will be scorched earth."

"What do we do when we find them?" Ivy asked, her hazel eyes sharp and intense.

"See what Gregory can do to defuse them. Flint, better go fetch him. He is still up at the temple."

"What are you going to do?" asked Nami. She looked like she wanted to rip something apart. Or someone.

Alexander could not blame her. He felt the same.

Max. He had no words to encompass the ache he felt for her. "I am going to see about Sterling. Oh, hell," he said as the wall of fire collapsed suddenly. "That is not good."

He backed away from the barn house and leaped up to the top of the roof. From there, he leaped across to another and then another. The Last Standers were thick below him, crowding into the spaces between the houses as they followed the angels.

The smell of torched dirt and an earthy wetness rose on the breeze. The flame wall had melted masses of snow in both directions, and now water ran in muddy deluges down the side of the hill, filling the wash at the center of the Heights with a tumbling torrent. The roofs of the buildings were slick with ice and snow, and Alexander skidded to his knees more than once, clinging to the eaves to keep from sliding entirely off.

Finally, he came to a grand house at the end of a dead-end street. It was brightly lit with witchlight. Behind it was a broad, flat apron of land that overlooked Missoula. Sterling stood at the center, surrounded by a half dozen men and women.

He was wearing robes of pure white. In one hand, he held an ornate gold cross that was big enough to choke a horse. In the other, he held a Bible. He was watching the two angels circle above him. Unlike his followers, he looked more angry than anything else.

"Come down and face me, dogs of Satan!" he called. "In the name of God, I demand it!"

He held up the cross, and a beam of gold light shot out of it. It nailed Xaphan in the chest. The angel folded inward with a jerk and jetted back through the air.

"Feel the wrath of the Almighty! Scum of the world, you and your master—Satan—will know the power of the Lord. I am the Hand of God. Bow down at His feet!"

With that, he unleashed another bolt of magic, this time at Tutresiel. The angel dodged it, and a moment later, Xaphan recovered.

Both angels attacked. Xaphan cast a spear of fire at Sterling, who batted it away with the hand holding the Bible. His body was encased in a gold shield, and the burning lance drove into the ground. Next, Tutresiel dove, his sword singing in the air. He brought it down on Sterling's shield. The cult leader thrust upward with the Bible, flinging Tutresiel back. He was very strong.

At that moment, the group surrounding Sterling moved in closer to him. They set their hands on his shoulders and back, bending their heads and chanting prayers. The smell of magic increased, and the gold light surrounding him brightened, turning brassy and hard. It had no effect on the men and women pouring magic into him. He had a coven, and they were giving him their magic. It poured into him.

More of his minions crowded in. They set their hands on one another, making a chain of prayer and power. Alexander gaped. The intensity of Sterling's power grew by the moment. He was a blood witch, drawing his power from blood and death, joy, pain—all the emotions of humanity. He had surrounded himself with thousands of people whose sole desire was to charge him with strength and energy. They were flooding him with all the fervor of their faith, hopes, and dreams. It was a potent cocktail.

Alexander scowled. There was no good way to combat that power. Even slaughtering the Last Standers wouldn't help. The magic that came from spilling blood was even stronger. Sterling would just gorge on the magic.

He started as Tyler, Oak, and Thor leaped up onto the roof beside him.

"The people down below are getting curious. They are starting to move up," Thor said.

"It's not every day people get to see an angel," Oak said.

"If they had any sense, they'd be running for the hills," Tyler said.

"Train wrecks and plane crashes," Alexander said. "Everybody has to get a look."

"Might be the last thing they do, if this keeps up," Tyler said as Sterling unleashed several quick bolts of magic at the hovering angels. They dodged, but the shock wave from the magic sent them spinning. They caught themselves, maintaining a more healthy distance.

"Neither one of them is at full strength," Alexander said. "They've used a lot of energy since they woke up. I do not know if they can handle this bastard." And if Shoftiel returned, they would need the two angels to hold him at bay.

"Got any bright ideas?" Thor asked.

"A bullet to the back of his head would work well enough," Oak suggested.

"If his shield allowed it," Alexander agreed.

"I'll go find out," the Blade said, and dropped down off the roof. Finding a rifle among the many-armed minions was not going to be a hardship.

Five minutes later, Oak clambered back up onto the roof. He carried a .30–06 rifle slung over his back. It was a standard hunting rifle for the area. Oak paused to check the weapon, making sure it was loaded.

"Are you any good with that?" Tyler asked.

"I can hit a squirrel in the eye at a thousand yards," he said. "Hope it's sighted in," he said, kneeling at the edge of the roof. He wrapped the strap around his forearm and raised the rifle, peering down it.

He squeezed the trigger. The rifle crack echoed over the valley. Oak shot the bolt and pulled it back, the cartridge flying out. He aimed and shot again, then lifted the gun, shaking his head.

"No good."

Suddenly, a hail of bullets launched up at the roof. The four Blades dove flat as bullets whistled past. It seemed that every single one of Sterling's minions was taking potshots at them.

A flaming ball smashed into the building. The place exploded, and the four Blades went flying in the air. Alexander's clothes ignited, and pieces of wood and metal debris pierced him all over. He bounced off the edge of another roof and plummeted to the mud on the other side. Hands grabbed him, dragging him onto pavement. A couple dozen guns pointed down at him.

"Who is it?" someone asked.

"Don't know. But shit, he looks like a pincushion. Who can survive that?"

"He's a devil," a woman said. "A demon. Benjamin said they were out to destroy us. Kill him."

"No," another woman objected. "Take him to Benjamin. Demons don't die like us. Let Benjamin lay hands on him and banish him back to hell."

There were all-around agreements to that, and suddenly, Alexander's hands and feet were grasped, and they were carrying him. He held his head up to keep it from bouncing along the road.

They cried out for the crowd ahead to make way. A path opened up, and he quickly found himself dropped onto the ground in front of Sterling. The witch looked down at him, his blue eyes shining like jewels. He pointed the cross down at Alexander.

"What manner of demon are you, foul thing?"

Alexander sat up slowly. The fires on his clothes had gone out, thanks to the mud he had fallen into. He pulled an inch-wide splinter out of his side and tossed it aside, then yanked several more from his arms and legs. He was lucky he had not been stabbed in the heart.

"I am not a demon," he said, staring up at the witch. "And you are no prophet of God. You are nothing more than a witch. The same kind you stuck on poles on the hill."

"Blasphemer!" shouted the Last Standers. "Devil scum!"

Sterling lifted a hand, all the while staring down at Alexander. "My Lord is slow to anger and great in power. He will not leave the guilty unpunished. His way is the whirlwind and the storm. He rebukes the sea and dries it up. He makes the rivers run dry. The mountains quake before Him, and the hills melt away. Who can withstand His fierce indignation? Who can endure His righteous anger? His wrath will pour out on this world and drive Satan and his minions back to hell."

He lifted both hands into the air. "Lord in heaven above, visit your wrath and justice on this creature of darkness! Send him back to the netherworld with your fallen children. My Lord, your glory is great, your strength immeasurable, your mercy wondrous. These creatures must not be allowed to destroy your children, those for whom you sacrificed your only Son. Bring your light and shatter the darkness of evil. Save us, oh, Lord!"

The performance was stunning. He clearly believed every word. His face was a study of passion and ecstasy. Alexander tensed, certain that Sterling was going to strike him down with one of his bolts of magic. Instead, hell broke loose.

Gunfire rained down on them. People screamed and jostled to get away. Bodies fell and were trampled under panicked feet. Alexander lunged for Sterling. He was shocked when his arms went through the barrier surrounding him, and he drove the cultist to the ground. His skin blistered, and magic raked him.

Sterling smashed at him with the cross, and it was as if Alexander had been jabbed with the hot end of a power line. His hair stood on end, and his body sizzled. He convulsed, his body bouncing and contorting violently, as Sterling continued to unleash power into him.

Someone shouted, and the barrage of magic stopped. Alexander's body continued to shake and twitch. He tried to sit up and slumped to the ground. He tried again, rolling onto his stomach and shoving himself onto his hands and knees. It was all he could do to hold himself up.

He lifted his head, searching for Sterling. His mouth fell open. The witch lay spread-eagle on the ground. Above him stood Max. The first thing he noticed was that she was wearing a red blouse that was several sizes too big. Then he took in the rifle in her hand. She'd clubbed Sterling over the head with it.

She looked at Alexander. "You okay?"

He stared at her, drinking her in. "I love you."

She blinked, then shook her head. "You got hit hard. Stay here. I'm going to go help." She disappeared.

Alexander slowly pushed himself to his feet. He swayed, trying to put together the pieces of the scene before him, his head whirling all the while. She was alive. Max was alive! Gunshots continued to pop all around him. He glanced up. Tutresiel and Xaphan were diving down, trying to drive a wedge between the two small armies. Uphill, an explosion sent a burst of flames boiling up into the night. Another followed, then another. Then none.

He reached out with his senses, getting a feel of the battlefield. But he homed in on Tyler. The other Blade's spirit flame was flickering gray. He was sliding into death.

Alexander ran.

He found Tyler lying unconscious on a mound of firewood. Like Alexander, he'd been burned, and bits of wood and debris pierced him. But the real problem was that he'd been impaled on a branch attached to a chunk of firewood. It punched through the middle of his chest. His head and arms hung down, and blood puddled on the ground below him.

"Xaphan!" Alexander shouted, knowing there was no way the angel could hear him.

Alexander whipped off his shirt, pressing it to Tyler's stomach to help stanch the blood. He did not dare try to move him. Taking out the branch would likely kill him at that point. "Hold on, Tyler. Do not die. Not today. Today we get to win, understand? Max is okay. It would kill her to lose you. You have to hold on."

He shouted again for Xaphan and then Gregory, then turned all of his attention on Tyler, forgetting the battle, forgetting everything else. He pulled himself close, focusing all the force of his Prime on making the other Blade obey. "Stay put. It is not your time yet. You stay."

Dimly, he was aware of time passing. He and Tyler seemed to be in their own private world. No one looked at them. Tyler's heart was slowing. Alexander lifted his head and howled his frustration. "Xaphan!"

"Alexander? Oh, fuck." Nami stood on the ground beside the firewood.

"Get Xaphan or Gregory," Alexander urged. "Hurry."

She ran. Minutes later, Xaphan plummeted out of the sky. He set his hands on Tyler's shoulders, his face set.

"I need you to pull him off the branch," he said.

Alexander reached under Tyler's body and braced his hand against the log. He slid his other hand under the prone man's back. "Ready?" he asked.

Xaphan nodded.

With a quick jerk, Alexander pulled Tyler up while pushing the branch down. He pressed the palm of his left hand over the wound in Tyler's back and the other over his chest. He stayed that way, praying to whatever gods might be listening that Xaphan could heal him before he finished dying.

"Come on, come on, come on," he muttered. Then, almost imperceptible, he saw Tyler's spirit flame strengthening. The gray was fading, and the oranges, reds, greens, and yellows pulsed stronger with every breath.

He felt the wounds under his hands closing. Slowly, he shifted, sliding underneath the other man to brace him. It was another full five minutes before Tyler's eyes blinked and opened. He looked up at Alexander for a long moment.

"Tell me you aren't my Princess Charming," he said. "If you kissed me awake, I'm going to have to wash out my mouth with bleach."

Alexander grinned. "You wish. Sadly, Xaphan gets the honors."

Tyler sat up. "My hero," he said to Xaphan, batting his eyelashes.

The angel shook his head and grinned, then launched himself back up into the sky.

"What's going on?"

"No idea. Been playing nursemaid to you." Alexander paused, relishing the moment. "Max is back. She is okay."

Tyler stiffened. "Tell me you're not joking," he said quietly.

"Not joking."

The other man closed his eyes, his head falling forward. After a moment, he lifted it. "And Sterling?"

"Max bashed his head in. He could be alive. But if you are done napping, we had better go check on things."

Alexander stood, catching himself as the wood shifted beneath him. He held out a hand for Tyler.

"I am not an invalid," he said sourly.

"Humor me," Alexander said. "I like holding hands with you." He grinned and waggled his brows.

Tyler rolled his eyes. "Next you'll be wanting to line dance."

"Now that you mention it . . ."

Alexander led the way down the hill. Xaphan and Tutresiel stood between the two ragged armies. Lined up on the uphill side were what was left of the Last Standers. They milled uncertainly, watching the angels fearfully. Without Sterling, they had no one to pick up the reins of leadership. They were sheep. Tutresiel stood before them, his legs widespread, his wings raised, his sword held out before him.

"Think people are more freaked out by the fact that he's an angel with a big sword? Or the fact that he's a naked angel with a big sword?" Tyler asked.

Xaphan had his back to Tutresiel. He, too, stood with his wings spread wide. Fire sheathed his body.

The two angels glanced up as they approached. Alexander now began to notice the bodies littering the battleground. There were at least a couple of hundred and plenty more wounded, by the sounds of the moaning and screaming he could hear.

Thor prowled over to them. "What now?"

"Now we finish this," Max said, striding down the hill behind them.

Tyler swung her up in a bear hug. Thor grabbed her and did the same. Alexander just watched her, devouring her with his eyes. She frowned uncertainly at him.

"Make the Last Standers lay down arms," she said to Alexander. "I'm going to talk to Kara's militia." She walked down the hill past Xaphan.

Alexander walked up around the two angels to face the Last Standers. "You people have been under the influence of a witch," he called out. "You may not believe me, but he is not the hand of God or anybody else. You have been committing crimes in his name, and the folks below think it is time for you to pay for what you have done. Lay your weapons down, and if you have someone who can speak for you, send them out now. I do not want any more bloodshed tonight, but if you do not surrender yourselves, I promise we will slaughter you. No more good people are going to have to spill blood for your idiocy."

The words were cold and brutal. However they had come to follow Sterling, they were responsible for feeding him power, for answering his orders, and for everything he had done. At the moment, he could feel no mercy for them.

"That's a bit harsh," Tyler observed. "I like it."

"Go start taking away their guns," Alexander said. "Anybody resists, drop them like a bad habit."

He walked down to where Sterling lay bound and gagged. His Bible and cross lay a few feet away.

Alexander cut his legs free and helped him to his feet. Sterling sagged and then straightened. Just then, Gregory came around the corner. He was carrying a length of silver chain. It was round and woven like a rope. Witch chain. It was designed to suppress a witch's powers.

"Where did you get that?" Alexander demanded.

"Giselle's truck. I pulled it out before we left the farmhouse. Just in case. I'd forgotten it in the kayak.

Flint and I got it when he came back for me at the temple. I thought it might be useful."

"You thought right," Alexander said, and took the chain. He wrapped it around Sterling's neck twice and tied it tight. It knotted like a good rope.

The three of them headed down to where Max met with a half dozen people, including Kara. They looked at Sterling and then exchanged nervous looks as the three approached.

"He's toothless," Max said. "That chain suppresses his magic. You don't have to worry."

Kara glared at Sterling, then slapped him hard. "I wish I was sadistic enough to do to you what you have done to so many," she said. "But unlike you, I'm a good Christian. We'll kill you quick."

She introduced the others she had with her. "These two are Ethan and Buck Mercer," she said, gesturing at two older men with stoic faces. "They came with me. Over there is Professor Larry Hollins and Lorna Sill. They brought the university crowd with them."

Alexander nodded at them. The man was thin, with wire glasses and a full beard. The woman was tall and thick around the middle, with iron-gray hair. Her hands were punched down deep into her pockets, and if looks could kill, Sterling would be DOA.

"The one on the end there is Forest Driscoll." He was young, with a square face and quick, dark eyes. "He brought a group down from Rattlesnake Canyon." She looked at Max. "You're welcome in our compound any-time," she said, then glanced around. "Any of you. We owe you a huge debt." She paused. "Those are *real* angels?"

Max rubbed her ear, her expression rueful. "Yes, but

don't go thinking they're kind and gentle. These are angry, vicious angels. Rude, too. They weren't sent by any god. They are just creatures of magic, same as dragons and trolls and goblins. Don't be fooled into thinking otherwise."

"What now?" Lorna Sill asked. "What do you plan to do with the Last Standers? Sterling?"

"We still have some cleanup to do," Max said. "I am going to leave it up to you to deal with the Last Standers. I'll warn you, though, don't be too merciful. Sterling used magic to persuade them to follow him, but they still did what they did from their own free will. In the end, you have to figure out who needs to be punished and who you can trust. If you choose to lock them up, you'll have to feed them and keep them warm, and that's already going to be hard to do for your own families this winter. If you turn them out, they're just as likely to turn around and come after you again. On the other hand, killing them all has its own drawbacks."

Alexander smiled grimly, watching their faces. They were going to be making some tough decisions. Better them than him. Humans should judge humans.

He held out the end of the witch chain, handing it to Kara. "While he is wearing that chain, Sterling cannot do magic. If you do not want to deal with him, we will."

He and Max started to turn around.

"Wait," Forest said.

Alexander stopped, his brows rising.

"That's it? The fight's over, just like that?" He sounded faintly bewildered. "No more Sterling? No more Last Standers?"

Max nodded. "There's bound to be magical trouble cropping up. We'll be around to take care of it. We'll help you in other ways, too. Kara, if you're willing, I'd like for you to set up a meeting with all of the leaders in Missoula. You can tell us what you need, and we'll see what we can do to help."

"I'll do it," said Kara.

"We aren't going to put up with another Sterling," Professor Hollins said. "We run our own area, and we don't want any interference."

"We're just offering help," Max said. "I don't want to tell you what to do any more than you want to be told."

He nodded, somewhat skeptically. Alexander did not really blame him. History was littered with wannabe dictators. But in time, he would learn that Horngate was different. They all would.

28

I T TOOK THE REST OF THE NIGHT AND DAY TO BREAK everyone else free of Shoftiel's prison pillars. The angels and Max shuttled her Blades back to Horngate before sunrise. She made a special effort to avoid Alexander.

He had changed again. His looks were once again possessive and full of seductive promises. How long that would last, she didn't really know. Neither did she care. Her heart was bruised and battered, and she had no interest in going down that road again. She loved Alexander, and maybe he loved her. But it wasn't enough. She couldn't trust him not to bag on her, and he needed someone safer, less prone to dying. Love just wasn't enough.

Max slept alone and held Alexander at a friendly distance. She checked in on Tris, Kyle, and Tory. Tory, as usual, was defiant, and Kyle was unrepentantly sheepish. He was too excited about the angels reawakening to remember what an idiot he'd been.

The night after everybody had returned, Max sat down in the dining commons. It was early yet, and only a few people had come in. Magpie came out with a quiche and a basket of biscuits. She set them down.

"Are you all right?" she asked.

"Healed up fine," Max said, perfectly aware that Magpie was not referring to her physical health.

"What about things with Alexander?"

Max lifted her shoulder in a half shrug. "I—" she said, flushing as he walked in and started immediately for her table. "It's dead in the water," she said.

"Is that because you're scared? Or because that's what you want?" Magpie asked, and walked away, not waiting for the answer.

Alexander gathered up some butter and honey and dropped down in a chair opposite Max. He ate silently, his eyes boring into her with dark intensity. It made her shiver and ache with want.

"You need to stop that," she said finally, getting irritated.

"Stop what?"

"Don't. Don't pretend. You quit me. Turned yourself off like a water spigot, leaving me high and dry. I get it. I'm a pain in the ass. I haven't been in a relationship in more than thirty years, and they scare the piss out of me. I don't blame you for walking. But I can't do it again. So you need to back off, Slick."

He reached out and grabbed her hand. "I need another chance."

"That's too bad. I'm fresh out."

She pulled her hand away, stood, and strode out of the dining commons. Her stomach was in knots. His touch had sent flames of hunger flickering over her whole treacherous body.

She wound through a maze of passages, looking for a place to hide, to collect herself. She felt him coming. He was stalking her. No use trying to hide from him. He could find her anywhere in Horngate. His emotions were molten, bubbling with a potent mix of hunger, greed, desire, fear, and longing. Max hardened herself. She wouldn't survive him walking away again.

She ducked inside a small lounge. It was being used as a sewing room, with piles of fabric and baskets of yarn and several magically operated sewing machines. She crossed to the other side of the room, turning around to wait for Alexander. He arrived less than a minute later.

He stopped just inside the doorway. His eyes were dark, the edges rimmed with a thin ring of white. His gaze skewered her, sending darts of heat and ice burrowing through her. She watched him warily.

"You're following me," she said, breaking the silence.

"Yes," he said, and stalked forward until he was just beyond arm's reach.

"Why?"

"I cannot help myself," he said with a rueful shrug.

That struck a match to her anger. Not that he wanted to be with her but that he couldn't help himself. As if the devil made him do it. She bristled, heat rising in her cheeks. "You'll get the hang of it. Practice makes perfect."

"I do not think I will," he said, then prowled the room, picking up bits and pieces and putting them down. "I do not want to."

The silence was wearing on her, and her temper thinned. "What exactly do you want?"

"You," he said, as if that meant anything.

She snorted. "You had me. You dropped me like a bad habit. Game over. Move on."

"I love you."

She balled her hand into a fist. "Right. That's today. How are you going to feel tomorrow? Or the next day? Or maybe next week or next year?"

"The same."

"And I'm supposed to believe that because your track record is so good?"

Desperation flickered in his eyes. "I need another chance. I need you to trust me once more."

Max drew a breath and blew it out. "Okay, let's say I believe you. Fine. Great. Hurray. But flip the coin, and you go ballistic whenever I get into a little trouble."

He snorted at "a little."

"You're right. Let's call a spade a spade. I'm in trouble a lot, Slick. I'm made out of the stuff. I breathe it. I eat it. That's never going to change. There's never going to be a world so safe that I won't find myself in the middle of some kind of shitstorm. The problem is, you can't deal with that. You don't love that part of me. In fact, I'd be willing to bet money you hate that part of me."

She broke Alexander's lock on her gaze and looked up, blinking back the tears that burned in her eyes. *Stupid.*

"You are wrong. I love all of you. I have no choice," he told her softly, and a thorny ache blossomed in her chest.

"Oh, wow," she said as a tear slipped out of the corner of her eye. She sniffed and turned so that he couldn't see. "That was truly beautiful. Heartrending, really. Like when you have to eat your brussels sprouts in order to get your dessert. Or someone puts a gun to your head to steal your car. No choice at all. I am so fucking touched that I could just puke."

He closed the distance between them, reaching out to brush a strand of hair gently from her cheek. She shook him off. Undaunted, he slid a hand down to cup her jaw and neck. He gently turned her to face him. She did not look up to meet his eyes. She was too fragile . . . exposed. Like a turtle on its back, its legs kicking in the air.

He refused to let her hide. His thumb pressed her chin up until she was forced to look at him. His lips were inches from hers. His breath was warm on her skin.

"I did not mean it like that," he whispered, pleading. "I admit that I let the fear get the best of me. It was too much, and my mind locked down. I put my feelings for you in a box so that I would not go over the edge. I was close to going feral. Too close. I have been there once. I almost did not come back.

"Not caring felt good. I felt free. Joyful, even. I understood myself. I was in control. I had not felt that way since before I met you."

"Sounds terrific, Slick. I can't blame you." She couldn't, either. She could barely handle her feelings for Alexander and her grief over Niko and Simon. Half the time, she wanted to kill everybody in sight, and the rest of the time, she wanted to crawl into bed, pull the covers over her head, and cry like a colicky baby. Commitment of any kind made her panic. "I get it."

"No," he corrected, his thumb rubbing along her lower lip.

It sent shivers wobbling down through her gut. *Not fair*. She did not pull away.

"You *do not* understand. What I feel for you is too big to stay in a box for long. It was not long after the locks broke open that I understood." His mouth curved, his eyes full of memory. "I went mad. Or maybe what happened was that I woke up from my madness. I realized that I could never walk away from you. I could never want to. There is no sanity without you. I am whole only with you."

Her lips were dry. Max licked them, and his gaze fastened on the movement. The shivers in her stomach turned to shudders. His thumb stopped rubbing.

"I love you," he said again. Third time. "Can you believe me?"

She chewed the inside of her cheek. Could she? More than that, could she trust him again?

Slowly, she reached up and traced the sides of his face with her fingertips. His body quivered beneath her touch. He was strung tight. She pushed up on tiptoe and touched her lips to his, light as gossamer. He remained rigid.

Then she pressed harder, her tongue tickling along the seam of his lips. They parted, and she continued her slow assault. Back and forth she feathered. She flicked her tongue in between his lips, tasting him, then withdrew. His chest heaved, and he inhaled sharply. Max grasped his face between her palms, pulling him to her. His fingers curled over her hips, but he still held himself away from her.

She teased along the edge of his lower teeth. She went slowly, tantalizing him with soft, delicate touches. She could feel his body shaking, and it matched the tremor inside her. She pulled back and nibbled his lower lip, then started back at the beginning, sliding her tongue sensuously along his lips. It was too much for him. He yanked her close. His hands roamed possessively up to her head and back down over her ass.

His kiss was demanding, desperate, apologetic. Max moaned into his mouth and slid her hands under his shirt. His skin was satin fire. He made a sound in his throat as her fingers glided up his back, over his shoulders and chest, and back along his ribs. His grip on her tightened convulsively. His tongue thrust inside her mouth. His greed for her was endless. Max delighted in the knowledge, pressing harder against him, as if she could climb inside his skin. Need for him seared her. She throbbed with want.

Abruptly, he pulled back. He was panting. He pressed his head against hers, his fingers fisting in the fabric of her shirt.

"*Tell me*," he grated. "Tell me you believe me. Believe *in* me." That he wouldn't let her down. That he wouldn't break her heart again.

It wasn't enough. There had to be more. He had to trust her, too.

Max stepped back, and the fear and uncertainty in his eyes flared. She took his hand. "Come on."

She led the way back toward the dining commons. Alexander didn't speak. His Prime was climbing toward the killing edge, and he was holding on to it with all his strength.

She came around a corner to find Thor and Tyler coming down the corridor.

"Perfect," she murmured. She shot a look at them. "Stay there."

"If we do, do we both get biscuits?" Tyler asked.

"Shut up," she said, and turned to face Alexander. "Say it again."

He frowned, his gaze boring into hers. "I love you."

The words made him flush, and her heart rattled in her chest. She opened her lips to speak, but nothing came out.

"You do not have to say anything," he said, cupping her cheek with his hand.

"So I have your permission to be a coward?"

"You can be you," he said simply, and she knew he wasn't just talking about whether or not she could tell him she loved him. He was talking about all the rest, all the trouble and near-death experiences to come. This was his promise: he was not going to shut her out again.

It wasn't enough. Not for her. It shouldn't have been enough for him. It was a sign of how much he needed her, how much she could hurt him if she wanted to. That's what had driven him away before. She knew that now. He was giving himself entirely into her power without demanding the same. Except that he had it. She just had to tell him.

It turned out the words were there after all.

She stood on tiptoe, nose-to-nose with him. She stared deep into his eyes. "I love you," she said, loudly enough for Tyler and Thor to hear. She heard Alexander's indrawn breath. His eyes widened. Then his arms clamped around her, lifting her off the ground and holding her tightly against him as he kissed her.

Max's legs wrapped around his waist as she lost herself in his touch and taste.

"Ahem. Not to be rude, but weren't we going to get some food? I don't think the kind of eating you're doing is going to be particularly filling," Tyler said.

"On the contrary. It will be filling. For Max, anyhow," Thor said.

Max snorted and pulled away. "You two are ruining the moment."

"Oh, good. That means you're done. Can we go eat now?" Tyler asked plaintively.

Max's stomach growled, and she winced. Alexander grinned and set her down, pressing a hard kiss to her lips.

"You need food. I want you to be strong for later," he said, his eyebrows lifting suggestively.

"Back atcha, Slick. I don't want you running out of stamina."

Tyler came up beside her and slung his arm around her neck. "If you two don't shut up, I'm going to puke."

"My, but you've got a weak stomach," Max said.

"Naw, he's just never been laid," Thor said. "He's scared of women and sex."

"Ha! I'm legendary in bed," Tyler retorted.

"Uh-huh. Just like Big Foot. A story that someone made up and no one believes."

"You wound me."

"Only because the truth hurts," Max said.

"You, too?" Tyler said, his eyes dancing. "I thought you were my friend."

"I am your friend. And as your friend, I need to help you see reality."

"The reality is that women everywhere want me." He leered.

Thor shook his head. "I think you've got it wrong, son. It isn't women who want you but sheep. Sheep everywhere want you."

"Oh, now you've gone too far. Now you're going to pay. I demand a challenge. Sparring room, right after we eat. I'll smear the floor with you." He looked at Max and Alexander. "You can judge."

"I don't know," Max said. "We were thinking of doing something a bit more private."

Tyler waved his hand dismissively. "It can wait. You've got all the time in the world."

All the time in the world.

Max grinned.

"Okay."

KICK-BUTT
URBAN FANTASY
from Pocket Books!

Available wherever books and eBooks are sold.
SimonandSchuster.com